CONVERSATIONS FROM THE EDGE

CONVERSATIONS FROM THE EDGE

THE GALAXY'S EDGE INTERVIEWS

JOY WARD

CAEZIK
SF & FANTASY
ARC MANOR
ROCKVILLE, MARYLAND

*

SHAHID MAHMUD
PUBLISHER

www.caeziksf.com

Tarikian, TARK Classic Fiction, Arc Manor, Arc Manor Classic Reprints, Phoenix Pick, Phoenix Science Fiction Classics, Phoenix Rider, The Stellar Guild Series, Manor Thrift and logos associated with those imprints are trademarks or registered trademarks of Arc Manor, LLC, Rockville, Maryland. All other trademarks and trademarked names are properties of their respective owners.

Hardcover edition published by Phoenix Pick, 2019.

Library of Congress Cataloging-in-Publication Data

Names: Ward, Joy, interviewer.
Title: Conversations from the edge : the Galaxy's Edge interviews / Joy Ward.
Other titles: Galaxy's edge.
Description: Rockville, Maryland : Phoenix Pick, an imprint of Arc Manor, [2019]
Identifiers: LCCN 2019012711| ISBN 9781612423340 (hardcover : alk. paper) | ISBN 9781612423395 (paperback : alk. paper) | ISBN 9781612423401 (eISBN)
Subjects: LCSH: Science fiction, American—History and criticism. | Fantasy fiction, American—History and criticism. | Authors, American—20th century—Interviews.
Classification: LCC PS374.S35 W37 2019 | DDC 813/.0876209—dc23
LC record available at https://lccn.loc.gov/2019012711

ISBN: 978-1-64710-011-7

First Paperback Edition. 1st Printing. March 2021
1 2 3 4 5 6 7 8 9 10

An imprint of Arc Manor LLC

www.CaezikSF.com

■ CONTENTS

■ INTRODUCTION

How often have you read a book or a short story and finished only to wish you could find out more about the writer? Me too. When I would read a particularly moving or entrancing story I would feel a connection to the writer in that way you feel when you meet someone and enjoy spending a few hours chatting about philosophy and history and whatever. (You know what I mean or you wouldn't be reading this.)

After twenty-plus years of interviewing all kinds of people about almost every topic you can name (really!), Mike Resnick kindly gave me the chance to interview some of science fiction's most iconic writers! Thrilled? You bet! What reader or writer wouldn't want the chance to ask writers like Connie Willis, Robert Silverberg, George R.R. Martin, Gene Wolfe, Mercedes Lackey and Larry Dixon, Terry Brooks, and many others about their lives, their work, and their writing?

So, I chased all these writers across the country and they kindly let me into their worlds and sometimes their houses. Walt and I brought our trusty cameras into homes and hotels. There we would be entranced by the marvelous truths and experiences of some of the best talebenders of our generation!

Sometimes respondents would tell us about times that made them laugh. We went with them and laughed too. Other times, the writers would tell us about frustrating times and we would tense our hands in frustration with them. Then there were the times we would be moved to tears with the writers. And those times were many as they opened their hearts to us, and you. How lucky are we!

I hope you can feel the honesty in these interviews. As an interviewer, that is the one thing I want to convey. I want you to feel the reality and truth in these words. Science fiction writers, especially these folks, convey a form of truth through their fiction. I hope that these words can share the beauty of their souls with you.

Each and every one has made an indelible and immortal mark on our shared dreams, both science and fantasy. These are the men and women who have led us and our genre with their visions and sometimes fears. You and I may not agree with everything they said, but they have all earned the right to say it.

My one regret is that I only have a limited number of interviews. There are other women and men I would have loved to interview. Some of them are already on record for upcoming columns and (hopefully) future volumes. We were sadly limited in this first volume by geography and sometimes writer trepidation. I hope that some of the writers who may be afraid of being interviewed will open their doors to us in the future.

I look forward to interviewing many other women and men of all ethnicities who have made a contribution to our shared passions—science fiction and fantasy.

On behalf of all of us, thank you to every writer who opened him or herself to us and our questions!

Also, thank you to my husband, Walt Boyes, for getting us to the interviews and wrangling the cameras. I couldn't do this without you!

Joy Ward, 2019

GEORGE R.R. MARTIN

George R.R. Martin is a famous science fiction and fantasy author who received a BS in journalism from Northwestern University, Evanston, Illinois, in 1970, graduating summa cum laude. He went on to complete a MS in journalism in 1971, also from Northwestern. As a conscientious objector, Martin did alternative service 1972-1974 with VISTA, attached to Cook County Legal Assistance Foundation. He directed chess tournaments for the Continental Chess Association from 1973-1976, was a journalism instructor at Clarke College, Dubuque, Iowa, from 1976-1978, becoming a full-time writer in 1979. Martin signed on as a story editor for *The Twilight Zone* at CBS Television in 1986. In 1987 Martin became an Executive Story Consultant for *Beauty and the Beast* at CBS, then Producer in 1988, moving up to Co-Supervising Producer in 1989. He was Executive Producer for *Doorways*, a pilot he wrote for Columbia Pictures Television, which was filmed during 1992-93. His series, A Song of Ice & Fire, has been turned into the HBO sensation, *Game of Thrones* (2011-2019), and the SyFy series, *Nightflyers* (2018), was recently adapted from Martin's book of the same name.

Joy Ward's original introduction: George R.R. Martin, one of the most important writers of our time and a man who is considered by many to be one of our greatest living writers, was kind enough let me visit with him in his den, overseen by a full-size functional replica of Robby the Robot and numerous other fascinating models and collectible space toys, including his first set of spacemen.

Joy Ward: How did you get started writing?

George R.R. Martin: I've always written. As far back as I can remember. When I was a little kid I used to make up stories about my toys and write them down. Give them all names. I had a collection of spacemen. I learned later they are called Miller Aliens. You can actually see them right behind your camera. Yeah, those are my original gang of Miller Aliens. They were made by a company called Miller in the 1950s, and they were sold for fifteen cents apiece in five-and-dime stores like Woolworths, Kreskes, W. T. Grants, and Big Ben's. I would buy them for fifteen cents. I got the whole set and they were some of the best toy aliens ever produced on the basis of where they were from, like being from Mars or the dark side of the Moon, but that was enough for me. I gave them all names and I decided they were a gang of space pirates. This guy was the brains of the operation and here was this lieutenant. There's a little guy there who's holding a weird weapon that looked to me like a drill so I said "Oh, this guy must be in charge of torture," because he drills people with that little drill. They had weird guns and all that, so I invented personalities for the whole thing and adventures of them, this gang of space pirates. I couldn't have been more than nine or ten at that time.

I would also write monster stories that I would sell to the other kids in the projects for a nickel so I could buy a Milky Way bar. Usually, the stories were two pages long, handwritten. They had a werewolf, and I would howl for them. I liked to frighten the other kids.

It was a short-lived career, though, because one of the other kids was having nightmares. His mother came to my mother and said, "Stop frightening the other kids. You can't tell them these monster stories anymore." So it dried up my source of extra Milky Ways and comic books.

JW: What did you do then?

GRRM: I just went back to not scaring the other kids for a few years. I read a lot. Books were my comic books.

At a certain formative age one of my mother's friends gave me a Scribner's hardcover copy of *Have Space Suit, Will Travel* by Robert A. Heinlein. That, of course, is still one of my favorite science fiction books; one of the great science fiction books of all time. Up there with the best of Heinlein, I think, even though it was part of his juvenile series. It works for adults too. I can still read that book with pleasure.

That got me into reading science fiction. I had my dollar-a-week allowance so I had to decide, because paper books were thirty-five cents, did I want to take the equivalent of three comic books and spend it on one paperback? It was a hard decision to make sometimes. You had to figure out these budgets. Well, there's a new *Spiderman* and *Fantastic Four*, but oh, look at this: here's a Robert A. Heinlein I haven't seen or an Andre Norton or A. E. van Vogt. The Ace Doubles. I liked the Ace Doubles because you got, for thirty-five cents, you got two stories. The Heinlein *Have Space Suit, Will Travel*, which was actually a beautiful first edition Scribner's hardcover, I read that to pieces. For a decade it was the only hardcover book I owned because we didn't have much money.

JW: What other writers did you read?

GRRM: Well, I mentioned a few of them. Andre Norton was the other big writer that was part of the Ace Doubles. I loved her stuff.

I liked Jerry Sohl. He wrote some good Ace Doubles. I read A. E. van Vogt, but I didn't quite get into him. It was interesting but his stories were kind of confusing in some ways and they're still confusing. But he was certainly an original. Münster, Isaac Asimov, Jack Williamson; all of the people who were writing back then and from previous decades.

I discovered Doc Smith at one point and devoured the Skylark series, *The Skylark of Space,* and its sequels.

Then at a certain point I discovered fantasy. The first discovery was a little book called *Swords and Sorcery* by L. Sprague de Camp, and I picked that up off a spinner rack and it had a Conan story. I was hooked, particularly by Conan.

I got into horror, which I didn't call horror; I just called them monster stories. The same way, there was an anthology that I found on a spinner rack—Boris Karloff's favorite horror stories or something. In that book I encountered "The Whisperer in Darkness," my first H. P. Lovecraft story. I'd never read anything so terrifying as what Lovecraft did.

JW: What's the first thing you sold?

GRRM: Before a pro, I was a published fan. I wrote for fanzines initially.

I've been outspoken on the internet and other places in not being in favor of fan fiction. Sometimes I get criticized by fans who don't understand and say, "You say you wrote fan fiction, and now you're against fan fiction." What I wrote was not fan fiction like that term is used today. Today when people say fan fiction, they talk about taking my characters or Robin Hobb's characters or Robert Jordan's characters or Kirk or Spock or any characters from a television show or movie and writing stories about them. Writing stories about someone else's characters. I never did that and I never approved of that.

I did write what we called fan fiction. In the '60s it was simply fiction written by fans and published in fanzines. They were original stories about original characters. Yeah, some of them were pretty derivative. You could sort of look through the thin layer of cloth there and see, wow, this is Batman, even though they've changed his name to Kookaburraman.

I wrote stories about Manta Ray and Powerman and Doctor Weird and numerous other characters, some created by me, some created by other writers who then solicited me to write about their characters. They were published in the fanzines, and I became pretty popular. I got a lot of praise, which encouraged me.

I was a very shy and introverted kid. I think the life of the imagination was a refuge for me—daydreams and books and comic books.

I was always a little hesitant to put myself out there. I don't know, fear of rejection or whatever. But actually having these things published in fanzines and having editors say, "This is great, one of the best stories we've ever gotten here," and readers writing in and saying, "This George Martin is terrific," was really encouraging to me. I think it was a crucial step in my development.

JW: What did that say to you, that people were writing in saying you were a great writer?

GRRM: It says to me they were high school kids who didn't know any better. So was I. I mean, comic fandom in those early days was 90 percent high school kids and younger. There was a [group of about] 10 percent college kids and adults that were sort of in the leadership position that got things rolling, but the guys I was dealing with were all high school kids. So you were in the little leagues. You weren't in the major leagues. You were a star in the little leagues. But that didn't mean you were able to play in the majors. I always dreamed of playing in the majors.

I knew that eventually I wanted to write comic books professionally. I wanted to write stories professionally. But I was hesitant even then to make that leap. What if they didn't like it? What if they rejected me? What if they said, "You're no good?" So I always wanted to save it until I got better. A few years I'll be a little older, I'll be a little better.

By this time I was in college. In college, at every opportunity, I took courses that would allow me to write fiction. I took creative writing and short-story writing.

Even in other courses I would say, "Instead of a term paper, can I do fiction?" I made that offer, it was my sophomore year at Northwestern University in Evanston, Illinois, and I was taking a course in Scandinavian history of all things. History was my minor. We were supposed to do a term paper for a big part of our grade, and I approached the professor and said, "Could I write, instead of a term paper, historical fiction?" He had never had this offer before, but he was intrigued by it. He said, "Sure. See what you can do with the history that we've taught you."

So I wrote a story about the Russo-Swedish War of 1808 and the surrender of the Great Fortress of Sveaborg, the Gibraltar of the

North. It's a great mystery of history in that part of the world. I wrote a story where I explained it. It was called "The Fortress." It got an "A," which was great. But not only did it get an "A," the professor liked it so much that he sent it to a professional magazine called *American-Scandinavian Review*. They liked it too, but they didn't publish fiction. They sent a very nice rejection letter to the professor, which he passed on to me. That was my first professional rejection. I said, "Okay, this is a professional editor and he said it was good. Maybe I don't have to be afraid."

So the next year I took a creative writing course, and I wrote some science fiction stories and some mainstream stories. For the first time I started sending them out myself to professional magazines. The mainstream stories I never got anything but straight rejection slips on those. But the two science fiction stories I wrote, both of them eventually sold, though one of them took a decade. But the other one sold within a couple of years. That was "The Hero."

That was my first professional sale. I wrote it, I think, in my junior year at Northwestern for the creative writing course. I started sending it out and I got a rejection letter from John W. Campbell Jr., which was quite a feather in my cap. He wrote personal letters, too. Then I got an acceptance from *Galaxy* magazine. It appeared in *Galaxy* in early 1971. I got $94 for it, which was real money back in those days.

I remember when it came out in February 1971. I was with my friends scouring all of Chicago to look for copies of it. Buying two copies at this newsstand and two more at that newsstand and oh, this doesn't have it, and carrying it home. They didn't send you authors' copies in those days. You had to go out and hunt it down yourself.

It was pretty exciting. Your first time is always pretty exciting, whether it's publishing or sex. And you always remember it. Opening that envelope and seeing that check in there. It was pretty amazing seeing it on the news stand, seeing my name in print. This was my name in print attached to a story, and that was pretty amazing.

I was very lucky. I know many people who have struggled for years, have collected a lot of rejection, and certainly I did collect a lot of rejection. I wrote four stories in that creative writing course, and the other three of them all got more than forty rejection slips. Some of them never sold.

"The Fortress," obviously, I sent it out a couple more times after the Scandinavian magazine sent it back. I tried it on places like *Argosy* and *Men's Adventure* and stuff like that. They were interested in a lot of stories. They published a lot of stories about Nazis and World War II. They weren't interested in the Russo-Swedish War of 1808.

Having had one story that broke through made the other rejections not seem so bad. If all of the stories had gotten forty rejections I may have been so discouraged that I might have stopped, but instead it encouraged me to persevere. Then I wrote more stories and those started selling, too—science fiction, fantasy. So all through the '70s I was publishing everywhere. There was one month in '73 when I had three stories come out simultaneously in three different magazines—one in *Analog*, one in *Amazing*, and one in *F&SF*.

It felt great. It felt like I was conquering the world.

I wrote short stories and published short stories all through the early and mid-'70s. I was nominated for the Campbell Award. I didn't win. I was nominated for Hugos and Nebulas, although I didn't win. Finally, I was nominated for a Hugo, and I did win. "A Song for Lya" in 1975. Best Novella.

At that point I thought it was time for me to do my first novel. *Dying of the Light* was published in 1977. Once again, I was very, very lucky. All through the '70s new writers that I knew who were breaking in were getting $3000 for their first novel.

In 1977—just as I was completing my novel, and I had no confidence I could work in something that long because I had only worked in short ones so far—a lot of people were selling their novels on the basis of chapters and an outline. You write three chapters, and then you write an outline, and they give you an advance and a deadline, and you have to finish the rest of the book by the deadline. I didn't want to do that, because I wasn't sure I could finish the rest of the book. I said, I'll write this entire book and then I'll give it to my agent to sell. Let's see if he can sell it. So that's what I did.

During the time that I was writing the book, which took me a year, the great science fiction boom of the late-'70s hit. Science fiction books were beginning to hit the bestseller list for the first time. The great writers of the Golden Age and the '50s, Asimov and Heinlein, were having bestsellers for the first time in their lives. The publishers that had them were happy, but there were more publishers in those days. It wasn't the Big Five; it was the Big Thirty. The others were all looking around. Maybe that's the next Heinlein, the next Asimov. There were auctions going on, crazy auctions where people were bidding for a lot of money on first and second novels by younger writers.

I was in the right place at the right time. I got four publishers bidding on *Dying of the Light* so it went for a lot more money than I could have gotten, even in a year. That made it possible for me to contemplate actually being a full-time writer.

Up to that point in my career I always worked other jobs. I'd been a chess tournament director. I'd done some journalism. I worked as a VISTA volunteer for two years. I'd done public relations. I was looking at the careers of other writers and thinking there's Heinlein who has been a professional writer since the beginning. But there is also Clifford Simak, who was never a full-time writer. He always wrote his fiction on the side and I thought that's the kind of life I was heading toward until *Dying of the Light* sold for so much money.

After *Dying of the Light* I wrote *Windhaven* with Lisa Tuttle and *Fevre Dream*. It kind of brought me out from straight science fiction.

Then I wrote a novel called *The Armageddon Rag*. It was a novel about rock and roll and the '60s. It had sort of a murder mystery element to it. It also had a supernatural horror fantasy element to it, and it had overtones of time travel, but it was largely a story about the '60s and the '80s and the time in between. It provoked great enthusiasm among the people who had read it and it got me my first really big advance and my publisher was really excited. He said, "This is going to be your breakout book, a big bestseller."

Up to that point in my life I had led a charmed career, really. I was looking forward to it being a big bestseller, and I was contemplating the book I would write next. Unfortunately, *Armageddon Rag* was nominated for the World Fantasy Award, it got some incredible reviews, and it's a book that's still close to my heart, but nobody bought it. It was commercially a huge failure. I quickly discovered that a world like publishing is not a world with a lot of security. You're as hot as your latest book or your latest movie or TV show.

JW: Is this when you moved into the Hollywood business?

GRRM: Yes. Suddenly I couldn't sell my next book—the one that I had partially written. I showed it around and they were, "It's good, but Martin, you know, look at the sales figures on *Armageddon Rag*. No, we don't want to do this." That was the point that I went to Hollywood because I had no choice.

Oddly enough, *Armageddon Rag*, that ended my career as a novelist, began my career as a Hollywood guy because it was optioned. Not a lot of people read that book, but the people who read that book loved that book.

One of the people who did was a fellow named Phillip DeGuerre, a television writer/producer. Phil had worked on numerous Stephen J. Cannell shows, earned his stripes there, and then he had created his own shows. And he created a hit show called *Simon and Simon*. Then CBS wanted more shows from him so he created a number of other shows. He created a show called *Whiz Kids*. It didn't last long but it was like the first show about computer hackers. And Phil was also a big deadhead—a Grateful Dead guy. My generation loved rock and roll, loved *Armageddon Rag*, and he wanted to make it into a big-budget feature film with the Grateful Dead playing the Nazul, the rock band in it. He optioned it and he flew me out to LA, and we had all sorts of meetings about the screenplay before he wrote it. He was going to direct it himself. He had great plans for *Armageddon Rag*. He wrote two drafts of the screenplay, a pretty good screenplay, I think. Never got it going. Never got the financing. But because of the *Armageddon Rag* meetings, I knew Phil.

A couple of years later, coming off of the continued success of *Simon and Simon*, CBS says to Phil, "What would you like to do next?"

He says, "I want to bring back *The Twilight Zone*."

And so CBS did own *The Twilight Zone*. That was unusual that the network actually owned a show. "If you could produce that at an in-house studio that would be very good. Yeah, go ahead."

Phil did some very unusual things. He put together *The Twilight Zone* and instead of just using regular established screen writers he looked for new talent. He found some great new talents like Rockne O'Bannon, who had never sold anything until Phil bought his story.

He also turned to prose writers who had never written screenplays or teleplays in their lives. He gave a dozen of them the chance to do a teleplay, and I was one of those. He called me up and he said, "Hey. How would you like to write a *Twilight Zone?*"

When I was a kid, *The Twilight Zone* was one of my favorite shows, so it was an amazing opportunity. I said "I don't know how to write a screenplay. I just write books and short stories." He said, "It's not that hard." He sent me some screenplays and the next thing I knew I was writing screenplays and I was on *The Twilight Zone.*

He liked the first ones I did. He hired me to be on staff and the whole Hollywood thing opened up for me, and I spent ten years out there.

It was great. It was intimidating, in some ways, because the original show had always been so good. We always felt we had a legacy to live up to, and Rod Serling's ghost was looking over our shoulder. The critics out there and the viewers out there were always going to compare us to the original show. We compared ourselves to the original show constantly. We wanted to make our own version of the show true to the tradition; something that Rod Serling would have liked if he had still been with us.

But, of course, times had changed. There were real challenges to that. The revived *Twilight Zone* did not actually last very long—a season and a half. I got to write five scripts for it and have them produced, which was pretty exciting for me. My first scripts *and* my first produced scripts.

But the audience had changed. In the original *Twilight Zone* there were still a lot of anthology shows on the air and quasi-anthology shows. Not so much by the time you reach the mid-'80s. *The Twilight Zone* came along the same time as Steven Spielberg launched *Amazing Stories,* and another network tried to revive *Alfred Hitchcock Presents.* It was like three different people were trying to revive the anthology format and we all failed. None of those shows lasted very long. The television audience didn't want different characters and stories every week. They wanted the same characters.

There were problems with the network, too. They loved the original *Twilight Zone* so much that I think they wanted us to replicate it more than we really wanted to do. They wanted us to remake old episodes and we did. We made a few of them. We made the Christmas episode which turned out very well actually. We remade the manikin episode which didn't turn out that well. It's hard to do. They constantly wanted twist endings. The 1986 television audience was far more sophisticated than the 1959 television audience. They saw those twists coming a mile away, because they'd all grown up watching *The Twilight Zone* marathons.

You couldn't get that sting in the tail so easily as you could have all those years before. But we got to work with some great actors, great directors. You know, William Friedkin did an episode for us. My episode was directed by Wes Craven. That was a real thrill to meet him. We had some amazing guest stars. And I got to work with probably one of the best writing staffs in television: Harlan Ellison, Jim Crocker, Rockne O'Bannon—what an amazing writer he was. And, of course, Phil DeGuerre himself. Michael Cassett. Boy, we had a hell of a writing staff!

I stayed in Hollywood. I did a couple of scripts for *Max Headroom*, which came and went very quickly; otherwise I might have done more. Unfortunately, neither of my *Max Headroom* scripts were ever produced, although one was in preproduction when they pulled the plug on that series. And then I got a job on *Beauty and the Beast*, which was just coming down the pike.

For three years I was on that show. I wrote thirteen scripts. Got promoted from story editor to co-producer to producer to supervising producer, up and up. When that show died, I was high enough up that I was doing development for the next five years, where I was trying to get my own show on the air or write a feature film.

I did both. I did half a dozen pilots and half a dozen features, none of which were ever made, and that was what really produced a crisis for me. Development can be quite lucrative. It actually paid better than being on staff on some of these shows. I had a big overall deal. I was being paid to come up with this stuff, but I found it tremendously emotionally unsatisfying.

Because I'm an entertainer. I need an audience. It's just not enough for me to write a script, spend a year creating characters and a world and stories and then nobody ever sees them except for four guys in a room who tell you for a year, "Oh yeah, it's great. It's great. It's great. It's terrific. This is going to be wonderful. Nah. We decided not to do it. We're doing this other thing instead. What else you got? Come up with something else next week." Then you go through the whole process again with a different story and all that.

After five years of that I said I'm going to go back to books. I love books. Books are my first love. I never really left them entirely, 'cause I had been doing the Wild Cards series and occasional other short stories. The result of that, my coming back, was this little thing called *A Song of Ice and Fire*, so the world is strangely ironic.

JW: How do you see that progression in yourself from probably television's best love story ever, Beauty and the Beast, *to* Game of Thrones, *which is very different?*

GRRM: For me it was not that different. I've always been different. As a kid I fell in love with science fiction, with fantasy, with horror, and I wrote all three. You look at my earlier stuff, "The Hero," that story I sold to *Galaxy*. That was a hard-core science fiction story. Military SF about a warrior in an exoskeletal suit. Straight out of *Starship Troopers*—fighting a war on an alien planet in the far future. The second story I sold to *Fantastic* was a ghost story set when people have stopped driving automobiles. He's a hobbyist. Everyone is using hover cars and jet packs and stuff like that. But he still likes to drive the old cars, and he's driving on a highway and he encounters this ghost of an Edsel driven by people who were killed in a horrible traffic accident a few years ago. "Exit to San Breta" was the name of the story. That was a fantasy, a little bit of horror story and ghosts, and the first one was science fiction. Even in my first three stories I was hitting all three bases. I kept moving around.

Dying of the Light, my first novel, is pretty hardcore basic space opera set on alien planets thousands of years in the future with a lot of exotic human cultures clashing, but I followed it with *Windhaven* with Lisa Tuttle. That one is a science fiction technically, but it feels like fantasy because it's on a planet that basically has reverted to feudalism. Then *Fevre Dream* was completely out of genre totally. It was a historical horror vampire story set in the 1850s on riverboats on the Mississippi River. *Armageddon Rag*—again, I never like to repeat myself. I always like to move around and change things and wonder, "What should I do next?"

JW: What's bad about repeating yourself?

GRRM: You get bored, and you just go through the motions. I see that in some writers, even writers that I love. They write some great book, and their later books seem like they are rewriting the same book that they wrote before.

Not all writers do that. There are writers, like Jack Vance, who I think was the greatest science fiction/fantasy writer of my time, who was amazingly fresh and inventive right up to the end. Incredible. You're inspired to do that.

Vance moved around, too. He had a very distinguished career as a mystery novelist. He won the Edgar Award for his mystery novels and wrote some of the most unusual horror mystery things of all time—*Bad Ronald* and things like that.

I was a child of the spinner rack. We didn't have any bookstores in Bayonne, New Jersey, when I was growing up. I bought my paperbacks off the spinner rack next to comic books. There was no sorting there. Dumas was next to Vance and Norman Vincent Peale was on a shelf below and Dr. Spock—not Mr. Spock but Dr. Spock and *How to Raise Babies*—was jammed in next to F. Scott Fitzgerald and Raymond Chandler. All the books were together. I've always read a lot of things, and I like to write a lot of different things.

JW: How do you use death in your writing?

GRRM: I don't think of it in those terms, that I'm using death for any purpose. I think a writer, even a fantasy writer, has an obligation to tell the truth and the truth is, as we say in *Game of Thrones*, all men must die. Particularly if you're writing about war, which is certainly a central subject in *Game of Thrones*.

It has been in a lot of my fiction. Not all of it by any means but certainly a lot of it, going all the way back to "The Hero," which was a story about a warrior. You can't write about war and violence without having death. If you want to be honest it *should* affect your main characters. We've all read this story a million times when a bunch of heroes set out on adventure and it's the hero and his best friend and his girlfriend and they go through amazing hair-raising adventures, and none of them die. The only ones who die are extras.

That's such a cheat. It doesn't happen that way. They go into battle and their best friend dies or they get horribly wounded. They lose their leg or death comes at them unexpectedly.

It's even worse in modern war than medieval war. I've talked to, even though I never went to war myself, people who went to Vietnam and Desert Storm and things like that. It used to be in medieval times that if you had good armor, and you were a good swordsman, and you were well-trained in the military arts, you had a pretty good chance of surviving. The guys who died by the hundreds and the thousands were the arrow fodder, the peasants they rounded up to fill out the armies. So this kind of skill as a warrior would get you through. Then you hear stories about Vietnam. It didn't matter if you were the best rifle shot in the platoon or you were a fat kid who was just drafted. You had an equal chance of dying 'cause some sniper blows your head off or something. You drive over a bomb planted on the road or something.

Death is so arbitrary. It's always there. It's coming for all of us. We're all going to die. I'm going to die. You're going to die. Mortality is at the soul of all this stuff. You have to write about it if you're going to be honest, especially if you're writing a story high in conflict. Once you've accepted that you have to include death, then you should be honest about death and indicate it can strike down anybody at any time. You don't get to live forever just because you are a cute kid or the hero's best friend or the hero. Sometimes the hero dies, at least in my books.

I love all my characters, so it's always hard to kill them, but I know it has to be done. I tend to think I don't kill them. The other characters kill 'em. I shift off all blame from myself.

JW: What kind of advice would you give the young George Martin?

GRRM: I would say it depends on who he is and what stage of career he's in. For young writers in this market, I say don't quit your day job because you may need it. The field is constantly changing. It has booms. It has busts. We live in a time when the midlist, as they call it, has largely evaporated. So you have a lot of writers who get paid small change. You have a few writers who get paid a whole lot of money, and it's difficult to make the transition from one to the other. I think the career I actually anticipated before the big boom of 1977 is the one a lot of young writers need to look forward to. Simak's career, not mine or Stephen King's. The career where they work at a full-time job and pay their mortgage that way and put their kids through school. But they write nights and they write weekends and they keep writing and they publish their stories. Maybe eventually they break through and get to the point. But you can't count on that.

Writing is a terrible career if you're looking at it as a way to have a career. You should not choose writing as a way to make money, to make a name for yourself, or any of these other external things. If you have to write, if the stories are in you, if you made up names and stories for your toy spacemen when you were little, if the stories come to you, ask yourself the question, "What if no one ever gives me a penny for my stories? Will I still write them?" And if the answer is yes, then you're a writer. Then you *have* to be a writer. It's the only thing you can do.

If the answer is, "No, I'm going to quit after a few years because I'm not selling," then maybe you should quit right now and learn computer science. I hear there's a real future in these computer things.

Everybody looks at the writer's lifestyle. There are a lot of cool things about it. You are your own boss, you get to travel, people ask you for your autograph. Those are not reasons to write. The reason to write is you have stories to tell. You have people inside you clamoring to get out. That's what I'd tell the young kid.

JW: Moving into the future, a couple of hundred years from now, when historians look back at George R.R. Martin—all the stuff he has done, his impact on society—what do you want historians to say about you?

GRRM: Listen, I don't worry about anything like that. I hope my books are still being read a couple of hundred years from now. Are these historians or literary scholars? That's great because the vast majority of writers are forgotten. It's terrible, the ones that are forgotten in their own lifetimes. That can be heartbreaking.

But even ones that are very popular in their lifetimes tend to be forgotten a generation or two generations later. Sometimes they are then revived. Literature is a fickle bitch, and you never know who is going to be forgotten and who is remembered. So I don't worry about that.

I'm going back to *The Winds of Winter* and writing the next scene—I've got Dany in a particular situation. I've just got to worry about how does this scene resolve? How do I end this chapter? How do I phrase this sentence? I can't start thinking, "What will the historians of three hundred years from now think about this sentence?"

Most writers have enormous egos, so I'd like them to say, "Hey, he was the greatest writer who ever lived."

But reality is, they are probably not going to say that. But it's nice. You know, we all like applause. At least people like me, who are entertainers, like applause, to feel validated. We all like good reviews, whether I'm writing a Dr. Weird story in high school for some magazine, and there's a letter sent in saying that was a great Dr. Weird story. You like that just as much as you like people in *The Rolling Stone*, and the *New York Times* and *Vanity Fair*, doing features on you and saying that you're terrific. So that's cool. I hope the good opinion continues.

JW: What do you want to do that you haven't done?

GRRM: I want to be thirty years old again. I want to travel around the world. I never traveled when I was a kid growing up, so it's great that the success of these books has given me the ability to visit Australia and New Zealand and England and Croatia and Germany and Morocco, and all the amazing places that I've been. I want to keep going to amazing places and having adventures there. But I do want to work on that being thirty years old again.

So, dammit, I read in classic science fiction stories that they were supposed to come up with that immortality or perpetual youth serum by now.

Oh, and flying cars! Where's my flying car? I *am* getting a Tesla next week, though....

Expanded version of the interview that appeared in Issue 10 of
Galaxy's Edge, *September 2014, and then again in Issue 20, May 2016.*

■ JERRY POURNELLE

Jerry Pournelle was the author or co-author of numerous *New York Times* bestselling books including *Lucifer's Hammer* and the *The Legacy of Heorot*. He has been science editor of *Galaxy*, and his columns in *BYTE Magazine* were important in the computer revolution of the '80s. Well-known for collaborating with Larry Niven, he is a former aerospace human factors and operations research/systems analyst scientist, and was chairman of the committee that wrote space defense policy for the Reagan Administration. This included strategic defense (called Star Wars) and other military/aerospace Cold War projects. His most recent projects include an anthology on Planetary Defense.

■■■■■■

Joy Ward's original introduction: Jerry Pournelle was not only the co-author of several of the all-time classics of science fiction, **The Mote in God's Eye** *and* **Lucifer's Hammer,** *he was one of the architects of the most controversial space programs in the history of the United States, the strategic Defense Initiative (SDI), otherwise known as Star Wars. He was one of the first presidents of the Science Fiction and Fantasy Writers of America (SFWA) and active in* *helping to build the California Higher Education Board. Called a "Communist" as a teenager in Memphis, Tennessee, this acid-witted writer was considered for a high position in the Nixon administration. Pournelle was nothing if not a surprising sage of our times. He did us the great honor of meeting with us at his California home prior to a recent stroke.*

Jerry Pournelle: If I don't write, I don't eat.

I learned that from Mr. Heinlein. When I first started in this business Robert used to say, "Don't owe anybody any money. You never know what your income is, so don't owe anybody any money." I'm always being asked for advice for new writers, and I can give it to them real simple: don't stop writing. Don't worry about what you've written, worry about what you're going to write. Keep writing rather than arguing with people. Keep on doing. The other is: don't owe anybody any money.

JW: How did you start writing?

JP: I was in aerospace. I was a so-called systems analyst. I started at Boeing as an aviation psychologist. I was designing controls and control panels. I could write. When I met Mr. Heinlein, I told him I'd probably written more science fiction than he did. I was writing progress reports on research, and I didn't have to put any characters in mine.

I was part of the space program. The space program kind of dwindled out. I was the science project manager for Apollo 18. Now you say there was no Apollo 18, and I say, "Yes, that is why I became a professor at Pepperdine."

Then I got involved in city politics and became the deputy mayor of Los Angeles, but I didn't like it and I was looking for something to do. If it weren't for the Regents of California and the California Master Plan—which didn't pay any attention to anything we did. We were trying to build what we thought was a university system for the state of California. They weren't. They were building a university system to pay the faculty and the administration a hell of a lot of money, charge the students more than the students could afford, and never fire anybody. I didn't like that much.

While I was in college I had written a couple of mysteries under a pen name. As it so happened, when I wrote the mysteries I had been corresponding with Robert Heinlein for some years about the space program and what was going on. When I wrote the mysteries, I said, "Robert, I've given you a lot of stuff about the space business, can I ask a favor of you?"

He said, "I'm afraid I know what it's going to be, but what is it?"

I said, "Yes. I have written a book. Would you read it and tell me if it's worth doing?"

He said, "Well, okay." So he read it and he gave me a bunch of suggestions. I did it, and he said, "All right. I like that."

I said, "What will I do?"

He said, "You don't have to do anything else. I'll send it to my agent to see if he'll sell it for you."

That's wonderful! I didn't have to worry about that. Two years later it sold. I was a published writer, and I had a major agent if I wanted one. I was looking for something to do and I wasn't doing too well. I sold some stuff to *Analog Science Fiction*.

I called up my friends in the aerospace business and I got offered a GS-13 to be an assistant manager in the army's aviation design program. But that meant moving to St. Louis. I was about ready to sell the house and do that. I had the formal offer, and all I had to do was sign the papers. I was ready to do it and the earthquake happened. This was in the early 1970s and it was the Northridge earthquake. It didn't do much to this place, but you can see there are a lot of books around. Out of all those books, one book fell on the floor. The Los Angeles library was so full of books they were asking people to just come in and put them on the shelves; don't try to sort them just get them off the floor so we can rearrange them. I looked at [the book on the floor] and it was called *No Wonder We Are Losing* by Robert Morris, who had been a judge and the counsel for the Senate Internal Affairs Committee. It was basically an anti-Communist tract by an anti-Communist lawyer. That's interesting. I knew who he was, but I'd never met him. So I put the book back on my shelf and then thought maybe there's a message there. That's the only book that fell off. Maybe I should pay attention to that one.

That was on a Tuesday. The phone rang at eight in the morning. I got up and went to the office and picked up the phone and said, "Hello."

This voice says, "John Pournelle?"

I thought what the heck, at this hour of the day, so I said, "Yeah."

He said, "This is Robert Morris. I am the publisher of *One Circle, the National Catholic Press Weekly*." It was one of those tabloid weeklies sold in the back of Catholic churches. "I want you to write me a piece about the earthquake in Los Angeles."

I said, "Yes, sir."

He said, "I need it by Thursday morning. I'll pay you $800 for seven hundred words. No more, no less."

Yeah, all right. That's better than I'm making now. This is in the early 1970s. I believe the payment on this house was $400 a month. So that's good money. I wrote it and the editorial offices of the paper were down in Century City. I took it down there. The editor read it on the spot, and he said, "I like this. We've been looking for a science correspondent. Would you like to be the science correspondent?"

I said, "What does it pay?"

"It's weekly, to be seven hundred words, and I'll pay you $600 a week to do this."

In 1972, that's money. That was enough money that I could afford to pay for the house and he said, "I want you to go to the big AAAS meeting in Mexico City and you can take your wife if you want to. I want four or five articles out of that because we have been getting a lot of pressure from the Jesuits about not having enough science in the magazine."

So I became the science correspondent for the national Catholic press, and I told the Civil Service Commission thanks for the offer, but I guess I'll stay in California. I had to write seven hundred words a week, but the rest of the time I could do what I wanted, which meant that I could get into a big science fiction project with Larry Niven called *The Mote in God's Eye*, which I did.

So, meanwhile, the rent was paid. You could live on $600 a week then. That was decent money. It wasn't a hell of a lot less than what they were going to pay me for the civil service job. Of course, it was just a contract job. It didn't have any benefits.

But I started writing *The Mote in God's Eye,* which started selling and became a bestseller. That's how I started my career. I found out I could do it and make money at it.

JW: So you weren't one of these little boys who was writing in grade school?

JP: No, I had a reasonable classic education. Actually, I have edited and published this online: It's the *California Sixth Grade Reader* and there's all these stories by fellows like Longfellow and John Ruskin. That's the sort of thing I was raised reading. Kids nowadays are never exposed to stories like this, which is why I have published it. It is public domain, of course, but I published it as the editor. You can buy it online for four bucks or something. I make a fair amount of money out of it because homeschoolers like it and they should.

I didn't make much of a personal contribution to it. I wrote a couple of pieces for it, and I wrote an introduction on why you want to read this book to the kids. What I said was, "Of course you don't want to read this book. You were given this book and told to read it by somebody who either has the power to make you do it, or reward you for doing it, but let me tell you why you probably really *do* want to have read it, even if you don't." This was the kind of stuff that was the common factor of Western civilization when I was growing up, and I think I'm better for having done this book. Nobody in his right mind wants to read long books when they're eleven years old. But it turns out that if you do read enough of the stories you begin to like them, and after a while people quote Kipling at one another, and so forth. Modern kids don't understand that, but that's how you got an interest in reading, then writing. That's why I did that.

Anyway, now I've had five bestsellers since then and I've made a lot money. I make more money off of it than most people do on whatever else they're doing. I've got a decent house in Studio City. The house next door is owned by an actress on Tim Allen's shows. Ed Begley Junior lives about five houses down. Bill Nye, the science guy, is down on the next block. I've got a pretty good neighborhood. There are probably more studio writers and third-rate actors and that type. I've done well. I'm in good company. I've got more toys than I need.

JW: Here you are in LA. Have you been tempted to write for television?

JP: I have never wanted to. Niven and I have done a number of best-sellers, and we have sold the movie rights to a bunch of our stuff. No one ever made one, but they paid us a lot of option money. The options are better than if they make the movie because if you sell the option ten times you've made more money.

Our agent took us around to a bunch of studio places with the idea that we might create a show. This was back before the SyFy channel got big. It was just starting up. We might come up and be co-producers or chief writers or something. The first interview was with Joss Whedon's people. We got along fine with them. I thought working with guys like this would be interesting. There was plenty of mutual respect. We just didn't have anything. We had an idea for a series and that wasn't one he liked.

The next interview was with CBS or ABC. It was like five guys, twenty-eight years old, all of them looked alike, dressed alike, and had that kind of cynical what-have-you-talents-got-for-us type of attitude. It became obvious that none of them had ever read a book. They had read treatments of books, they had read scripts, other things, but never read a book. They didn't care about stories or storytelling. We left there thinking, "I'm glad we didn't make any deals with them."

We had two more interviews. I think it was at Disney. It was like it was the same five people every time. In the middle of the interview I stood up and I looked at Larry. I said, "Niven, do you understand that if we do everything just right, we get to spend a lot of time with these people?"

Larry said, "You're right. Let's go." And we walked out. We left our agent there to explain it to them. We didn't care anymore.

Every now and then I'm tempted to do something with the Hollywood people, but when I do I have a sure cure for it. I call up Harlan Ellison and let him tell me about his experiences, and I think, Harlan, you've got more patience than I've got. I just don't want to deal with those people.

There was one exception. James Cameron bought one of my novels to do it as his next picture. Instead he did *Avatar*. He paid a lot of money for my option. He was going to do it, but in the meantime, we went down to his office to talk to him. Golly, he knew more about my book than I did. He knew more about a lot of my books than I did. He knew a lot about Niven's stuff. Working with somebody like him would have been fun. But I don't think I've met more than ten people I could stand to work with for any great length of time in the Hollywood business, so I go to the parties instead.

My agent takes me to the parties. I've been going to them a long time. I met Arnold Schwarzenegger at one of them back when he was just an actor. Nice guy. I didn't know who he was at the time. I was talking to him for a while and then I realized, I am talking to the strongest man in the world. But he was just a nice fellow with an accent.

JW: Talk to me about your collaborations with Larry Niven.

JP: Larry has done a lot of collaborations, and in fact I wasn't the first one. He did something with David Gerrold before me, but *The Mote in God's Eye* and *Lucifer's Hammer* are very commercially successful.

I decided if I'm going to be a science fiction writer, what I've got to do is get famous quick. I looked around to see who I knew or could know who wrote the kinds of stuff I liked, that I could do something with. No point in trying to collaborate with somebody who's doing the same thing you are. I realized Larry writes better than me, but I think I'm better in the sense of plots and interweaving plots and subplots and a lot of that formal stuff. So I went to him and I said let's do it together.

He said, "We can talk about it." So we sat around and talked about it all night in his house with coffee and brandy, a lot of both. By dawn we had an outline for *The Mote in God's Eye*.

When we started, I said, "What would you like to write about?"

He said, "I've had this alien that I designed. I've had a vision of this asymmetric alien with two arms on one side and one on the other. But I don't know what to do with it."

I said, "First thing is, how the hell did it get that way? That's clearly, probably, an intelligent design, but we don't need God for it. It's obviously an intelligent design of an intelligent species that altered itself to be like that." We went on to do the whole history of this outfit. We've got notes that thick. By dawn we had a huge pad of paper about the Mote and what you'd find if you went on an archeological dig. That was the point. We got all the detail done, and I already had an empire I had invented for my stories so we'll just discover it in this book. How did it happen that they didn't know these guys were there? Well, if we put them behind the cold sack and we give them this problem that they can't get out of there, we made sense out of it. We finished with it and looked at it, and I told Larry: "You stick with me, buddy, and I'll make you rich and famous."

Larry said, "I'm already rich."

I said, "Yeah, you are. We'll both get famous, and I'll get rich."

He said, "Oh, all right. But you are going to do most of the work."

I said, "Of course I am. You're the senior author."

Well, that was the first one, and it worked that way. We have always had [an agreement about] who would be the senior author on a book. It's been me about as often as him, depending on the book. On the first one obviously it was going to be him. It was his reputation that was at stake.

We get along fine when not writing, too. I taught him to do backpacking and he came with me as my assistant, taking the Boy Scouts up into the High Sierras, back in the days before cell phones. Back when going up the mountains meant you were isolated up in the mountains. You weren't going to send for the rescue patrol because there wasn't any way to do it.

Larry had never done that before. The thing was, I had a bunch of kids, mostly movie kids but not all. Their parents couldn't do hikes, but the kids wanted to do it. It requires two adults if you're going to take that kind of hike. You can't do it by yourself. You have to have someone who can. Well, who do I know who can take two weeks off and go hiking? Of course, Larry Niven can, so, "Larry, you want to go?"

JW: What made you decide that you wanted to do that?

JP: Oh, I love hiking. I was raised by wolves. I was raised on a farm in World War II. My father was a radio station manager and my mother was an executive at the Crane Company and always busy, so I was raised by wolves. I like camping out and building fires with no matches. I must have read Kephart's *Camping and Woodcraft* forty times when I was a kid.

JW: What does that do for you to be able to take these kids out like you're talking about?

JP: It was a good way to get out on my own. I had four boys. You've got to do something with them. I took them all into the mountains—fifty, seventy miles into the High Sierras before there were cell phones.

JW: I'm assuming you brought them all back.

JP: Oh yeah. We had a couple of so-called emergencies when we went up the local mountain. A snowstorm started and we made camp. Somebody reported us missing and my wife got a phone call from a TV station. "How does it feel to have your husband lost in the mountains?"

"He's not lost."

As I told the parents, "I'd rather come home a day late than a boy short." There is no danger in making camp. I wouldn't go if we didn't have the equipment. We never went unequipped. Sometimes we would have to survive for a night in a storm. We'd make a fire.

JW: How have you used "being raised by wolves," as you say, in your books?

JP: My characters tend to be fairly competent and self-competent. Larry's don't, and the interaction between them works that way.

JW: Is there anyone else who you have wanted to work with?

JP: If the internet had existed in the '60s and '70s and early '80s I would probably have done some collaboration with Poul Anderson. Poul and I—Larry is kind of my best friend—but Poul and I were very close friends. I had to officiate at his funeral, which I hated. If we had lived closer, if he had a house in Berkeley and I had a house in Los Angeles, that would have worked. Mailing things back and forth, in the days of typewriters—it wouldn't have worked.

With Niven and I, we wrote our first two books on a typewriter, but we'd get together and work together every few days. Of course when they started doing computers, Poul wouldn't do it because he liked to rest his fingers on the keys of his old manual typewriter. He tried that with my computer and it jumped. So I probably would have worked with Poul if I could have.

JW: Any advice for people who are looking to collaborate?

JP: Yeah. Don't do it unless you have a good reason. Each of the collaborators does about 90 percent of the work. It doesn't look that way, but it is. Don't work with people you don't have respect for. Larry and I never have any big arguments. If he doesn't like something I did, there must be something wrong with it, something that needs changing. It's the same the other way around. If he does something I just don't feel right with, we don't argue about that because it's obvious something needs to be done so we do it. That's all.

You need rules as to who's going to do the final cut, and of course, that was me in our first book. That was part of the deal. I will do the integration so that it looks like only one guy wrote it. All our works are that way. I don't think you can tell who wrote what. You can tell some scenes must have been Niven's simply because he's crazy. I'll give you an example. *Lucifer's Hammer*. A comet is going to hit the Earth. We had a lot of technical details in it, some are mine, some are his. He's good at explaining things.

A year or two ago, *Nature* magazine, which is that big British heavy-duty publication like *Science in America*, did a four-page reminiscence on whatever anniversary of the publication of *Lucifer's Hammer*. Four pages in *Nature*. That's pretty good. I felt pretty good about that. But of course what did they open it with? They opened it with that scene of that crazy surfer trying to surf the mad, huge wave, the tsunami. Of course they did. Anybody who has read the book… they remember that scene. That's an image. There isn't any possibility I could have written that or even thought of that. As Larry says, "He's not mad enough to have thought of things like that." But in general, you can't tell who wrote what in our stuff. We try to make it smooth.

My advice to people who are collaborating is: don't do it unless you have a good reason. Don't do it unless you've got enough mutual respect that you are not going to fight about it. Now, that's not the case with all collaborations I know of. I know of collaborators who hate each other, but I couldn't live that way. I don't want to be that close to somebody I don't like.

JW: What about high points in your life? You have won so many awards.

JP: I suspect that biggest accomplishment we have is not a book at all. When Reagan was elected he asked General Schriver—retired General Schriever, a four-star general of Systems Command—to do a plan on space and defense for his incoming administration. This was in October of 1980, since the inauguration is going to be in January.

Schriever turned to Colonial Francis X. Kane, who died about six months ago. General Kane had been Schriever's Director of Plan for basically forever. Kane—this is a very complicated story—got his doctorate at Georgetown University from a man named Stephan T. Pusoni, who nobody has ever heard of nowadays. But Pusoni was a major intelligence officer in the United States. Well, he had been.

Pusoni got his doctorate in Vienna in 1930 or thereabouts. He was an advisor to the Schusnick government when they were trying to keep Austria independent of Germany, and they had Mussolini as an ally at that time. Well, that didn't work. When Hitler came in, Pusoni went to Slovakia and that didn't last long. He went to France and that didn't last long. He was in the air industry in France and that didn't last long. So he came to the United States and went to the Pentagon. Then Pusoni became a professor at Georgetown. He then became a Fellow at the Hoover Institute.

Pusoni and I were old friends and in 1970s when Pusoni and I published a book under our names called the *Strategy of Technology*, which you never heard of, but it was a textbook for West Point and Colorado Springs and I think even briefly for Annapolis; for a long time in Colorado Springs it was a textbook there.

Well, that book had a third author. The third author was Colonel Francis P. Kane, PhD, who, at the time the book was published, was an active duty Air Force officer and did not want his name on the book. So when Schriever asked Kane to hold a conference and come up with a space plan, Kane immediately calls up Pusoni and me and says, "What can we do about this?"

I said, "I know where we can have a meeting."

He said, "How?"

I said, "Have Larry Niven host it. Having it in a house rather than a hotel is going to make it a lot more congenial. He, being a California millionaire, has a big enough house to do that."

Marilyn, Larry's wife, agreed, so she end[ed] up doing gourmet meals for seventy people, starting with Buzz Aldrin and Edward Teller. Teller wasn't there but his deputy was, and a whole bunch of people, like the manager of the aerospace program at Northamerican, Max Hunter, who was probably the most eminent rocket scientist in the country at the time.

Because its Niven and I doing it, we can invite anybody we wanted, so we invited Heinlein, Poul Anderson, his son-in-law Greg Bear, because, as Larry said, "We're going to need people to write the reports, and if we get a technical writer to come in here, he's going to tell us how to design a wrench. We want someone to write something people will read."

That's how a bunch of science fiction writers and General Morris and General Graham and whole bunch of other generals—some of them *still* on duty, so their names are *not* on the report, some retired and their names are on the report—were in the same room. So we did this paper and we sent it in.

Well, there's one more piece to this. One of the people who got his doctorate from Pusoni at Georgetown was a chap who was courted by Reagan to be his national security advisor. So we had direct access to the president.

Either way, we wrote it. We invented SDI [Strategic Defense Initiative] basically and Larry likes to say we saved civilization. I don't know about that, but I think we had something to do with it. I think it was important and when Reagan made his Star Wars speech two years later, a lot of it came right out of the stuff we had done; we had five meetings of this council and I wrote most of the final drafts of the report.

JW: How did that make you feel?

JP: There was a time Henry Salvatore, who was the finance chairman for the Republican Party in California, had recommended to Nixon in '68 that I should be the assistant secretary of the Air Force for Research and Development, which is a job I am qualified to do. I thought I was going to do that, but it turns out that two of Nixon's staff members didn't like me. Their names were Haldeman and Ehrlicmann and they didn't care for me, and in fact the phrase one of them used was "too inflexible." I don't know what that means but my guess is "too principled." I don't know. All I know is that was the reason I was put out of a job and the reason I became a writer was basically because I did not get that appointment to the Air Force.

JW: So you're telling me that we can thank Nixon for your writing?

JP: Not really Nixon himself. I think Nixon actually was going to make the appointment and the two staff guys vetoed it. In any event, I did not go to Washington, and I did not sell this house, which I am very glad I did not do.

JW: You've been in the science fiction field during a large part of the heyday. How are you seeing science fiction change?

JP: In the first place, fantasy is much bigger than science fiction. It wasn't when I started in this business. *Analog* was the big, important magazine. When John Campbell died, they offered Poul Anderson the editorship and Poul didn't want it and he recommended me. So- They offered it to me, but they were only paying $13,000 a year, and I couldn't live in New York City on that kind of money. I'm sure they paid John a lot more than that, but that was what they offered me.

Well, I wasn't going to go do it. Fortunately, Ben Bova, although he lived in Florida, had a house in Connecticut. He could afford to take the job, so they got a good man to be the editor at *Analog*. It's a good thing because *Analog* was terribly important to the science fiction community in those days.

My world changed. People ask me, how do you become a successful writer? It's simple. Write a bestseller. After that, everything you do is successful. The publishers love you. But you may say, how do you do that? I've told you how to do it. I leave the details up to you. You will recognize that as a parody on a Will Rogers story. They asked him what to do about the submarines and he supposedly said, "Boil the Atlantic Ocean. They'll have to come up and you can sink them."

The navy guy knows his leg is being pulled by this time, so he says, "How do you do that?"

He said, "Don't bother me about details."

Before I had bestsellers, *Analog,* and selling to *Analog,* was a very important part of science fiction. No longer. Some people do. Some don't. But it's not the major source of income anymore.

In those days you didn't have many books. My first science fiction novel was serialized in *Analog* before it ever was a book. The book is still in print, and it is up on *Analog* as an e-book.

JW: Are you seeing any trends in science fiction?

JP: The trend is there aren't any. There are a lot of schools in science fiction. There's a lot less demand for consistency. The kind of stuff I did was what you used to call "hard science fiction," which was to say if you make an assumption, then that assumption is going to change other things. You have to deal with that. You just can't assume that we're going to have anti-gravity. That changes everything we think we know about physics. The old school that I come from, it means you have to think of other implications for having done that.

They don't do that anymore. Now it's just, oh boy, we've got anti-gravity. We're going from there. I can't write that kind of story. Larry's better than I am at writing things he doesn't really believe in. When we work together I keep pulling it back to reality. That's one of the reasons why our collaborations sell a hell of a lot better than either one of us does individually. Part of that is because I do keep it to reality while it's still got all that sparkle that Niven's prose puts in. When he's doing it by himself, he will take an idea and run with it until it's so far out of sight you don't know where he's gone. It's all right. He doesn't care. Sometimes he does that very well, but it's a different kind of story than what we would have written together.

I don't know, the trends are strange. There's a whole bunch of different avenues. There are people who think we need more diversity in science fiction. Well, what do you mean by that? We've got all these people of color and women. What do you mean? Do you mean we are supposed to favor some story because of the race of who wrote it as opposed to how good it is? At which point I was told I was insulting, and I should be thrown out of the club.

I didn't mean any insult to anybody. Just that I don't know what it means to promote diversity as diversity. I have never in my life been in favor of rejecting a story because it was written by a woman or by somebody of a different orientation than me. That's all irrelevant to me.

I seem to be in trouble with the diversity crowd in the science fiction business because people are taking it as a personal insult because I don't think we ought to promote things on the basis of *who* wrote them. That's not my intention. In fact, I think I would have been insulted if they promoted one of my books because I'm white.

JW: There's a lot of discussion now about being a member of SFWA. Is it still valuable to be a member?

JP: You're not going to get me to say much on SFWA. I was the former president. I rewrote the constitution on coming into office. I was tricked into being president. Harlan Ellison said he was running for president, and he wanted someone to oppose him. Would I run against him so it would look like a fair election? I'm a new kid. I've only just joined. Okay, Harlan, I'll do that. Then he said, "Fine. I quit. This guy, vote for him. He knows how to manage things." I'm not kidding. Ask Harlan.

Harlan and I have a very peculiar relationship. We are pretty close friends and have been for forty-plus years. I don't think there's much of anything we agree on. I can think of almost nothing we agree on other than movie producers are not nice people. Anyway, he's a great guy, but he likes to give the impression that he isn't though.

JW: As you look in the future, what do you want your legacy to science fiction to be?

JP: I never thought of it. I have no idea. I don't win awards, I never have. On the other hand, I know for a fact that I outsell most of the award winners by a lot. I know we have done very well, but I don't win awards. I'm not allowed to say what I actually think of awards.

JW: How do you want to be remembered?

JP: From my point of view I would rather be thought of as the guy who came up with the strategy that ended the Cold War. At the time we were just trying to get through it. Most people nowadays don't remember what the Cold War was. They don't remember that in 1980 there were 26,000 nuclear warheads aimed at the United States. There were kids sitting in silos on Christmas night, sitting in these L-shaped things with these keys around their necks listening for that claxon. Something could have happened at any time. That was a pretty scary time. I grew up in World War II. I was never as afraid as I was during the Cuban Missile Crisis. Well, if I'm going to be remembered I think I want to be remembered as one of the designers of the Strategic Defense Initiative.

It means my kids don't have to grow up being scared *to death*.

I don't exaggerate my own importance in things, but I've been pretty influential. I've been president of the Science Fiction and Fantasy Writers of America. I've been an influential writer. I've been invited to be a speaker at a lot of places. Mostly I tell stories for a living. I think science fiction is important, but I don't think it's the only thing in the world.

I wrote a piece for the *Encyclopedia Britannica* on science fiction. I'm sure they've got something else in there now, but my essay was that "We're the Bards of the Sciences." We're basically like the old Homeric singers. We go around with our lyre on our back and our cup. We see a campfire over there and here's a bunch of Bronze Age warriors sitting around roasting an ox. We say, hey fellas, cut me a chunk of that ox and here's my cup. Fill me up and I'll tell you a story about a virgin and a bull that you just wouldn't believe. I'll tell you about when men can fly and bronze men run around.

I sing for my supper, and I think I earn my money.

I sing for my supper, and I get well paid for it. I haven't had any audiences walk out on me.

Expanded version of the interview that appeared in Issue 13 of Galaxy's Edge, *March 2015.*

■ NANCY KRESS

Nancy Kress is the author of thirty-four books, including twenty-seven novels, four collections of short stories, and three books on writing. Making over one hundred short-fiction sales, Nancy's work has won six Nebulas (for "Beggars in Spain," "The Flowers of Aulit Prison," "Out of All Them Bright Stars," "Fountain of Age," "The Erdmann Nexus," and "Yesterday's Kin"); two Hugos (for "Beggars in Spain" and "The Erdmann Nexus"); a Sturgeon (for "The Flowers of Aulit Prison"); and the John W. Campbell Memorial Award (for *Probability Space*). Her most recent novels are the first two books in a trilogy: *Tomorrow's Kin* and *If Tomorrow Comes*. In 2015, Subterranean Press released a 200,000-word volume of *The Best of Nancy Kress*.

■■■■■■

Joy Ward's original introduction: Nancy Kress is one of science fiction's crown jewels. She is a writer of powerful science fiction, having won Hugos and Nebulas. She also is known as a talented writing teacher.

■■

Joy Ward': How did you get started writing?

Nancy Kress: By accident. I had never planned on being a writer. When I was a child, I thought all writers were dead because the writers I was reading were Louisa May Alcott, and the like. I really did not realize that writing was a commodity that was still being produced. I thought it was like oil—there was a finite amount of it.

Then I discovered that there were actual writers living and this completely shocked me, but I come from a very conservative Italian-American family, and I grew up in the 1950s. My mother sat me down when I was twelve and said, "Do you want to be a teacher, a nurse, or a secretary?" Because those were the only possible things she could think of, and I thought it over and I said, "Okay, I'll be a teacher." So I became a fourth-grade teacher, and I was for four years. I enjoyed it.

Then I got married and had my children. I was pregnant with my second child. We lived way out in the country. There were no other women at home. They were all older and had gone back to work. My then-husband took our only car to work, and he was taking an MBA, so he often didn't come home for dinner; he stayed for classes. I was there with my one-year-old to eighteen-month-year-old, very difficult pregnancy, and I was going nuts.

I started writing to have something to do that didn't involve Sesame Street, and I didn't take it seriously. It was a thing I was doing while the baby was napping, to try to have something of my own. I would send them out. They'd come back. I'd send them out. They'd come back. After a year, one sold. After another year, a second one. After another year, a third one sold, then it started to pick up and I began to take it more seriously, but I didn't plan on doing this.

I remember [selling the first story] very well. It was to *Galaxy*, which is a magazine long-defunct. What I didn't know is that everybody else had stopped submitting to *Galaxy* because it was trembling on the verge of bankruptcy. I had no connection with fandom. I didn't know it existed; I didn't know SFWA existed. I didn't know conventions existed. When I first sold it, it turned out that nobody else was submitting anything, and they were desperate. So they published my story immediately, then it went bankrupt. It took me three years to get my $105. I wanted it, and I kept writing and I'd say, "This is my first sale. I want my $105." And for that, eventually, I think he had pity and he sent me the check.

I did it. That was what goes through my mind. Three words, "I did it." I didn't think I could, but I did it. It felt really good. I still wasn't taking it seriously as a career, but it felt really good. What I remember more vividly, is that sale of my first novel.

This was five or six years later and my then-agent, called me up on Valentine's Day in 1980, and she said, "Well it's been three years or whatever, but Pocket Books is taking it." I was stunned. It was a minute or two before I could even talk, and I'm just holding the phone there and she said, "Are you there?"

I said, "Yes, yes, yes, yes." But yes it was an incredible moment.

For me, I guess erroneously, I thought that now I had sold a novel it would all be smooth sailing from then. I have talked to other writers who have had the same experience, who thought, "I'm in." That's it. It's now going to go on like this, and of course it didn't. David Hartwell, who had published the first novel, rejected the second one—rightly, it's not a good book. Eventually somebody else published it, but when I get it in line for a signing, I write in it, "Don't read this one, this is not good. Read some of the others." Because I don't like it anymore. It was not a good book. But you learn. It's not a straight line for some people like it is for Silverberg. For most of us it's an up and down, and up and down, and up and down, and that's what my career looks like.

So many writers have told me that. I think a rollercoaster is much more the norm than the straight line, but I didn't know that. I didn't know anything. I didn't know that the whole apparatus of fandom, and SFWA, and conventions existed.

Then somebody gave me a copy of *Locus*, and I said, "Oh." *Locus* did conventions listings then. I thought, "Look at this! There's a whole community out there. There's an apparatus. There's stuff." So I signed up for a local convention. There was no online portal, but I mailed it in. I threw my stuff in the car and went. I didn't know anybody, and I was too shy to introduce myself. Even though I'd sold three stories, I was too shy to introduce myself to any of the pros.

I went to every single panel I could because I wanted to see these writers that I've been reading since I was fifteen, and it was just so interesting to me. I wanted to see what the writers I've been reading look like. My second one was a real con in Boston, so there were a lot more writers, and nobody looked and sounded like I expected except Robert Silverberg. He looked and sounded exactly like I expected him to, but everybody else was a revelation. It was interesting to me to hear what they had to say about writing, and it was interesting to see the camaraderie, the joking that went on during panels. But mostly I just wanted to look at them.

I learned that there was an apparatus, that there was a dealer's room. There were lots of science fiction books in one place, and jewelry, and knives. This was before the peace-bonding of weapons, so there were a lot of knives and evidence that there was sword fighting, even in the hall. I learned that this was a place I wanted to be.

But the place that really came through to me was a few years later at a Boskone. The old Boskone was in the Boston Sheraton and with two towers, and I could stay up later then. I had been to a party at one tower, and I would go back down and cross the lobby, and I was waiting for the elevator to go up in the other tower—it was 1:00 in the morning. And because that Sheraton was near Logan, the airlines maintained a lot of suites for their pilots and stewardesses that were doing layovers. So I'm standing there, waiting for the elevator, and a pilot and three stewardesses come up dragging their little suitcases, and they looked dog-tired. I mean they looked like they can barely stand. We all stood in there waiting for the elevator and it opens, and there are three guys dressed as barbarians holding spears, with goatskin wine bags, and they're chanting to Ra the sun god and as if it had been choreographed—the pilot and all the stewardesses took a step backward.

I got on the elevator, and I thought, I just made a decision here. This is my community, I just made a decision. If I hadn't been so tired it probably would've felt great. But it was clear that I was throwing in my lot with the strange ones. And you notice I still don't look like I've thrown my lot in, but I have.

I spent most of my life living in my imagination. My mother is a wonderful person but a very realistic, practical one. She would read, but she would only read romances. Not that those are realistic and practical but you could follow them, and they were in a world she understood. She never understood why I wanted to write science fiction. She never really understood—neither did my father—anything about my attraction to the genre. So much of my life had gone on in my head. I discovered science fiction when I was fourteen, and the reason it happened so late is that there was a girl section in the library at school and a boy section. All the science fiction was shelved in the boy's section, with little rocket ships, and I never went over there because I was a goody-goody. When I did, the first book I ever read was *Childhood's End* by Clarke. I thought, "This is a canvas big enough. This matches what goes on in my head."

I like to be able to visualize in my books people from different societal levels, different classes, and different positions in life. Much of modern-American literature, much as I like a lot of it, focuses in a very small range. This family, this marriage, maybe this community, but it doesn't cover a lot of time and it doesn't cover a lot of space.

The Victorians did do that. In many ways, the modern science fiction novel is the inheritor of the Victorian novel. Dickens for instance, because it covers larger societal sweeps, even though our societies are often invented and theirs are not. But I liked that, I liked the grandness of it, the size of it.

I think one of the best things about being a writer, maybe *the* best, is the feeling of getting out of your own head. What it makes me feel is when the work is going well and you're in that flow state, you forget the room around you, you forget the keyboard, you forget yourself. You're not there. You're in the story, and you're not you. It's a method of out-of-body experiences that doesn't involve a lot of drugs.

Then if the doorbell rings, or the dog barks, or my husband comes in, there's a moment of disorientation. You get it when you're reading too, and you're really immersed in a book, although I can no longer read that way and I'll tell you why in a minute.

But there's that transition where you're back into the real world, "Oh, I'm here." And sometimes there's a little feeling of disappointment. So what it makes me feel to get into that writer tapestry, whether I'm writing it or whether reading it, is an escape from self, that is non-dangerous and non-permanent.

I can't do it when I read anymore because one of the things about being a writer is you can't read like a virgin anymore. When I'm reading, if it's good, I stop and say, "How did he do that? Can I steal it?" If it's bad I'm thinking, I have a mental red pencil and I'm thinking, "That's a misplacement. What if I move it over?" Consequently, I can no longer completely immerse myself in a piece of fiction in the way I could when I was young. The editorial me takes over.

Oh, it's a loss, like everything is a loss. Innocence is always a loss, but ideally, it's a gain as well. It's a gain because I can better differentiate what is good and what is not, and I can better admire the good in a way that I couldn't when I was younger. You always lose something when you go forward.

Whenever I'm writing a book, I love it—or a story. Later that may not be true. For a short story it may not be true, a week after I finish it. For a novel, maybe six months. Some objectivity sets in after, but while I'm writing something I'm always wildly enthused about it. There's lots of high points while this is happening.

Writing *Stinger*, I fell in love with Robert Cavanaugh, my major character. That'll happen every once in a while. He became so real and so solid to me, that I would dream about him, and I would also sometimes find myself thinking if I saw something, "What would Robert think about that?" And Robert doesn't exist. Robert is only in my head. So that's some sort of a high point, although it's a high point that's verging on the edge of multiple personality disorder.

One of the great things about being married to another writer is that not only are there practical advantages like you know the same people and you can critique each other's manuscripts, which he does for me, but it also means they understand the strange mental processes that writers go through. I can understand why Jack is standing there staring out the window saying nothing for twenty minutes, but he's not looking at whatever's outside the window, he's looking at whatever's in his head.

JW: What does that say to you when you look at the six Hugos and two Nebulas lined up on your shelf? That's pretty good for somebody who didn't plan on doing this.

NK: They say to me they're validation; that somebody liked my work. Creating the work is half of it, and I have to say that for me it's the bigger half, although I realize this is mathematically imprecise. It is the bigger part, the creation, but having created it, the other half is to say you want people to read it. The Hugos and the Nebulas say to me, "Enough people read this and liked it, that they voted for it." That pretty much has to be the only thing because God knows it hasn't helped my sales any. I think it's the validation, is what I've gotten from it.

It's a part of my identity. It's not the whole thing because I'm also a mother, and a teacher, and a wife, and a friend, and I'm close to my birth family, especially my sister. It's not the only piece of my identity, but it's a big one, If I were to stop writing tomorrow, I would still be me. I'd still have many facets from my identity, but there would be a hollow.

The hollow would look like lostness I guess. It would look like a constriction. It would look like my life had shrunk a little bit, in a way that I don't want it to shrink. But writers don't retire. Like all soldiers, like MacArthur, we just fade away, and I expect that that's probably what's going to happen. I'll just write less and less when I get older. I'll still be Nancy, but I'll be a diminished Nancy.

There's either something added to people like us who would like to imagine what isn't there, or something missing from people who don't, depending on how general you want to be here. But I think there is that quality of imagination where something that doesn't exist is as interesting to you as the things that do exist, and for me if you ask how I feel about that, it gives a different and an added dimension to life. There's reality and there's also hyper-reality or invented reality. So I get two dimensions, and that's a source of pleasure.

JW: Where do you see your writing going?

NK: I don't know. My first three books are fantasy. Then I switched over to science fiction. I don't know why, except a story occurred to me I wanted to write, and then I wrote several books of science fiction without any actual real science in them. Then I became interested in genetic engineering, and I don't know why. The last several books have all been much more hard SF as each one goes along, and *Yesterday's Kin* is very hard SF. It's very closely allied to what actual scientists do, and how they do it.

I'd like to write another space opera. I wrote the *Probability* se-ries—*Probability Moon, Probability Sun,* and *Probability Space.* I'd like to do that again. I've been doing some smaller focus ones, and I think I would like to do that.

JW: Well, what's attractive about that?

NK: The largeness of the canvas. Heavily influenced by *Childhood's End* and how much larger canvas, how much wider canvas can you get than that? I—it's always a balance, the character himself or herself is a small canvas, and then the whole setting and plot is a large canvas. How much verbiage do you spend on each? If you're Olaf Stapleton, you have no characters to speak of. You're dealing only with the large canvas. If you're a modern-American literary writer, you don't have a large canvas, you only have the small one. The more verbiage you spend in one, less verbiage you have for the other, and it's always a balancing act that I think we're always striving to get right.

JW: How do you see yourself being seen in the future?

NK: Very hard SF writer. That's what they're saying now, and I think they're going to go on saying it. I've been on three science panels and I was scheduled for a fourth, but the timing didn't work out. I'm not a scientist. I'm not trained, and here's what I think happened. Some-body says, "Oh we're going to do this panel. We need a woman. Get Kress." There are not a lot of women writing very hard SF. I'm glad about it in a way, but I also wish they would put me in some writing panels because this is something I'm more familiar with than genetic engineering, even though I love genetic engineering and I talk about it endlessly. I'm not trained.

First published in Issue 28 of Galaxy's Edge, *September 2017.*

JOE HALDEMAN

Joe Haldeman is a science fiction author, lover of music, artist (a gallery in his hometown recently showed his work), and astronomer, who lives with his wife, Gay, in Gainesville, Florida. His first novel, *War Year*, was published in 1972, following his tour in Vietnam. That novel helped him get [accepted] into the prestigious Iowa Writers' Workshop at the University of Iowa, where he wrote a science fiction novel for his master's thesis. You've heard of that thesis: it's *The Forever War*, which has become one of those rare books that wins all the available awards, has gratifyingly large sales, stays in print forever, gets optioned for Hollywood, and is made into a play and even a graphic novel. From 1983 to 2014, Joe spent each fall semester teaching science fiction writing at the Massachusetts Institute of Technology.

Joy Ward's original introduction: Joe Haldeman is a treasure. He's a storyteller who loves weaving tales which enwrap everyone. He is a science fiction Grand Master who has published poetry, novels, short stories, and if anyone invents a new literary form, this gentleman will be one of the first to master that field as well.

Joy Ward: How did you get started writing?

Joe Haldeman: I've written since I was four years old.

JW: What were you writing?

JH: Cartoons. Comic strips, basically. Graphic novels before the term had been invented. I'd draw them and color them, and my mother would sew them with bindings. I wish I had a few of those. I could probably retire on them.

It's so far back I can't say. I would tell the other kids stories. One thing, I would go into the basement of a friend of mine and I would give lectures for ten cents. I would lecture about volcanoes or tides or the Moon or whatever. And basically it was Saturday morning, and so all the neighborhood mothers would send their kids over with their dimes. That would free up at least a little of their mornings so the ladies could get together and have some coffee. Get the kids out of their hair. And I got some valuable experience in lecturing. Oddly enough, they were called lectures. And so I was a lecturer at that tender age.

JW: How old were you when you were doing that?

JH: Fifth grade? I guess ten years old.

JW: How did you get into being a lecturer even at ten years old?

JH: I don't know. It must be in your blood. 'Cause my father wasn't a lecturer. He had been way into school, a PhD. I grew up in a family that respected education and thought it was necessary. But I don't know. It was just show-offy. That's what kids do to get attention, so I got attention.

I was never any good with sports. That was a crucial part of my growing up. I couldn't throw. I couldn't catch. I couldn't hit a ball. I couldn't even run. A kid ought to be able to run, but I was uncoordinated.

JW: What's the first thing that you wrote that actually got published?

JH: When I was ten years old I wrote a poem that was published in the *Washington Post*.

I guess my first real fiction was published the last semester I was in college. Or rather, I sold it my last semester in college. It wasn't published until after I got out of the army.

I took a writing course. My advisor absolutely wouldn't let me take writing until the last semester. I had all my coursework done in physics and astronomy and she said, "Do whatever you want. It's a waste of time."

So I did, and I wrote two stories and sold them before I was drafted. Then when I came back from Vietnam they came out in magazines. I began writing more.

The first one was called "Out of Phase," and it was in *Galaxy Magazine*. The second one was "Eye of Newton," which was in *Fantastic*. "Eye of Newton" became a story on *The Twilight Zone*.

"Out of Phase" was about an alien left on earth as part of his maturing processes, an embryo, and it destroys all life on earth as a part of a growing-up exercise. I thought: it works. It's kind of hard to get a sequel, but in fact I did.

"Eye of Newton" was just a silly deal-with-the-devil story. I had a short story due for this course and put it off and put it off. The night before it was due I just started typing like a madman. So, I typed up this story and gave it to the professor.

The next class he came over to me and he's a little annoyed. He said, "You're a ringer, aren't you? You've published before. This story is publishable."

"No, I haven't published before." But yeah, I sent it out and it sold. I sent the other one out and it sold. And then I sent out a novel and it sold. I did not have the rejection slip collection most people have, and I have found over the ensuing decades that maybe a quarter of the professional writers I know have the same experience, and it's not quality of writing. It's largely the first publication is a crapshoot. But then with subsequent ones you are a published writer, and so it is much easier to get over the transom.

At first (when the professor said I was a ringer) I was a little insulted. I said, "I am not cheating. I just wrote this." But he was of course being humorous, so I talked with him a little bit. He didn't know anything really about professional publishing, but he was a literary guy. Looking at it now, I say, yeah, it is publishable. This is as good as most magazine fiction. What can I say? Some people don't need a lot of practice.

JW: *Then you were drafted.*

JH: Yeah. I was a combat engineer.

JW: *What of that time did you bring back with your writing?*

JH: A lot of the experience. My first novel was basically a recounting of the year I spent in Vietnam. *The Forever War* is basically that put into a science fiction concept.

In fact, being drafted gave me my writing career. I don't know what I would have done if I had not had the army experience. I would have written science fiction, I think, but it would have been quite different. I'm not a particularly employable person, and so writing was very attractive in that it didn't require bosses or hours or anything like that. So it was really made for me. I would have been a bum of some kind.

I see this in my students all the time. I see people who are just ready for a job and before they've got their degree they are searching, looking through the possibilities. They know what they want to do. They probably won't do that in the long run, but they know what they want to do as soon as they get out. And then over at the other end of the spectrum are the, "Jeez, they want me to get a job after this?"

The thing is, I wanted to be an astronomer; but the kind of astronomer I wanted to be they don't have anymore—get paid for looking through a telescope. Nobody does that, literally. How can you get paid for looking through a telescope, when the only things that look through telescopes now are cameras and spectrometers and things like that?

So I got a job with the Naval Observatory. This is going to be gold for me. Because I want to be a writer, and I also want to be a scientist and the job enables me to write. They would send me down to this little observatory in Chile. Gay [Joe's wife and inspiration] had a degree in Spanish so she would be able to work outside, and I would be up on this mountain with a dome and a telescope. The terms of it were, I would spend forty hours on the mountain up there and then come down and spend forty hours doing nothing and drawing a paycheck. Well hell, I can write for a week and then go up, be an astronomer for a week. It was just a perfect opportunity. The Naval Observatory said, "Yeah, okay we'll employ you," but then I got drafted. When I came back the job wasn't there anymore.

I had started writing in Vietnam. I wrote to her [Gay] every day, literally a letter a day. I wrote poetry. I didn't write any fiction when I was overseas, but I really wanted to. When I got out of the army, I did.

My father had sent me *Conan the Barbarian* and *Conan the Conqueror,* and I thought "This is pure crap. I can write this." It's probably the worst thing for a new writer to think. Yeah, anybody can do this, and that includes me. I started a *Conan the Barbarian* rip-off while I was in Vietnam. But because I am an artiste I wrote it in linked couplets as I was on this great poetic thing.

JW: Do you still have it?

JH: No, in fact the enemy got it—the Vietnamese. Yeah, they read it and said, "Oh shit, we're done."

No, actually, I went out on an assignment and things got all strange. When I went back about two weeks later, the bunker where my story had been was a crater and it was gone. I found a couple of pieces, and I thought, God says I'm not going to be a writer. Who's going to argue with God?

JW: I'm hearing a theme right through your life. You're still only in your early twenties and everything is centered around the writing. What is it about writing?

JH: You always look for hints in a child. Writing was a sort of a special blessed kind of thing. My mother taught me how to write and read. You know Chinese children learn how to write because their mothers hold their hands and move the brushes around. I guess I was sort of like that, because my mother paid attention to everything that I did when I was about four years old and starting to just find my way. And she loved my poetry, my verse, and she bound it into these little books. I drew colors for my little books. So I haven't fallen far from that tree, I guess. Except I have a publisher instead of a mother.

53

I'm really a rather quiet and private person. Being a writer has forced me to be more public and communicative, and so forth. I would have been a much different person than I have been, if not for writing.

JW: What did writing do for you once you came home from the war?

JH: Well, in the broadest general sense it gave me someone to be, something to do that wasn't just turning out a paycheck. But that happened very, very fast thanks to science fiction. If I had just been ordinary Joe with my talents, I'm not sure what would have happened. With science fiction I came virtually out of Vietnam and straight into the conventions, science fiction's social circuit.

The people I admired were science fiction writers, and, as it happened and still happens, I knew them as friends before I could write. I could write, but I wasn't doing anything very public about it. But at the same time, I came in and started writing for my brother's fanzine. So [I was] doing little bits of fan fiction and reviews and stuff like that. He had a great big old Gestetner press, and he made a real professional fanzine. So I inched into it that way and, I don't know, I wrote stories. And once those were published, I just started doing more.

I went to the Milford Writer's Conference and that's when I knew, you have to write books. There's no living in short stories. This is where I started making contacts, although my professional contacts were outside of science fiction. My first novel was *War Year*, which is not science fiction. I started with this identity as a mainstream novelist. It was parallel to my identity as a science fiction writer. Basically with *The Forever War* it came together because *The Forever War* was published as a straight novel. They didn't have a science fiction department at St. Martin's Press at the time. It was reviewed as a mainstream novel set in the future, which actually made for fewer sales at first. It gave it permanence and gave it a large audience. It was reviewed in places like *Harper's* and the *New York Times Book Review* as a mainstream novel with aliens and spaceships.

JW: I've heard over and over that you're one of the people who began military science fiction.

JH: Yeah, but who knew? I didn't think about it that way. I had read *Starship Troopers* and really enjoyed it, but I didn't see it as a genre or something. It was just a natural thing to write about among the interesting things to write about. It's automatically dramatic. It automatically has structure. And it's interesting. It's full of detail stuff. I mean, a lot of stories, science fiction or whatever, fail because of a lack of supporting detail, because you know everything about the inside of this guy's mind and write a fascinating story about what's going on. Boring as hell unless he rubs up against the environment and does this and that and the other thing. That's rule zero of writing fiction. People have to be interested in what you're doing. So war, even for female readers—which was a distinction we used to make—war is kind of interesting too because it is so basic, so primal.

It was my personal experience. That was the most dramatic thing that ever happened to me, and every soldier has his own set of experiences, and I think everybody has his own war. This is mine, and since it was the most dramatic thing that had happened to me it was the natural thing to write about. I was of the age to write about it. Twenty-four, twenty-five. I mean, if you've written short stories, it's time to start a novel.

I went to the Iowa's Writers' Workshop, which is where a lot of academic writing careers started. I wrote them a kind of naïve letter. "I've heard the Writers' Workshop is such a wonderful place. I've only written one novel, but it's gotten good reviews." I sent them my first novel and this full-page review from the *New York Times Book Review*. And it was a snow job. I dare you not to accept this guy. They actually gave me an assistantship.

I don't know how it's done now, but, in that time, if they liked the fiction sample you sent, they would assign you to one of the professors and they give you some sort of make-work job for a year, maybe two years, turning a mimeograph handle or something. Then, if you were okay the first year, they give you some classes the second year. I wound up teaching bonehead English. It's called Rhetoric Ten. It was essentially a writing course for people who couldn't pass the writing exam. That was the most valuable course I ever taught, for me.

Basically, here are a bunch of people who are probably never going to make it through college, but I want you to give them a real solid writing assignment. Find out whether they have a shred of literacy, basically. So I did and probably half of those people will never graduate from any meaningful program and probably a quarter of them were pretty good writers, but they needed a fire lit under them. They needed an assignment so they could practice. But for a teacher, a person who might want to teach, it's a wonderful experience because you had to motivate these people, most of whose motivation is to stay out of the army. And that started to dwindle away because the war was over. It was good and I got introduced to the academic life.

A pretty interesting part is Iowa is competitive like Harvard. It's really a hard place to start out. I'm a killer. Throw me a challenge. I will wrestle it to the ground and tear it into little pieces because that was the way I was taught in my previous company, my little job there. I was not a standout as an academic. But I was publishing stories and getting paid in real folding money for them, and everybody at the workshop was [thinking], "What's wrong with this guy?"

We'd be throwing dinner parties and taking people out for drinks. We were church mice ourselves, but we had money to spare because I was not just a veteran, I was a combat-disabled veteran, so I was getting huge checks by graduate-student standards. Then I was selling stories. We both had assistantships. Your wealth depends on where you are in relation to the people around you, and we were fucking loaded.

Looking back at what I wrote in those years it gave me a kind of contact with the snobbish side of writing, and I saw I could use my skills in various ways. To make a crude comparison, one of them was to sell stories and get a lot of readers, and the other was to demonstrate how sophisticated I was—the stories and the style of writing—so I tried to do both.

As an index of my own popularity at the time, I think that I was trying to stay in both camps. It's like one of those fun house things where you have one foot on this disc and one foot on that disc and they're going different ways. If you can stay up, you are making a living. That was what I was doing. People who liked one story wouldn't even read the other story. I was covering a lot of ground; not so much carving out a niche for myself as being like a film of contamination all over the conceptual universe.

People don't have expectations of me doing the same thing again because how can you extrapolate from two separated examples? I mean, I was successful in lyric poetry, to nuts-and-bolts science fiction, and a lot of real estate in between. So as a young writer I was getting a lot of chops around the place, which is probably not the best advice to give to a young writer.

I could write anything I wanted, go anywhere I wanted. If I had stuck to hard SF, stuck to *Analog* writing, I probably would have advanced faster as an *Analog* writer, but as it was, I did *Analog* one out of four times. I've never had [John W.] Campbell as an editor. He died with my story in his slush pile. I grew up in my early writer-hood playing all these markets all the time, and the fact that I could hit *Analog* all the time made me kind of an *Analog* writer, but I was all over the other magazines, too. Then I was writing within and without the genre. I was doing hardcore adventure stuff, too, so nobody could say I was being too fancy.

Jack of all trades, master of none, I think. It's a way to go. Not all writers go that way, but many of them do. On a day-to-day basis I wake up in the morning and I can do anything I feel like doing. I don't say, "Uh oh, I [have to] get back to that damn novel again." I can always write a poem or something. That's been really my whole thing except for a few years when I had to do contract work and basically had to get adventure novels done on time.

I've also done movie work and, of course, that is pretty much like being a bricklayer. Which is fine. You understand that when you sign the contract. I hate bricks. Have you ever been a bricklayer? That's a baaad job. Fuck up your hands. They don't make any light bricks. Nobody has ever thought of that.

JW: Tell us about a high point in your career.

JH: I would say quite honestly that would be the day I got my first check. I was back from Vietnam and I knew I'd sold a story. Gay was in school. I had picked up the mail and here was this check, $165. Our apartment was a hundred dollars a month at that time. I ran down to the bank and cashed it, and I got tens and twenties and one fifty-dollar bill. Oooooo!

I made Gay get a little Christmas tree because it was November. And I put little dollar bills all over the Christmas tree and put it out on the table. So, that was my graduation into professional writerdom.

I realized when that check came: I don't have to be a wage slave. I can be a freelance writer for the rest of my life, which was such a relief because most of the people I admired had that as a job description. All the guys who I wanted to be when I grew up were basically bums. I mean really bums. That's what their parents would say and their children's teacher. "Your father's a bum." A bum who can make a living being a bum is a smart guy.

I can do what I want to do every day.

That's important, being able to do whatever you want. The opposite is doing what somebody else tells you to do every day, which sucks massively!

JW: What would you say is your driving impetus in your writing?

JH: Aside from very practical things like groceries, that's always got to be in the equation. The worst thing that ever happened to me was being a soldier and killing people and all that stuff. In the broadest most vague kind of way, trying to make a world where that can't exist or where it becomes marginal. I suppose I choose themes that are congruent with that. You don't wake up in the morning saying, "How can I change the world?" or "Oh, what important thing should I write about?" Basically, if you're anything like me, you either face the keyboard with a wild static going on in your head, "Oh, what am I going to do now?" or you have an assignment, usually from some outside source. You've got seven days and you better have him out of that dragon's nest by Monday, which is what I like. I like that kind of writing. Though I don't even do it. I have never done it for a long time but being *able* to do it is very important.

JW: What is the most important thing to know about being a writer?

JH: Get up and do it every day. There are all kinds of exceptions to that, and in my life there have been a couple of periods when I didn't do that. But basically it is that, and this is what separates—what I always thought when I was a young writer—the real writers from the wannabes. You do whatever you feel like doing, but first write.

You get that out of the way, and then you can do whatever you want. You know some people are physiologically different because they can only write at night or in the afternoon or something like that. It's a great rule of life if you need a rule. This is the rule that says: you can do anything you want if you do this one thing for me, which is put in a good day's writing. A good day, usually it takes a couple of hours. Sometimes it takes a long time. But if it takes a long time, I've agreed to do something that required me to work longer than I want to.

JW: What piece of work are you most proud of?

JH: Oddly enough, it would be a very commercial piece called *Tool of the Trade*. I'm writing science fiction and everything, and I thought, I'm going to try to write a suspense novel. I was teaching at MIT, and so I wrote this opening to a novel. I was going to give it to my class as one page. Now continue this. See how you go with it. They hated that, and almost nobody did anything with it. But I thought, this could be a really good story, so I just kept going with it. After the semester was over, I'd written about half this novel, and the next year I guess I kept writing on it. I was on a manual typewriter—tic, tic, tic, tic, tic, tic, like that. I remember the day that I finished that novel with extreme clarity. Because I'm typing along, I guess it's a weekend and I was teaching. I typed the last page to the novel and I put it down, and I thought it was the last page of that chapter. I put the new paper in the plant and then—wait, the novel's over! I looked over and yeah, the novel's over. I had finished a novel unconsciously.

It was very strange. I thought, "Is seven in the morning too early to make a martini? No, it's never too early to make a martini."

The thing about this one is that it's not connected to anything else. It sits there as a single creation which I wrote in the course of three and a half months. It's sort of my baby for that year. I would be hard-pressed to remember anything else I did at that time. Sit and write and had a wonderful time.

JW: How does this relate to your SF work?

JH: I was doing science fiction short stories to maintain my actual identity. It's where I started. At my age, I don't have to do anything.

Take a breath every now and then. Don't forget to get dressed in the morning. Somebody would notice.

I am Science Fiction Guy. I have been Science Fiction Guy since about, I don't know, 1961 or thereabouts. That's what I keep returning to. Also, I'm comfortable with science fiction. I'm confident in the way I can work through it, even though I know my stuff is very old-fashioned.

It seems old-fashioned because most contemporary stuff bores me. Most of it is not very interesting, and I take that to mean I am not its audience. I know that the people who write it are very serious and have a lot of skill, but it is not my stuff. Maybe I'm just an old dinosaur, but that's the way it is. Fortunately enough, people are writing stuff I do like.

You know what looks so strange, I can look at any engineering magazine or *Popular Science* or something like that, and I find something out about what I was writing fifty or forty years ago, and it is all just there as reportage. I was not trying to do that at all. It was just because I grew up reading science fiction, and so I just continued that in my own present.

JW: Where do you see science fiction going in the future?

JH: I haven't tried to keep up with science fiction because I got out of the habit when I started writing it. I guess I said, like a lot of people do, science fiction can keep with me. Or not. I kept writing it and didn't feel I had to read too much of it. I'd read my friends' stuff. Sometimes I'd read award winners. And sometimes somebody says, "You ought to read this. It's really cool!" I'll read that.

But I don't make any effort to try to stay current. I read the "year's best" every year and the Nebula winners, so it gives me this weird feeling. I know the cream of the crop, but I don't know anything about the hulking icebergs that go by me because I don't have time to read these big fat novels. So to me science fiction is the evolution of the short-story form from the mid-twentieth century to now. I think it's a wonderful, wonderful field. I'm continually surprised by it. Now I'm a very slow reader, and it takes a huge amount of noise for me to even pick up a whole novel of science fiction. But when I do, it will often change me.

I'm basically a storyteller. I'm not a stylist. I don't want to be a stylist. I want to be a storyteller so good I can reach everybody. I love science, and what I know is science and engineering and nature. My fiction is in that direction.

I write what I want to read. If I saw a story by Joe Haldeman, I would probably just snatch it up and enjoy it. This guy gets my dollar.

JW: There seems to be a discussion going on in science fiction right now between the storytellers and the stylists.

JH: As such, it has been going for half a century. Judy Merrill was the focus of it for twenty years, and she was all about traditional science fiction being so old-fashioned and who needs it? Spaceships and all that bullshit. What's really important is feminist ideals and social histories. And you know that's an enduring second wave of science fiction. The arguments are still there and they will never be settled. But it's a good thing it's still there, because it's part of what energizes science fiction. I wonder whether the readers care.

Expanded version of the interview that appeared in
Issue 18 of Galaxy's Edge, *January 2016.*

Peter S. Beagle is a science fiction and fantasy author most recently named the Damon Knight Memorial Grand Master by the Science Fiction Writers of America (SFWA) in 2018. Known best for writing *The Last Unicorn*, which *Locus* subscribers voted the number five "All-Time Best Fantasy Novel" in 1987, he then wrote the coda, "Two Hearts," which went on to win the coveted Hugo Award for Best Novelette and the Nebula Award in 2007. He started developing his screenwriting credentials in the 1970s, eventually writing the screenplay for the Ralph Bakshi-animated version of *The Lord of the Rings* in 1978. A highlight of his career in television came when he wrote the teleplay for "Sarek," known as one of the most famous (and memorable) episodes of *Star Trek: The Next Generation* (episode 71).

■■■■■■

Joy Ward's original introduction: Peter S. Beagle, who began his writing career at an early age with the beautiful and intensely moving **A Fine and Private Place,** *spoke to us at the 50th Balticon. He is known as the author of the fantasy classic* **The Last Unicorn.**

Beagle has also been known for his screenwriting and his almost-magical vocal and guitar performances.

Peter S. Beagle: My first agent was John Steinbeck's agent, and Harper Lee's agent (I met Harper Lee in her office once). Elizabeth (my agent) became my aunt. I don't know how else to describe it. She was my agent until she died, twenty years later, and after her death my mother told me she had said to her—they were good friends—"I can't judge John's [Steinbeck] work anymore. He was my first client. If he had never sold a book and I'd never had a client, there's no way I can accurately judge his work of any period. I'm getting the same way about Peter."

I cherish that. Knowing Elizabeth, she would not have said that to me while she was alive. She told my mother. She would never have told it to me directly. And yet, I knew Elizabeth loved me.

I was also growing up in the wake of World War II. One thing I knew, and had drummed into me, was just part of the atmosphere: the word "holocaust" was never mentioned. All I remember was a sense that everybody in the world right now had it worse than you do, so don't complain. So, I never really learned how to complain.

My father was a history teacher. I am very much aware of how lucky I am to be here at all. Every now and then, when I'm by myself, sometimes I lift a glass to a family I never knew, a gentile family in the Ukraine who would take in my mother and her entire family when the Tsar's Cossacks were in town looking for a little R and R in the Jewish quarter. They would head straight for this family and they would hide them in the cellar, at the risk of their own lives. They had to be very quiet, even the baby, because the Cossacks were just upstairs. I don't know who those people were. My mother never mentioned the name. I just know I wouldn't be here if it wasn't for those people.

I was raised culturally Jewish, but I was never interested. My mother and brother were but I was never interested in being bar Mitzvahed or anything like that. Studying Hebrew meant taking time away from reading.

I was ill a lot as a child. I had respiratory problems a lot when I was a boy. I was home one time, at age eight or nine, and one of my teachers sent me this book to read while I was convalescing. It was *The Wind in the Willows*. I still know huge chunks of it by heart. It has, in the first edition, an introduction by A.A. Milne, and he writes what I would love to have somebody write of me.

He says to the reader, "Let's understand one thing, this book is not on trial; you are."

JW: When did you decide you wanted to be a writer?

PB: I almost can't remember making that decision. I tell people I can't remember if I fell in love with words first or story first. Probably story, but either way it was close.

I was generally thought to have learned to read at a very early age. Bah. I couldn't read. I could memorize. I would sit in the kitchenvreading *Jean and John Are Still Six*, and I'd read it aloud to myself and I'd turn the pages when it seemed to me to be the right time to turn the page.

I still do that, even at my age.

JW: What was the very first piece you had published?

PB: I won a *Seventeen* magazine fiction award. If I remember, it was a piece from *A Fine and Private Place* that I was writing in college. I also actually sold a story, "A Telephone Call." I remember that it was $500, and I quit my summer job because I wasn't going to make $500 at the job, so I could stay home and write.

It was simply reinforcement. I can do this. I actually can do this! The thing I will always remember is that suddenly I married a woman with three children. No matter how much my parents worried about me, they never said, they never suggested, that I couldn't support a family. They never urged me to get a backup job, a breadwinning job. They just let me believe I could do this. That was a blessing. I knew people who hid what they did, the fact that they were writers or poets, from their families. You become aware of people who you would envy if you wanted to do that.

It is a curious thing. Oh, it is a curious business to begin with. I lived in Berkeley. It was the beginning of the folk-music explosion. One of my friends there was a young guitarist—brilliant, brilliant folk guitarist, brilliant finger picker, who went with me to see a banjo player who was going through town, who supposedly had developed a technique to allow him to play three times as fast as anyone else. We went, and yeah, he did play three times as fast as anybody. There was not a trace of soul in the music, but the technique was incredible. I remember sitting with my friend Perry beside me, thinking, "Wow, I'd really like to know how to do that, and then not do it." I've felt that way about a number of writers. Great admiration for the technique, but no, it would never occur to me to do that.

I come from a generation where it was understood that all the writers you were supposed to imitate, to learn from, were all white and male. The one female writer I can think of was Edith Wharton. Generally it was Hemingway, Fitzgerald, and John Dos Passos at the time. I was never taken by those guys, although I liked certain stories of Hemingway's and certain, oddly enough, poetry of Fitzgerald's. But I was already into the strange guys.

What's there underneath everything I do is a certain bittersweetness. As the Latin poet says the same thing, I laugh so I may not weep. Everything of mine is in some way funny. It needs to be. I'm strongly drawn to Irish literature and Black music. Well, I grew up around Black people. It's the same humor. It's the storytelling. Very much part of the culture and it's the same humor. If it wasn't for bad luck, I would have no luck at all. There's an immediate sort of empathy.

I once asked [my mentor and friend writer] Robert Nathan, "Why is it that half the writers who mean something to me are Irish?"

He said, "As an amateur anthropologist I always supposed that the Semites and the Celts are part of the same wave of immigration into Europe out of Asia Minor, only the Semites took a left at Canal Street down to the Mideast and the Celts just kept going until they ran out of land." He said, "I bet they were pretty well acquainted in the old days."

The humor is people keeping defeat at bay.

There was one Irish family in the neighborhood, the Goeghans, whose New Year celebration I always tried to get to if I was in town because Mr. Goeghans always would utter the same toast at New Year's. He would look around at his sons, around the table. He'd say, "Well boys, we're through with having a bad year. Here goes for another just like it."

JW: You are known as a musician and a writer. How do the two feed each other?

PB: Even when I was too shy to speak to people, I could always sing. It always seemed I had a trash memory for lyrics. My mother remembers me marching into the local grocery store, where we were customers, and singing all four verses of the *Star-Spangled Banner*.

But I acted. I loved theater. I usually memorized not only my own lines but everybody else's.

But singing is special. It's a way of speaking. You can't lie singing, at least I can't. It's another way of telling a story.

JW: What's different in that way of telling stories between music and writing?

PB: One of my very favorite songwriters, Johnny Mercer, was known as a lyricist/singer, a very good singer, but also musically literate. He created the music for some of his hits. Not all, some. Mercer was asked in an interview about the difference in writing words and writing music. He was silent for a little bit, and then he said, "I think it takes more talent to write music—but it takes more courage to write lyrics because music goes straight to the heart." That's it, and words have such a long way to go before they get there." Words have to go through your own personal sensor. They have to go through the brain. They have to go through your training. Finally they get to the heart. He was dead right.

When I went to my first Hollywood party it was really a Hollywood lunch, a lot of tables at a big house. I was seated with a charming woman, someone older than I, who was wonderfully literate. We mostly talked about books.

We got on very well, then she had one glass of wine too many and she said, "Writers. I know about writers. I was married to a writer. Fucking emotional misers, the lot of you! You are so afraid you are going to wake up one morning and it will all be gone."

The hair stood up on my arms because there is one of those three-quarters near truths that's just close enough to the real truth to scare the hell out of you.

JW: How do you as a writer prevent "it" being gone?

PB: I take great comfort in the fact that Shakespeare had days like that. There's a sonnet of Shakespeare's:

> *"When, in disgrace with fortune and men's eyes,*
> *I all alone beweep my outcast state,*
> *And trouble deaf heaven with my bootless cries,*
> *And look upon myself and curse my fate,*
> *Wishing me like to one more rich in hope,*
> *Featured like him, like him with friends possessed,*
> *Desiring this man's art and that man's scope,*
> *With what I most enjoy contented least."*

It's a great comfort to me to know that Willie the Shake had days like that.

You can't ever really know; all you can do is keep your heart open. Finally, that's what it comes to.

JW: What have been the high points of your career?

PB: My great moment in show business would have to be doing the script for a television movie in 1977 called *The Greatest Thing that Almost Happened*. It was adapted from a novel by a Cleveland writer named Don Robertson, who is dead now. It was largely a Black cast. Debbie Allen was in it. It was built around Jimmy Walker, who was hot at the time. James Earl Jones insisted on being in it over the advice of his agent although it wasn't the lead role. He played Jimmy Walker's father.

I brought my son; he was fifteen at the time. I brought him to LA to see some of the filming. The driver sent to pick us up at the airport walked right past us. When Jones, meeting us, did a double take, it was only then that it hit me. Oh my God, he was expecting a Black writer. I told you I grew up around Black people. I didn't think about it. I've lived with Black people, including my wife.

When Jones realized that [I was the writer], he got up and took my hand and said in front of my kid, "I don't know where you get it or why you should be able to do it, but you write Black dialogue like a poet."

I couldn't talk. I was dazed. It was too much to take in. It really was.

A lot of this I'm slow on the pickup. A lot of times when I have been truly, deeply honored to my heart I realized that's what happened. That's what that was.

My first roommate in college was black. He was a senior, and his friends largely had been in the Army in Korea. They had come back to college. I just listened to them talk, being very aware that they didn't all talk the same way. Some were from the South, some were from Pennsylvania, some were from the East. After they'd left, I badgered him, saying, "Okay, Ben, I promise I'm not going to bother you after this, I know you're studying, but does this sound like the way Boz talks?"

Ben would look at me and say, "You're getting there."

I thought about that when Jones said what he did.

Then there was a moment when I was on the panel at the Institute for the Study of Fantasy and the Arts, the MLA of the fantasy world. I was there as a guest, not a panelist, and I was sitting next to a great English writer, Brian Aldiss. At one point, Aldiss, apropos of nothing, got up and left the table and went out of the room. He came back with a glass of wine with a rose in it and he handed it to me.

I was stunned. I said, "Brian, that is very sweet but there are other people at the table who could use a glass of wine and a rose."

Aldiss said, "Ah, but they didn't write *A Fine and Private Place*."

It's moments like that where there's nothing to say.

I'll tell you. With Jones it was specific. But it mostly comes back to either an event of learning something or studying something because I so badly want to learn it.

There is a wonderful essay by somebody's name I don't remember, called "Growing into Molly." Discovering how much Molly was in her as she grew older.

That's real. That's stunning for me. That's real people. That's not necessarily from other writers, that's from people I've never heard of writing from nowhere. That's real. That knocks me off my feet.

I have friends in Florida whom I see whenever I'm there.

They're lovely people. I treasure a review more than any other I ever got, when I was staying at their house; I'm comfortable enough to work there. I was working on the book, which will be out in September, *Summer Long*. Strangely, I had not read any of it aloud to anybody. For some reason I read a passage aloud to Mary [the wife]. It's a take on the legend of Persephone. One in which Persephone reluctantly realizes she can't make a break from this. It is her destiny, going back to the Underworld with Hades, who has come looking for her. She stops in to say goodbye to one person, one of the main character's daughters, Lily. Lily is gay and her mother's never minded or thought one way or another about Lily being gay, but she has such lousy taste in women. Persephone is really the first woman who has ever been kind to her and treated her like a valuable person. Of course, Lily fell totally in love with her and even made a clumsy pass at her. Persephone turns her down in such a way that she never felt ugly, stupid, dorky, a jerk, or even rejected. But Persephone has come to say goodbye.

I think it's the best love scene I ever wrote. There's no physical contact between them, but she falls asleep with her head in Persephone's lap and Persephone is gone when she wakes.

I read that section to Mary.

She didn't say anything for a moment, then she put her hand on the back of my neck and said, "You poor, poor bastard. You really do know what love is." Then she got up and went to the kitchen to make dinner.

I think that's somehow, speaking as a writer, the most wonderful thing anybody has said to me.

Just that she hit something on the head. Something. I don't even know what it was, but I can tell you it went straight to my heart when she said that.

JW: What does that mean to you when someone says something like that to you?

PB: Damn, I've been here. I've been here. Whatever happens, it's much bigger. It's like a friend of mine long ago in Santa Cruz, was a guitar player and a songwriter. He wrote a song once which I remember still. The refrain is:

> *I'm going to make it a good one boys,*
> *Gonna make it lean and sad,*
> *I'm going to sing about the hippies and the hard uck chippies*
>   *and the horrible times I've had.*
> *When my song is over boys, the crowd will understand.*

They may not like my style, boys, but they'll know who I am.

That's it, all I can hope. Because there are people I met at Elizabeth's office [my first agent] who were publishing everywhere at the time, who simply vanished when they died. The same thing could very well happen to me. I won't know. But I was here. Some people will know I was here.

JW: What would you tell a young writer?

PB: I have known some people who have told me they've never read because they are afraid of affecting their styles. I've bellowed at them, "You don't have a style yet! Imitate enough people and you will have a style. You can't help it."

So many people have told me, they read too much, like me, and they are intimidated by their heroines—I could never write like that. I just say, don't worry about falling prey to your heroes. Read everything and try to write like anybody you admire.

I've said to a class, I'm not going to make the mistakes you make because I've already made them fifteen, twenty times. I'm on to a much higher class of mistake. Don't even try getting it right. The thing in your head is different than the thing that comes out. That's just the way it is. But you try again. Maybe you get closer to getting it right. That's all it is, chasing getting it right.

When it's just flowing and you can't believe how easy it is, naturally it comes straight out of you. For every one of those, there are fifteen or twenty when you are just hacking it out. That is not right, but that's going to have to do because I can't think of a better word. There's a lot more of those. But you're supposed to make it look easy. The great actors make it look easy.

I guess a lot of my life as a working writer has been spent. All right, that's not it. But I look back afterward; it does look easy, doesn't it? It always comes down to you're not going to get it right. When you think you got it right, look back in a year or two.

JW: How do you want to be remembered?

PB: One of my favorite books is James Thurber's, *The 13 Clocks*. It has one of the great villains of all time, the Duke of Coffin Castle, who says, "We all have flaws and mine is being wicked." The duke goes down fighting until the last, but his world is falling apart. There are children laughing somewhere, the ones he got rid of. The prince has climbed the tower and is beating the hell out of all his guards and rescuing the princess. Something very much like something that no one had ever seen before came trotting down the stairs and ran across the floor. The duke clutches his henchman and says, "What was that?" The henchman clutches back and says, "I don't know but whatever it is, it's the only one there ever was."

I would like that as an epitaph. Whatever it is, it's the only one there ever was. Beyond that, who the hell can predict?

Just have fun, do the best you can, take care of your responsibilities.

First published in Issue 22 of Galaxy's Edge, *September 2016.*

▮ ERIC FLINT

ric Flint is known for his alternate history novel *1632*, first published in 2000. In addition to his fifteen novels in the 1632 series, several of which making the *New York Times* extended bestselling list, he has edited twelve anthologies of short fiction set in that universe, and was the co-editor of *Baen's Universe*. He also publishes the *Grantville Gazette*, a bimonthly electronic magazine devoted to the 1632 series, which has now produced over sixty issues. He has collaborated with David Drake, Dave Freer, Mercedes Lackey, K. D. Wentworth, David Carrico and Ryk Spoor. His latest projects include working with David Weber on a series of novels set in Weber's Honor Harrington series, and writing an alternate history series that takes place in Jacksonian America. He now lives in northwest Indiana with his wife Lucille.

▮▮▮▮▮▮

Eric Flint: The very first piece of fiction I wrote was a hanwritten military SF novel I wrote when I was fourteen or fifteen. It was a novel about World War III. I don't think there were any main characters in it. I think it was a kid playing toy soldiers. But I discovered I liked to write, so then in high school I wrote a lot. I wrote a total of three novels, one of which I thought was good enough, I paid a typist. Cost me $60, which was a lot of money for a sixteen-year-old kid; it was 1962 or '63. But I paid a professional to make a real manuscript out of it and I sent it in to Ace Books.

It came back, rejected in three months. Thank God. I did get a very nice rejection letter from John Campbell which unfortunately I lost decades ago. But I was impressed. It was two pages long, handwritten and a detailed explanation of why he was rejecting the short story. He encouraged me to keep writing. "Kid, you're talented. Keep at it."

Then in college one night, myself and my three best friends were all kind of plastered and probably high on grass, too. I don't remember. Not sober. That was shortly after Harvard Lampoon's *Bored of the Rings* had come out. We had all read it, and we all didn't think very much of it.

We all said, "We could do better than that!"

Right there on the spot we vowed we would write our own satirical fantasy. And so we did. We completed the novel. This would have been 1969. I was twenty-two years old. We then lent the manuscript to a friend of mine, and she lost it. I have lived in deep fear ever since that someday that novel would resurface.

I don't remember what it was called but it was very sophomoric. It was college, male humor in the 1960s so that means it was very sexist. Some of it was pretty funny sexism, but it was sexist. What actually happened though was that by the time we finished it, we kept going and the story underwent a transmogrification.

It started as simply a parody of fantasies. Then we actually started taking it seriously. Parts of what I then wrote eventually did get published. Parts of *Philosophical Strangler* go back to that time. So something real came out it. But that first manuscript, like I said, didn't wash. I don't know what Berenice did with it, but I hope to God it is long decayed away in a landfill somewhere or is feeding the fish somewhere at the bottom of the Pacific. Or is *anywhere* that someone can't read it.

I like to tell stories and think up stories. And I was good at it, [at] a level of a sixteen-year-old guy. But it was way better than most sixteen-year-olds could have done. Actually, interesting, during that same stretch my best friend and I—who was one of the three guys I was writing the novel with—he and I were in drama class together and we would write skits that our drama teacher allowed us to perform at lunchtimes. We would pack that classroom with kids every lunch. They would come to hear what we had to say.

I was at my fiftieth high school reunion just a couple of months ago and ran across one of the other students in that drama class, a lady I had not seen in fifty years, and she still remembered the skits. She still remembered them. We were talented within the limits of that age and what that age finds funny. Which is not particularly what I find funny today.

I always liked doing it and writing comes easily and naturally to me. I did well in college writing essays and later on, when I got politically active, I did a lot of writing. I've always found writing pleasant, easy, and something I find fulfilling. Once I became a political activist, I had been politically active for some years when I devoted myself to it full time, which started in the summer of 1970. At that point I stopped writing fiction because that kind of political activity was too all-engrossing intellectually and emotionally. You just don't have enough energy left over to keep writing, so I did not do any fiction writing in those years. In fact, any time I wrote any fiction for the next twenty-two years was a couple of stretches when I was inactive politically for a while. I would go back to writing.

Joy Ward: You spent about twenty-five years in political and union organizing. What drew you into political action?

EF: I had been active in the civil rights movement from a very early age. I've been interested in politics since I could remember. I've always been interested in history since I could remember.

As a teenager I considered myself a conservative. I took that very seriously. I read Edmund Burke and I read the American theorist I liked the most, and still do—a guy named Peter Viereck. He was not well known, but he was kind of William F. Buckley's mentor. But the one issue where I parted company was on civil rights; which did not seem to me to be parting company with conservatism, but when I got active in the civil rights movement I became uncomfortably aware that I was the only conservative in the civil rights movement.

There were no others, and that was when I became disenchanted with conservatism.

I still have a lot of conservative attitudes but there's a point at which I decided that while there was a lot about conservatism I find attractive, the problem is, if you put it together and make it your guiding philosophy, it is way, way too easy to slide into a justification for what exists.

So I had a kind of mixed political attitude, and then I got involved in a rather bizarre group that was a spin-off of the civil rights movement that I got involved in. This was not uncommon. It was the late '60s. It was kind of a hard, heavy counter group that concentrated on race issues.

It was called the Family. It was a group in Los Angeles that was multiracial, mixed race. I say all race—there was one Asian. The group was pretty screwy, but one of the things that came out of that was one of the leaders was a Maoist. So, he insisted we study Marxist theory, which we did. I was expelled after about three months.

JW: How come?

EF: For petty, bourgeois individualism deviation. Basically what happened was that they would say things I just knew weren't true, and I would say, "No, I know that's not true." Basically, things wrong in history. I wasn't trying to be a troublemaker, but they would say things I had to refute. "No, no. Sorry, sorry. That's actually not true." After three months of that I got the boot.

JW: What was important for you about you being involved in the civil rights movement?

EF: It's the whole situation with race relations in America. When I was a kid my parents moved to France. I started out going to French schools. One of the things I like to tease my American conservative friends about, who talk about how there ought to be more discipline in schools, is you would love French schools because I used to get beaten in French schools. French schools are tough. When my dad realized that the headmaster of my school was regularly beating me, he blew his stack and went down there and chewed him out. I'm sure this French headmaster thought "Who is this crazy American?" because it is just taken for granted in France that naturally you whack kids with a ruler. My parents yanked me out of French schools.

There was a very wealthy school, a very well-known private American school, the American Community School in Paris, which is still in existence. My best friend was the son of the American Ambassador to France. My sisters' best friend was the daughter of the Indian Ambassador to France because any kid who came from a place where the people spoke English—could be Indians, could be Indonesians—would send their kids there. It was a very multiracial school. I didn't really think anything about it because kids don't. But my first conscious awareness of anything involving race [was when] I was eight years old and I learned the word "n*****s" from somebody. I wasn't really quite clear what it meant, but I came home and I used it at dinner. The minute I used it I knew I was in serious trouble because there was dead silence at the table. My mother gave my father an apprehensive look. He got up and he said, "Eric, come with me."

We went into the study. He pulled out a book with pictures and opened it up. It was a book about lynchings in the South. He showed me a number of these pictures of Black people being lynched. The one that I really remember, the thing that is most vivid about the picture, is there was this young white boy right in the foreground, about my age, maybe eight years old, with a smile pointing up at the corpse of the Black man hanging. I remember that. It was just appalling.

It's really easy to understand how people get sucked into this. It's one of the things to this day when I hear people, usually but not always white people, criticizing some Black kid for doing something really dumb or vicious. I really understand how easy it is for people, when you're brought up in an environment and there's no clear counter to it. And I will use this example; I've seen pictures of white kids cheering on a lynching, so people do this kind of stuff. You have to have a strong moral compass and as a child you have to get that from someone else. You don't get that from yourself. Another thing I remember thinking at the time was what kind of sicko would bring a kid to something like that? I still have never gotten the answer.

But, in any event, then my father said to me, "The word 'n****r' is a Nazi word." This is right after World War II. He had fought in World War II. He was a combat pilot in World War II in the Army Air

Corps and he had come out with a Distinguished Flying Cross. He was quite highly decorated. He said, "This is what I fought against in World War II. This is what we were fighting. It wasn't just Germans. That's where it was worse. You can find this anywhere. That word is one of the manifestations of it." I don't even remember if he used the word racism, but that's what he was talking about. And he said, "So we don't use it." And that was it.

My dad was kind of an interesting guy. He had a lot of faults. His main one being one reason I'm so hostile to capitalism, is that he was quite a successful businessman. He was good at it, but he would end up screwing up. The problem was, I don't know why, but my dad seemed to measure himself by the amount of money he made.

It wasn't that he was greedy. It wasn't because he was a generous man. But somehow his success at making money seemed to be a critical point by which he gauged himself and his own worth, which I've never, ever done and I don't romanticize poverty. I've been there. I've been dirt poor and an alcoholic. I know exactly what the world looks like when you don't got a dollar to rub together but you scrape together. Having said that, it's nice to be well-off, but the amount of value people place in that just seems bizarre to me.

I know when I was growing up as a kid in college, neither I nor any of my friends had as our ambition in life getting rich. If somebody had dropped a million dollars on us, we would have been perfectly happy to take it, but we certainly weren't going to organize our lives around making a lot of money. I've never understood it. To this day it's like it seems a lot of people, their biggest ambition is after they die. Six months later they can be in a grave and, "Ah ha! I'm rotting slower than everyone here because I can afford a better sarcophagus." Who cares? Well, my dad did, and a lot of people do. But there were things about him I really admire a lot.

I first found out about feminism from my dad. It wasn't my mother. My father, when I was about thirteen, I don't remember the context, but he said to me one day, "Women get a raw deal in this world." The thought had never crossed my mind. You're a kid. You don't think about stuff like that. I said, "What do you mean, dad?" Girls are girls, you know. So he explained it to me.

This did not stop him from being a shameless womanizer. I mean he had his own set of feet of clay.

I felt very strongly about civil rights. I actually wanted to go on the Freedom Rides in Mississippi that summer. I wasn't old enough. No way my mother would let me do it. It's probably just as well because I don't really have the temperament. A couple of years later in '64, '65, when I graduated from high school, I went to college and joined CORE right away. Congress of Racial Equality. What they did is they put us through a training session on non-violent resistance. I went to Santa Monica City College, and it was held at the Quad, right in the middle of campus. A bunch of us were down there and we were play acting. The instructors were sort of showing us this was how you're going to get harassed. Well, there were onlookers. There were these white young guys who were a bunch of racist assholes and they started making remarks. I had lived in a rural area and I had gotten into a lot of fist-fights because I was the only—well I wasn't rich by the time we got finished, but we started off rich.

I was the city kid. I was thirteen or fourteen. I showed up my first day of class and I was carrying a copy of Hans Reichenbach's *The Rise of the Scientific Philosophy*. Boy, did I fit in. I got into a fist-fight my first day of school. Anyway, I just bounced right up and got right in their faces. I was ready to have it out with both of them. And the guy who was teaching said, "Maybe you should find some other way." But I still went to a lot of demonstrations.

Where I actually got more active was when I got to college. When I got to UCLA there was a South African Freedom Action Coalition. I probably spent more of my time involved in that than American civil rights because I was studying that and I had friends of mine who were Black South Africans.

JW: Your degree is actually in African Studies…

EF: Yeah, that was actually from my interest in civil rights because I always liked history, and I had decided I was going to major in history when I went to college. I pretty much had decided I was going to become a college professor in history, but I still didn't know what particular branch of history I was going to get into because I found all history interesting. In those days there was a very high-end glossy magazine called *Horizon*. One issue came in that had an article by a writer named Basil Davidson on the lost cities of Africa. It turned out that there was such a thing as African history. I wasn't aware it even existed. That was part of Davidson's point, that one of the manifestations of racism had been the kind of obliteration of the fact that Africans actually had a history of their own. The impression that most white Americans had, including me, was that they were a bunch of people running around in the jungle somewhere. It turned out it was an introduction to African history.

Davidson, in those days—he has been dead for a long time—he was actually a core workhorse model who came out of World War II. He wrote a book on the Yugoslavs. I used to have it but don't know if I still do. But after the war he got interested in African history. He wasn't a professional historian although he was well respected by professional historians. I said, "I'll do this. I'll specialize in African history." UCLA, as it happened, was one of the three centers in the world that had African history. The others being the School of African Studies in London and the Sorbonne in Paris. And actually UCLA was probably the biggest and best of them. Still is to this day. But anyway, I was in the right place.

I went to junior college for two years because my grades in high school were cruddy. I couldn't get into the university system because I didn't have good enough grades. What you could do in California was to go to a secondary school and when your grades were good enough you could transfer. When I got to UCLA, I majored in history. You couldn't major in African history. I took every African history course. I got to know the African history professor. Then I applied to UCLA, Columbia graduate school. I got accepted in both, but UCLA offered me a full scholarship. Actually, I kind of wanted to go to Columbia. It would have been nice to go to New York, but, on the other hand, this was a full scholarship. I wound up spending three years in graduate school, and eventually I got politically active. I decided I did not want to become a professor, but by that point I had picked up a master's degree. I was ABD, all but dissertation.

The single most important epiphany I ever had actually involved Chinese history. It was around the same time, but I was at a friend's house. I can remember looking out over one of the hills in Los Angeles. I had been studying Chinese history. I actually was interested in non-European history. I got to thinking about all those generations of Chinese peasants that nobody remembers their names; nobody will ever know their names. Their families don't remember their names. But each one of them, just like every human being who has ever lived anywhere in the world, made some contribution to the human race. It may have been nothing more elaborate than providing food for other people as well as themselves but there was something.

Of all political philosophies the one I probably detest the most—it's not the worst, but I personally detest it—is libertarianism, this attitude that libertarians seem to have, that of ME: I did it on my own. Nobody ever, ever does it on their own. You come into the world as part of a species that is a quintessential social animal. You would not exist without that entire species. You cannot continue to exist. Whatever your accomplishments might be, you can't ever say, "That was me." I know some part of that might have been you but you owe something. That is the basis of my own personal morality. You have a debt and you have to repay it. I leave it up to each individual to figure out what they think is the right way to try to do it. But I do think you have a debt. I think we can't say our job in life is ME, ME, ME and make as much money as you can and just "screw you." Like I said, it's not the worst philosophy. It's not like the Nazis.

I just remember looking out that window thinking how connected we are, not only to all other people but to our own history. I think it was Faulkner—I've forgotten who it was—who said something like, "The past is still with us and not even past. The past isn't dead. It's not even past." I think it was Faulkner. And really that's true. So, my interest in history has always been there. I can't remember a time in my life when it wasn't.

When I was ten years old, I read Thucydides' *Peloponnesian War*. Your average ten-year-old kid does not do that, but I did. Partially I did it just to do it. But I've always been fascinated by history.

I've always thought we should try to understand the world from viewpoints different than our own. That's why I've always been interested in non-Western histories. This is not multiculturalism because I do not think cultures are equal. There are a whole lot of cultures out there that really sucked. We're probably way better off when they finally go away, but you should still understand or look at them.

I think it was also tied in with my interest in science fiction. That goes back to at least when I was twelve. I've always thought about aliens and non-human intelligence as another angle to look at us. Now you can only do that in your own imagination. We never met any but it's probably why, in a lot of my novels, the aliens are looking at us.

JW: What's important about looking at things from another point of view?

EF: If nothing else, to make sure you're not screwing up. One of the things that really drives me nuts when I hear—it's not true of all but it's true of most—evangelical Christians, is that when they talk about compassion they don't seem to understand what the word means. They seem to think it means "I am somehow a nice person." That's not what it means. It means the ability to see your kinship with anybody, including people who are really screwed up, either because of objective circumstances or poverty or disease or 'cause they are just screwed up in other ways because they don't behave well.

It doesn't mean you have to accept them, but it does mean you should try to understand them. I run across people—I hate to say this, but it seems like it's way more prevalent among Christians or religious people in general—who seem to think that just because they are religious they automatically partake of this virtue. They don't. There are some very outstanding exceptions, but I think that interest of mine is also a valuable trait if you're a writer because that is what writers are doing. Whether they realize it or not, they are exercising their compassion when they write, in the sense that they are seeing the world through someone else's eyes and trying to make that make sense. It's the reason for the kinds of things I write when so much of what I write is based in history. Even things that don't look like it. *Mother of Demons*, my first novel, is really an alternate history taking modern humans and transplanting them into a Bronze Age world. How would they handle that? I made it a Bronze Age world of aliens, not humans, so it gave them some freedom.

JW: What does that do for you to translate that into science fiction?

EF: When I decided to become a writer, I had been a political activist over twenty years, and I was kind of a little burned out. It's a pretty hard life. I had done twenty, twenty-five years of it and I figured whatever debt I had to the human race had been paid off. One other thing I really wanted to do was write. I did have to think about, "What are you going to write?" I've always enjoyed science fiction more than other writing, but I've read a lot of other. I've read a lot of mysteries. I've read a lot of historical fiction. The reason I picked science fiction was because it would give me the most artistic latitude. Modern literary fiction is basically a genre of its own. It's very rigidly circumscribed.

JW: What's important about that for you?

EF: I want to write stories that I want to write and not worry about whether I'm fitting into a mold or not. I enjoy Westerns, and actually I probably have been more influenced by Westerns than anything else in how I write. But I wouldn't want to write Westerns because it is too restrictive. Also the market for it has kind of blown up. I enjoy mysteries, but I don't want to write mysteries because basically there are only three characters: the murderer, the victim and the detective. That's about it. All the mystery novels basically revolve around those three characters. Well, I enjoy that, but I wouldn't want to spend a lifetime revolving in that narrow a line.

There's a lot of romance in my writing, but I don't want to write romances because there are a lot of restrictions on what you can do there when you start off. So-called literary fiction is really circumscribed. If you want to make it in literary fiction what you have to do is create a character who is some way or another pretty dysfunctional, and then the plot is how he or she underachieves. I just don't want to write this because I don't care. It's not that I'm not sympathetic, it's just not what I want to write. It's very hard in literary fiction to break out, plus there is an incessant concern about your prose.

Science fiction gives me a lot of leeway. I could write about issues. You call it speculative fiction, and you can write pretty much what you want. Actually, the majority of what I write I don't think is alternate history. Alternate history is what I'm best known for and is certainly where I make the most money. Alternate history—how is that science fiction? In the case of the 1632 series, fine, it's a time traveler story. In the case of the Belisarius series it's a time travel element involved. In the case of the series I've done two books, the Trail of Glory series, there's no science fiction element at all. It's just different history. But you can do that in science fiction. I can write pretty much anything I want. I can do comic fantasy, which I do. I can write straight hard SF, which I do.

Right now I'm working on a novel with Mike Resnick that is anything but hard science fiction. It's about as loose and sloppy science fiction as you can get, and we're having fun with it. I just have an enormous amount of latitude. I can bring in a lot of the things that I care about, that I think are important.

The trick or the key is not to try to shove your specific political opinions down people's throats. Which I don't ever do for a couple of reasons. First of all, I think its dishonest. I think it's false advertising. If I wanted to write political tracts, I could do it. I have done it. I'm never going to make a living at it. But I can do it. I think it's cheating to try to smuggle in your own political viewpoint and call it a novel. Really, it's a diatribe. The second reason is, I think it is completely ineffective. I could go on about this at length but all political theory, it doesn't matter whose it is—libertarian, communist, socialist, conservative, liberal, it doesn't matter—all political theories have one characteristic in common, which is that they factor the individual out of the equation. You have to, because all individuals are different, and if you try to figure out anything based on all individuals you just get lost in the morass. So you have to factor out the individual and focus on whatever they all have in common. Whatever that might be. Nationality, race, class, sex, whatever it is that you're trying to focus on, and you strip out the individual. You have to. Well, except you can't tell stories that way.

I don't know if you've ever read *Socialist Realism* but the reason it is such God-awful stuff is because what they do is they strip the individual out of the story and then they just stamp names on what are, in fact, political interacts. So Bill the Worker wakes up and he goes and gets exploited by Mike the Capitalist. This is not a story. You have to make them about individuals but if you do that then they are quirky. So, trying to use stories that impart political lessons irritates your reader. That's not why they bought it. They want to be entertained, but it doesn't work very well anyway. Things are much more complex when you deal with them on the level as individuals, which is what the story has to be about. A characteristic all stories have in common, going back to *Gilgamesh*, is there are recognizable individuals.

Now on the other hand, what fiction is superbly good at is imparting broad ethical or moral lessons. It's very good for that. But you're not really trying to force anyone to accept your particular political viewpoint of the world. I call this algebraic. It's a term that's used in the social milieu I came out of. Which is that I will present something, and I will let you fill in the exact arithmetic. To give an example from the 1632 series, in the first novel *1632* someone once asked me how I would summarize it and I said, "Well, one way I could do it is say to you that these Americans are transplanted in history and find themselves in a really, really tough position and they have to make a number of critical, important life-and-death decisions."

At every single point they do the exact opposite of what Dick Cheney would do. That's what happens. But I don't ever say that, so even people who like Dick Cheney can read it and if they want to live in a delusionary world and think Dick Cheney would do any of the things my heroes do, it's fine; I'm not going to tell them otherwise. It's obvious it's not true, but I'm not going to force anyone to say yes or no way. I also went out of my way to make sure the central hero is not a Socialist. There is one Socialist there who is based on a couple of people. But I'm not trying really to shove my political opinions down people's throats. What I end up doing is using my novel to express a broad base of values that I believe, which a lot of people agree with or like even if they don't agree. I mean, I have fans of the series who are conservative. Quite a few and that's fine.

They are pretty much the same values that came out of the American Revolution, the French Revolution, and the Enlightenment. It's equality, number one. That goes beyond the silly nostrum. A lot of people say equality of opportunity, but it goes much deeper than that. Every human being's life is as valuable, no more, no less, than any other human being's life. You have to respect that. What they do with it is some degree up to them. To some degree. A lot of it has to do with the social possibilities open to them, which vary a lot. Liberty and personal freedom—although there is also libertarianism. On a philosophical level, libertarians have a basically platonic, mystical concept that there is such a thing as the individual who needs to be free. "I want to be free to do whatever the hell I want to and the hell with the rest of the world."

Whereas my way of looking at that is similar, if you want to call it this, to Aristotelian, but what it is, is the attitude of a historian. We have lots of historical experience and evidence and what is by now absolutely crystal clear is that societies, especially advanced industrial societies that allow their citizens the maximum amount of individual freedom and personal dignity, are stronger societies and do a lot better than those that don't. That's a plenty good enough reason. You don't have to posit some mystical, individual whatever to come up with proof that all so-called totalitarian societies have in common is that they are anything but totalitarian. They all collapse. Hitler lasted twelve years. The Stalinist regime—and we can argue if you want to date that from Stalin's seizure of power in 1929 or go back to 1917. Forget that—but it collapsed in one of the most bloodless revolutions in history when the Soviet Union collapsed in 1991. And so it's like, what kind of society collapses with a smaller loss of life than we saw here in the United States with any one of the major race riots in the 1960s? Of the people who died, half of them died in one incident in Latvia.

Obviously this wasn't much of a totalitarian regime. Because regimes like that are incredibly brittle. They may be very rigid and look tough, but you crack them anywhere and they collapse. Whereas a democratic, egalitarian society is really tough and resilient. That's good enough reason to do it. You don't have to go any further than that to support it. Not discriminating against or punishing people because they belong to a particular race, sex, creed, or any particular sexual orientation, whatever—there's nothing particularly esoteric about it. It's pretty well, I think, the common, the generally shared value of the history of Western civilization. They are shared to one degree or another by most all other civilizations. There is a way in which you can say we're all Romans. The same way I hope two thousand years from now everybody will be able to say we're all Americans. I don't expect the United States of America to still exist. Political entities don't last that long.

JW: In the 1632 series, you have quite a few people who come in and write in the series. A lot of the people are known and a lot are not. What is important about that for you?

EF: Well, I did that for a couple of reasons. One very mundane and simple reason is that it's a lot of fun. This series is very, very rooted in a fan base, much more than most. All series have a fan base. This series is challenging, and it violates, believe me, all marketing precepts about how to do a series. You're supposed to, when you write a series, basically every book is supposed to be kind of pretty much like every one that went before, so people pick it up and read it. They know what they're getting. 1632 is not like that at all. Depending on who I'm working with, who my co-authors are, the books can read radically, wildly different. A book I write with Virginia DeMarce is not going to read like a book I do on my own or one I do with Dave Weber or one I do with Chuck Gannon or with Gorg Huff and Paula Goodlett. They are all going to be different. You lose a certain number of readers when you do that.

What I've always hoped would be true would be that we would keep a certain number of readers that like that complexity. What's striking to me about the series—the first book now came out fourteen years ago—is that it's by no means a bestselling series. It's popular, four of the titles are *New York Times* bestsellers. But there are any number of series—I mean, Jim Butcher's Dresden Files will hit *New York Times* every time one comes out. David Weber's Honor Harrington series won't go quite that high in sales, but it will go up there. David will outsell anything I write.

JW: So why do you do it?

EF: 'Cause I want to. The other thing I'm trying to do with it is—in this series, not necessarily any other series—I'm trying to capture, firstly, the complexity, the chaotic quirkiness of real history. Now understand, I am a Marxist. I do subscribe to a political or historical philosophy that does believe there are certain patterns and logical ways in which human history unfolds. But as Karl Marx was the first to say, you can't predict what is actually going to happen. Yeah, you can see broad patterns, but that does not mean that real history is going to be perfect. The way Lenin put it—and I think it was originally from Hegel—is you don't really know what's going to happen. Any theory you have is a guide. That's all. I'm trying to capture that. And the thing about that is, intrinsically there are certain logical dynamics in the very process of telling narrative stories that tend to work against that. Narrative stories always are coherent and make sense. They have to or you can frustrate your reader. So, in a way, you are always tidying little things up as you go on.

The other thing that happens with narrative history is you're almost always giving credence to the Great Man theory of history, which I personally detest. Because you can't write about everybody, you focus on a few characters, so what those characters do better be pretty important or why are you telling their story in the first place? At least, on an emotional level, no matter what, you wind up making those people more central than they really would be.

Now there's something around one hundred and twenty different authors and letting—which I do to a very large degree—letting them shape the way things happen. I keep overall control over it, but I am anything but a control freak. I kind of like to see what unfolds, and as much as possible I try, sometimes I have to put my foot down and say, "No, you can't do that," but I don't do that very often. As much as possible, when somebody comes up with a new idea in a short story or a novel I say, "Let's go with it." We'll see what comes out of it at the other end.

I think when readers get to read the 1632 series it is a much more complex picture of an alternate world, an alternate history, and also one where, although there are some central characters (central historical figures), it is very clear that they are not the only people shaping this history. But what I also have to say is, I can do that with the 1632 series because there is an objective framework we can work with in that the history is fixed at the starting point, and the technology was fixed at the starting point.

We start with a small West Virginia town. It's modeled on the real town of Mannington, West Virginia, and the rule is that if it doesn't exist in Mannington, it doesn't exist in Grantville. There are a couple of exceptions but not many, which means I don't have to decide everything. Anyone who wants to write a story in that framework can start from a certain established historical framework that I didn't create. I didn't invent Charles I or Oliver Cromwell or Richelieu.

Secondly, [this series has] a clear-cut, fairly defined technological base. I would not try to do this kind of massive joint project in, for instance, David Weber's universe. He doesn't try to do it in his universe where he invites other writers to write stories. Well, of course not. Because he would have to technologically design everything. It would drive him nuts. He would have to make every decision because it's all in his head, rather than based on history. I wouldn't try to do it with other kinds of stories, but it works in the 1632 series. So far, the books have sold well enough that we keep going.

I feel good about [the 1632 series running for fourteen years]. First of all, I enjoy the series myself. I like those stories, so I think it's a very good series. Beyond that, it's always a nice feeling to create something that's never been done before, and there's nothing like this in the history of science fiction. The closest you can probably come is Marion Zimmer Bradley's Darkover series. But she kept a lot tighter control over it than I try to. There are a lot of different dynamics involved in this. There have been some series based on media stuff ,where they bring in a lot of writers—Star Trek—but that's different because the basic framework is set, and you can't really change it that much. So, that makes me feel good. Nobody has ever done this before and kept it going.

The thing to me that is most fascinating about the series is, like I said—the sales of the books have been good, no question about it—is that at the center of that series is one of the most successful electronic magazines around, *The Grantville Gazette*, which has now been chugging along as a professional magazine for over seven years. It comes out regularly, it makes a profit, it pays for itself, and it's primarily devoted to this one series. What that tells you is that there are two ways to gauge your fan base, a book or a series, although you really need a whole series to gauge it over time. And that is, how wide is it, how many people follow it, but also what's the depth of it in the sense of what's the emotional commitment to it? What this success tells me is, that there are a lot of series that have a wider fan base. But I don't know if there's any that have a fan base as deep that they're able and willing to support a professional magazine devoted entirely to a book series. There has been, to the best of my knowledge, no other magazine in the history of science fiction that's done that. It's been done in mysteries. There have been magazines devoted to TV series or media like *The Man from Uncle* had a magazine and *Alfred Hitchcock's Presents* had a magazine. But they always depended on a big movie or TV audience to keep them going. Whereas all I have is a very modest book series compared to—I don't even come close to having the kind of mass base as a successful TV series. And yet it's been quite successful. Now we're up to fifty-five issues and it's doing fine. So that tells us something about the series.

JW: How is this series, including the magazine, a continuation of that initial interest in compassion and understanding the other point of view?

EF: It's still there in the series, but I'll be honest, that part is being somewhat attenuated, because the series is being spread out so much. So there is a degree to which I would say the 1632 series is less about that than, a) basically having a good time and what the hell, and, b) we're seeing a lot of the complexity in history insofar as I want to write books that focus more on the kind of issues you're talking about. If that were all I was trying to do I probably would have dropped the series some books back, because there are other things that I am writing. I'm really looking forward to getting back to my Sam Houston series. I started writing American history.

You write books for different reasons, a different mix of reasons with each book. The book I'm writing right now with Mike Resnick, it's pretty much kooky. There's a certain serious element in that I'm writing the alien side of the story. My aliens are all a bunch of religious fanatics. Their religion is very different from any human religion in that they are much less given to abstractions about ultimate gods, and they consider human beings insanely optimistic. The idea that there is some good divine deity that created it all, this obviously flies in the face of all evidence. It should be clear that whatever gods exist are probably a bunch of assholes. I just finished a chapter in which my heroine recites the three principal prayers of her particular tenet or creed: the first one of which is, seek not revelation lest ye be revealed. You don't want to call the attention of the gods to yourself, because that always ends badly. The other two are along those lines, so when they encounter humans it's kind of like, "These people are batshit crazy." That's fun to write. If I can poke some fun at some of the way human beings look at religion, God! It's a lot of fun to write because I don't have to do research. I can just sit there, and I don't have to even think through the science.

JW: What does collaborative writing do for you?

EF: Honestly, on an emotional level, probably the reason I do so much collaborative writing is I like it because you've got to remember I spent most of my adult life working in workforces where the work was one way or another collective. There was a lot of interaction in the workforce. On top of that I was a political activist and organizer, so I had a lot of interaction with co-workers. It's a social life on the job.

There's two things I don't like about being a writer. One of them is, you wind up being able to read a lot less—at least in reading whatever you want to 'cause there's always something you've got to read. The other thing I don't like is my job is to go down to this room that measures thirteen feet by seventeen feet and talk to myself all day. This is a really weird way to make a living. The reason I go to conventions is it's good for my mental health to get out of here and go somewhere and meet people I don't know, I didn't invent, and I can't predict what they are going to say. I don't get to do that on the job.

The other reason I do it—I do a lot of collaborative writing so I'm constantly interacting with other writers in all kinds of ways. I do a lot of editing, too. So the truth is, I actually have at least as many friends in my life through the science fiction, and I interact with them constantly, and one of the main ways that takes place is collaborative writing. That's one reason.

Another reason is I can write a wider range of books. I can tell more stories than if I were simply working on my own because there's an old joke that in collaboration everybody does 70 percent of the work. Which is probably true but that's still not a 100 percent. So you can get more done collaboratively than simply by yourself. There are some things you have to do solo because you do lose a certain something with every collaboration. It's not quite as individual as something you did by yourself, but the flip side of that is that you can do stories you could not do on your own.

JW: What do you look for in a co-writer?

EF: The first thing I'm looking for is, can I get along with this person? My very first collaborative writer was David Drake. I remember David saying to me—he's done a lot of collaborative writing—"You know, Eric, it's really a bad sign when the first part of the paper you turn to each morning is the obituary section hoping you'll see the name of your co-author." He said, "But that happens." All my experiences have been good.

The second thing is, do they have or are they bringing into the partnership a level of knowledge that I don't have, or would be very hard for me to duplicate? The final thing is, as much as possible, I want them to be people whose writing skills have strengths. They may also have weaknesses—sometimes they do. Some of my co-authors are really uneven. But there's really something there.

What I don't want is a writer whose kind of—I'm trying to figure how to say this so it doesn't sound arrogant—I don't want them to be second-ringer as a co-author. I don't want them to be me. I want them to be whoever they are, whatever their strengths and weaknesses might be and we'll go from there. Some of my co-authors—like David Weber and Misty Lackey—are extremely capable, accomplished, better-selling authors. So that's not an issue, but even there we're meshing well, because we are bringing different things into it.

These are the three things. That I can get along with someone, they bring in a level of expertise or knowledge I don't have, and that they are strong writers, whatever problems they may also have. I can live with that and fix problems. But what I don't want—I'm not going to name any names—there are some writers that are just kind of blah. I mean, it's like, "What's wrong with this?" Well, nothing exactly but there's nothing exactly right about it either. I don't want something like that. I want something that may need to have the edges filed off or may need to have problems corrected, but it's really strong.

There are some people I would not co-author with simply because I think their values are just too antithetical to mine. By the way, these are not necessarily people I dislike. They're not people I necessarily think are bad writers. You have to look at the world enough the same way. David Weber and I, for instance, you can put us down and talk politics and we will argue for hours. It will be a cordial, friendly argument, but it's going to be an argument. But we've always been able to write novels together because the issues over which we argue are pretty much contemporary issues that are kind of irrelevant, and I don't have any problem with his basic values and he doesn't with mine. We both like the same kind of story and he gives me a great deal of leeway when I'm working in his universe, and I give him a tremendous amount of leeway when he's working in my universe. Neither one of us feels cramped or crowded. So it works fine.

It's hard to answer this because collaborative writing is an art, it's not a science. I just have a feel for it, if it will work or not. I'm doing a book right now with Mike Resnick. Mike and I disagree at least as much as I do with David Weber. But we're writing a book about Indiana Jones meets the Alien Terminator. He doesn't have a grudge against humans. He has a grudge against other aliens. The human expression is, she's going Grendel. Who cares whether we agree about who the governor of Iowa will be? It's not about that. I like Mike personally. We've always gotten along.

JW: What advice would you give to this next generation of writers?

EF: The single biggest piece of advice I give to new writers, the same advice I give to kids trying to figure out what to major in college, is study what you're interested in and write what you want to write. Don't try to second-guess the market. Don't try to figure out what people want to read. Don't try to figure out what's going to sell. You do have to be practical about stuff. If you have a burning desire to tell a story that looks at the world from a viewpoint of a turnip, I suggest you wait until you're a very well established writer. It takes months to write a novel, even if you're a fast writer. You're having to put a whole lot of your own self into it. Don't do that with a story you're not interested in. Do something you find interesting. Figure out a story you really feel passionate about and write about it. Let the chips fall where they fall.

Expanded version of the interview that appeared in
Issue 11 of Galaxy's Edge, *November 2014.*

■ MERCEDES LACKEY & LARRY DIXON

Mercedes Lackey is one of the most prolific fantasy authors of all time, with approximately 140 books in print (so far!). She is able to write at a rate of five and a half books a year, ensuring the creation of multiple popular series—solo and in collaboration with writers such as Eric Flint and Anne McCaffrey. Best known for her Valdemar books, Mercedes created a series known for embracing diversity, long before such diversity was the norm in real life, with one of her protagonists, Herald Mage Vanyel, becoming a favorite among readers. Mercedes is also well known for her Bedlam's Bard, SERRAted Edge, Tales of the Five Hundred Kingdoms, The Dragon Jouster, and the Diana Tregarde series. In addition to her fantasy writing, Mercedes has written lyrics for, and recorded, nearly fifty songs for Firebird Arts & Music, a small recording company specializing in science fiction folk music—winning five Pegasus Awards, mostly for her song writing over the years.

Larry Dixon married Mercedes Lackey in 1992, working in collaboration with his wife as the co-author on The Mage War trilogy, The Owl trilogy and two SERRAted Edge novels. As an artist he has also illustrated many of her books, as well as contributing artwork to the *Dungeons & Dragons* source books for the Wizards of the Coast. Commissioned by "Save Our American Raptors" and the United States military, Larry has also provided photographs of a stuffed Golden Eagle (held for a local tribe elder), to Weta Digital in New Zealand, which were used to help create the digital model for Gwalhir and his eagle companions. Larry and Mercedes live in Tulsa, Oklahoma, in an unusual two-and-a-half dome house with an octagonal wooden shell over it, and their menagerie of birds.

Joy Ward's original introduction: Mercedes Lackey and Larry Dixon are one of science fiction and fantasy's power couples. With well over one hundred and forty books and numerous short stories to their credit, this multi-talented duo have set their mark on both literature and cover art. Mercedes (Misty is her nickname) and Larry work together on the writing, and Larry is a much-sought-after cover artist.

Joy Ward: How did you get started in the arts?

Larry Dixon: As a very young child I got the idea that I wanted to write and illustrate my own books, because I found that was what was really influencing me. I entered a library reading competition. I read a record number of books for our small-town library. I discovered that I had greater comprehension with the illustrated books than with straight text. I decided this may be what I want to be when I grow up. But at a time when most of the other children my age wanted to be football stars or astronauts or whatever, I developed a fascination with state-level diplomacy. I thought that the idea that the fate of nations could be changed by one person talking to one person was one of the most amazing things humans can do.

Then the connection was made inside me that I would be able to affect other people for the better by doing stories. So, while other kids were saving up their money to buy skateboards, I put a Royal Model 3 typewriter on layaway, and I still have it. And that's where my very first short stories were written. Eventually it led up to characters in the books that the lovely and talented Mercedes Lackey and I have written together.

JW: Mercedes, how did you get into writing?

Mercedes Lackey: My father was an avid science fiction reader. As soon as I could comprehend books, which was fairly young, I started reading his books. There weren't enough of them being published to satisfy me, so I started writing what was essentially fan fiction, even though I didn't know what that was. When I discovered science fiction conventions I discovered fanzines, and I started writing more of it. Eventually I just moved into trying to get myself good enough to become a pro.

JW: How did you move into becoming a pro?

ML: Practice, practice, practice.

JW: What was your big break?

ML: That was Marion Zimmer Bradley buying a short story for *Free Amazons of Darkover*.

I got to know Marion, and I volunteered for one of the Darkover Cons. I was the person who made sure all the gophers ate and slept, whether they wanted to or not. Marion asked me if I was trying to break into publishing, as she always did with her protégés and followers. She told me to submit some stories for the *Free Amazons* anthology and the *Sword and Sorceress* anthology. I did not sell to the *Sword and Sorceress* anthology. She gave me some good advice on how to revise my story. I subsequently sold that to a magazine called *Fantasy Book*, but not before I had sold a *Free Amazon* story to her.

JW: Larry, how did you become a pro?

LD: I can tell you almost the exact moment that it happened. I went to my first convention in 1984. There were two people that were there that I admired very, very much, Anne McCaffrey and Michael Whelan. They did something for me that I thought was quite wonderful: they took me seriously. During the course of that weekend they just talked to me and gave me twenty minutes of taking me seriously. Right there, that first weekend of my first convention, I decided if this is what the professionals are like, this is the field I want to be in for the rest of my life. Last year I celebrated my thirtieth year as a full-time professional. It all goes back to that twenty minutes that first weekend. Since then I've been a guest or guest of honor at two hundred and fifty-eight conventions around the world, and it's all thanks to those two.

Ever since then I've tried to be the one to give others that twenty minutes, and dozens of careers have been started. Even more importantly, many, many people have been made happy just because somebody would take the time to listen to them, give 'em some time, take 'em seriously.

We're all in it together. You hear that phrase but it's especially true whenever it comes to fantasy and science fiction as a field because we support each other. We like to take on protégés. We like to take on apprentices. We like to help other people because when it comes down to it, we're still fans. We just happen to make our mortgage off of it. Part of the motivation in wanting to help new people come up in the field is we want to geek out over what they make.

There's a lot of fan art that happens, and I will see people's take on characters that we've created. You realize that this beautiful piece of art that somebody spent hours upon hours upon hours painting would never have existed if we hadn't written that particular story that inspired it. So we kind of build the sandbox and other people come and play in it. Then we get to walk in and say, "Check out that cool sandcastle! It's shaped like a griffin! That's so awesome!" That's a lot of fun. They remember the details better than we do sometimes. It's an honest truth that sometimes when we've been working on our own books we can't remember a detail, so we will go to a fan site to double check. Their memories are way better than ours for our own material.

ML: One of the things that writers have a problem with is insomnia, because you're working out the details of whatever you're working on. Then what you're planning on working on after that is always running through your head, which kind of keeps you from going to sleep at night.

LD: I can't count the number of times that Misty has glanced over and I'm on a laptop just writing down story notes. I've been in bed for two hours and I'd better write this down. I open up the laptop and start typing.

It's like that, too, whenever we're on road trips. I'll drive and Misty will be in the passenger's seat just typing away. We will plot out entire books during the driving hours just talking back and forth.

ML: It's very useful because there's no such thing as writer's block. Once we start talking about it, you see the way through the block.

LD: Whenever people think of the term "writer's block," I think they're picturing it as if it's a corridor and there is something in the way in the corridor. I always look at writing and the art of storytelling of any kind, something like a plane. If there is a writer's block it means it's just something that can be skirted. You simply go around it. You don't have to run into it.

ML: Or you go to another direction entirely. I keep saying there's no such thing. It's your subconscious telling you that the story's not going to work the way you planned it. Your subconscious is a lot smarter than you are when it comes to plotting.

LD: It is. I teach master classes in art. I tell people, "Trust your intuition," and here's why; I define intuition as the assimilation and processing of great amounts of information so quickly that you are unaware of the process but are left with the answer. When you trust your intuition you've already thought it out. You just weren't aware of the process of thinking it out. You're just hit with, "This is the right thing to do." Whenever you develop intuition as a professional skill, you wind up saving a lot of time because you're learning to trust yourself. As a result, you can go off in directions where other people would simply muddle about trying to think it through. Instead, you take a moment and you see how it feels. You know that the back of your brain has worked it out, and there is no writer's block. You're ready to go.

JW: Tell me about working together.

LD: Misty is one of the most prolific living fantasy writers. I'm often Misty's editor. I'm going to brag on you. There was one day where she was really doing a heavy burn on a book. She turned over to me forty-two pages of finished text in one day and it was flawless.

ML: That was the end of the book.

LD: There were no typos. There were no misspellings. There were no grammatical errors. Nothing. But that's forty-two pages and most writers do that in a month. For her that was one day of very, very good focus.

ML: The front end of the book is always hard. It's like pushing the rock up the hill. Once you get to the middle of the book then the rock goes down the hill and picks up speed till you come to the end.

LD: Then it can go pretty darned quickly. We've been able to work together in some very interesting ways, where I'm able to bring in a slightly skewed perspective. Misty, on the other hand, has a very laser-like focus, and she has a clear idea of where something is going to go. I'll come in and say, "Did you notice this reflection? Did you see that you foreshadowed this here?" And she'll go, "I wasn't even aware of that, but I'd better play that up." It's awesome how that happens where we get to bounce back and forth like that. One of the great things about co-writing is that you each get to write the best part of the book.

JW: How did you come to have this flow with co-writing?

ML: I just naturally co-write well.

LD: I have a gift for the social side of things. I consider it part of my job. I can write just fine as a solo writer, but I feel my rarer gift is the ability to work with others. Part of my job is keeping it fun, is making sure that everybody is having a great time. We're in to create something awesome, and that will help other people feel something in their lives. That's how she and I work so well together. Any time we hit a rough spot in our lives we're there for each other emotionally and professionally. That makes it a great privilege to be able work with this woman and I love it.

ML: Part of being a good co-writer is you always check your ego at the door, because no matter how junior somebody is to you they may have better ideas.

LD: To talk about how we work together, let's go back to the moment we met.

ML: I was the writing guest of honor [in Meridian, Mississippi] and he was the artist guest of honor. I think it was my second GOH gig. I was literally picked up at the airport. He was already in the car and they took us off to do an interview on a TV show back when there were little tiny TV stations everywhere.

LD: It was just a spot at the end of the news show.

ML: We came right after the report of the UFOs being seen in the swamp. I am not making this up! There was a report of UFOs being seen in the swamp by a couple of good old boys on their trolling boat.

LD: This is our portent? Okay. But here's the thing. I'd read some of Misty's work by then. When we met she thought I was the ugliest person she'd ever seen!

JW: Did you tell him that?

ML: Later.

LD: By the end of the weekend we had plotted our first book together. It was called *Ties Never Binding*. I did the first sketches of the characters that weekend. Whenever you train as an artist there is a tremendous amount of self-image and ego involved. You need that to keep you going because the better you get at your craft the more sensitive you become, and that's a trap. When I met Misty, when I was around her, I realized that as impressed as I was by myself, I had just met somebody that the world needed more than me.

ML: Well, I just thought he was a tremendously good artist and certainly deserved all of the ego that he was exuding. He's basically a griffin.

JW: How did working together on a book actually morph into the life-long relationship?

LD: We were kind of what we needed, and we were lucky enough to come across each other in that way. Mostly we just maintained forward motion.

JW: What are you looking for when you're looking at co-writers?

ML: Cooperation. They have to recognize that I have a certain level of expertise and they also have to recognize I'm the final editor. I'm the one who has to make the final decision because right now they don't have the reputation, I do. My reputation could be ruined by something that they insist on.

LD: We may have our own emotional baggage, and we have things that stress us out. We have things that frankly crush our spirit from time to time. Twenty years from now no one will care, because all that will be left is the book. That's why "the show must go on" is a major part of our philosophy. It does not matter how miserable we are, the pages must come out. The show must go on.

I realize we've probably got between sixty and eighty people whose income depends upon what we turn in. If you add up all the different publishers that's the money they're going to send their kids to college with. That's the money they are going to pay their mortgage with. If I have a drama fit and my book comes in late, I'm holding up the money that goes to their children. I'm not that much of a dick, so I get over it. I move on. Part of the skill set you develop is coping.

ML: With the co-writers, the other thing is that everybody's ego gets checked at the door. In spite of the fact that I'm the boss, it's not an ego thing. It's an experience thing.

LD: An expertise thing. It's really interesting too because sometimes the newest people will notice something that we missed. I've said before that the worst hell is the place where everybody agrees with you. How can you ever learn anything new in a place where everybody agrees with you? We've seen so many examples where nobody dared disagree with the guy in charge and everything jar-jared out. So, we like the idea of a little bit of conflict going as far as questioning things. But we don't dig a lot of drama. We don't have time for a lot of strife. That's where the selecting of the partners carefully comes in.

JW: Tell me about a real high point in your careers.

ML: Virtually every day. I get to do what I love for a living. There are not very many people in the world who get to do that. So, that's pretty much it.

I get to do exactly what I want to do every day for as long as I want to keep doing it.

LD: My exciting things are things like whenever you meet someone who has named her kid after a character you wrote or created, then you meet the kid after they've graduated and you realize, "We've been doing this how long?"

ML: That just makes me feel old.

LD: There's something to that. I've seen people take my art and do full-sleeved tattoos which I've autographed. Then they got the auto-graph inked. So I've signed people. It's been nose art on aircraft, and all kinds of military equipment. You discover that people incorporate the things you make into their lives and they are significant to them.

Misty and I know that we are never going to cure cancer. But we might write the book that will get somebody through the darkest time in their life—that will help them to cure cancer. Anybody can hit a dark point in their life where they need something just to get them through. Just that one little bit that will tip them toward keep-ing with it, staying in. We get letters sometimes from people where we've been that for them.

JW: About a hundred years from now, when people pull up your name and they pull out your books…

ML: I have absolutely no freaking clue because if you look at people who were considered great writers one hundred years ago you cannot find them at anything but Project Gutenberg. You look at people who were considered hack writers one hundred years ago, people like the

Kiplings and the Dickenses—they're the ones who are being taught in school, so who the heck knows.

LD: Hack is an important term.

ML: As Harlan Ellison told me once, "A hack is a perfectly reliable horse that is guaranteed to get you where you want to go."

LD: We've had to look at ourselves very honestly as far as the work we do and the quality of work that we do. We make comfort food. We make a really great mac and cheese and every once in a while, you'll go, "There's bacon in this too." There are people in our field who are gourmet chefs. We will look at what they're writing, and we'll go, "Holy crap! They're amazing!"

We don't get an ego trip and we don't get crushed by it either. We understand what we do. When we talk about the Valdemar books, for instance, I say that we like a Valdemar book to always feel like you're coming home.

You'll come across writers that are absolutely deadly serious about their work and what they write is deathless prose.

ML: No. Not even cast in concrete. It was written in sand.

LD: It's kind of brittle plaster and soggy too. You get writers that think that their work should be taken absolutely seriously, and as a result the fans expect that it should be taken seriously.

If you only take something seriously and you don't pick out what's hilarious about it, what's silly, you're not getting the whole picture.

Being serious about it isn't the point. Taking it seriously, is because we're professionals.

ML: Well taking it professionally, is the point.

JW: You made the comment earlier that you're kind of the mac and cheese. You're not the gourmet food of fantasy.

LD: Sometimes you really want the mac and cheese. That doesn't make it a lesser thing.

ML: You can't live on truffles. You can't live on gourmet chocolate. And I guarantee you that you cannot live on steak. It will make you sick and kill you.

I wouldn't say we are mac and cheese. I would say we are a good home-cooked dinner, probably balanced with lots of broccoli.

The idea is just because you're aware of your talent level doesn't mean that you're doing a bad job. We give it the best we can, but we know it's not going to be as good as some of the greats in our field. We give it the best we've got, and as a result I believe it's solid.

JW: What do you look for in science fiction writing by other people?

LD: Time. I have stacks of books by people I adore on a personal level that I've never gotten to read.

ML: I want somebody that makes me forget I'm reading a book. Immersion.

LD: I learned a wonderful word recently from William Gibson. It was the perfect word to close it on because you've spoken as a theme that we have influence.

ML: And we have a lot of longevity at this point.

LD: He used the word we were looking for. What is the right word for when you find that other people have been influenced by your work? Derivative is not the right word because there is something vaguely insulting about using the word derivative. I learned it from William Gibson: echoic.

ML: They are echoing you. They echo your voice but it's now their voice.

LD: An echo is shaped by what it encounters. So there are times when I'll read somebody's work, or they'll send me something to proof or whatever. I can see an influence, or in the fan art and things like that, and I'll get a letter that you're the first artist I've wanted to be. I can see the art I did twenty years ago influenced this person and their whole career. I can't take credit for it, but I did make the sound that caused an echo.

Man, what a great thing to be. I hope it never ends. I just hope it continues to get better. Then I get to see what cool stuff comes from those echoes, because it will reverberate too. We do a lot of looking forward. Science fiction is supposed to be the only inherently hopeful form of fiction, because it assumes there will be a future. We really are custodians of the future. Fantasy fiction tends to be more about relationships, about understanding how people work and why people work. We find that the fantasy books that we write are often embraced by people who are just trying to figure out how the world works. We have a responsibility to not screw them up.

First published in Issue 9 of Galaxy's Edge, *July 2014.*

Gene Wolfe was born on May 7, 1931, having the misfortune to develop polio as a small child, only to soar to great heights as a prolific science fiction and fantasy author. He was drafted into the Korean War, earned a degree from the University of Houston upon his return to the United States, and became an industrial engineer. Senior editor of the journal *Plant Engineering,* his professional engineering achievement was to contribute to the construction of the machine that is used to make Pringles potato chips. Wolfe became most famous for writing the four titles in The Book of the New Sun series. Winning many awards, Gene has won six Locus Awards, four World Fantasy Awards, two Nebula Awards, a BSFA Award, a Rysling Award for a long poem, the Edward F. Smith Memorial Award, a World Fantasy Lifetime Achievement Award, the Damon Knight Memorial Award, and more.

Joy Ward's original introduction: We're here with Gene Wolfe, Grand Master of science fiction and a grand person as well. It is a pleasure to interview him.

JW: Gene, how did you get into writing science fiction?

Gene Wolfe: When my wife and I married, we had no money at all. We were living in a furnished apartment that had once been an attic. All the rooms were pointed at the top, if you know what I mean, and we needed money for furniture. I came across a notice in a magazine somewhere, mentioned in a magazine, that said Gold Medal books was paying a guaranteed $2,000 [which was much more in those days than it is today] for any book they would accept. I thought, "I will write a book for Gold Medal books, and we will have money to buy furniture."

So, I tried and it was not a saleable novel, but I got the bug that way and I kept writing all sorts of stuff, frankly, and the stuff that sold was science fiction or fantasy. The first thing that I sold was a story called "The Dead Man," which was basically a ghost story. It's about a man who discovers that his body is in a crocodile's cave. Crocodiles dig lairs under the riverbank and they stash bodies in there until the bodies get ripe enough to eat. Crocodiles can't chew by the way. Anyway, that was my first sale and my second one was a science fiction story that I sold to *Galaxy*...no, pardon me, it wasn't *Galaxy*. It was *Worlds of If.* I sent it to *Galaxy*. I was going down an alphabetized list of markets and it was sent back with a form rejection slip, which is how all my stories came back.

I then sent it to the next magazine on the list, which was *Worlds of If,* unaware that they were being edited by the same man, who was Frederik Pohl. This time I got a letter from Frederik Pohl that said I think the rewrite has really improved this (and there had been no rewrite), and I will buy it if you will accept one cent a word. And, God knows I have been stupid all my life, but I wasn't so stupid as to say I would not accept one cent a word. I said I would be happy to accept one cent a word. Sold! And so he bought it.

I thought, the first thing that sold was a ghost story and the second thing that sold was a science fiction story, so maybe that should be telling me something. I started writing that type of story more than other types of stories. I had written some things like straight love stories and some detective mystery stories, and what do you know—I could not only write those stories, but I could sell them if I wrote fantasy or I wrote science fiction. So that's what I wrote.

JW: Which type of story did you enjoy writing most?

GW: I enjoyed writing both. I still do and I kind of ping-pong back and forth between the two. I wrote a number of fantasies recently. Then I wrote *Home Fires*, which is a straight science fiction novel. Then I wrote *A Borrowed Man*, which I just sent to the agency. That is a straight science fiction novel. So I'm kind of correcting the deficit of writing so much fantasy, and I'm writing more science fiction.

They are both interesting forms in themselves. Fantasy has the danger that you will play so fast and loose with it to make things easy for yourself, which you must not do.

I teach creative writing sometimes. When I read students' stories I often get stories in which things change simply because it is convenient for the author. I have read some stories written by good established authors who have done the same thing. The man is rich when it is convenient for the author that he be rich, and he is poor when it is convenient for the author that he be poor, and so on. A character is helpless at one point in the story and far from it at another point in the story. Supposedly it's the same person because that's convenient, too. This is not realistic and it's not artistic. You shouldn't do it. When you say so-and-so is a wizard you're in danger of saying he can do anything and that's not interesting.

JW: What's bad about that for both the reader and the writer?

GW: It's unrealistic and it's obviously cheating for the writer. It's like the story I was talking about earlier where the author is plainly working out a grudge. He has this rather ordinary woman whom he hates, and it comes through all the time...I hate this damned character and I'm going to tear her to pieces in my story and it will feel so good. And that's not art. It's not literature. It's not anything that a reader is going to enjoy. You tend to look at this poor woman and pity her because you know that the author hates her and is going to do really ugly stuff to her. You think she doesn't deserve this. "Come on. Why do you hate her so much? Put it down." And of course he doesn't, and the reason he hates her so much is some stupid trivial thing like she doesn't want to watch football with him or something. Come on. Grow up.

JW: Who, as an author, has really had an impact on you?

GW: Lots and lots of people have. G. K. Chesterton…Rudyard Kipling. I'm not deliberately sticking to Englishmen. It just so happens that those are people who had a real impact on me. Earlier than that, a woman named Ruth Plumly Thompson who continued the Oz series after the death of Frank Baum. As a kid I liked the Plumly stories better than I did the Baum stories, although I liked the Baum stories…. They just appealed to me more. There was more an open, pleasant feeling to them than there was to the Baum stories, as far as I was concerned.

JW: Who else has had a real impact on you?

GW: H.G. Wells, for one. H. G. Wells for me started with his *History of the World….* I had the odd experience of having a father who had been one of the really early science fiction fans. He was an H.G. Wells fan. As a result I would not read H. G. Wells because I was a kid, and kids are that way…. He put H. G. Wells' *History of the World* into my hands, and I kind of skipped around in that. I looked up things I was interested in and all that sort of stuff. Then I was reading pulp magazines and Famous Fantastic Mysteries came out with *The Island of Dr. Moreau.* I failed to notice that it was H. G. Wells, the author that my dad was so fond of. I read it and it was wonderful! And it's still wonderful after one hundred years now. It has to be close to one hundred years old, and it's still a terrific book! So he was certainly early science fiction.

The first downright science fiction story I ever read was "A Microcosmic God" by Theodore Sturgeon. I had been reading *Flash Gordon* and *Buck Rogers* in the Sunday funnies. I was a Sunday funnies reader at that age. I fell off my bicycle and injured my leg sufficiently badly that I could no longer ride my bicycle to school, so my mother was taking me in the car until my leg healed. And she was waiting outside the school one time for me to come out so she could drive me home.

She had a mass-market paperback on the car seat beside her. My mother was a fanatical mystery reader. She had been reading those and I had been reading them behind her.... So here she had this book and I could tell from the cover that this was something like *Buck Rogers* because it was a futuristic city with spaceships coming out of it. I said, "Can I read that after you when you're finished?" She said, "Well you can read it now because I don't much care for it." So I read it, and the first story I read was "A Microcosmic God" by Theodore Sturgeon. That just turned me on to science fiction and blew my mind. I thought, "This is marvelous stuff." And I was right. It is marvelous stuff. And I would point out to those who insist on rocket ships, ray guns, and robots, that "The Microcosmic God" has no rocket ships, no ray guns, and no robots in it, but it is science fiction and it is really, really good science fiction.

JW: If you could set up a writing school now and include any writers from the past and any who are currently writing, who would you put in it?

GW: That would be a neat idea! I would of course have Wells. I would have Sturgeon, Chesterton, and Kipling, if I could get them. I think I would take Dickens, although I would have to give him a lecture, seriously, on the uses of punctuation. Dickens writes correct punctuation for the period in which he was writing, and correct punctuation has changed considerably since his books and stories were written. So he needs modernization on the punctuation. Nobody, I think, could resist the temptation to get William Shakespeare to teach. He was so good and so versatile.

JW: You've obviously had a lot of students, many of whom have gone on to become excellent writers. What does that do for you?

GW: It doesn't do anything for me except make me feel happy and proud and feel like I have not wasted my time.

If you can pass on the flame, hand on the torch, you like to be able to do that. I had a mentor. My mentor was Damon Knight, and Damon taught me a heck of a lot. The one thing I always remember... he used to say he grew me from a bean. I had written this crazy story in which everything was in two panels, two parallel columns, one by an Earth man and one by an alien, describing the same events: one from the Earth man's viewpoint and one from the alien's viewpoint. And what Damon said what we needed to do was cut this thing, so that we would go from the Earth man to the alien and then back and forth. He said, "I have tried cutting it up. See how you like this." And I spent the evening after I got it trying to cut it up better than Damon had, and I couldn't. Everything he did was right, and I couldn't do anything righter than he had done. But I learned a hell of a lot in going through that story and seeing how he had divided things. The story is "Trip Trap," for anyone who wants to find the story and go after it.

JW: Are most of your stories still in print? I know there have been collections.

GW: A whole lot of them are still in print. Yes. I am primarily published by Tor Books and Tor Books has been very good to me about keeping my stuff in print. I know that…[some] writers I could name who have been prolific are now getting no royalties at all from some of the things that they have written; books they have written. You don't normally get royalties from short stories; although occasionally somebody pays you money to reprint the thing. But you do get royalties from books, if the books are still out and available from the publisher. Theirs aren't. The publisher is not keeping these books in print. So they bellyache about it, and they do what they can to try and get them back into print. I was very, very lucky because *The Book of the New Sun* was sold to a publisher who did not keep it in print. [The publisher] would not revert it because my contract said that the book did not have to be reverted as long as it was in print from any source licensed by the publisher. It was in print from Science Fiction Book Club, licensed by that publisher, so the publisher could have the book out of print but not revert it, because it was still available from Science Fiction Book Club. And what happened then was that my then-son-in-law worked for the company that had published the book, and the president of the company was leaving for a new job and they threw him a party. At the party my then-son-in-law went up to the president and said, "Would you do me a favor, please, mister?

Revert my father-in-law's books." And the president said, "Sure, I'll be happy to," and he did. On his last day, just before he cleaned out his desk, he reverted those books. And the result was that my agent got to sell them again, this time to Tor Books. I got more money and they are still to this day in print from Tor Books.

JW: Any advice you would give newbie writers who are facing the great crocodile of publishing?

GW: In the first place, write short stories. I'm assuming, you say newbie writers. I'm assuming these are writers who are interested in writing fiction. If they are interested in writing non-fiction the answer is write magazine articles. But for the fiction writer, the advice is write short stories.

JW: Why start out with short stories?

GW: Because that is the easy way to learn to write. It takes you so much less time and less effort to make your mistakes in short stories and realize, one hopes eventually, what you have done. I know a lady, a friend of mine, who wrote some good short stories and also wrote six novels, none of which ever sold. I have never read her six novels, so I don't know what she was doing wrong, but I know she wrote some good short stories, and she should have been able to look at those novels and see what she was doing wrong. But she was not a person who accepted teaching from someone else.

I had a male friend who was the same way. He was a wonderful person. He was extremely intelligent. He had all sorts of talents, and he wanted to write. But when you said, "Don't do this," instead of learning from what you said, he argued with you that what he did was right and acceptable and so on. He was wrong; just plain wrong. He used solecisms and things that are not found in good writing, except when a character is speaking. If you want to characterize a character you can have him do all kinds of things and make grammatical mistakes. Sometimes that is what you want to do, but when you are just writing the text you don't do that. You write literarily acceptable English, and that is what he would object to.

I tell my classes, "Look, if I tell you to take X out of your story, I could be wrong. I'm often wrong. I'm just one person. And if so-and-so also tells you to take X out of the title we could both be wrong. But if everybody is telling you to take X out, for God's sake, don't screw around with it, TAKE X OUT! Throw it away!"

Don't be so stubborn that you kill yourself! The person who insists on driving at eighty miles an hour, icy roads or no icy roads, ends up dead.

JW: Any other rules or suggestions you would have for newbie writers that maybe you would have even told yourself when you were starting out?

GW: Read good writing of the type you want to do. If you want to write mystery, read good mystery stories. If you want to write fantasy, read good fantasy. That doesn't mean just pick out a few books because you like the covers. Try to find out what has reputation, what is well thought of in the field, and read some of those books and look at them. Insofar as you can, read them as a writer. How is this written? How does the book open? And does the book's opening really draw the reader in? And if I'm really drawn in by this opening, what is it the writer has done in that opening that draws me in?

I used to workshop often with Kate Wilhelm. Kate Wilhelm would always bring a red pen to her workshops. One thing that she did frequently to a story was to take her pen and draw a line halfway down page three or wherever it was, and say, "This is where the story starts. This stuff before is stuff you have written to get yourself into it. It's for you. Take it off of the story that you are going to submit. Start your story here."

I read advice from a Western writer one time who said, "Shoot the sheriff on page one." Of course he didn't mean that to be taken literally, but he meant to do something significant on page one. Don't begin your story or book with twenty or thirty pages of scene setting and ranch life, and what it's like at the spring roundup, and so on and so forth. Shoot the sheriff on page one. Get it going. The rest of that stuff you can put in later as needed.

I taught Clarion West at one time. There was a man there who, I thought from his background, was likely to be one of the best students.

He sure as heck wasn't. I'll call him Bob. At the end of your week teaching Clarion West you had one-on-one interviews with each of the students, talking about their work and trying to help them. When Bob came in, I said, "Bob, I have your most recent story here. Whenever you introduce a new character you stop the story dead and give us anywhere from half a page to two and a half pages on what this character is like—what he looks like, how he dresses, what he enjoys doing, what he likes to eat, what he does for a living, what he used to do for a living, how he treats his wife, and so on and so forth. Now I know I'm the sixth and last instructor on this six-week course. I know who the other instructors are. You had four good writers and you had a good editor who were your instructors in the earlier weeks. I know damned well that those people have been telling you not to do this ,and I've been telling you not to do it all week and Bob, you're still doing it! Why the hell are you still doing it?" And he said, "Well I think we need that." What can you do?

JW: So how did you get him out of that?

GW: I didn't get him out of it. I've never seen his byline anywhere, so he probably is unpublished if he's still writing.

I read a while back and probably you did too, about a man in Australia who has written fifteen novels and none of them have sold. I told you about my female friend—she's now dead—who wrote six novels, none of which sold, and there are people like that, and they write for twenty years and they never have any success because they are doing something or some things wrong and they never catch on to it. Read other people's writing. If you are doing something distinctly different from what those other people are doing, look at the thing really hard because it may not be what you want to do.

JW: Switching gears here a bit. You are a Grand Master of science fiction. In the future, how do you want to be seen?

GW: I was trying to remember the little rhyme, about, "When I die, may it be said that his sins were scarlet but his books were read."

First published in Issue 8 of Galaxy's Edge, *May 2014.*

■ JACK McDEVITT

ack McDevitt started his first novel, *The Canals of Mars*, at age nine. He wrote a column for his high school newspaper, South Catholic's *Rocket*, and won the Freshman Short Story Contest at LaSalle in 1953 with an SF story, "A Pound of Cure." LaSalle's literary journal, *Four Quarters*, published the story, and Jack thought he was on his way to a career as a professional SF writer, but he did not write another word of fiction for twenty-five years. He became a naval officer, an English teacher, a customs officer, a taxi driver and worked for the US Customs Service. Eventually his wife, the former Maureen McAdams, persuaded him to return to his original passion. He wrote "The Emerson Effect," which sold to *Twilight Zone Magazine*. Since then he has written twenty-two novels, twelve of which have been Nebula finalists, and more than eighty short stories. He has won the Philip K. Dick Award, the John W. Campbell Memorial Award, the Georgia Writers' Association Lifetime Achievement Award and, most recently, the International Astronomical Union named an asteroid for him.

■■■■■

Joy Ward's original introduction: Jack McDevitt is a writer who always makes us think. His heroes are women and men with hearts of gold and feet of clay, like many real people.

Jack McDevitt: I can't remember a time [when] I didn't want to write. It might be that it had to do with when I first became enthusiastic about science fiction and I realized they were doing stories and stuff. I thought I would like to do that too. But I developed an absolute connection with science fiction when I was four years old, and I never recovered.

I grew up in south Philadelphia and my father used to take me to the local theater called The Bell. They ran Westerns. I remember the movies of pilots and war. It was World War I movies about pilots, and I didn't really care about those. I didn't know what was going on, but they also ran serials and the serials I remember. There was *Buck Rogers* and *Flash Gordon*. *Flash Gordon* has this great rocket ship that Dr. Zarkov built it in his garage—this thing, it had no air. I didn't realize at the time it had no air lock. They went to Mars in this thing in one of the episodes, in one of the series. There were three serials actually. They went to Mars in this thing and it had no air lock and it had no washrooms [that] I could make out.

I absolutely loved the serial. I remember, though, I got annoyed with it. I can remember telling my dad one time coming out of the theater, "Why is it he's got this great rocket ship and he can go anywhere he wants and all he can do is pick fights with this guy who looked like one of my uncles?"

It was really pathetic, but I loved the rocket ship and I never got past that. I remember one night we came out and there was a full Moon up over the rooftops. I asked my dad if we were ever going to go to the Moon, and he said he didn't see it was going to happen. The reason is—well, it was, unfortunately—it would never happen and the reason for that was that rockets need something to push against. You can't just take them out into a vacuum and expect to be able to steer the thing, which I understand later was a fairly common view back in the '30s. But anyway, I just loved that stuff and I never got over it.

I go, once in a while, to speak to groups. Not science fiction groups, the library group or something like that. Whenever I do there's always, at the end, there's some guy who will come up and say, "You know, I don't read the stuff myself, but I've got a nephew..." The tone is that the nephew does other idiot stuff as well, but he likes it. I usually stand there and I feel sorry for this guy because the train has missed the station.

He's stuck in south Philadelphia or wherever and he never really gets out. He lives his life bound to the Earth. Those are the sort of science fiction enthusiasts we get clear. We don't do it physically, but we get clear all the same, and it counts for a lot.

JW: What's important about that, that we get clear?

JM: We're born with a natural curiosity. What's out there? What's going on? Look at this thing recently where they were talking about taking people on a one-way flight to Mars. They had all kinds of people volunteering to go. I'm not saying that's rational but there's something going on—we look around us and we see this universe, this wide universe is out there and we know so little about it. Right now it's what science fiction does. What science fiction does, [it] plays games with astronomy and other sciences. We get to look at what is, and, as far as we can tell, what's possible.

It's an indicator of who we really are. We're something better than somebody who wants to kind of live at the end of the street and we got a place in the garage. We have our families, and everybody grows up, and after a while we die and go into the dust. I think most of us want more. We're curious. It's a reason. If we weren't curious we never would have made it to the Americas.

It makes me feel very happy. I, I feel honored when people come to me at places like this and say nice things. They talk about how their lives have been influenced by some of the stuff they read. That is true for me. My life without science fiction, it would be like.... I've been a baseball nut all my life. I can't imagine my life without baseball, and it's the same thing with science fiction. There are certain things that make my life seem worthwhile other than the usual stuff. You know, having children, having a family, that's all great. You can't get along without that, but there's got to be more to life. There have to be other things to it. For a lot of us the other things are wondering about what's out there, what the possibilities are, where we're headed—and that's a big thing. Where are we headed?

The average human being pretty much ignores the possibilities of what's going on until we get surprised. It's not the way nature intended or God intended. We don't really know what God intended so much. But I think the future is coming on us very quickly. We are getting close to a point now, for example, where women are going to the doctor and the doctor's going to say to women who are going to conceive, "Well, there's something we can do for you if you like. We can arrange things so that your child will have a much higher IQ than the people around him. Do you want that? Or we can make him pretty handsome or we can…we can arrange things so that child is going to live an extraordinarily long life." We're not far from that kind of thing.

For most people, when it arrives it will be like having the roof cave in. Suddenly, [there's] this huge surprise that they cannot completely handle. They're in shock. They don't know what they want to do. So maybe it's something we should think about. Would you really want a child whose IQ is one hundred points higher than yours? I'm not sure whether that's a really good idea or not. Maybe we ought to think about it before we do too much more research.

I have a friend; his name is Michael Fossel. He's a neurologist and his specialty is life extension. He tells me that we're getting very close, not only to being able to stop the aging process, but to reverse it. Now imagine some kind of pills that you could take that would send you back to being twenty-five years old. Aside from the potential consequences from something like that, how do we arrange something like that? People stop dying. Your boss never goes away. Nobody ever retires. Where do we put everybody? We've already got a huge population problem.

I think what we try to do is to get people accustomed to the fact that the world is changing, and that it's a good idea to look not only for what happened yesterday and what's in the news today, but what the potential is in the future. What is the future going to look like, and what do we really want to do? For example, the question about global climate change. We've got a lot of people who absolutely refuse to accept the notion that there [is] global climate change, even though the science seems to indicate that yes, in fact, something has changed. Look what's happening. We have people who refuse to accept that idea. That is very serious. From everything I've read, we are past the point now where we could have moved in time to stop it. But at least we could slow it down. We could recognize that, whether you won't admit that [it has] anything to do with automobiles running around or whether it's some kind of cyclical thing, is irrelevant. The thing is, we don't want to continue adding carbon to an atmosphere that's already got too much.

It should teach us to be a little bit smarter. I have a friend who's always talking about his grandchildren, but who refuses to accept the climate change. His grandchildren will be facing a pretty dismal world if the scientists are right and he's wrong. But he doesn't take that into his confidence, [he] ignores it because it's inconvenient. It reflects ill on his political views for one thing.

JW: What's been a high point of your life as a writer?

JM: I guess there are a couple. One—I think most writers will tell you this—that's the first sale the first time. I always had wanted to be a writer. I started my first novel when I was about seven or eight years old. It was a Batman novel, and I never got past the title page, I don't think. Then I started the science fiction novel a couple years later. Fortunately, that never went anywhere either, but the title for that one, I'll tell you how good it was going to be—it was called, "The Canals of Mars." I wanted to write science fiction. That's the only thing I ever really thought about seriously writing.

When I was about fourteen, I submitted by first story. I submitted a story to *Fantasy and Science Fiction*. I was either in eighth grade or [my] first year of high school, I forget which. And I got a letter back from [the editor] in which he said he liked the story, but they were full up at the time. So it was like he really couldn't use it but he encouraged me to continue. I got mad because I thought I was getting rejected. I didn't like it, and I just remember crumpling it and tossing the thing away. I didn't write again after that for a long time.

JW: When did you sell your first writing?

JM: When I was in high school I was a columnist for the high school newspaper. That was South Catholic in Philadelphia, and I enjoyed that. I went to La Salle and they ran a short story-contest every year, a freshman short story contest and I won that. I wrote a science fiction story for it—one that they published in the school's literary magazine.

So I was off and running, and I thought well, maybe I do have a future at this stuff. I made a mistake. I read *David Copperfield* and I thought, my God, I'm never going to be able to write at this level. I can't compete with this guy. I did not realize that I didn't have to. I didn't have to compete with Charles Dickens, but I didn't know that. I did not attempt another piece of fiction for, I don't know, somewhere [between] twenty-five to thirty years [later]. Then I went back and tried again.

What eventually happened is I married Maureen McAdams. This is after I spent several years in the navy and I became an English teacher. I ran into Maureen while I was in my teaching years. I mentioned to her a few times about how I would love to be a science fiction writer. At one point, after we'd been married for, oh boy, twenty-three years—something like that, a long time—and it was around 1980, I discovered I couldn't make enough money. I was the English department chairman in a system in New Hampshire. My father died, Maureen's father died, and Maureen was about to have our first child and we just couldn't afford it. I was supporting both our parents, both our mothers and a child coming. The newspaper was going on about how teachers were overpaid and I was making $10,000 a year. So I quit teaching and became a customs inspector. I looked at people's suitcases and I made twice as much money as a customs inspector as I did as the English Department chairman.

I was in Pembina, North Dakota, for a few years and then I worked there and they sent me to the academy in Brunswick, Georgia. I guess I had mentioned again to Maureen what I was missing with my life. And she said, "Well, [why] don't you try it?" So I did.

To keep her happy I wrote a story about a guy who worked at a post office who falls in love with a young woman at the other counter down the way, but he's afraid to make a move because he's afraid of being rejected. I didn't get the connection at the time that I was doing this story of what my life had become. I wrote this story and we sent it to *Asimov's,* and they said, "Thanks, but no thanks." I had a lot who rejected it.

That's it, I had enough. I just don't need the rejection.

Maureen brought it to her friend, by the way, before we sent it out again and I rewrote a little bit. She went down to the local store one day and came back with a copy of *The Twilight Zone Magazine*. This was about 1980 and, uh, she persuaded me to send it to *Twilight Zone*.

We were wrapping up our assignment here at the time. We closed everything out and drove back to North Dakota. I had a postcard waiting for me when I got back to North Dakota, which is now framed and hangs over my desk in my office, saying in effect we can't pay you a lot of money, but you'll get a national audience. At that point, I had sold the story. It was a *Twilight Zone* and I was on my way.

Incidentally, I should tell you a little bit about the story, that there is a little more irony in this than I realized at the time. What the story is about—I mentioned the guy's a post office clerk. What really kicks the story off is a letter comes in that had been mailed by Ralph Waldo Emerson to a friend, I guess, eighty or ninety years before. Of course, the friend's long gone. There's nothing they can do with this ninety-year-old letter. So the clerk opens the letter and looks at it, and I used some lines that Emerson actually had written in his essays. One of the lines being that if you can learn to believe in yourself, you can do almost anything. I think that's what took hold of me. I didn't at the time—I didn't realize the point of that whole business, but that's exactly what happened.

There has been research done that almost all of us tend to be smarter than we realize. What happens to us is that authority figures in our lives spend a lot of time showing us what we do wrong, what we screw up, telling us, "Just stay clear, leave it alone. You'll just mess it up." After a while we start to behave that way as if that's really the truth.

I was a communications specialist when I was in the navy and during that period I attended a cousin's wedding. Afterward, I was looking around the house while they're having a big party, and there was a new FM radio that they had. I was kind of toying with the radio. My father said, "Don't touch it, you'll break it." My father was a good dad, but that's the way we do things.

One of the things that is so good about writing science fiction—and I suppose about writing in general, particularly science fiction—is that you're not just sitting in a room, as I was in the beginning with a typewriter, an electric typewriter, and making this stuff happen. To a degree, you actually live the experience. I feel as if I've actually traveled to Mars and been to various stars. Priscilla Hutchins, who's a major character in seven or eight of my novels—I feel as if Priscilla is an actual person in my life. I love her.

You get a sense that the universe opens up and I can make things happen. It's particularly effective when—I don't do good guys versus bad guys and stuff like that. My interest in science fiction is in discovery. What's out there? What could be out there? What could happen? What does happen to the woman who goes to a doctor and when she's getting ready to have a child the doctor says, "All right. I can arrange things so that your child will not grow old. Your child will hit about twenty-four, twenty-five and stay that way indefinitely, okay? But because of population problems, your child will not be able to reproduce."

What do you want to do, Mom? Which way do you want to have it? It just makes for a fascinating approach to the kind of world that we live in. The world is changing so quickly that it's becoming increasingly hard to keep up with. What really matters? When I sat down to write that story, I had no clue what the mother was going to [do], [or] what the mother's decision was going to be.

I think I created a problem for a close friend of mine. I went to lunch with a close friend in Philadelphia. His wife went along. I told them about the story I was working on, and I asked Art, I said, "What would you do?" She didn't think that living a long life was good. She said, "Listen, I wouldn't want to go through this again for anything." That's what makes science fiction so much fun, really. If you are writing a Western you know who the bad guys are. There's a little shoot-out at the end and that'll take care of them, and that'll be it. But with science fiction you have to deal with stuff like this. The one that I'm working on right now is *Beyond Centauri*. Priscilla Hutchins lives in New York two hundred years from now. She's a starship pilot and they're shutting everything down. A lot of scientists are saying right now, including Stephen Hawking, that we should not be sending out all these signals because we don't know what's out there—that somebody might come down here and have us for dinner.

In Priscilla's time, it's become a political issue. The president wants to shut it down. They've got interstellars, they've got starships, and it's crazy. A lot of people think it's absolutely nuts to go out there and draw all this attention to ourselves. The way the storyline sets up, we detect a signal coming in from a place that's seven thousand light-years away. It's a waterfall. Just a picture of a waterfall. It's a directed signal, and they want to go out and take a look. We go, we've got to. We've got really very fast ships. We're going to go out and take a look, see what it is. You just don't know. You don't know what you're getting into.

So they do launch what everybody is saying is going to be the final mission and they almost get stopped. The orders come in to stop it before the whole takeoff. They go out there and they discover several things, but one of the things that they run into is a world which is mostly an ocean world and there are creatures on it that look like dolphins, except they walk around on the islands.

They go down and take a close look. The lander that they're operating has a malfunction and crashes. Priscilla could've landed on the beach. They could have probably made it to the beach, but there were a lot of these dolphins that were in the water and she would have killed some of them, probably, if she had tried. So she goes down in deeper water. They lose the land. They have no way of getting back to the starship. And the dolphins do a rescue.

The thing that sets the story line in motion is the waterfall—that they saw from the seven-thousand-year-old signal—had to do with black holes. There was a pair of black holes in the neighborhood, and those black holes are now approaching on this world where the dolphins are. The dolphins have very limited technology. And now your problem is, can you go home and persuade the people back home to put together some starships, to build some starships and come back out and do a rescue for people who think that it's deadly dangerous to do stuff like that.

JW: You are one of these people who can write about these issues, who can do it. You know you can do it now. How does this change your life?

JM: I have people who tell me how much my work has meant to them. That means a lot. I've had things like that happen before with some of my former students, who are still in touch with me. I get emails on a pretty regular basis from people who thank me for my books and tell me what it means to them. I hear periodically from scientists telling me that they got started in sciences because of science fiction. Sometimes they specify it's my work. I got an email not too long ago from Dr. Wasserman, first name is Larry. He discovered an asteroid, a new asteroid, and they named it after me. I'm up there with Tina Fey, George Washington, all kinds of people like that. He said that he wanted to thank the science fiction people for making stuff available that drove a passion in him, effectively, to go to the stars.

I hope it doesn't hit the Earth at some point.

JW: Where do you see your writing going now?

JM: I think I'm going to continue much in the same direction I've been. I enjoy dealing with discoveries—especially discoveries, advanced technological advances, whatever, that has an impact on the way we live, things we learn. Are we ever really going to be able to get into space? You know, the radiation out there is pretty severe. We might never get there in any way. I just enjoy this, science fiction that really just turns you loose.

That is the point. It makes me feel that I'm having an impact, that it's not just a matter of earning money and getting my kids through school. There's more to it. That's one way of looking at it. Another way of looking at it is the fact that I get to live in these worlds. You know, I go through this. So does my wife to some extent. I know Priscilla Hutchins. I live with Alex and Chase and solve these historical mysteries that they're always in. What on earth happened to those people who went out in the Polaris to get a look at that star that was going to be destroyed out there because there was a big dead star plunging into it? There are no aliens around anywhere, and they go out there to take a look at it along with two other ships and then the two of them start talking about coming home?

JW: What advice would you give a young or new writer?

JM: Too many young writers, new writers that I see when they went through high school and college, they did a lot of talking about conflict and how important conflict is to fiction. And it is, there's no question about that. But be aware that conflict is not very exciting when it's simply a good guy versus a bad guy. That the real kind of conflict that works, that carries drama, is the sort of conflict that you have with another person whose ideas are just as valid as yours are, and there is no easy answer. Or better yet, [it] is when you have a character who can't make up his own mind as to what is an appropriate course of action.

I've got one book in which there's a chaplain on Moon Base, and the title of the book is *Moonfall*. There's a giant asteroid that has appeared and is heading straight for the Moon. It's going to blow the Moon out of the sky. It wasn't an asteroid from our system, and no one knew it was coming out of the Sun. It had been invisible. There wasn't time to get everybody off the Moon. Now the chaplain is about twenty-seven to twenty-eight years old. He's in love with a young woman back in London. He does not want to get killed, and they have already announced that he's more or less inconsequential. They've got certain people who are there, who they can move out of there in a hurry, but they're not going to get everybody out.

He finds himself stuck because they're telling him he can go and they're going to leave somebody else to die in his place, effectively. He thinks, "What would Jesus do?" He asks would Jesus really jump on the next bus out of town and leave somebody else to die in his place?

On the other hand, he doesn't want to die, and he keeps looking at the telephone. He could call them and tell them, "I'm going to stay. Don't move me out of here," but he's got that young woman back in London. He does not want to die. That's the kind of thing that works for dramatic stuff, not simply the fact that you're hiding behind a barrel shooting it out with some guy down the street. It always seemed to me that there is no stronger conflict than the one where you, yourself, cannot decide on a correct course of action.

What are the big mistakes new writers make? They talk too much. It's true. They explain too much. They underestimate the intelligence of the reader very frequently. They explain things that don't really need to be explained. And the old line is, you know, show, don't tell. They overwrite.

Hemingway says somewhere that you let the nouns and verbs carry the freight and get rid of the other stuff. Anything you have, any word, any verbiage you have in there that does not contribute to the scene that you're painting that the reader's supposed to be living in, brings the reader out of it. You use words that you don't need, and it reminds the reader sitting there they're reading a book.

JW: How do you want to be remembered?

JM: That's—that's a tough one, Joy. I would like to be remembered as a decent science fiction writer, and that I've written something somewhere that is memorable—that people will remember and enjoy. Something that's had an impact on people.

That's the point of being alive. We're all that way. You're the same way, Joy. You would not want to go through your life and not have an impact on the people around you. I mean, why are you doing this? It helps to feel that you're having an impact, making the world a little bit better for what you've done.

Expanded version of the interview that appeared in Issue 29 of Galaxy's Edge, *November 2017.*

■ GREG BEAR

reg Bear is the author of more than thirty books of science fiction and fantasy and has lectured around the world on literary, scientific, and technological subjects. He has served on political and scientific action committees and has advised Microsoft Corporation, Xbox, the US Army, Sandia National Laboratories, Callison Architecture, Inc., SAIC in Maryland, The American Philosophical Society in Philadelphia, and other groups and agencies. Recognition of his fiction works are many and impressive. He has won five Nebula Awards, two Hugo Awards, and has been nominated for five John W. Campbell Awards. Nominated twice for the Arthur C. Clarke Award for Best Novel, Greg has won the Prix Apollo Award and the Endeavor Award. He has also been gifted The Monty Award, The Heinlein Award, and the Galaxy Award (China), for "Most Popular Foreign Writer." He and his son, Erik, collaborated with Neal Stephenson and others on *The Mongoliad*, a serialized novel published in trade edition by 47North in 2012. His daughter Alex works as a copyeditor.

■■■■■■

Joy Ward's original introduction: Greg Bear is the award-winning author of numerous science fiction classics. He is also known as one of the founders of the infamous San Diego Comic-Con. He began his writing career at the ancient age of fifteen and later grew into his own works and collaborations with some of science fiction's greats. Listening to Greg Bear is like taking a stroll through science fiction history.

Joy Ward: How did you get into writing?

Greg Bear: I don't really remember. I was wanting to tell stories ever since I started seeing movies and reading comic books back when I was six and seven years old and could read. I was reading lots of comics and went to see a number of movies, and because I was a military brat, we would see them in strange places like the Philippines. I'd go to an officer's, not to an enlisted men's club in the Philippines, and they were showing *20 Million Miles to Earth* in 1957, I assume, and Ray Harryhausen scared the pants off of me. I loved it, and I went back and started considering writing stories. By the time I was eight, a couple years later, I was writing stories and putting them in little manila folders and all that kind of stuff, and by the time I was eleven or twelve I was trying to submit stories to be published. With the help of my mother and my school teachers in Kodiak, Alaska, at that point I was sending off cartoons. I wanted to do everything: I wanted to illustrate. I wanted to write. I finished my first short story when I was, I think, nine years old.

Telling stories is a way of kind of expressing your emotions but also getting other people to feel emotions that you regard as important and/or cool or interesting. If the readers agree with that, you've got a career. If what you write about interests other readers and makes them feel emotions they like to feel, or perhaps feel is useful to feel, then you're on your way.

JW: What's good about that for you, to be able to make people feel those emotions?

GB: Interesting question. That comes back to why people do art to start with and it's to express the inner self, maybe to dominate the world, which you can't do [in] other ways, maybe. But also to write and create your own world in which you have complete control. The demiurgic kind of response. I think that's true of all artists. We really like to be kind of left alone in a world that we can create, where we can try and figure out the parameters and then fit them over our world like a mask or a glove to see if they have congruence, if they make sense or if they can lead to changes in our world. And there's always been what Wells called the novel of adjustment interest: we want to change society, so we will write this novel with this attitude, and if it changes society, it will have adjusted it. He thought science fiction was a perfect vehicle for adjustment-interest stories or for commenting on society.

It's part of that dialogue. We're born into this world and we talk to people and we listen to them, and we get advice from our teachers, and we pass along that advice when we become teachers. We all like to be interactive with the other humans around us. And we all like to feel that we're valuable and have a part in all of this. So everyone who's out there doing everything- from, you know, harvesting vegetables to doing medical work or whatever, wants to feel that they're having an influence on the world around them. They do. Whether you're famous or not isn't really in it. It's just that you're working, you're contributing, and there you are. So, if you're working, you're a valuable part of the society.

For a writer to work, you're telling stories that people want to listen to. That can be great fun. Especially if they come back to you and say that was a pretty good yarn, to use my father-in-law's kind of perspective on this whole thing. I once told Poul [Anderson], "How did you feel when you finished that book?" and he said, "Oh, well, it was another good yarn." I think there was a little more humility there than might have been on the surface, but you never could tell with Pooul. He was a pretty straight forward man.

I'm happy to hear [positive reinforcement], but it also makes me feel, "Oh my God, I've got to write another one now. Can't just stop here." If you're relying on your greatest hits, and that's all you're doing out there—selling K-tel records, greatest hits of whoever—well that's fine. You can get a retirement bonus that way, but you've got to keep on writing and keep on trying to see if you still got it. Keep the challenge up between you and the readers.

I was fifteen years old. I was doing all sorts of stuff and I was fond, fond of magazines called *Magazine of Horror, Startling Mystery Stories* and *Famous Science Fiction*. All were edited by Robert A. W. Lowndes and published by the Health Knowledge Publishing Company, which also did sex manuals and all sorts of stuff. But he was an old-line science fiction writer, and he was publishing his magazines. He published Stephen King's first short story, and I was also writing letters to Forrest J. Ackerman, *Famous Monsters [of Filmland]*, and trying to sell him a story and trying to enlist him to be my agent. I was fifteen years old. I designed a cover because I thought the magazine of horror had blood-curdling, blood-dripping letters, and I thought that was a little uncool. So I tried to design a cover. Robert Lowndes wrote back and said, "Well, this is very nice, and thank you, but we like to sell our magazines and these covers sell our magazines." So then the next thing I sent him was a short story. He bought it.

I was a junior in high school, fifteen years old, and a year later they published it. I got all of ten dollars for it. Also, at that point, I was hanging out with a lot of really interesting guys at Crawford High School in San Diego, and people like Scott Shaw and David Clark and John Pound and other people we would meet later on. We would hang out with science fiction fans that came into the area like Ken Krueger and Shel Dorf, and they knew a lot of comic book artists. So while I was writing these stories and trying to sell them at the same time, our enthusiasms were guiding us to help found Comic-Con in San Diego.

That was one of the most interesting things at that point, which I didn't realize at the time. I thought, "Oh, Comic-Con. Great. Okay. Good fun." I would go off and do other stuff, and then Comic-Con would continue to grow and grow and grow and it's like, "Oh my God." Come back and there's a hundred thousand people there. The thing was, my whole point in being alive was to meet people whose work I loved, to express my love for their work, and to try and write something that they might want to read.

In many cases that actually happened later on. But also, we were being supported as youngsters by a lot of cool people like Ray Bradbury and Jack Kirby and Forrest J. Ackerman. The old-line fans would run into them at conventions and talk with them and they seemed to see something was going on here with these young San Diego fans.

Also, they were just very enthusiastic to talk about what they loved, and so if you loved something you were doing, that was very important. That became very obvious to me, and the example of Ray Bradbury, totally enthusiastic about everything and very supportive—that was really nice.

I began to realize that I probably wasn't going to be able to work a day-to-day job with my attitudes toward being told to do stuff and having to do stuff and everything. And so I just kept writing and writing and hoping that something would peel out and become a career. By the time I was twenty-seven, twenty-eight it was happening.

JW: Well, you're telling me that you're a fifteen-year-old boy and you've got this acceptance letter. What goes through your mind?

GB: No one is ever going to be able to teach me about English literature again. Because I know the stuff. I've sold a story. I got ten dollars for my story. That's what Edgar Allan Poe got for his first story, by God. It was great fun. But also to take my friends with me to a local magazine shop to buy the issue when it came on the stands—that was very cool.

It was great. 'Cause we were all high school kids and we're all showing up at this magazine shop and I'll pay, what? Fifty cents or whatever for this magazine and put the quarters out on the counter and say, "My story's in here." You know?

I was just on the foothills. Within two or three years I'd written the starters for many novels and the starters for many stories. I didn't sell another story until about 1970. To David Gerrold of all people: *Alternatives.* I published a story which I still reprint. It's still a pretty good story. David bought that. I started selling to *Fantasy and Science Fiction.* I started selling artwork too. I had a cover on *Fantasy and Science Fiction* that I thought was pretty good.

I already helped found Comic-Con so there couldn't be anything bigger than that; although, Comic-Con in '83 was doing pretty well. What I knew as I was going into this was, a) I liked to work with some of the people as long as they're smarter than me, and b) I like to work with people who can do interesting and new things. So in '83 I was also starting to work with Jerry Pournelle, who I first met back in the '70s. We had the first book publication we had the awards going on. I was writing novels and selling them. First fantasy novels started coming out. It's always a long slog when you're dealing with professional publishing, trying to convince people that you're the greatest writer alive is not easy to do. Fellow writers don't believe you either. They say, "Nah, you're not."

So hanging with Benford and Brand and watching their careers take off, and reading their books and loving them, and then hanging out with Ray Bradbury, who was still publishing quite regularly and was a great guy—oh, and all these writers we met at conventions: Poul Anderson, who made a huge impression on my career and as a gentleman on my life and watching his interactions with Karen while they were sort of collaborating on things—that was all very informative. So I put it all in my mind, putting together what I could call the history of science fiction, from many different perspectives because that is what I do. I sense what's going on. I sense the culture around it, and then I can write it into a story. That's what happens when you write a science fiction story. You take the culture of the science and the scientists and you make them characters in your story.

If you get the dialogue right, the story works. You've got to get the story and the dialogue right. That's one of the real challenges of science fiction. But also scientists like to read this stuff, for a couple of different reasons. One, they like to be amused. Two, they sometimes like to be astonished. And three, they sometimes like to think, "Oh my gosh. I didn't think of that." That's the rarer one, is when you can make a really good scientist do that.

JW: There's a suggestion that military science fiction has a part to play in people growing up.

GB: Fiction in general has a part to play because it allows you to model certain circumstances you may not want to have to live through. It puts your circumstances you are living through in perspective, so war novels that came out of World War II help us adjust to what happened in World War II.

Catch-22 is a cathartic novel, simply because it's so absurd, and yet it gets so much about the military correct. Any soldier, any airman reading this stuff is going to go, "Ah, I know that guy." You know? You get Joe Haldeman producing a version of the Vietnam War that is totally compelling for veterans coming back reading this stuff. Or what Heinlein was doing was kind of helping create a conservative approach to what will become space warfare, which was interesting, controversial.

Heinlein loved to stir up argument and controversy. He really enjoyed that. I don't think he believed half the stuff he put into the book. He watched people argue about it and that was great fun for him.

JW: What do you want to do?

GB: Most of what I want, what I've laid out to write, I've already kind of written. I want to write a big, thick fantasy novel. Everyone wants to do the George R.R. Martin thing without being George Martin. I've written nearly every aspect of imaginative literature. I suppose at some point I would write a historical novel, but I'm not sure what about. Mostly, I just want to slip gently into retirement where I can write the books I want to write, which is kind of what I've been doing all along. There's not much difference, but that's what I would like to do.

JW: How do you want to be remembered?

GB: That's how I want to be remembered, as a science fiction writer—a person who liked to write in the fields of imaginative literature and appreciated those who had gone before him.

Some good stories. Some scary stories. Some salutary stories and stories that inspire, frighten and expand your mind. That's fine by me. And if I come up with some crackpot theories of physics that are still around two hundred years from now, I would go for that, too. 'Cause I shook hands with Richard Feynman.

JW: What would you recommend for people who want to be writers, especially in military science fiction?

GB: I'm going to go outside that because if you want to write military science fiction that's one particular thing, but the advice applies and it's the advice that Ray Bradbury gave me when we were kids. When I was a kid and he was still a kid too, actually. He was a forty-seven-year-old kid: "Write what you love." I added to that: "Write about what scares you, and if what scares you is what you love, you may have a great novel, or a great story."

That's kind of the advice I would pass along. Understand your own emotions, know where they come from, and how they fit into other characters. Don't hold your characters down because you still want to express yourself only and realize you're expressing everybody when you write a novel. You know, here comes everybody. All showing up at once.

You have the duty to express the nature of the culture you're writing in, and to tell the stories of the people who lived around you. Science fiction quite often avoids that because we're writing about the stories that will live around us, about the people who will live around us. But even so, science fiction tells about the dreams and fears of the society around you. That is what's going to be its long-living impact—not predicting, but writing about what people were thinking at the time when things were changing so drastically and how they felt about it.

You read *1984* today and it's still scary as hell. But remember that Orwell wanted to write the title of the novel as 1948, 'cause he was actually writing about England in a very interesting sense. If you read *Brave New World*, c Olaf Stapledon, you're getting a lesson in the kind of books that Dante might have been writing if he had been alive in the twentieth century instead of the fourteenth century. And Dante was one of our earliest writers and he was speculating on the nature of the universe.

First published in Issue 31 of Galaxy's Edge, *March 2018.*

■ DAVID GERROLD

David Gerrold has been sitting alone in a room and talking to himself for more than fifty years. If he hears anything good, he types it up. When he has enough words, he sends it to an editor. Occasionally some editor somewhere is so desperate for something to publish, he sends David Gerrold a check. The result is a forest-killing avalanche of short stories, novelettes, novels, articles, columns, non-fiction books, television scripts, film scripts, stage plays, comic books, and mangas. His TV work, includes episodes of *Star Trek*, *Land of the Lost*, *The Twilight Zone*, *Babylon 5*, and *Sliders*. (He created tribbles for *Star Trek* and Sleestaks for *Land of the Lost*.) In 1994, Gerrold shared the adventure of how he adopted his son in *The Martian Child*, a semiautobiographical tale of a science fiction writer who discovers his adopted child might be a Martian. *The Martian Child* won the science fiction triple crown: the Hugo, the Nebula, and the Locus Poll. It was the basis for the 2007 film *Martian Child* starring John Cusack and Amanda Peet. (The book is better.)

■■■■■■

Joy Ward's original introduction: David Gerrold, the 2015 World-con Guest of Honor, has had a long and fascinating career. Trekkers know him from his years as a writer on the original **Star Trek** *tele-*

vision series. The rest of us know him from his hard science fiction writing or the magical realism of his **The Martian Child**. *Always outspoken, never boring, Gerrold is a writer consistently ready to share his thoughts and feelings.*

Joy Ward: How did you get started writing?

David Gerrold: It was almost accidental. I wanted to act and direct and produce, and it was very clear to me from the beginning that you have to know story structure, you have to know character[s], especially if you're going to direct. You have to know how to tell a story. And the writing was easy. It was fun, and one day they were paying me for it. So I said, all right, if they're going to pay me for it, I'll just keep doing it.

Everybody else tells these stories of, "Oh God, I sent story after story, rejection slip after rejection slip." I didn't have that. I sent in a story, they said here's some money, kid, write the script. So I'm absolutely the wrong person to talk to about determination and discipline and stick-to-itiveness and stubbornness and all that commitment stuff because I've been very lucky to have it very easy.

JW: You've collaborated with a number of others. What do you get from collaboration?

DG: There are scenes you don't want to write. You get to be lazy. I don't want to write this one. I never said it this way. And there was stuff Larry [Niven] didn't want to write or couldn't write. Larry is brilliant on a lot of stuff, but at that time neither comedy nor characterization were his strongest suits. I never thought I was good at punch lines, but a lot of people think my work is funny so I must be good at punch lines.

What happens is, I look at a line of dialogue and I say what's the obvious thing that someone is going to say next, and I don't say that. What's the opposite of the obvious? What's the punch line here? I don't think in terms of the punch line. What's the most interesting thing to say next?

I have certain strengths, and the reason they are strengths is because I know they're weaknesses. I always thought I was terrible with characterization, so I worked a lot on characterization. I thought I was terrible with dialogue, so I worked hard at it. I always thought I was pretty good with plot and structure, so I don't work too hard at it anymore. That's why my plots and structures are sloppy. So I have to work on that. I was taught to find your weakest aspect of your strength and concentrate on that to make it get stronger. Develop that writing muscle, and that has always been my goal. What do I *not* know how to do? Okay, that's my next challenge.

Here's a half century later and I look at people writing reviews of my work and they say, "David is versatile." That's interesting because there's a thing that the Beatles always said. They never wanted to do the same song twice. I have that same feeling. I never want to write the same story twice. So every story I do is different from the others. This is kind of self-defeating. I don't have a unique voice like Jack Vance did. I love Jack Vance. I don't have a unique voice like Harlan Ellison. Everything has to be a different voice. It's an acting trick really because I'm playing a different character each time I sit down to type. Because I'm playing a different character each time I sit down to type I get different voices.

I'll give you an example. Robert A. Heinlein, who I admired a lot, had a very distinct writing voice. So he writes *Glory Road*, which is a fantasy and reads like *Starship Troopers*, which is a military book, and it reads like *Farmer in the Sky*, which is a young adult book. They all have the same voice, so you tend to feel it's all the same character. But if somebody is versatile in voices—for instance take Theodore Sturgeon. He did a story "Mr. Costello Hero" which I just reread because I just wrote a sequel to it. He wrote the story from the point of view of a not-very-intelligent person. He's not an imbecile; he's an idiot savant. He knows numbers, but he doesn't know people. Sturgeon conveys that very well, and you read that whole story through the character's eyes. In the sequel I did, I also looked at Mr. Costello, but through another character's eyes. That person has a whole different attitude about life. It's a very frontier, Western kind of attitude. The reason you want to do that is you want your reader to get into the soul, the heart of the narrator, the protagonist, and feel that viewpoint. When you write first person you're becoming the character, and you're saying this is how I experienced it, this is how I perceived it. So the Jumping Off the Planet trilogy—I wrote that from the point of view

136

of a very angry thirteen-year-old in a very dysfunctional family. I succeeded so well that I had reviewers saying, "Obviously David comes from a dysfunctional family. He's a middle child, his parents were divorced, it was an ugly divorce and that's why he hates lawyers." All five of those are wrong.

My family was so white bread you could have put mayonnaise on us. My parents never divorced. We were not dysfunctional. I think the biggest dysfunction we had was whether I could buy a motorcycle, and I did anyway.

JW: You've had quite a journey in the human potential movement. How has that played out in your writing?

DG: I was living with a wonderful partner, a man named Dennis, and Ted Sturgeon invited him to do an EST [Erhard Seminars Training] and didn't invite me. So Dennis signed up for EST. Then Ted and Jane [Sturgeon] kind of monopolized Dennis's time after that. Dennis came out to me and said, "I would like you to do the training." "All right, fine." Part of my reasoning was I was going to be damned if I was going to let anyone be more enlightened than me.

Dennis and I stayed with EST for two, maybe three years. We went through every possible program they offered. We did the communication workshop.

We did the seminar leadership program, which is I think the entire reason for doing EST would be to do that course because it is about enrollment. Now most people hear enrollment as please sign up for something and give me your money. It's not. Enrollment, as I see it, is inviting people—you want to go to the movies, you want to get married, you want to be my playmate, you want to hang out, you want to go to dinner—that's all enrollment. You want to share my space? Learning how to be an enrolling person is probably the greatest human condition of all. It is learning how to be open and vulnerable and generous and giving so that people want to be around you.

How does it affect my writing? This goes back to EST. Bullshit is everything you explain to allow yourself to evade responsibility, so once I started taking out explanations and started focusing on experiential, focusing on what is the person experiencing, the writing shifted dramatically. Now I had already been sort of moving in that direction, but now I had a clear context of "Don't explain, just show." Don't explain, just experience it. Give the reader the experience. Evoke the emotions. What does it smell like, taste like, feel like, look like, sound like? What is the reader experiencing? What is the character experiencing viscerally, stomach, heart, hands? What's the experience? Once I was writing from the experience and not explaining, then there's room to do a lot of storytelling without bogging down. The story moves a lot faster. There's more impact.

What happens is that it's easier to get inside the character's head. My characters get didactic. There are long, long sections of dialogue I don't apologize for. I'm interested in this conversation. I want to hear what these people say. Most of my stories are conversations, because a really great conversation is a connection between two people.

As a writer you're having a conversation with the reader. He just doesn't get to answer back. He just gets one option—whether or not he's going to turn the page. So my job is to make sure that it's so interesting the reader wants to find out what's going to happen next.

JW: What is your favorite high point of your career?

DG: My favorite high point isn't a career thing, as much as it's a personal [one]. Adopting Sean and the day I met him. There was the day he was placed in my home. There was the day the adoption was finalized. They asked me, I had this wonderful caseworker, and she said are you planning to write a book about adoptions? I said, "No." One day after he moved in I just started writing a story about how much I loved my kid. It was rejected by the first six editors. It was editors who knew me too well. So I gave it to an editor who didn't know me very well at all, Kristine Kathryn Rusch. She bought it for *Fantasy & Science Fiction*. We started getting the weirdest, most amazing fan mail on it and it brought home a Hugo and a Nebula and a Locus award and some other stuff, and then we got a movie offer and I expanded it into a novel. So I think *The Martian Child* would have to be the career high point.

JW: What made you decide to adopt a child?

DG: It seemed like a good decision at the time. They asked, "Why do you want to adopt a little boy?" and I couldn't answer the question. I said, I don't know why. I just want to. I think even after all these years I'm not sure I can answer it completely. I think there's a biological, instinctual urge—your mommy clock goes off. Rrrring! Time to be a mommy!

We've had adoptions in my family starting with my grandmother who took in foster kids, and my aunts and uncles [who] adopted kids. We have more adopted kids in our extended family than handmade ones.

I finally recognized that the only way to get love is to create love, and I get to create something that couldn't be created any other way. So I think it was just that there's a thing about being complete, about having a family, and not being alone, but that wasn't the goal. The goal was I want a family of my own. Everybody else gets to show off pictures of their kids so I want to show off—there he is right there. I want a picture of my own kid to show off. Course, I got a late start. Everyone else was showing off their grandkids.

JW: Any advice for young writers?

DG: Quit. Quit. If you can be discouraged, quit now and save yourself all that time and anguish and energy and beating your head against the brick wall and the frustration and the anguish. Now if that sentence makes you pissed off, then maybe you have enough determination and stubbornness and commitment to make it, but most of the writers I know who have succeeded have done so because they are either too stubborn or too stupid to quit. I have seen writers of enormous talent give up because there's no push and I have seen writers of—I hate to phrase it any way that is negative—let me say, writers of lesser ability or writers whose work does not interest me, manage to have very successful careers because they don't quit.

You can learn almost all the skills of writing. You can take acting classes, read all the good books by Ray Bradbury and *Elements of Style* and John Gardner and Rita Mae Brown and Nora Ephron, and read all the great books about writing. All these great, great books on writing give you some insight, but it's really experiential. What can you experience? Then just be too damn stubborn to quit. I think the best advice I could give any new writer would be always look at what you don't know how to do and do that next.

JW: How do you want to be remembered?

DG: Well, anything other than the Rodney Dangerfield of science fiction. And I loved Rodney Dangerfield! But every so often someone comes out with this *Encyclopedia of Science Fiction* and so, of course, I look myself up. It's like, wait a minute, half a paragraph? A footnote?

Yeah, if somebody said, "Here is your Grand Master trophy," that would be very nice, but that is not the goal. I would love to have it, but the real goal is the keyboard. What comes out of the keyboard next? What am I going to write next? What's the next story? What's the next thing I can accomplish?

There's a wonderful movie, *Personal Best*. It's not about winning. It's about what is your personal best. What are you capable of doing? My personal best is I once wrote ten thousand, three hundred words in a single day. I averaged six thousand words a day for a week. That's a personal best. And it was good stuff. A personal best is I've never done this kind of story before. A personal best is I've gone somewhere I know where I've succeeded. I know when I've pushed the limits.

Going back to your question, how would I like to be remembered? I would like people to remember me saying, "You pick up a story by David Gerrold, you're going to have a good time with it." I think that would be a fine epitaph or eulogy. "Read this. You'll have fun." That would be good.

I am still a student. I know some people consider me a master. But a master is still a student. That's why he's a master. He's still a student of the craft. Yeah, I know a lot about writing, and I know that I know a lot more about it than a lot of people. But I know how much I still don't know and still want to learn.

What is important for me is to not be arrogant. It's very hard to not be arrogant when you're a writer because the mere act of writing is arrogant. I have something to say. I have something to say that is so important that it justifies chopping down a tree. That is arrogant. I have something to say that is so important that you should pay for the privilege of listening to it. That is arrogant. One of the things I have constantly been called out on in all of the courses I have done is

"David, you are very arrogant." No I'm not arrogant or aloof. I'm trying to figure shit out. But it shows up as arrogant, so I think being a student is about staying open and vulnerable because the minute you say "I know all this crap," the minute you say "I know how to do this," you start the process of dying.

There was a writer—I won't mention her by name—she attended a lot of conventions, went to all the panels, she took notes, practiced, and her first book was ambitious and sold well. Her second book was better because she was learning. Her third book was a little better, but somebody asked her to be on the panel. She became pretentious and she stopped listening. "Well. I'm an expert now and here's what I know about writing." I don't even know if she got to a fourth book. Her writing went downhill very, very fast because now she believed she knew it all. She's long forgotten, which is why I haven't mentioned her name. Long, long forgotten because she stopped challenging herself. I figure if I ever stop challenging myself, I will have peaked. There's always another rung on the ladder.

There's another part to it which comes back to Ted Sturgeon. As much as I loved and admired Ted, one of the things I would never want to be is Ted. I don't want to be Harlan. I don't want to be Heinlein. I want to find out who I am sometime before the next half-century is over and be comfortable being me. Right now it's still a learning process, as I've had the longest case of prolonged adolescence in history. I'm thirteen with a half century of experience. The Golden Age of Science Fiction is thirteen and that's exactly who I want to be. I don't want to lose my sense of wonder.

If you lose your sense of wonder you're dead. Your sense of wonder makes it worth getting out of bed in the morning. What am I going to discover today? What's interesting today? Sometimes it's what bad thing happened today, but even what bad thing happened is part of the learning experience. Life is not all about one great wonderful adventure after another, because an adventure means there's something at risk. So sometimes life is about being at risk. Sometimes life is the avalanche headed your way, and it's all bad news. So sometimes you have to say—and I have said this more than once, I've been through worse—I can handle this. So far, the universe has not thrown anything at me that I haven't been able to handle one way or another. So I guess I'll get out of bed tomorrow morning, too.

We have fallen into a terrible trap of judging our worth or our success by how much money we have, and I don't do that, which means money around here comes and goes in the strangest ways. My energy goes into the keyboard. The four or five years I was working with the training company I took a sabbatical from my writing. This past year I've turned out a lot of work because I'm on a writing binge. I will go away from writing for a while and learn something. I'll go drive cross-country. I spent a month touring around, staying off interstates, doing the back roads. When I get on the back road I end up with a story. So sometimes not writing is part of the job.

I tell people 90 percent of what I do is research and the other 10 percent is plotting revenge, because most writing is about revenge of some kind. Sometimes the research means that you stop, you walk away from the keyboard, and go and live a life. Because how can you write about life if you haven't lived one? So go fall in love. Go adopt a kid. Go climb a mountain. Go do something that requires you to stretch yourself.

I think when I'm not writing I'm stretching. Okay, where's the stretch here? What am I going to learn? That's why I spent so much time with doing the trainings, and I loved being a trainer. I heard so many great stories from people sharing, but I also got to make a difference for them by being a good coach. So how do I get to be a better coach? By being a better coach how do I get to be a better human being? How do I get to be a better dad for my son? How do I get to be the person I want to be? And the person I want to be is insightful, introspective, thoughtful, generous, open, vulnerable, giving, powerful, loving. That's the person I want to be.

First published in Issue 15 of Galaxy's Edge, *July 2015.*

KIJ JOHNSON

Since her first sale in 1987, Kij Johnson has published five books, a short-story collection, and dozens of short stories, winning speculative fiction's Triple Crown—the Hugo, Nebula, and World Fantasy Awards—as well as the Sturgeon and Crawford Awards and the French Grand Prix de l'Imaginaire. Her books include a Star Trek: The Next Generation novel, *Dragon's Honor* (with Greg Cox), two novels set in Heian-era Japan, *The Fox Woman* and *Fudoki*; a novella set in H. P. Lovecraft's Dreamlands, called *The Dream-Quest of Vellitt Boe;* and a sequel to Kenneth Grahame's *The Wind in the Willows*, called *The River Bank*. Award-winning short fiction has included the short stories, "26 Monkeys, Also the Abyss," "Spar," "Ponies," and the novella, "The Man Who Bridged the Mist." In the past, she worked as managing editor at Tor Books; collections and special-editions editor for Dark Horse Comics; and editor, continuity manager, and creative director for Wizards of the Coast. She received a master of fine arts at North Carolina State University and teaches creative writing and fantasy literature at the University of Kansas.

■■■■■■

Joy Ward's original introduction: Kij Johnson is a Hugo winner, and a three-time Nebula winner (in consecutive years, yet!) and is acknowledged as one of the field's leading short-fiction writers.

■■

Joy Ward: How did you get into writing?

Kij Johnson: It took me seven years to write my first book. It took fourteen months to write the second, and it took twelve years to write the third and then I just ash-canned it. The book is broken, and I can't figure out how to fix it. I realized I could spend the next ten years endlessly tweaking something that is fundamentally flawed and not do any new work, or I could put it aside and write three new works in a twelve-month period, which is basically what happened. So it was a good decision, but it was also one of the more painful decisions. And it wasn't until I made that decision—I made the decision to step away from the giant book—that I started to say, yes, I am a writer. So it took that. The awards didn't do it. Nothing else did it. It was the moment that I said that. Sometimes you just throw it away; that made me realize that this is what a writer does.

I think it is recognizing that I have many stories to tell and that if I want to tell them in my lifetime I'm going to have to tell them. You start to say, "If I have twenty more writing years and I just spent twelve years on a broken novel, do I really want to spend another ten years of those last twenty years working on the same goddamn novel?" and the answer is "No! No, I don't!" I want to write new things that make me excited *now* instead of things that made me excited at forty.

When I walked away from it, I realized I don't want to write something for an audience. I want to write it for love. So I wrote a book in a two-month period, which is coming out next year from Small Bear. I wrote that for my friend Elizabeth. It was something she and I both loved and it was pure joy to pour it on the page. I never had that experience with fiction before, but it was like this is what everybody is always talking about! I get it now. I had never gotten it before. I never had flow. I would talk about it when I taught. You don't need it. "Flow is for sissies," is what I would say. People who write, they are getting it done, even if there is no flow. I was saying that partially because I had never had the experience of flow.

So the first one just poured out of me and the second one poured out of me and the third one was slower because I was starting to write for an audience again. I noticed more tension as I was thinking, oh, yeah, it's going to be read by a lot of people and I'm not writing it for an individual as sort of a gift. Now I'm writing it for an audience. It was slower and was harder than *Vellitt Boe*. Now the next project is slower still because I told my workshop about it. So I have twelve people who think they know what the story is going to be. I don't know if it's going to be that or not.

The blinding insight I had about *Kylen*, which changed everything [*Kylen* is the giant novel], was what do you love in the stuff you read, the media you take in? What is it you cannot get enough of? I wrote a list and none of those things were in the book I had just spent ten years writing. So I said, "Fuck that!" I am going to write a book that has all the things I want. I want buddies. I want humor. I want linguistic playfulness. I want the stakes to be high for the characters but not necessarily high for, not real-time high but funny stakes where everybody gets all in a kerfuffle about something ridiculous because all the great comedies—that is what they are about. I want to write a comedy because the stories I like to read the most were romantic comedies. The movies I liked the most are generally just witty, crisp dialogue. I had strayed from all of that. At that moment I said, I'm just going to write for fun. Writing for fun is the best thing!

It was so cool! I was like bubbles all the time. The honeymoon period of me writing just for joy is kind of over, so now it's kind of like I'm back to the hard work of writing stories requiring a lot of research...it was just a different level of research and a different level of engagement with that research. It was so different to only do the parts that were fun and find out you could write an entire book and have it be a really good book, just by writing only the parts that are fun. So I am remembering that. I am trying to tattoo that on my forebrain so that as I move into books that are more driven by other motives: I can remember just only write the fun parts and you'll probably be right.

While I was working on *Kylen* I really had my eyes opened because it started out as—it started out in London and due to a series of machinations which are too complicated to go into, essentially 250 Londoners from 1778 find themselves teleported into Tashkent, which is now Uzbekistan. Originally when I first started to talk about this story it was going to be this big adventure, like good-looking people in exotic clothes doing exciting things, is how I saw it. But the more I looked at it, the more I realized I couldn't do that. Central Asia has its own history and it's a very complicated history. The more I read about it the more I realized I couldn't just write about white people having fun in a brown-people land. Part of why I put the book aside in the end is, I realized I can't do it justice. It really is too big. I started thinking much more about race. I started thinking much more about gender, and not just as it applied to me. So when I walked away from *Kylen* I had this newly sort of opened-up sense of experience, and I found I couldn't go back into the box.

I was trained as a historian first, and I'm a very impeccable world builder, but that's because I actually can't do anything but history and I have to be really careful about my history. Somebody noticed something wrong with one of my books; it was like a vocabulary thing. I used one anachronistic Japanese word and it was like, oh, I'll never forgive myself for that! For heaven's sake, one person noticed it. Probably forty people have noticed it in the twenty-some-year history of that book. So it's like, "You can stand down, Kij. It's okay."

In the background [there] was always this sense that people who like me critically, I have to satisfy them because I don't ever want anyone to ever read something I said and say, "She used to be a very good writer." Nobody ever wants that moment. So I was trying really hard not to write to them critically, but I was also trying to write something that was for an audience and I couldn't do it.

When I won the Nebula, I won the Nebula for a story that I didn't expect. I was so excited, so gobsmacked that I hadn't really prepared anything. There are two strategies, it turns out, for winning awards. One is you have your notes. The other is you didn't expect to win it so you didn't prepare for it. I guess the third strategy is you've gotten so many of them you can just do it off the cuff. I had nothing, so I just got up and gibbered helplessly for like two minutes. That was a huge moment for me because that was a story that I wrote from a position of absolute authenticity, without thinking in terms of how it was going to be received. Again, I wrote it for someone who was reading it. That was the first time that I said, don't worry about what people are going to think. Just write this story and if they don't like it or they don't read it or it gets totally ignored, you can deal with that later. Just get it done and then move on. That's your best strategy.

I remember the very first award I won, which was the Sturgeon. I had been lured under false pretenses to the University of Kansas. I was just sitting in the writing workshop, and the Campbell Conference ends that workshop. So we finished the workshop and I was going to stay for the Campbell Conference and leave early. I was going to leave on Saturday morning and they said don't leave. Jim Gunn invited me to his office and sat me down. He said, "We weren't going to tell you until the award." I was sitting in James Gunn's office, the first grown-up I'd ever met, really, and I didn't realize you could feel faint when you're seated. But it turns out, yes, you can be light-headed just sitting without doing anything. So I ended up just rolling forward and Jim said, "Are you okay?" "Yes, I'm fine." But it was dizzying, that very, very first award.

It was a real validation. It really was. We all use that language—validation—because the real sensation under it is the classic Sally Fields. Oh my God, they like me! They liked it!

For a lot of writers what drives them, and one of the things that drives me, is that this is a way to control people's understanding of me, but also a way to put parts of myself out there. So I can be both completely sincere and authentic and real and show people fundamental parts of my soul and my heart, but I'm doing it in ways they aren't going to see the other parts.

I'm perfectly happy with that. We have a duty as a human being to be as much ourselves as we can be but also to be healthy about it. So fiction is one way I'm both able to communicate with people but also control the interaction. I think there is an awful lot of false intimacy in the world. Fiction is a false intimacy, but it is a false intimacy based on a very, very careful attempt at honesty. It's the same thing that drives you sometimes to write a letter to say something hard to someone instead of face-to-face. Not because you're trying to distance yourself but because you want to be accurate and if you can't be accurate in real time then writing the letter is the right way to be accurate. Precision. So to my mind that's exactly how I feel. I try to be very honest but there's a lot of stuff that people don't need about me. Stuff that would be unhealthy for me to share, so I don't.

I started out teaching writing workshops, professional workshops, dealing with really motivated adults who were very interested in being better writers. So I started out being a very tactical instructor. I still am. I'm mostly a structuralist. That's why I write so much experimental fiction. I loved it. It played to my passion for standing in front of people and talking and having them listen, which is always fun. Showing off when I was in third grade—that's what they called it. I also found that it's something exciting when I say something that changes something fundamental. Teaching and changing a writer, showing her something she's never seen before, so she picks up the pen in the middle of class and starts scribbling and she doesn't look up for the rest of the hour. That's an exhilarating moment! That is the exact same moment as when I write a story and I know somebody is walking down the street, bumping into things because she is reading my story on Kindle. It is the exact same thing. I am changing those people and changing how they think by the things I do or things I say.

I have an uncomfortable relationship with that. Of course it's showing off. When I was a little tiny girl growing up in a very small town I was smart. My brother and I were both really smart. We both read encyclopedias, and we were both pains in the ass in class. We were both the third graders who raise their hands and say, "Actually…" So it was always gratifying to be in situations where people actually did want to hear what I had to say instead of teachers being like, "We need to hear from somebody beside Kij in this class," or "Kij, put your hand down," or even "Kij, that's not a real word," depending on the teacher.

One of the most important things I ever say to my students is, everything else I teach them is just tactics, but the thing that I am always proudest of bringing up is: figure out why you're writing. Really why you're writing. Not, "Oh I have things worth saying," or "Oh, I want to make a living," or whatever it is. But really if you go all the way down deeper and deeper and deeper—like spend two years in therapy with a therapist every single Tuesday. So why do you write? Usually the answer is somewhere in early childhood. So it's a little kid response. I'm not ascribing any value judgment to that. Because mine, when you get right down to it, is parents were sort of emotionally absent, and when I wrote I didn't get praised for my writing very much but I didn't get praised for anything else. So my writing ultimately was a way of saying I'm not my mother and a look-at-me to my parents. I also did a lot of art for the same reasons. That's my reason. We all have one, ultimately, underneath it all.

Whatever we say in interviews usually is the cover-up. It's the pat response we use to cover up the sincere response. I do it because the only time anybody took me seriously as a five-foot, ten-inch Amazon blonde was when I wrote and they didn't know what I looked like. Because they stopped staring at my chest [for however] long enough it took to read my story. So there are so many responses and so many of them sound venal or petty or small or something like that. Those responses are not any of those things. Those responses are the heart, that when we understand it, it gives us the spines that we build adulthood on. That's what I always think of, so to me knowing that is the most important part of your writing. If you know your reason for writing is because you're competing with your dad, it's like, as soon as you know that, now you can get away from writing your dad's story or the stories that are going to school your dad about you and now you're going to be able to tell the stories you want to tell. If you are doing it because you are insecure and you want people to look at you, that you're smart or clever or cute or whatever it is, as soon as you know that, you are in control. Until you know it you aren't.

So I'm always telling [this to] undergrads, but especially adults, because we get those super complicated defense mechanisms that allow us to never, ever look at ourselves. That's fundamental. That's my answer really. It's fundamental that we understand who we are and our smallest, pettiest, most selfish or narcissistic or greedy, envious little pieces. We can either counter or use to our advantage and make them work.

JW: How do you want to be remembered?

KJ: I would like to be seen as one of the bridges between mainstream literary and fantasy, speculative fiction. I think there are a handful of us and we're coming all at it. I'm over here and David Mitchell is over here and he's coming in. Sherman Alexie is over here and he's coming in and all these people are coming in. We're all sort of staking out a place where high literary, experimental fictions, are engaging in intelligent ways with science fiction, not just using it like a punch line. You can write something that is both high literary and true science fiction or true fantasy or true slipstream.

I'm coming at it differently from most of the others because I do these experimental works, but we are all pointing at the same thing. What I would love to see, but it probably won't happen, is that sixty years from now there will be an understanding that modernist fiction and post-modernist fiction [are the same]. That they have been for quite a while now as we all fold back into the notion that everything is literature. That's a new invention, being a subcategory. There's been a lot of writing about why science fiction and fantasy got split out. What does it mean and what disadvantages were attached to that? Marketing was an advantage but there were a lot of disadvantages including the escalating marginalization of genre literature and escalating contempt for it. But I do feel like sixty years from now there won't be that. Part of what I like to do is I like to feel that I'm part of that movement toward bringing it all back together.

I will have changed things. But I will have changed things on a different level, a bigger level. I didn't have children. I had no interest in children. I also didn't really believe that writing lasts forever. There are so many works that, as an Anglo-Saxonist, there are so many works that all that exists is one fragment. Which means how many works don't exist anymore but did? Some poet [years ago] wrote a 4,000-word poem about something that mattered like crazy to him or her and it's gone. All those women on the shelves who wrote a book in 1960 and they're gone. We don't even know their names anymore. So I never felt like you get immortal by being a great writer. There are a lot of the bestselling writers of the nineteenth century that are not read anymore. Ideally, will I be remembered as a writer sixty years from now? That would be awesome! It seems unlikely, but that's awesome! But if I am part of the movement to bring science fiction and mainstream back together that's good too.

I'm part of a larger thing. Science fiction is a literature of the species as soon as we start thinking species-wide, and right now I'm thinking about the species. I care about this literature and people are always going to care about this literature, and being part of this literature and knowing that I may be part of the reconciliation of this literature makes me feel great.

First published in Issue 26 of Galaxy's Edge, *May 2017.*

■ MIKE RESNICK

Mike Resnick is, according to *Locus*, the all-time leading award winner for short science fiction. He has won five Hugos (from a record thirty-seven Hugo nominations), a Nebula, and other major and minor awards in the United States, France, Poland, Spain, Croatia, Catalonia, Japan, and China, and has been short-listed for major awards in England, Italy and Australia. Mike is the author of seventy-six novels, twenty-seven collections, ten books of non-fiction, and three screenplays, as well as two hundred and eighty-five short stories. He has also edited forty-two anthologies, spent three years as co-editor of *Jim Baen's Universe*, and six years as the editor of *Galaxy's Edge* and Stellar Guild Books. He has helped the careers of over twenty young writers who are known as "Mike's Writer Children," and his own daughter is a well-known romance, science fiction, and fantasy author. He's collaborated with Robert Sheckley, George Alec Effinger, Mercedes Lackey, Nancy Kress, Jack Chalker, Eric Flint, Jody Lynn Nye, Jack McDevitt, Kristine Kathryn Rusch, Kevin J. Anderson, Barry N. Malzberg, Harry Turtledove, and fifty-one others, including more than thirty-five relative newcomers to the writing profession.

■■■■■■

Joy Ward's original introduction: Mike Resnick is more than simply a science fiction icon. Mike has won more awards than any other science fiction writer. In fact, Mike is so good at what he does he makes the very hard work of writing top-notch science fiction look almost easy. Besides numerous books and stories in print all across the world, Resnick is also the editor of **Galaxy's Edge***.*

Joy Ward: How did you get started writing?

Mike Resnick: My mother was a writer. I always wanted to be a writer. By the time I was in high school I sold my first article when I was fifteen. I sold my first poem at sixteen. I'm not a poet but I ran it in Facebook a while back.

Silky Sullivan came to the Derby with more prepublicity than Secretariat and ran twelve. I wrote Silky at the post (which was my answer to Casey at the bat), and I actually sold it. I sold some stories by eighteen. I married Carol in college. I was nineteen, she was eighteen, and after a year or two of fiddling around with a horrible year with the railroad, I figured it was time to get a job in publishing somewhere. And it happens that the only publishing job open in the whole city of Chicago at that point was at 2771 North Pulaski Road. National Features Syndicate is what they called it, but what they did is they put out three tabloids, very much like the *National Enquirer* but much worse, and three men's magazines. Within half a year this twenty-two, twenty-three-year-old kid is editing *The National Insider* with a print run of 400,000 a week. Our bestselling headline during all the years I had it was "Raped by 7 Dwarves." I would not testify to the veracity of our stories, but because we did not publish erotic books, adult books, that meant I was free to sell them elsewhere. I couldn't sell tabloid or men's magazine stuff elsewhere. We had our own publications. But I knew guys from other publishers in our field and I started doing that. By the time the dust had cleared ten years later, I had sold over two hundred of them [adult books], all of them under pseudonyms. As I explained, the only place we wanted our name was on the check, nowhere on the book.

You'd be surprised how many people (who have gone on and made it pretty big) learned their trade in that field because you can get very well paid while you are learning how to write. We only got a thousand a book, sometimes seven hundred a book, and no royalties ever, but if you turn out a book every two weeks or every week or so—this is at a time when the average American is making seven thousand bucks a year. We could do that every month and a half if we had to. We were twenty-two, twenty-three-year-old kids. You learned how to make deadlines and you learned how to differentiate characters since they were all going to do the very same thing.

One day in 1975 I turned to Carol and I said, "If I write one more four-day book or one more six-hour screenplay for Herschel Gordon Lewis,"—he was voted the second-worst director in history after Ed Wood—"if I do one more thing my brain is going to turn to putty and run out my ears. What else do we know how to do?"

At the time we were breeding and exhibiting Collies. We had twenty-three champions overall and we had twelve or fifteen dogs on the place any given day, and we figured if the two of us could care for fifteen dogs and I had time to write all that crap, think of what a staff could do. So we spent about eight months looking around the country and wound up buying the second-biggest luxury boarding and grooming kennel in America, which happened to be in Cincinnati. We moved there and within about four years it was going full force. We had a staff of twenty-one. Any given day we were boarding like two hundred dogs, sixty cats, and grooming about thirty or forty.

I was finally able to go back to writing, only this time writing the kind of stuff I wanted to write. I was sure there was no audience for it. That was why we had the kennel. Much to my surprise, it started selling and, in 1991, when the writing out-earned the kennel for the fifth year in a row, we sold the kennel. Then we figured we could live anywhere we want. We looked all over the country and said we kind of like it here, so we stayed in Cincinnati.

The first thing I sold after we bought the kennel was The *Soul Eater* in 1981. *Analog* called it a work of art, which surprised the hell out of me that anybody besides me thought it was any good. The next one I wrote was one called *Birthright*, which I have resold ten, twelve times. It created a future in which I've put about thirty-five of my novels I've written since then. I wrote thirteen books for Signet and they were getting phenomenally good reviews. They were selling okay because Signet kept buying them from me but they weren't selling anymore than okay.

My advances weren't getting any bigger. It was like I was standing still doing nothing. My friend Jack Chalker finally convinced me that the problem was my agent. I had made one foreign sale in four years. So, after he convinced me of that, I did the smartest thing I've ever done in my career: I hired Eleanor Wood as my agent. I hired her in 1983. She remains my agent. The first book she sold was *Santiago*, which got me three times the biggest advance I had gotten up to that point. It made the *New York Times* bestseller list and in the first two years I had her, she made twenty-six foreign sales for me of books, which are twenty-five more than anybody else had made for me. We have been together ever since.

I thought at the time, a rather stupid thought, that if you had something important to say, you had to say it in fifty, sixty, seventy thousand words. You couldn't do it in a short story. I only wrote seven stories the first ten years I was writing science fiction. Then in 1988 or '87 Scott Card asked me to write a story for an anthology he was doing called *Utopia* and by keeping to all the strictures he gave, which were interesting ones, I wrote a story called "Kyrinyaga." It made my reputation in a way. It won the Hugo. It made me just decide that, yeah, you can occasionally do something with short stories. From that day to this I've written three hundred and something short stories. I found out I like doing it more or better.

You have to understand that unlike most beginners, I wasn't [one]. I probably had ten million words behind me, so the fact that it sold wasn't the thrill that it would be for most people. Everything I wrote sold. Most of it I didn't want to sign my name to. It was very gratifying that I was able to get away with it. I didn't have to do Burroughs books and Howard books. I could do Resnick books and sell them. That was very satisfying and the fact that I had a legitimate New York publisher say, "Okay, I'll buy three a year from you, any subject you want." That was kind of nice.

It was gratifying to know that I could finally write what I had been training myself to write for fifteen years. I could write stuff I could sign my name to, that when people came over and said, "What do you write for a living?" I would say books, or I wouldn't give them any titles because I didn't want anybody to know those titles. It was very satisfying to be able to do that and to be able to write at a more elevated level. Howard and Burroughs were fine for their day and they wrote at the peak of their ability, but they are not the peak of most of our abilities. Totally different kinds of things.

They were rather outmoded and what happened was Lynn Carter was a friend of mine and he was probably the greatest literary chameleon of them all. One day I am in New York, probably around 1970 or so, having lunch with him. He was telling me what he was working on. He said, "Two weeks ago you did a Burroughs book and right now he's doing a Lee Bracken book. Next month he is doing a Robert E. Howard book." I said, "That's fine, Lynn, but when are you going to do a Lynn Carter book?"

He looked at me and I could tell he didn't understand the question. That made up my mind then and there. I didn't want to spend the rest of my life writing Robert E. Howard and C. L. Moore, the way Lynn did. So I stayed out of the science fiction field for ten years. I wrote more adult books. I wrote other things. It really made up my mind that I didn't want to write that stuff. I'd rather not write science fiction at all than imitate other people.

So it was really gratifying to be putting my own views down. This is the kind of science fiction I want to write, that nobody else was writing exactly like this. To be able to sell it, and be able to get good reviews, to have a publisher, and finally a number of publishers who continually encourage me and say do more of it.

I pretty much loathed everything I had written before, and I had written a lot. Because I had written a lot, I had done screenplays. Okay, they were for Herschel Gordon Lewis but they got made. I knew I was good enough to sell, and it just took me a long time to be able to figure out how to sell what I wanted to write instead of what I wanted to buy. Hopefully, now they want to buy what I want to write and we're in business for the last thirty years, fifty years.

It meant that I knew what I was going to do for the rest of my life, and I do a lot of it. I'm pretty fast. One thing you learn writing for a thousand a book, no royalties and publishers who may go to jail in three weeks—you learn how to be fast. Well, to give you an example, I'm seventy-two years old. I should be slowing down and in ways I am. But when I was seventy, two years ago, I had ten books out. Last year, at seventy-one, I had four books out. This year I will have either five or six books out. I've already got three books coming out at age seventy-three. This is what I love to do.

The most satisfying part of being a writer, probably for the last twenty-five, thirty years, has not been seeing my name in print. I do that all the time. I love winning awards and I've won my share, but the real highlight is at the end of the day when I look at what I've written and it comes out pretty much the way I hoped it would when I sat down in the morning to write. To me, that's more gratifying than any good review or anything else. I know the difference between good and bad. I also know when [what] I write isn't as good as it should have been, and I have to go back and do it again. But again, it's really very gratifying when it comes out the way I hoped it would.

The most memorable award was probably the first Hugo I won because you never expect to win one. Nobody expects to win one.

We were sitting in the audience right behind George Effinger in 1989 and I was up for best short story. It was the first time I had ever been nominated. I looked at the field and David Brin was up. David Brin was as hard to beat in the late '80s as Harlan was in the early '70s. I knew I was going to lose to him, so I was talking to George Effinger. Then Carol pokes me in the ribs and says, "Go up there. You won!"

I said, "No, you must have heard wrong. David Brin won."

She says to George, who had been turning to me. "George, will you tell him he won?"

What she didn't know is George was deaf in one ear, and he turned the good ear to me and the deaf ear was facing the stage so he didn't know. Finally a bunch of other writers who were sitting near us told me to go get the goddamn award so we can find out who won the next one. That was probably the most surprised and the biggest kick I got. Thereafter, not that I ever expected to win a Hugo, I now knew it was possible. I didn't know that the first time.

JW: You have a love affair with Africa.

MR: Yes, I do.

Off the top, it's a beautiful and fascinating continent. More to the point, it's as close to an alien society as a science fiction writer is going to find on this world. I think every science fiction fan will agree with two statements. One, if we can reach the stars, we are going to colonize them. Two, if we colonize enough of them, sooner or later we are going to come into contact with more than one. Africa offers fifty-one separate and distinct examples of the effects because it was colonized by so many countries, usually deleterious colonization, not only on the colonized but on the colonizers. Those of us who don't learn from these warnings—and humans aren't really good at learning anything—are doomed to repeat them. You add that to the fact that these really are alien societies. How alien? In Kenya in 1900, there were forty-three languages and not one of them had a word for wheel. That's pretty alien. There are many other examples. At the same time, as a tourist, it is beautiful. The animals are beautiful.

One of the interesting things is I made friends with our private guide. Whenever we're in Kenya or Tanzania I will write him ahead and say I'm going to be working on this, this, and this. Find me some old-timers who can tell me about whatever it is I'm researching. So we spend some time in the game parks, but we also hunt up a bunch of eighty-three-year-old guys with really weird stories to tell, who are going to die with them untold if I don't visit them. I'll ultimately transform them into science fiction. They end up in my books and stories.

The most powerful ones [my stories] are about Africa. My five Hugo winners are about Africa and, except for *Santiago*, my better sellers are about Africa, but that's because I feel very passionately about it and it comes through.

JW: You have your writer children?

MR: What happened was the *Alternate Kennedy* book, a closed anthology. Invite only. I had invited Nancy Kress to it. She was teaching a workshop and a kid called Nick DiChario, never sold a word in his life, gave her a story. She said that would fit [the anthology], "Send it to Mike." I should have cut her throat for that because she knew it was a closed anthology. The story came in and I must have

been in a bad mood because instead of putting in a little note saying politely, "Please don't do this until you are asked," I thought let
me read it and see just how bad it is. By page four I knew nothing
could keep it off the Hugo ballot. And nothing did. It was a Hugo
nominee. It was a World Fantasy nominee and Nick himself was a
Campbell nominee for that story. I finally met him a few months
later at the Orlando Worldcon and I said to him, "Nick, why did
you send it to me?" A story that good, the magazines at the time had
three times the circulation of an anthology. "A story that is ballot-
worthy should get to as many people as you can." His answer was
that he had sent it to every magazine in the field and got nothing
but form rejects. I thought, they are crazy! They are not going with
the story. Fire the slush readers. It never got to an editor. No editor
could read that and not buy it. About a year later we became corre-
spondents and friends. A year later he sends me a note and a novella.
"You know I'm having the same trouble with this. I think it's pretty
good, but it has been turned down by everybody. Can you tell me
what's wrong with it?" I read it and the only thing wrong with it was
it was by Nick instead of by Isaac, Arthur, or Robert. I knew Piers
Anthony was doing an anthology on that theme. I wrote him and
told him, "Read this. You are going to buy it," and he did. He gave
it the spot of honor, the last spot in his anthology.

I thought if we keep treating this poor kid like that, he's not going
to stop writing, but he's going to stop writing science fiction and go
write espionage or something else. We're going to lose a great talent.
So I figured what I better do is something to encourage him. I get
about eight or ten invites every year for anthologies. When they invite me it's a guaranteed sale. So I invited Nick to collaborate with me
on four or five of these just to get him in print. This was to keep him
enthused. He's still writing now and he's been up for another Hugo.

I thought, I bet there are more good writers out there than Nick
who can't sell. So it became my duty over the last twenty-five years.
Every time I find a good one, I collaborate with them to get them in
print, I buy from them for my anthologies and now for my magazine.
And at conventions I take them around, I introduce them to editors, I
introduce them to agents. I do everything I can to help them.

People ask why, and the answer is you can't pay back in this field. I'm seventy-two. Everybody who helped me at the beginning is dead or rich or both. So I can't pay back so I pay forward. It's very, very gratifying to see some of these kids go out and do things!

It means the field which I love, I have devoted my life to, isn't going to lose ten or twelve or fifteen really talented writers.

These are people who deserve to be in print. This field, like almost any other field, is limited. They can't do an unlimited number of books. They don't have an unlimited number of dollars. It's like movies or anything else, that once you're in, you fight to maintain your turf. If that means being a little tougher on the guy coming up behind you, you do it. This is a way to even the playing field for them because most people won't even define the playing field for them. You get an awful lot of platitudes out of how-to books on writing, but there aren't any how-to books on selling.

It makes me feel that I've helped pay the field back for being so good to me. For the last thirty or forty or fifty years I've been living a dream. When I was six years old I wanted to write a book called *Masters of the Galaxy*. Now, the subject matter has changed appreciably, but two years ago I did a book called *Masters of the Galaxy*. It happened to be a hard-boiled futuristic detective called Jake Masters, but for sixty-five years I wanted to write that book. This field has been phenomenal to me. It's given me everything I ever wanted. My spare time is spent going to conventions, associating with friends. The only people I tend to talk to now we [have no more] dogs—on the computer or anything else—are science fiction fans and writers. And I am as much a fan as I am a writer. How do you thank a field for giving you a lifetime? This is my way.

First published in Issue 25 of Galaxy's Edge, *March 2017.*

▮ TERRY BROOKS

Terry Brooks was born in Illinois in 1944. He received his undergraduate degree from Hamilton College, where he majored in English literature, and went on to earn his graduate degree from the School of Law at Washington & Lee University. A writer since high school, and heavily influenced by William Faulkner, it took him seven years to finish writing *The Sword of Shannara*, which published in 1977. It became the first work of fantasy fiction to ever appear on the *New York Times* bestseller list for trade paperbacks, where it remained for over five months. He published *The Elfstones of Shannara* in 1982 and *The Wishsong of Shannara* in 1985, both bestsellers, and was hand-selected by George Lucas to write the novelization of *Star Wars: The Phantom Menace*, which hit number one on the *New York Times* bestseller list. *The Shannara Chronicles*, premiered January 5, 2016, on MTV. It adapts *The Elfstones of Shannara* and features the creative talents of Jon Favreau, Al Gough, Miles Millar, Jonathan Liebesman, and Terry Brooks as an executive producer. Terry Brooks lives with his wife Judine in the Pacific Northwest.

▮▮▮▮▮▮

Joy Ward's original introduction: Terry Brooks has sold millions of books since his entrance onto the fantasy stage in the 1970s. His much-loved Sword of Shannara series will be unveiled as a series on MTV this January, starting with the **Elfstones of Shannara**. *Besides being one of fantasy literature's most popular writers, Brooks is also one of the nicest in the field. Despite having an overbooked calendar, he made time to meet with us at his home in Seattle to talk about writing and his life.*

Terry Brooks: If I were starting over today as a writer I'd be highly intimidated. I think that what is expected of you is much greater. You have a finite period of time to prove yourself. You have limited opportunities.

It wasn't like when I started out with the Del Reys, where I wrote one very good book in '77, and then the next book got turned down.

They said, "You've got to write another one and we'll give you five years to do it." You know they'd never do that now.

I really feel like there are more options for places to go with your work, which is a good thing, and there are more nontraditional types of publishing taking place, which is also a good thing. I think there's some independence for writers who weren't present ten or twenty years ago.

But the competition is severe, in part because suddenly fantasy is the eight-hundred-pound gorilla in all forms of entertainment when I started out it was, "Nobody cares about fantasy, nobody buys that except for Tolkien." Now, all of a sudden, *Harry Potter* made the world safe for fantasy. Now there are millions of people writing the great American fantasy novel and we've got so much competition.

I just walked into the bookstore again the other day. The young adult fantasy section was an entire wall, all by young adult fantasy writers writing those young dystopian, female protagonist novels that have become so popular. It really speaks to how popular the genre is, but also to the obvious interest in writers out there in doing this sort of thing. It's kind of fun to watch. A lot of it is good, actually.

Science fiction has been kicked to the curb. Science fiction dominated when I was growing up. Everybody read science fiction. Science fiction dominated to the point, really about the mid-'70s, when fantasy started to emerge.

I think there are a couple of things that speak to the problem. Science fiction, a lot of it is not immediately accessible, and the second thing is that it is more a fiction of ideas than story in many instances, and story is what most people connect with. They don't care about the tropes of science fiction unless it is a compelling enough story that they can skip past all that, ingest what they need to, make it part of what they're reading in an easy fashion. But if it gets too technical, most people won't give it the time of day.

Fantasy doesn't have any of that. We all grow up reading fantasy and fairy tales, being acquainted with different mythologies. That's very immediately accessible. To me, that's probably the single biggest reason.

It just may be that that's where writers have drifted to now. There are a lot more fantasy writers than science fiction writers and for many, myself included, science fiction is intimidating because science is not something I ever excelled at or have any personal knowledge of. Space opera I can write. I can do that, but when it comes to writing hard-science science fiction, I can't do it.

JW: How did you get started writing?

TB: Boy, we're going back in time now. Well, I was writing at ten. The first story I still have from fourth grade. I remember it very well because I was impressed with the fact that the teacher, my fourth-grade teacher, loved the story, and gave it an A+, and told me I was a great writer and all this other stuff.

It was a story about four boys in a haunted house who stayed there on a dare. Then there was a spaceship in the basement with aliens. It was typically weird but not too weird for a ten-year-old boy.

That was kind of the start of it. Then I wrote a story for a historical magazine in Illinois on Lincoln because every kid had to write about Lincoln. That got published. So I went, I can do this! And by golly, twenty years later, there I was. In the meantime, I just read everything.

I was still writing, but I wasn't publishing or anything. I was terrible, terrible for a long time. The college literary magazine asked me to please stop sending them things. They were terrible stories. They were coming-of-age love stories, but I was flexing my literary muscles. I hadn't really found myself yet. I was doing a lot of stuff, but none of it was any good.

So I got into law school. I was about twenty-six, I think, when I started *Sword of Shannara*. I started writing it because I hated law school and I told my parents. The first year I got crappy grades and I hated it, I thought, "What am I doing here?"

My parents said, "Tough it out. Hang in there. This will work out. Give yourself some space."

So I just said, "Well, I'm going to quit watching TV. I'm going to read books and I'm going to write something." The minute I did that my grades went right up, and I thought, well, something is going on, so I stuck with it. I actually graduated in a respectable middle-of-the-class position instead of at the bottom. I kept writing after that, and that was kind of a turning point for me in many ways.

At that point I really felt that I was into something with *Sword*. I thought I was making really good progress, and I would write it three more times, of course. Well, two more times before it got to Del Rey, and then another time after that, and some parts many times. You just sort of find that you get your teeth into something that you feel has got something to it—then you sort of feel like, well, maybe I can get there after all. Maybe this is the one that is going to do it for me.

Luckily for me it turned out to be the right thing at that time of the world, with the right people to make it happen and that saved me.

I really didn't hit my stride in that first book. Even though it sold a ton of books, I didn't really hit it until *Elfstones*. I thought I got it right with *Elfstones*. I still think that it is maybe at least one of the best books I've written.

If you talk to Judine [Terry's wife] about it, she'll tell you that you're either born to be a writer or you're not. You may not get there, even if you're born to be one, but you have to be born one. It doesn't just happen along the way. I think she may have a point because you're disciplined for doing something like this. Your bent for the way you look at life and analyze it is very specific. I really kind of think that if you're wedded to this—and I also think that for real writers, this is the most important thing in your life—and it is to me. It is the single most important thing. Not to denigrate my children or my marriage, but this is something I cannot live without. When I am not doing it, I become real weird, and I'm not kidding. I become unpleasant. You don't want to be around me, and I don't feel like everything is working. I'm not firing on all cylinders. So for me, writing is the thing that keeps me stable and content.

I don't know what would be missing in my life. I think it is more an emotional thing for me; that I am not as stable emotionally when I am not writing something. I feel incomplete, unfulfilled, and because I've been doing it for so long, and on such a regular basis, I've written a book a year forever.

I just can't imagine what would happen if I quit working because I know that even for short periods of time I start getting shaky, antsy, not happy with things.

I'm going through withdrawal and I've got to get right back into it. Maybe it's something else.

So I just think if I had to quit writing what in the world would I do for a living? I'd starve to death. Of course, now I am seventy, so, hmm.

JW: You have had a lot of high points in your professional life.

TB: That's a very tough thing for me to say because, believe it or not, I try not to dwell on the highs and the lows of my life. I find that it just screws you over. If you get too up about something, then you're going to come down hard at some point. If you get too far down, then you have to climb your way back up out of it.

I just think that it's like talking about critics. I was taught early on by Lester [Del Rey] who said, "Don't ever pay attention to critics. Go ahead and read them if you want to, but just remember that it's one person. Don't pay any attention to the good ones. Don't pay any attention to the bad ones. Look for something in the middle. It's probably closer to the truth."

So I kind of feel like it is the small victories that are more important than what seem to be the big things. I outlasted all of my critics, most of the people in publishing that I started out with. There's nobody left at my [publishing] house except for one or two people that were there when I started. There's nobody there who's read all my work; just me and Shawn Speakman, who runs my website. It's a weird thing to know that you have that kind of knowledge, breadth of knowledge. There are dozens of ten-year-olds out there who've read the whole series, and they can chime in any time they want.

It says, "You are so damn lucky, Brooks. You can't even imagine! You are so lucky, don't ever forget this." That's what I always feel about it.

It's like when you have a book go to the *New York Times* best-seller list. You think that's not something that just happens. You are so lucky because you can't plan this. I don't go out there and say, "Well, I'm going to have a million readers!" You don't do that! Nobody does that unless they've lost their mind! You're just trying to do the best work you can.

This whole TV show thing felt to me like an immense stroke of luck because it all came together so well. I think that it's the kind of thing that because you recognize that you're getting a break here that most people are never going to get. A tremendous break! You have to remember what that means. There's that tendency to go off the rails in situations like this, and I've seen people do it. You don't want to get too full of yourself. You don't want to say, "Oh, yeah! I sure deserve this, don't I?" You never want to be like that. It's just a terrible thing to do. What you want to do is just stay yourself, stay balanced in your life and in your work.

You know none of it means too much to me. This may be why I don't think too much about awards and all that stuff.

The point is, is that when you go out on tour you do bookstores or you do whatever events, and people tell you how wonderful you are, and they love your work, and blah blah blah. You do all this.

Then you come home, and your wife says, "Okay honey, now take out the garbage please, and when you're done with that, we have some tasks."

It's good to understand that your life isn't lived on the road in front of adoring people, and if it is, you're probably not doing anything besides being adored, which is even worse. You know you have to still write another book. You're a work-a-day writer. Remember that's what got you where you are. It's that you started out as a worka-day writer, sticking to the thing that got you there, writing every day, building up an oeuvre that means something to writers and readers. Remember that you owe those people! You owe those readers, and the thing that you owe them is not to let them down. They've spent money on you. They've put their faith in you. They love your books, so just don't give them a piece of crap. Don't disappoint them by suddenly turning into somebody who just goes to panels all their life and doesn't actually do any writing anymore.

I don't think that's who you are. That's who people want you to be, maybe, but that's not who you are. I think most of us are just writers, and that's what we should do, is write.

It's the most important thing we do. It's what pays the bills. It's what defines us. It's what readers are waiting for. I worry a lot about people, and there are some good people out there, who have written some good things, who are showing up regularly at waaaay too many conventions and too many tours and too many panels. They become celebrities, but at the end of the day, that's worth a handful of sand.

What counts in this world is what have you got to show for what you've done? Have you disappointed people? Have you let them down? Have you done your best? Have you worked hard and done your best? That's part of my midwestern work ethic as much as anything else. I like it that way, and I'm better off that way.

It means everything. That defines who I am. That pretty much is the person that I am, and I've spent my whole life doing it, since— certainly since the publication of *Sword of Shannara*. It's been almost forty years now. I've been writing for five decades, six decades—something like that in one form or another. So that's been the thing I've loved all my life, and I can't imagine doing anything else. It really does define who I am, to me, who I am.

When I started out, after my first book was published [I got] fan letters. I always, always answered those letters. I *always* answered those letters. Because you just want to say, "Thank you for taking the time to write to me. Thank you for reading my book, spending money on me, having some faith in me." People still come up to me, forty years later, and they've got those letters.

They say, "Look at this. You wrote this back to me in 1978. I've kept it."

And I think, oh, my God. You know it means something to people when you do that. That's just a small example.

JW: You said that Running with the Demon *is about your life?*

TB: I wrote it about growing up in a small town in the Midwest in the early '50s. It was about how kids believe in magic and how the realities of the world and parental units and adults grind you down, so that all of a sudden magic isn't real anymore and you lose that child-like love of things.

I have not lost that. I believe in magic. I am Peter Pan in many ways, and I probably always will be. I think it's better to have that side at the forefront of your personality than to be a cold stonyhearted realist who knows better than to believe in such foolishness.

It just makes me happy, being that way, I think. I just think you have to have a childlike appreciation of things. Children have such a wonderful view of life and they believe in so many things. Even if you know that they are going to get disabused of those things, it's good to keep in mind that there are permutations of that sort of thing that can be true and not to spend too much time trying to say, well you should accept the realities of the world and let go of all that childlike stuff.

JW: What do you see yourself writing in the future?

TB: I am working on a new book right now that I haven't got quite where I want it, but it is something entirely different. But I have faith in it, as they say. I am going to take as long as I need to take to get [it] to where it needs to be. But in the meantime, I'm also writing for a living, so I'm doing three more final books in the Shannara series to wrap that series up, because I keep saying, if I don't then Brandon Sanderson will write the ending after I'm dead. I can't let him do that, so I'm going to write it, and I'll fill in the gaps along the way if I want to.

JW: Is there a genre that you haven't written in that you'd like to?

TB: No. Every time I try to write some other genre I end up drifting right back into fantasy. Everything that I want to do seems to work well for me in the fantasy setting. I've done a couple of things that bordered on being something else, and this new book is actually more like futuristic than it is anything else. If I had a really good idea that required that it *not* be in fantasy, I'm sure I would do it. I just haven't had that good idea yet. I haven't been challenged in that way. I'll be around a while, so we'll see.

JW: You have written a book on how to write, Sometimes the Magic Works. *What's your best advice for young writers?*

TB: I think I'd tell them you have to be patient with yourself. The inclination is to charge into this and if it doesn't work out right away to get all discouraged. The fact of the matter is that you're probably going to have to write a whole bunch of stuff before you get to something that's pretty good, even by your own measuring stick. You have to persevere. This is a craft that you learn by doing. So start doing it. Do it every day. Do some portion of writing every day. Be patient with yourself and try to learn. It's hard to come out with just one thing. I also say you have to read books. If you're going to write books, you have to read books; otherwise you aren't going to learn anything.

You have to see what other writers are doing. You have to measure yourself against what they are doing, and you have to see what the tricks of the trade are, which you can figure out by seeing how they handle structures of scenes and character development and so forth. You accumulate this information. So I would say all those things are pretty darn important.

We didn't talk about this, but I am a writer who believes in having a strong editor. I just am extremely grateful that, from the get-go, I have had strong editors. We haven't always agreed on things, and they've been a mixed bag in terms of personality and so forth. But in terms of what they've done for me as a writer, it is immeasurable. Immeasurable how much I've gotten from them and how much I've learned. I was lucky enough at the beginning to have a teacher in Lester Del Rey, who basically was a very strong teacher.

When something wasn't right, he'd say, "This isn't right, and this is why." Since then I've had editors that have made every book I've done stronger.

When somebody says, "Oh, I don't need an editor," I think, "Bye! There goes your career!"

You know you can't see everything. You are not God. You can't see everything about your own work in an objective way. You need to have that editorial help. Those things have all made me successful and I owe those people tremendously.

Humility is a good thing. It shouldn't be underrated, I'll tell you.

First published in Issue 17 of Galaxy's Edge, *November 2015.*

▋ DAVID BRIN

D avid Brin is a scientist, tech speaker/consultant, and author. His new novel about our survival in the near future
is *Existence*. A film by Kevin Costner was based on *The
Postman*. His sixteen novels, including *New York Times* bestsellers and Hugo Award winners, have been translated into more
than twenty languages. *Earth* foreshadowed global warming,
cyberwarfare and the World Wide Web. Dr. Brin serves on the
external advisory board of NASA's Innovative and Advanced
Concepts program (NIAC). David appears frequently on shows
such as *Nova* and *The Universe* and *Life After People*, speaking
about science and future trends. He has keynoted scores of major events hosted by the likes of IBM, GE, Google, and the
Institute for Ethics in Emerging Technologies. His non-fiction
book—*The Transparent Society: Will Technology Make Us Choose
Between Freedom and Privacy?*—won the Freedom of Speech
Award of the American Library Association.

▮▮▮▮▮▮

*Joy Ward's original introduction: Dr. David Brin, the brilliant
and puckish author of some of science fiction's most innovative work*

such as **The Postman, Sundiver, The Uplift War,** *and many others kindly opened his home to my interview team.*

Joy Ward: How did you get into writing?

David Brin: I've always known that I would be a writer. I come from a family of writers going back generations. It was fun, and I always knew I would be good at it.

But as a teenager I did something that all science fiction writers do. I read a lot of history and something struck me. History is gruesome. It's awful. It's filled with errors, and, above all, delusion. Delusion is the great human talent. We authors cater to it by providing incantations that can cause miracles of subjective reality to erupt in the readers' heads. This art is great. It's wonderful. But when artists tell you that art is rare, that's when they lie.

Art fizzes out of the pores of probably 50 percent of all human beings. All the great scientists I've known practiced an artistic avocation at almost a professional level.

There has been almost no civilization that I know of without art. It is the most natural human undertaking after sex, love, and eating. If you kill all the artists in a society, and it's been tried, the next year you'll get more art. Art is not rare. Great art may be, but the essentially delusional nature of human beings makes art one of the most profoundly easy things to do. All the propaganda spread by artists notwithstanding because it is in their best interest to talk about how rare and brilliant they are.

When I realized this, I also saw that my life in 1950s, 1960s America was pretty good, and for the first time we had a civilization that at least paid lip service to rights, decency, and knowledge. Something different was happening.

For the first time a civilization was employing millions of people not to reinforce what they passionately believed to be true, but to honestly experiment and find out what is true. That had never happened before.

So I decided I was going to join those people. I would be a scientist and do my art part time.

I'm told that when I was three years old my father took me to watch Einstein play the violin. I have no memory of it, but perhaps it struck me that you can be more than one thing. Probably the most evil limitation on human nature is the zero-sum game—the assumption that for every victory there must be a loss, for every winner there must be a defeated. If you are good at something it means you can be good at nothing else. This propaganda that we are inherently limited beings.

The most powerful concept that a modern person can grasp is that of the positive-sum game—that the notion is that one person may win more than another, but the other doesn't have to be a loser. Competitiveness in marketplaces or science can result in everyone getting richer. You can be a good parent, spouse, citizen, co-worker and still find a way to be an artist.

I'd be the last to deny that being a trained scientist affects what I write. When I studied to be an astrophysicist, I maintained my hobby of writing with the full intent of being published—having a nice sideline. My role model would have been Robert Forward or Charles Sheffield—possibly, if I was lucky, Gregory Benford. Who knew that the tail of my avocation would wag the dog of my profession? Civilization deemed my time writing incantations to be worth more than my pretty good work. Appraising the science of comets—which, by the way, my dissertation was proved last week, with the LA Lander. And that is what I recommend to young people who have both a scientific and artistic side. Do the science first because it's hard. But passionately maintain your art. And never let it go. If you are both talented and lucky and if you work hard, your art will rise to some level that pleases you, and it may drag you kicking and screaming away from your day job. I curse you with that dilemma.

But to answer your question, science fiction was very badly named. Just the name "science fiction" helps to foist a pallor of hostility across the genre in a thousand university campuses in America. In only twenty or thirty has the science fiction instructor been given tenure, even though science fiction is the literature of which Americans should be most proud: perhaps the name has something to do with it. Only 10 percent or so of science fiction authors are scientifically trained as I am. But that doesn't stop many of them from doing terrific scientific science fiction.

There are English majors out there who write the hard stuff as easily as I do, with bold extrapolations and adventures that will be mediated by science and technology. Some of the best examples would be Kim Stanley Robinson, Nancy Kress, Greg Bear, none of whom could parse a simple derivative if their lives depended on it. They learned the simple trick in our field which is that scientists, the best of them, will give very cheap consultations to science fiction authors for the price of pizza and beer or naming a character after them. One or two of the best experts held out for their character to have sex on stage or to die gruesomely, depending on their personalities. I was happy to oblige, especially the latter. The point is that if 10 percent or so of SF authors are scientifically trained, almost 100 percent read history voraciously.

Quite frankly, the field was badly named. It should have been speculative history because that's most of what we do. We speculate what history would have been like if this or that had happened or the rules had been different. What might that past truly have been like, but above all how might we extrapolate this gorgeously stupid, poignantly horrific litany of errors that is called the human experience?

By far, the most tragic and transfixing tale. Indeed, that may be one explanation for the Fermi Paradox of why we haven't been contacted by aliens out there. Because our struggles may be so interesting to them. We're the miniseries that they want to see renewed and never end.

I think George Martin has kind of captured the essence of human history.

JW: You were talking earlier about how humans are really deluded in this idea of zero-sum game. How has that come through your writing?

DB: First off, this is a concept that is absolutely essential, and if I urge your readers to pick up any nonfiction book from the past twenty years it would be Robert Reich's *Nonzero* because once you understand the concept of the positive-sum game all your politics change. You start to understand 99 percent of human history across six thousand years was kept tragic by zero sum or sometimes negative-sum cultures in which cabals or gangs of large men would pick up large instruments, call themselves kings, lords, and priests, and took away the wheat and women from other men. I say this in a sexist manner quite deliberately because women were in no position to object across those six thousand years. It quickly became the natural human social order, variations on feudalism, societies shaped like a pyramid with a few at the top lording over others. Those lords, their top priority over competing with each other was to suppress the ambitions of those below.

Fantasy novels portray this kind of social structure. It is the one common thread in most modern fantasy novels, except urban fantasy and steampunk, which fields I respect. It is the assumption of society's changelessness that I consider to be the grotesque but highly natural storytelling riff that distinguishes science fiction from fantasy.

This was best expressed by the great author and my dear friend, the late Anne McCaffrey. Regularly in interviews she would be referred to as a "fantasy author." Always she would rear up in anger and deny this. She would say, "I'm a science fiction author." People would smirk because she had dragons—people riding dragons with swords. She had sword fights. She had castles and keeps and long passages about medieval crafts like macramé, sewing, and weaving. The ambiance was very similar to a fantasy novel, so why would she say that?

It's truly simple. In her dragonriders cosmology the people of the planet Pern have a feudal social order. They have lords, tenant farmers, they have their great knights on their charging steeds of the sky, but at some point in the second novel they discover a truth that they were colonists on this planet who had been beaten down by a catastrophe. The feudal order with all of its lovely crafts and its ornate culture and all the cool aspects, were all fallback positions. Once their ancestors had flown through the sky, they had had the germ theory of disease, and their children didn't die in their arms. Once they had flush toilets, printing presses, and networked tablets. The thing that distinguishes Anne McCaffrey's characters from those who wallow in mindless sameness in Tolkien and so many fantasies is this: Anne McCaffrey's characters want those things back. They are determined to get them back, and if their lords and the dragonriders help them get these things back, then there might be nominal lords in the future.

If they stand in their way, they will be grease spots. This is what made Anne McCaffrey, without a scintilla of doubt, a science fiction author.

The true distinction is that science fiction admits to the possibility of fundamental change and deals with it. Fantasy hearkens to an older tradition going back to the *Iliad*, the *Odyssey*, the *Vedas* of India. The notion that the demigod is more important than the citizens and the social order, there may be dramatic variations on who gets to be king, but there will always be kings.

JW: Your work flies in the face of that. I'm thinking about your work dealing with nonhumans.

DB: I'm not the first to speak of uplifting animals to human levels of intelligence. But those authors did what perhaps I would have done in their situation. They told the simplest possible version of that story, one that writes itself and that is a Frankenstein situation. We created these new beings in order to be slaves, we're cruel to them, and we get our comeuppance for having the arrogance and hubris for picking up God's powers.

Well, this has been done and I'm not convinced that picking up God's powers is automatically punishable. There are passages in the Bible that suggest it's what we were made to do. So in my Uplift universe I decided to try something different. What if we give the Promethean gift of sapience to other creatures with the very best of intentions, openly, submitting the project to endless criticism, avoiding as many errors as we could and correcting those we come across? Wouldn't that still be a fascinating story? Wouldn't there still be dramatic and tragic errors? Would not the intermediate generations suffer from a poignancy of both progress and pain? That could make for good art. In fact, I think the potential mixed feelings of such creatures would be made more interesting in a milieu of kindness than deliberate grotesque caricature of cruelty.

JW: Is there a lesson that we need to learn from the way the creatures— the chimps, the dolphins—come across in your writing?

DB: We need to become unafraid of complexity. I believe that one of the attractions of fantasy stories is the notion of the simple, old-fashioned social order. You knew who you were; you knew what your role was. We know what our role is compared to the other animals on Earth. If they start talking to us, if the robots start asking for rights, if aliens come here, perhaps domineering or curious or as refugees, life becomes ever more complex. We have dealt with complexity so vastly more intricate and so much more successfully than any of our ancestors ever would have predicted. Our only chance of survival is to do the same. That is the real contribution of science fiction.

JW: On a more personal level, what has been your highest point in your career?

DB: Well, the 1984 Worldcon was in my hometown. It's still, to this day, the record holder for attendance of a Worldcon and I owned it. Oh, I was Guest of Honor and at a Worldcon much later, 2007 in Yokohama. That was very nice. But I was the hot young twit in 1984. Everywhere I went at that con, people stepped back and whispered to each other. It was my brief taste of Hollywood, I suppose.

It's a terrible thing if it lasts. I've known people who settled into that frame of mind and it never did their personalities any good. Mine is a difficult, enough personality as it is. My ego does not need more inflation. I settled into being a venerable old fart of science fiction and that will do nicely.

JW: In 1984 you were a fairly young guy.

DB: I said I was the hot young twit. There are attractions to it. Certainly one has to create, on one's shoulder, the servant who rode alongside a Roman general when he received his triumph through the streets of the city wearing his laurel crown, receiving cheers and adulation while the slave leaned into his ear and whispered "sic transit Gloria." All this will pass. In my case, I got that reminder in 1984 when I looked at the base of the Hugo Award I had just won, received for *Startide Rising,* and it was toilet porcelain with black rats all over it and I realized, "Okay, this is not something to take too seriously. Enjoy."

JW: How have you seen science fiction change?

DB: I am no stranger to writing dark fiction. Certainly my graphic novel, *The Life Eaters,* set in a future where the Nazis and the Norse gods won World War II, is plenty dystopic. But there again, I like to veer in a different direction.

The Postman was not about an individual or a small gang achieving triumph, instead a complex and fretful demi-hero reluctantly coming to realize that he had the power to lie and that his lies could inspire survivors to remember one simple thing—that once upon a time they had been citizens.

Dystopias are useful and interesting to the extent that they point out errors or possibilities. The greatest dystopias include George Orwell's *1984*, Harry Harrison's *Soylent Green*, *Silent Spring*, *On the Beach*, *Dr. Strangelove*. What did all of these have in common? They were self-preventing prophecies. Each of them pointed out a potential failure mode so vividly that millions became determined to prevent it from ever coming true. This trait cannot be ascribed to the tsunami of simple-minded, grotesquely clichéd dystopias and post-apocalyptic tales that we're seeing today.

If you want to get your heroes into pulse-pounding action by starting with a premise of a holocaust, fine. That's lazy, but go for it. On the other hand, if your failure mode has nothing interesting or realistic or chillingly likely about it, then your only reason for taking us to this place is authorly laziness.

I had an essay in *Locus Magazine* that got a lot of attention. People can see it on my website. It's called "The Idiot Plot." It describes the underlying reason why Hollywood and so many authors are pounding us flat with dystopias after apocalypse.

It's not that they really believe that they live in such a world. Were any of the directors or authors to find themselves in trouble they would dial 911 and they would be pissed off if skilled professionals did not leap to their aid. Yet none of their characters ever do that. Or if they dial 911, the phone lines are down, or if they get through, the operator is incompetent. If the police come, they come late. If they come on time they are incompetent. If they're incompetent that's the surest sign that they are in cahoots with the bad guy. With one exception: there is a sliding scale of competence that civilization is allowed, depending on how badass the villains are. When you have someone unlike the Joker in Batman, the cops are allowed to be haplessly competent—just enough to get in Batman's way. When the villains are as humongously badass, as the *Independence Day* aliens, the government and military of the United States of America is allowed to be simultaneously good and competent.

I don't begrudge authors and directors for making this choice deliberately, that the simplest way to keep their heroes in pulse-pounding jeopardy for ninety minutes or three hundred pages, is to assume no institution works and that you can never count on your neighbors because they are hopeless sheep. But for them to make this clichéd choice out of habit and sheer laziness, that's contemptible, because every dystopia that's like this. That says, "I'm not offering you a failure mode that you could do something about, you viewers or readers. I am immersing you in gloom with the fundamental lesson that thou shall never trust any institution, no matter how many citizens fight to make it useful and better and above all, never put any confidence in your neighbors."

The exceptions are actually very heartwarming. In every Spiderman movie, and they are not great art, the hero saves New Yorkers in 90 percent of the film. But there is always a scene wherein the New Yorkers save Spiderman. Now that's sweet. It's an homage to a civilization that has actually been pretty good to all of us, and this notion is that civilization might be a character in your work, it's flaws, it's failures, but also the good aspects the hero might call upon.

This is the fundamental distinction between *Star Wars* and *Star Trek*. In *Star Wars* the ship is a World War I fighter plane. The heroic pilot, silk scarf and all, is the demigod, going back to comic books, going back to World War I, going back to Achilles. And there's room on the fighter plane for perhaps his brave gunner or droid. The ship is a knight's charger; there is no room for civilization.

In George Lucas's epic saga, you never see civilization doing anything. The Republic never does anything. It never even takes any actions that may be called mistakes. It does nothing. The other institution, the Jedi Council, is dumber than a bag of hammers.

This is an ancient storytelling motif. It writes itself, which you can tell from the writing quality of the three prequels.

In *Star Trek* the ship is a naval vessel. The captain is, at most, way above average and needs the expertise and skill of not only main cast members but also [in] every episode somebody from below decks must rise up and contribute to the team effort. The ship deals with complexities. One of the major cargoes and passengers of the Enterprise and Voyager is civilization, the Federation. Does it make mistakes? Absolutely. These are topics of shows: mistakes to correct, mistakes to reveal and expose, but also thought experiments about how our grandchildren might be better than us.

All of these are possible when civilization is a topic and you don't fall for the old demigods trap. When the Enterprise encounters a demigod what is the reaction? Folded arms and a skeptical expression, looking at this pretentious being and saying, "Okay, what's your story?" Individualism is a core message in our culture, and those who use the demigod motif actually convince themselves that they are writing stories in praise of individualism because they have a hero—the hero overcomes all odds and villainy, and caricature villains with red-glowing eyes. In fact, they are wrong. They are deceiving themselves. They are not promoting individualism because individual human beings can be cantankerous, egotistical, and self-centered, but they only achieve really valid goals, ironically, in the context of the civilization. It is indeed ironic that those tales that have a functioning civilization in the background are the ones that speak to individualism most valuably, most realistically, and offer insights that go beyond resentment, revenge, and rage.

JW: Moving more back toward you as a writer, who or what other writers have really influenced you?

DB: Orwell and Aldous Huxley, certainly. Who would have thunk that because Orwell wrote a self-preventing prophecy, that some of the failure modes in *Brave New World* are indeed more likely to come true? I have found it very interesting to explore cultural memes from the past. The *Hindu Vedas*, the *Bible*, the great works of the East, and while I'm there, let me mention that probably one of the greatest works of science fiction ever to emerge from Asia has just been published by Tor Books. It's called the *Three-Body Problem* by Liu Cixin. It was translated into English by our own Ken Liu. They have the same name. It is about a three generations leap forward in Asian science fiction. It's stunningly of the first rank.

Within our genre my influences range from hard SF of Charles Sheffield and Robert Forward, [to] the deeply moving quasi-hard SF of Octavia Butler, Nancy Kress, [and] Ursula K. LeGuin. Of course, the great old farts. I had a collaboration with Arthur Clarke and had the honor last year of helping to establish the Arthur C. Clarke Center for Human Imagination here at UCSD. I was among the Killer Bees, Greg Bear and myself, who were asked by the Asimov estate to write the second Foundation trilogy. These are standalone novels that also tie together. Mine, entitled *Foundation's Triumph,* tied together all the loose ends I could find from Isaac's universe, including not just the Foundation and Robots books but obscurer titles like *Pepper in the Sky* and *56:57 The Currents of Space.* Isaac's widow was very kind calling it the best non-Isaac.

But putting that braggadocio aside I find a lot of the new folks truly wonderful. Paolo Basset Giulupia, Michael Chabon. They are very bright, knowledgeable and better writers than I am. Still, I like to think that I'm one of the last truly great science fiction authors for one simple reason. Dentistry.

These new whippersnappers are geniuses, brilliant writers, but they have got almost no fillings in their mouths, so they don't pick up radio waves from Aldegeberon Six in the Twilight Dimension and places like.

Hence, I have an unlimited supply of ideas.

JW: Where are these ideas going to be taking you in the future?

DB: My novel *Kiln People* was a cry for help. I have a substantial public speaking career and I consult about many future-oriented issues. This plus three kids, teaching—all in all, I've been neglectful of my core writing career. Hence, I dreamed of having a machine where I could make cheap copies of myself every day. In *Kiln People* everyone gets such a machine. The notion in so many science fiction novels is here's a new piece of scientific progress, let's assume it's hoarded in secret and hence you get all Michael Crichton plots.

I like to see what happens if everybody gets it. So, in this world, any morning you could put your face on your home copies and out steps a cheap, clay golem image of yourself. Good for one day. It will melt after twenty-four hours. It knows everything you know, has your personality, and it's one chance of continued existence is to do what needs to be done and come home and download the memories of the day. As a result, you were five people yesterday. You had five days yesterday. Today you might make six copies because there's a lot to be done. It's a world in which you have a list of things to accomplish—you can do them all. Can you see now why it is a wish fantasy? You make two cheap green copies to do all the errands, fix all the things around the house, and do all the cleaning. You make an expensive ebony copy to go to the library and study. You make a battle version to go to the arena and get killed, but have its head put on ice so that you can remember.

In *Existence*, we have the genre of novel that I conveyed also in "Earth." These are my two, big, sprawling near-future extrapolations from *Chronos*. The motif is based upon John Brunner's *Stand on Zanzibar*, filled with extracts from media and events happening around the characters, portraying a complex society that we might plausibly live to see. By the way, folks can go to DavidBrin.com and see a three-minute trailer for *Existence,* with gorgeous art and portrayals of the characters by the great web artist Patrick Farley. I guarantee you [it will be] the most fun you'll have in three minutes with your clothes on. My wife made trailers for two older novels, *Glory Season* and *Heart of the Comet*.

JW: how do you want to be remembered?

DB: I'd like to be remembered by sci-fi fans on Earth as one of the good ones whose explorations might seem quaint in the future, but nevertheless worth picking up, and who makes Earthlings wait impatiently for a stretch for the next novels that have to come by radio from the colony worlds of Tau Ceti Four. That's how I want to be remembered on Earth. However, I'm willing, grudgingly, to be remembered the way Isidoro Galilei is remembered. He helped to establish pools and creative potential of Italian opera and the only way we know of him today is because he was the father of Galileo Galilei. I expect that a hundred years from now a few fans, a few million fans of the writing of my daughter, Ari Brin, will say, "Do you know that her father also wrote?" And I will live on. We do live on through our children.

In most fields of art there are two ways for the creator to succeed. One is to be noticed by the mavens and doorkeepers of the high level professional status and to be plucked up and announced to the world. The other is to climb up the pyramid via the ramp. For example, you have a local band; they win amateur night. They serve as an opening act for your town's hot band. You cut an album; you play a concert in the park. You work your way up. You get some local radio play.

Published fiction never had a real ramp. There was vanity press, but that was meaningless. Today the ramp is filling in. You can self-publish in ways that are sort of quasi-professional. There are partially professional publishers, quote unquote. There are ways to get your work out there and have it be discovered and rise up, either by dint of quality or lack of it. The result is a yin and a yang. This happens with all kinds of progress. True talent, accompanied by endeavor and courage and hard work, will see the light of day today. It may not achieve great success, but somebody out there is going to read it. This is better. On the other hand, it means there is so much crap, and to distinguish the good from the bad requires crowd vetting of a degree that is still highly uncoordinated and so we need the professional maven gatekeepers.

Expanded version of the interview that appeared in
Issue 14 of Galaxy's Edge, *May 2015.*

❚ CATHERINE ASARO

atherine Asaro is known for her beautiful singing and the heart-tugging romance and hard science concepts she infuses into her fiction. She had enrolled at UCLA as a dance major where she discovered her love of math and science. She went on to earn a BS with Highest Honors from UCLA, a master's in physics from Harvard, and a doctorate in chemical physics, also from Harvard. As part of her academic career, Catherine has also published reviews and essays and authored scientific papers in academic journals. She was a physics professor until 1990, when she changed careers to become a writer (and consultant). Over the years she has been nominated for the Hugo Award, the RITA Award, has won the Nebula and Sapphire Awards several times, and also won the UTC Readers Choice Award, the AnLab Readers Poll, the HOMer Award, the Prism Award, the Affaire de Coeur Award, the RT Book Club Reviewer's Choice Award, the Outstanding Achievement Award (WRW), and the Book Buyers Best Award. Catherine was also given the Wallace S. North, Jr., PE Award for Contributions in the Maryland State Mathcounts Program, 2017.

■■■■■■

Joy Ward's original introduction: Catherine Asaro is more brilliant and talented than any of the heroines she has written, win-

ning numerous award-winning science fiction and fantasy works. She holds a doctorate in chemical physics and directs the Chesapeake Math Program. It might be easier to list the awards she has not won than those she has won. Dr. Asaro has served twice as president of SFWA. She was a jazz and ballet dancer and is still a musician.

Joy Ward: How did you get into writing science fiction?

Catherine Asaro: When I was a kid, I used to make up stories. When I was really little, they were about this sort of nebulous girl who was, when I was five, she was seven, and she'd go out and save the galaxy. I didn't know I was making up stories. I thought everybody did this. I would daydream.

Then I found science fiction. *Space Cat* was my first set of science fiction stories. I thought this was just cool, the idea [of] these kids going to the moon or this cat going with this astronaut to Venus and so I started reading science fiction voluminously.

I had a brother and a father who liked it so I'd steal their books. Until my father found out I was stealing books with sex scenes. Then the books all disappeared. I didn't quite get them [the sex scenes]. But I just loved the science fiction, and I always made up stories. I didn't know at first why many of the books didn't quite work for me. All I knew is that when I made up stories, the central character—and I didn't think about it for many years—but she was always a girl.

Around the time I was twelve or thirteen, I started making the connection. There are no girls that play substantial roles in these books. Even when [girls] are there, they're usually there to support a male character. It wasn't that I was making some great statement by stopping reading. I just kind of lost interest. I couldn't find books that spoke to me since I was becoming a teenager and I'd figured out that boys were different than girls, in very interesting ways—ways I wanted to explore more. The books didn't really speak to me, but I did keep making up the stories in my mind. I never made the connection with that and the fact that I was making up stories about very strong female characters who ruled civilizations and went out on adventures until the boy next door—actually it was the boy across the street. We were down in the park doing that sort of flirting thing that teenagers—thirteen- and fourteen year olds—do. He said, "Tell me your stories." So I started telling some and he listened, and he goes, "Well that's cool." Then he said, "But how come all the main characters are girls?" Until that point I hadn't made the connection. Then I thought, well should I make main characters the guys? I thought, well, sure yeah, but then I thought I don't have to do it; it's my stories. But I did. I mean it wasn't on purpose. The guys are in there, the romantic interest. So the cats got replaced with handsome young pirates.

JW: When did you start writing down the stories?

CA: I tried once when I was about maybe nine. I drew pictures of the characters. Then I tried to write a story and I realized that the main character, it was a girl, she's going to rescue the male, the handsome pilot. He'd been captured and was in the enemy military installation. She went to this installation to help him escape. I got her into the military installation, and I got stuck. I finally realized I had no idea what went on in military installations. I could have just gone to my parents and asked how do you do research? But I didn't. I just quit writing.

It was strange. I knew I had to do research, and I didn't know how to do it. I just kept making the stories up in my head. They matured over time. Then in college I started writing. My last semester at college I only had to take one class. I had all this free time. I wrote a book by longhand on yellow legal paper. There's two things. I wanted to revise it extensively. I knew it needed it. I also didn't know at the time I'm dyslexic. I just knew that I was having trouble writing it in longhand. I thought two things. To revise this the way I want is going to take a huge amount of time because you have to rewrite it, and I said it's hard for me to write. The other thing was the way it took over my life. I knew if I went to grad school I had to concentrate. So I didn't write for about another three years.

Then in grad school when I was working on my doctorate I thought, I need something. I can't look at equations anymore. I need a break. I started writing what, at the time, was the *Last Hawk*. I wrote some other stuff first, and then I wrote the *Last Hawk*. And it took over again. I mean I didn't know at the time I was the classic writer who can't think of anything else but writing. I just knew it took over, and it delayed my thesis by at least six months, maybe a year.

But I finally knew how to do research. I finally knew what I wanted and what I had to do to get it and how to write the stories. I don't think I've ever stopped since then. Things got in the way, like I was a professor for a while.

JW: You've got two really distinct worlds you're working in. What is it that you get from the science fiction world that you don't really get from the mathematical and physics world?

CA: I love math, I couldn't imagine not doing it. I love writing. They are very different. Often the question I get is, what's the difference between ballet—I was a ballet dancer for many years. But I trained for years. I performed, and I established dance companies when I was in graduate school. So that's often the question I get, and, to me, the math and dance are not that different. Just like there's a connection between music and math.

Now that more girls are going into math and more boys are going into ballet, they're finding out there's a very strong connection between being good at ballet and being good at math. They both involve understanding spatial perception. All the music-math connection is there. But dancers are incorporating it into their body. It's not surprising that dancers and math go together. Writing for me is different. It accesses a different part of my brain.

I usually know when I've done enough, because I write it and then I go back and I go through the whole thing again revising. I write really fast the first time through and it's a mess. Then I go back and it's like cleaning it up. Every time I go through I clean it up, and I finally reach a point where I'm not stopping and rewriting. But I'm never done. I could keep doing this for another year. There comes a point when you have to say, alright. I never feel like the prose is as beautiful as I want to make it. I know if I spent more time and effort I could make it even better but you have to stop at some point.

For each story there's usually a scene that is close to my heart. Often there's more than one scene. I choreograph them in my head and I listen to music. There'll be certain scenes, like in *Undercity* there's a scene where this person is supposed to bring members of the Undercity to this shadowy, mysterious place to be tested for these special abilities. That scene meant a lot to me when I wrote it. I imagined it in my head and choreographed it to music. I had music and I choreographed the whole thing over and over and I'd listen to it. When I finally got to writing it, I had to write it and rewrite it to get it right. When I finished that I was glad. I said, "It's done. I'm happy and this is pretty good." Then of course it got edited and edited and edited because it was too long. I put everything I imagined into it and I actually weakened it because it was too long.

It had a lot of revising, but I think for me the high point was actually imagining it in my head. It does something. All my life I would imagine these things in my head to music, long before I was writing. It did something for me, to the point where my personality, my psychology, is connected with my ability to turn on music and imagine stories. I'm not as satisfied—happy with my life—if I don't do that at least a little bit.

The times when I haven't been creating, when I've had a nine-to-five job, like being a professor and going home, doing homework—there's not a whole lot of time when you're a professor to do anything else—were very frustrating for me. I was not happy with that world. I sometimes almost regret that because, had I been happy to do that, I could have done a lot. I could have become well-known in my field, and I could have pushed harder and been a better role model for young women who want to go in sciences and math and all this stuff. I sometimes regret that I didn't enjoy living that way, but I didn't. I love writing and I love running this math program because I'm in charge of it.

I just would like to see more young women go into math and science. I'm trying to think of ways to get girls interested in math, because right around the middle school level they start dropping out in huge numbers. I understand better now that I'm so directly involved with it. There's a very different dynamic between boys that age and girls that age. The girls just seem to grow up a little faster. When you put those groups together they're charming. All of them are charming but they interact [in] very different ways, so the boys are still boisterous, youthful and most of them are very young. The girls just sit there very quietly kind of looking around. Then they don't come back because they don't feel comfortable. So I'm trying to figure out ways to make the girls more comfortable. One thing I'm trying is dividing the classes up. Give the girls their own class. Then they come out of their shell more. I'm just trying to think of ways to involve them.

I know a lot of women write to me about reading the books and I did not set out to write strong female characters because this will have such and such effect. I just wrote them. But they apparently speak a lot to a lot of women. The books are not YA. They're read a lot by teenagers, including some that I told my daughter she couldn't read but she did anyway.

I was the guest of honor at a convention. I remember a young woman; I saw her walking by and looking like she wanted to say something and then she went away. Later she came back, and she had a card for me. She said, "I hope I'm not imposing." She was so apologetic and, I said, "No, no, not at all." She said, "I just wanted to give you this card." The card said that I had changed her life with my books. She's very apologetic and shy about it and I thought, I can't imagine anyone doing me a greater honor than what my readers do when they say my writing speaks to them, or I changed their lives. They're not imposing but it's like, wow! It reached somebody.

I almost cried. I teared up. She walked away quickly, so I was by myself by the time I was reading the card. It felt really, really good like, wow! It reaches somebody. It changed somebody's life in a good way. It just surprised me. I thought, my crappy writing actually did something. I'm very hard on myself. I don't have a very high opinion of a lot of things I do. I think I'm lazy and I mess around, and I don't do what I should do. I don't finish things when I should. Someone says something like that, and it just gives you a little bit to keep you going.

Winning a Nebula, that was a high point. It was so funny. I was sure I wouldn't win. It was for the *Quantum Rose*, which is a very romantic book. I'm probably the only science fiction writer who's been nominated for the Hugo, the Nebula, and the Rita from the romance writers. It's a retelling of *Beauty and the Beast*. I thought there's no way this is going to win, and it was going against Connie Willis and several brilliant hard SF novels, one by Jeffrey Landis. I thought there's no way. I said Connie's going to win or Jeffrey's going to win so I didn't even write a speech or anything. I didn't bother.

I did go to the ceremony because it's kind of fun to go and have people say, "Oh, you're a nominee." I'm sitting next to Nancy Kress and we're talking. She says, "Catherine, you ought to write something down." She said, "I didn't think I was going to win when I did, and I wrote something at the last minute because somebody told me to do it. So I'm going to tell you to write something." I said, "No, Nancy. Don't be silly. Nobody's going to vote for a romance for the Nebula." Nancy said, "Well you should do it anyway." I took my [name tag], turned it over and I scribbled some stuff on the back. They're doing the announcement. It's two people. They were kind of joking about the various nominees for novel and they said, "And there's Connie Willis and then there's these hard SF writers." They didn't name me as one of the hard SF writers. My agent was over there looking really mad because she knows how much criticism I got when I first started writing hard SF. It wasn't canonical, and because I'm a woman it got a lot of criticism. There are romances in it or it wasn't so much that there was romance in it but there was a lot of touchy feely stuff about emotions that people didn't associate with hard science fiction. It was controversial when I first started. So when they didn't mention me, she started looking kind of mad. I didn't care at that point. I was just waiting to hear who won. It had never occurred to me that they didn't mention me because I won. Then they're going on and they say, "And the winner is Catherine Asaro for the *Quantum Rose.*" I swear to God I just sat there with my mouth open. My agent was about to get up and come over and pull me out of my seat when finally Nancy kind of did this and I got up and I went up. Thank God she told me to write that because I was fumbling with my thing and I said, "Okay, Nancy Kress told me to write this." If it wasn't for her, I would've just stood up there with my mouth open. I couldn't believe it. I mean I literally couldn't believe it.

It almost was like I couldn't process it. I just kind of, "What? Is this a mistake?" Did you ever see that scene in the Olympics where all the runners run together? It's a really funny scene from the Olympics maybe ten, fifteen years ago. They all run together and they fall over. The guy who was behind them runs past them and wins the gold medal. That's what I felt like. They're all these really good people and they probably split the vote so I won. My agent was going, "No,

Catherine, it was a good book. Don't put yourself down." But that's what I felt like when I won.

It was an award given by my peers. It's the highest award science fiction has to give along with the Hugo Award, and it came from my peers. It was incredible. Maybe I wasn't as bad as I thought I was I'm still not happy with the book, but it is one of my better ones.

There's some sexual violence in my earlier stories that I just don't know if I'd put it in as explicitly now as I did then. I think I've changed and become more aware of the effect that such scenes can have. That they're more upsetting to some readers than I realized. They're triggers. I don't know if that's what I wanted to do—if my intent was to trigger certain reactions but it wasn't. I deal a lot with questions of role reversal, of violence, of gender issues. I'm not sure the methods I chose to deal with it were always the most successful to achieve what I wanted or the comments that I wanted to make. I may not have made them so explicit. They are aspects of the stories. You can't deal with those kind of issues without having them there to be dealt with. I think I would have made them less explicit. I think my writing now is a little bit less explicit than it used to be.

The writing is the most important. I do like running the Chesapeake Math Program. I like doing that, but it does take time from the writing so it's a constant tension. My writing, slowed down a lot since I started running this program. I want to write. That's really what I want to do, but it's hard to walk away from something that you also very much like to do. I've made up stories since I was old enough to think. I started imagining alternate worlds when I was two or three years old. I've done it all my life. It's so much a part of what I am, I don't know how I could do anything else.

JW: How do you want to be remembered?

CA: When I first started I didn't get a lot of acknowledgement for [hard science in my writing]. I would get people saying, "Oh well maybe she knows a little bit of physics." I have a doctorate from Harvard in this stuff.

Now, the world's changed. Even in the twenty, twenty-five years since I started, people are more willing to accept a woman in that role.

I'd like to be remembered for that. I'd like to be remembered for starting a conversation on the representation of women and challenging literary gender roles. I think I was born a feminist, and I grew up very aware of all these differences in how women and men were viewed. It was implicit in how I saw things and nobody else saw it. I grew up in a world not long after the 1950s where "father knows best" and a strong female role model is Donna Reed. At the time, I respected her in the sense that she was the only one woman who had a television story, she and Lucille Ball. They were not in any way role models that I wanted to emulate.

I wanted to go out in space and be the fighter pilot. I almost took that for granted that that was a good thing to write about. I never had trouble writing about it, even though I grew up in a time when women did not do that. I mean period. There was no representation. I've seen the world change so much since then. It's become so much more accepted, and I like to think that maybe I played a little bit of a role in making that happen. And I still enjoy writing those characters. I have more freedom now because there's less pressure not to do it. It's more accepted, so I have more freedom in what people will publish. I think if I'm remembered for anything, I would be—I would be honored to be remembered for that. Maybe I made a little bit of a difference in the world.

First published in Issue 32 of Galaxy's Edge, *May 2018.*

■ DAVID WEBER

David Weber has over sixty titles published, and is the author of the well-known Honor Harrington science fiction series. Completing undergraduate studies at Warren Wilson College, Swannanoa, North Carolina, he then attended graduate school at Appalachian State University, in Boone, North Carolina. While finishing his master's thesis, he decided to return to Greenville to take over Weber Associates, Incorporated—an advertising agency—from his mother, who was retiring. However, it was David's work in the development of the StarFire board game series, from Task Force Games of Amarillo, Texas, that started his writing career. It led to the writing of his first published novel, *Insurrection*, in collaboration with Steve White. Baen bought the book in 1989—literally within a week of receiving the manuscript. It was published in 1990, by which time Baen had also bought three of David's solo novels, so he pitched the Honorverse series in 1991. Having wanted to buy a "Horatio Hornblower" tale in space, Baen immediately bought the first four novels, and the rest, as they say, is history.

■■■■■■

Joy Ward's original introduction: David Weber is the author of one of the most-loved characters in science fiction, Honor Harrington.

His readers know him as a gentle giant who inspires loyalty from fans and friends.

Joy Ward: How did you get into writing?

David Weber: I started writing when I was in the fifth grade, writing poetry first and then eventually doing some shorter fiction. In the sixth grade I started doing some longer fiction.

At seventeen, I began writing ad copy for my mom, and I learned how to do paste-up art—not well, but I learned how to do it. I became a typesetter, and eventually I became one of the world's last trained Linotype operators. Yes, I was looking at Y2K and thought I might have a new career opening back up, but no…no…

Aside from that, everything I've ever done has been associated either with writing of one form or another, or with research and teaching.

The three careers that I almost went into, other than writing, were the US Navy; choice number two was the Episcopal seminary, and choice number three was that I was going to teach history on the college level and write on the side. I was just finishing up my master's degree when I saw a demographic study of the field [at] which said that more than half of all tenured history positions were held by people forty years old or younger, and that the field was shrinking at the rate of about 1 percent per year.

At that point I decided that I would go back down to Greenville, and I would take over my mom's small ad agency, partly because she wanted to go down to Georgia to take care of *her* mom. So I did. I took over Weber Associates. I'd also done some war game design, but I've written just about anything you could write. I've written newspaper copy. I've written magazine articles. I've written book reviews. I've written travel reviews. I've written TV and radio advertising, annual reports, informational brochures, and, as I like to say, when I couldn't get honest work I've even done political campaigns.

I think of myself as a storyteller who happens to use the written word as the medium through which I tell the stories. I'd need a really, really, really big campfire to tell the stories to everybody I'd like to tell them to. That is the reason I tell people that I think of myself more as a craftsman than an artist. My art is storytelling; my craft is writing, if that makes sense. Even as a storyteller, I see myself more as a craftsman than an artist. If I was going to weight the scale one way or the other, that's where I'd put the artistry.

I have been told by at least one very well respected writer that the worst thing that can happen to a writer is to allow his fans access—in the sense of inviting them in to discuss with him where the stories are going and so forth. Because then they begin to be influenced by the fans, and if the fans could write, they would write and the work will suffer. That's exactly how he put it to me. "The work will suffer, when that happens."

I told him that was the biggest pile of bullshit I'd ever heard. Because storytelling is an interactive art. Yes, I need to be in control of the story I'm going to tell, but I need to know how the way in which I am telling the story is working with my audience before I can judge how well I am succeeding in what I am trying to do.

You can get some view from dollar sales, and I suppose in this person's case that would be part of it if the reviewers kind of like you or don't like you, but I don't care about reviewers. Now, I like good reviews and don't like bad reviews, don't get me wrong.

What I care more about is the degree to which people are willing to invest themselves in the stories that I am telling them. That is where my emphasis, my objective, is. I feel that I have an obligation to the reader not to be the greatest stylist who ever lived, even though I do have passages that I'm proud of here and there. Not to necessarily come up with the most brilliant plot twists that could possibly exist, but to come up with a story that has in it a world and characters in whom they become invested, about whom they care, that entertains them, that speaks to them in some way. That's what I am supposed to be doing. That's my job.

It is important to me that I am doing my job well. I don't want to do it poorly. Every writer, whether he or she realizes it or not—the instant that person starts to write, they step up onto a soapbox. Books are kind of like protest songs. Good protest songs don't have to make any sense at all. They are there to motivate, to engage the emotions in some way and so forth. They are insidious. You sing the song and that brings you on board with whatever cause that song espouses.

A writer who takes a political view that you might otherwise find objectionable and puts it into the belief structure of a character you find admirable, makes that political concept more available to you. You're saying to yourself, "Maybe there must be something to it because this character who doesn't seem to me to have any jagged inconsistencies shares this belief." Or maybe it's a way of kind of getting inside somebody else's head. I try not to do that. And I try to make it clear to the readers where I am coming from, when my own views are involved.

No writer can write without doing that, whatever his intention. That happens because what you write springs from the basis of who you are. And what you believe and what you think are important human qualities. So you incorporate those important human qualities into the characters that you find admirable or that you find deplorable, and the way that the story works out is to at least some extent bound within that framework. You can occasionally deliberately write counter to it, or whatever, but ultimately, I think the reader will see which of the characteristics you truly think are admirable and which you think are abominable.

I think that for me the satisfaction is having somebody come to me and say, "I would like to meet Honor Harrington. I would like to know Honor Harrington. Boy, I'd like to be Bahzell's friend." Because it means that I've created a person who is real to them, and a person who they too find admirable.

I have to say that the quality of your fans also is a validator as a writer. As is the number of people who have come up to me, and who over the years have become friends, who've joined the Royal Manticoran Navy, which is the official fan club. The quality of the people who have chosen to invest themselves in my novels tells me that I got it right, because, so far, I haven't had any serial murderers among them, but I have found a great many people who I have come to like and respect very much.

I don't like doing things wrong. I don't like to do anything poorly, whatever it is. I will sometimes do things less than perfectly because I'm in a hurry, or they aren't things that I am as invested in, or so I can get this out of the way so I can do something more important. But by and large, if I don't feel that I have done the job right, it eats at me. That's one part of it. The other part of it is that I have an obligation to people who are going to read the books and people who are going to invest themselves in the characters. I have a job to do. I have a responsibility to do the very best job I can in presenting that world and those characters to them. It is a moral, ethical thing, not just, "Oh my God, I feel so good because those people think I'm the greatest storyteller in the world!" It's great if somebody thinks that. There are going to be quite a few people who don't think that. I'm good with that, too. Everybody has a different writing voice that they respond to. They like different kinds of stories. You can't change that.

If someone is going to do me the incredible courtesy and favor of not simply reading my books but actually buying them, helping me put food on the table, put my kids through school, and all the rest of that then I owe them full value, both as a reader who is investing himself in the book and as someone who paid money for the book. If I don't provide that value, if I look at the book afterward and think, I really didn't do my job on this one, then I become very disappointed in myself, and angry at myself for not having lived up to my side of the deal. Storytelling is communicating. Communicating is human interaction. What makes it human interaction is the sense that there is a degree of connectivity, and that connectivity is mutual obligation. The obligation is more on my side than on the reader's side. That's the way that it should be.

I've never had a problem with collaborations. Storytelling is an interactive art. My rule of thumb is that I won't do a collaboration just to increase output. I will do collaboration if there's a story that I want to tell, that I don't have time to tell all by myself, but only if my other criteria for collaboration are met. Those criteria are that the final product is what I can teach or learn in the process. The best writer, the best storyteller in the world can learn something from almost anyone that they work with. The second thing that I am pretty insistent on is that the collaborator will bring something to the project that I don't already have. The third thing is that the final product has to be at least as good as either of us would have done solo. If those criteria are met, then I am perfectly interested in doing collaborations with almost anybody. The problem is that almost anybody probably won't fit all of those criteria for me.

I did two of the YA novels, *Fire Season* and *Treecat Wars*, with Jane Lindskold. I've known Jane for twenty years now. We have been very close friends for a long time. I really like and respect Jane's writing. She has actually done more YAs than I have.

I have very strong views on what constitutes a good YA. I hate, loathe, and despise dystopian YA fiction. It is, to me, a perversion of what YA fiction should be.

If you're talking about an adolescent, barely pre-adolescent, or adolescent, this is the period in someone's life when they are most at sea about who they are and where they fit into the world. Nobody understands me, mom and dad hate me, and everything else. The last thing they need is a literature that is going to confirm to them that all adults are idiots or malevolent, or that there are all these destructive forces waiting out there. It is all very well to say that kids who are in trouble need something that they can identify with and communicate with, but I think the authors are mentally masturbating when they write them. To me this is the writers venting. That's fine. That's what writers do.

There are a few authors out there who write more dystopian fiction that I have enjoyed. Usually somebody, a kid who is in a horrible situation, wins through. But why do we have to emphasize the ugly and the vile? Why do we have to inculcate the child who's thirteen or fourteen with the belief that most of the people in the world will cut your throat as soon as look at you? If that's the view of the author, then the author obviously had an unhappy childhood. If it is not the view of the author, why is the author projecting that for young readers? If you read the YAs that Jane and I did, there are malevolent adults in them. There are stressful social factors.

JW: Isn't that part of YA?

DW: It is, but it is also possible to have competent adults involved. Stephanie Harrington has parents, and these parents are not the uncle keeping Harry under the stairs. These are parents who are involved with their daughter, and they still can't keep their daughter from getting into trouble. She has to deal with it. You can give the protagonist in [a] young adult novel serious challenges to overcome without creating a situation where they are cut adrift from all adult supervision or input. That's what I wanted to do in these YAs. I think it has worked.

I always had strong views, but they got stronger once I had kids of the age where they started reading for themselves.

What brings the reader back is the individual voice that that writer evolves; the way that the writer tells the story rather than trying to figure out how someone else would tell it. When the voice of the storyteller is not up to telling a YA ugly, destructive story in a way that makes the ugliness and destructiveness accessible to the reader without submerging the reader in it, then that dystopian fiction fails. It seems to me that there is more of that out there than some people want to admit.

I write largely military science fiction, and I think that any writer of military fiction has [an] absolute obligation to play fair with the violence and the ugliness of combat. I think that people who don't are guilty of writing a form of "splatter porn." I mean, if you write fiction in which only bad people get killed and if good people get killed they die instantly and cleanly from a single shot when they're hit.

People talk about the United States as a violent society. But the fact is that compared to a great deal of the world, we are not very violent at all, and most American citizens' personal experience with violence is limited. Now there are specific subsets of the population that's not true for. There are specific subsets of the population who live in communities where violence is quite common. But for most people living in the United States, violence is not something they experience every day or every week or every month, and therefore their view of what violence is, is vicarious. It has to be. They can gain that experience through fiction, through reading the newspapers, through going to the movies. There are all kinds of avenues they can take. But one thing we don't need to do is to glamorize it in the sense of ever forgetting that this is ugly and hurtful.

That doesn't mean that we have to say that anybody who engages in it is a brute. It doesn't mean that we have to say that it is not patriotism, that it is not love for their fellow soldiers that drives them. But in the end, if your best friend steps on an IED [improvised expolosive device], it doesn't matter that your hearts were pure and you were really committed to your mission and that you would have died to prevent this from happening to him. It still happened. If he survives, he has to live with the consequences of it and so do you. You have to live with the consequences of it even if he doesn't survive. There's a cost involved, there's pain involved. To my thinking, that's something that has to be made clear in the books. I cannot possibly write anything that will truly show you how terrible combat is, so what I will write is something that will make combat as terrible as I possibly can. I'll come as close as I can. It is my obligation.

What you get frequently is a situation in which the reader actually gets desensitized because they can't escape from the drum roll of violence and bloodshed and, "Oh, God, somebody else just lost an arm."

I think it is more effective to hit the reader occasionally with a scene in which the reader and the characters are brought face to face with the violence. You have to be able to communicate that to the reader: that sense that this is the price you pay when this happens. Sometimes you have got to show them the carnage. You got to show them the guy who aspirates on his own blood because he got hit in the vac suit and nobody can get to him. You have to do that. But you do that in a way that provides what the story needs to keep moving with the focus on the characters and the price they are paying—the price of combat.

JW: How do you want to be remembered?

DW: I want to be remembered as a storyteller who respected his audience, who wanted to give his audience full value, who created characters that people could actually identify with, and care about—even if for some of them it is, "I can't wait for that SOB to get his!" Characters that were real enough for them that they gave a darn about what happened to that character.

To be completely honest, that's not what I really want to be remembered for. What I want to be remembered for is somebody who gave a damn, somebody who loved people—not everybody—and somebody who tried his damnedest to be there for his kids, for his wife, for the people in his life.

There are two things you can want to be remembered for. One is who you are and one is what you are. I am different things to different people. To be remembered and respected as a storyteller, that's important to me. That's being remembered for what I am to them. I would far rather be remembered for who I am to the people who know me than for what I am to the people who don't know me. I think that probably infuses part of the stories I choose to tell and the ways I tell them. It's who I am that helps to determine the stories that I want to tell.

People have asked me what I think the essential characteristic of the Weber hero is. The essential characteristic of a Weber hero or heroine is responsibility—owning your own actions and the consequences of them that's a huge part of it. But another part of it is taking the responsibility when something is broken, something is going wrong, and it enters your orbit. Then instead of saying "It's not my fault," or excusing yourself for something that you did by saying, "Everybody does it. Anybody would have lied to get out of this particular situation." It's not lying. It's saying, "Yeah, I did it, and I will take the responsibility for it." It is saying, "Okay, here's a problem. Somebody is getting hurt, and I can do something about it." I didn't create the situation. It is not my fault, it is not my responsibility for their being in this position, but it is my responsibility as a human being to get them out of it if I can. That's what makes most of the heroes in my books. Some of them are the Honor Harringtons, who are superbly gifted; some of them are not superbly gifted, and some of them die trying. To me, if you know how to put a meal on the table for your kids and you take that responsibility. You see somebody hurt and you try to fix what's wrong. You be there for somebody who's losing someone they love to cancer. That's what heroes do. My characters get an opportunity to do that sometimes on a bigger scale. I can manipulate the situation so that they either succeed or they fail, but the characters are still in there. If they die trying, they die trying. To me, that's the summation. Now I don't necessarily want to be remembered because I died trying. But I do want to be remembered as somebody who was trying. I think I would like [to have] on my tombstone, "He always tried."

First published in Issue 19 of Galaxy's Edge, *March 2016.*

■ ROBERT SILVERBERG

Robert Silverberg has more than a hundred books and close to a thousand short stories published and translated into forty languages. His collaboration with Isaac Asimov, *The Positronic Man,* was made into a movie starring Robin Williams, called *The Bicentennial Man.* He has won four Hugo Awards—the first (of all his awards) for Most Promising New Author (1956)—six Nebula Awards, the Damon Knight Grand Master Award (2003), and three Locus Awards. He was also named to the Science Fiction Hall of Fame in 1999, and a Grand Master by the Science Fiction Writers of America in 2004, of which he is a past president. Silverberg has also been the editor of dozens of science fiction and fantasy anthologies, and is currently a columnist for *Asimov's Science Fiction* magazine. A book of collected conversations on Robert Silverberg's life and career, *Traveler of Worlds: Conversations with Robert Silverberg,* was transcribed and written by friend and collaborator, Alvaro Zinos Amaro. It was nominated for the Hugo Award for Best Related Work in 2016.

■■■■■■

Joy Ward's original introduction: Robert Silverberg is one of the living giants of science fiction. His writing has been in constant print for well over fifty years and has been a defining influence on more writers than we will ever know. No science fiction reader can ever consider him or herself to be well read without at least one of Silverberg's masterpieces under their belt. We were lucky enough to catch up with him at his lovely home in the San Francisco Bay area.

Joy Ward: How did you get started writing?

Robert Silverberg: I started reading science fiction when I was ten or eleven, and by the time I was thirteen I decided I could do this too. This was not actually correct at that point. I did send some stories to magazines and, when they figured out it was a boy sending them and not a demented adult, they sent me very gentle rejection letters. But I continued writing. By the time I was sixteen, seventeen I was getting published. That's how I began writing.

JW: Tell me about the early days of writing. What kind of stories were you writing?

RS: Probably not very good ones. I lived in New York then and I sent the stories, nearly all of which were edited in New York, and they sent them back with encouraging letters. Then they started sending checks. The editors invited me to come down and meet them. I hastened to do that. I think they were surprised to discover I was eighteen or whatever, but I got to know them, became part of the New York science fiction writers group as a kind of mascot, really, and as the editors discovered that I was a very dependable craftsman they began calling me and saying, "Bob, we need a story of 5,500 words by Friday to fill a hole in an issue. Can you do it?" I would say, "Yes," and I did do it.

JW: How did that feel to be with all these literati?

RS: Well, I was accustomed to that because, more or less against my knowledge or will, I got skipped through the early grades very quickly. I could read when I was about four. I didn't spend much time in kindergarten. I zoomed through. Suddenly I was in the fourth grade and I was a year and a half younger than everybody else, and when you're seven and a half and they are nine that's a big difference. So all through my childhood and adolescence I was younger than everyone else. Then I started my career and the same thing was happening, so I assumed this is what life is like.

What is really strange is now I'm practically eighty, and I'm older than just about any functioning science fiction writer. Not that I'm functioning much anymore, but I'm still up and moving around and it's a very odd experience for me after having been so precocious, to be older than everybody that I know.

It's kind of lonely. I've always gone to the science fiction convention every year, Worldcon, and I formed friendships with writers who were fifteen or twenty years older than I was. People like Frederik Pohl and Lester Del Rey and L. Sprague De Camp and Gordon Dickson and on and on and on. Because they were fifteen or twenty years older and I am now eighty, they are all dead. There's one writer left, James Gunn, who is ninety-one, of all the writers that I knew from those early conventions. So I've had to form a new set of friends among young people like George Martin and Connie Willis and Joe Haldeman, who are only sixty-five or seventy or so.

It's been a conscious act on my part to form new friendships, because otherwise I would be all alone. [I would be] that guy with the white beard standing in the middle of the convention hall saying, "Where did everybody go?"

Science fiction writers are a very collegial group. Before science fiction was big business it was a downtrodden minority. It was a funny little pulp-fiction field—[with] gaudy looking magazines with names like *Amazing Stories, Astounding Science Fiction,* and we were considered pretty weird. So we banded together, a league against the world. Of course that all changed, changed almost frighteningly, and science fiction became such big business that it's impossible now to keep up with the whole field, to understand what's going on. When I go out into what I laughingly call the "real world," I hear people talk about aliens and alternative universes. All of those esoteric things that were our private property are now in everybody's vocabulary because you can't go to the movies without seeing five trailers for what they call the new sci-fi movies. I hate that sci-fi word.

So science fiction writers tend to choose other science fiction writers as their friends. Not exclusively. Also, I have no family to speak of. I have a wife and a brother-in-law and sister-in-law. That's about it. I have no ancestors left. I have outlived them, all and I never had children. So the science fiction writers are sort of surrogate family for me. That's why when I go to the convention I don't want to stand there and say, "Where did everybody go?" It's an unpleasant feeling. But I don't. I've known a young whippersnapper like George Martin, I've known him for thirty-five years or so. This is not a recent friendship.

The big high point of my career, not a very difficult one to understand, was 2004 when the science fiction writers gave me the Grand Master trophy. What was special for me about that, [was that] I had been a member of SFWA since it was founded. I was there when the Grand Master award was invented and given to Heinlein and to Jack Williamson and to Clifford Simak and to Sprague De Camp—and these people I'm naming are all writers I read and admired and idolized when I was twelve, thirteen, fourteen years old. Suddenly in 2004 I'm getting the same award they got, which told me that I have achieved something in my career. I have found a place for myself among them. I never really—I don't see myself as being among them. I'm just that kid that managed to get a lot of stories published back there in 1956. But from the outside I know it looks different.

It feels wonderful because I was a reader, a fan, and came to conventions when I was fifteen, sixteen and looked at these demigods and grew up to be a demigod myself. I can only feel that I did it the right way. That's a good feeling. You don't want to know that you have wasted your life or you bungled your ambition. I haven't. I remember at a convention about twenty-five years ago I was standing in the lobby of the hotel talking to Isaac Asimov and Arthur Clarke, both of whom I had known for many years and I regard as friends. But the teenage boy within me could not help thinking, "You're talking to Asimov and Clarke." Then I heard somebody about twenty feet away say, "Look. There's Asimov, Clarke and Silverberg." It put everything in perspective when you see it from the outside like that.

To them, standing over there, that was a group of big-name writers. To me, time traveled back to 1953. I'm a kid who myste-

203

riously finds himself talking to these titans of the field. A lot of double vision was involved.

I've done a lot of writing that isn't science fiction. I wrote a number of books about geography and geology and scientific subjects. I wrote a few Western stories. I wrote some detective stories, even though I wasn't very good at that. Mostly what I thought (when I did this) is this is what I do when I'm not writing science fiction. A lot of hardened science fiction writers have felt that way, that it's not really sensible or justifiable. I remember James Blish, a writer who I revered who has been dead a long time now, Jim was a great science fiction writer, but to pay the rent he wrote for sports pubs and Westerns, which was funny because I don't know Jim knew which end of the baseball bat to swing and as for Westerns, he was a New Yorker through and through. But still that's what he did. and he always regarded the other stuff as something you did when you didn't have a science fiction idea, but your main business was writing science fiction. On some level, I think that too.

JW: Is there anything you would have done other than write science fiction?

RS: Well, when I was in high school when people would ask me "What are you going to do when you grow up?" I couldn't say, "I want to be a science fiction writer," because that's like saying, "I'm a lunatic." You didn't say that back there in the 1940s. So I said, "I think I'm good at writing," and they translated that into journalism. It was assumed that I'd become a journalist. And indeed, I was the editor of my high school paper and I was a fairly important figure on the college paper, but I knew what I was going to do. Then midway through my college years I began doing it, and I've been doing it ever since. So I guess this was what I was meant to do, and I'm glad that I did it pretty well. How sad to have spent the last sixty years writing bad science fiction.

JW: Is there anything you haven't written that you want to write about?

RS: Not at this point. I've written everything, and I don't feel any hunger to tell some story that's untold. Not after all this time. My bibliography is the size of the phone book. I don't mean the Podunk phone book; I mean the Manhattan phone book. So I'm really done so far as conquering new worlds goes. I'm very far from young. I don't have the energy I once did, and I don't have anything left to prove. What I am happy about is keeping everything I wrote in print and seeing the stories of yesteryear printed in places like *Galaxy's Edge* or in anthologies, and of course there is the wonderful world of electronic publishing. I confess I don't own a Kindle or any such gizmo myself, but I've taken great pains to see to it that the people who do can find my work very easily and I'm all over the electronic world. So I'm still here; I'm just not writing anymore or feeling the need to do so.

It says that I'm still alive. I still go to conventions. I still go meet editors. I make deals. I have a real agent, a very good agent, but I make the connections. Roger Zelazny, dear man, has been dead for twenty years and James Blish almost forty years. It's very hard to keep your career going when you're just a ghost. You need a passionate agent or a very capable widow, and widows get old too. So that's the easy part of the answer that yes, I'm still here and still doing deals for myself. It also says to me the stuff is probably pretty good. I think it was. I gave my best effort but it's nice to have the confirmation coming back in the form of new editions, Grand Master awards. There's nobody so sure of himself he doesn't mind validation.

JW: *As you look forward, what do you want people to say about you in the future?*

RS: I hope they will still be reading me. I hope they will still be reading anything. I don't give much thought to what people will say a hundred years from now. I can barely understand what they are saying right now. The language has changed so much in my lifetime, the mental attitudes, the political attitudes. Occasionally I wander through the internet to see what people are saying, or it comes to me. I don't go looking for it. Some of the comments, other than the praise, are incomprehensible to me. I assume that a hundred years from now nothing would be comprehensible to me if I was reading it, but I won't be reading it.

I've already seen the world morph beyond recognition in my lifetime. I began writing professionally, I guess, in 1954. That's sixty years. I'm living the science fiction world that I wrote about and then some.

These little machines that everybody holds in his hands and keeps his nose in, well, there were computers, or what we used to call thinking machines, back there in the '50s and it took a whole gigantic room the size of this and they had punch cards and things like that. Now everybody has one in his hand and has a million times the computing power of those giant IBM mainframes of the '50s. So I'm living in what for me is a very weird futuristic world.

I can't keep up with it. I don't even try. I don't have a smart phone. My need for one is small. I do have a computer, in fact, several of them. I do know how to drive. A few of my late colleagues couldn't drive. Ray Bradbury, for example, a man who had a vision of the future that was splendid, but in the present he needed somebody to drive him around. Well, I can drive. What I feel now looking out at the world of people with telephones in their hands and the strange clothing that they wear and the strange apparel of the body, the people of the shaven heads and the unshaven cheeks, I realize I've lived on into a different time. I'm not a man of this era and I take that very calmly most of the time. When I go to restaurants—I go to restaurants a lot—I wish things were not so noisy. But it's a different culture.

Remember I am a science fiction writer. I spent my life writing about people who traveled in time and found themselves embedded in some strange era that they could barely comprehend and learning the ropes as they were dumped down in the far future of, say, 1979 back in a story written in 1955. So I expect change. I'm not astounded that the world has changed out of recognition all around me. I'd be pretty upset if it hadn't. The fact that I'm now old and no longer living in the world that is familiar to me seems quite normal to me. I don't object to it and fortunately I don't have to get out there and deal with it very much. I'm not looking for jobs. I'm not worried about my privacy issues. I don't live the life of an active forty-year-old. I would be surprised if I did.

JW: What advice would you give to someone trying to get into science fiction?

RS: I don't know how you go about starting a career today, but I edited a book called *Science Fiction: 101*, which has thirteen of my favorite stories—thirteen stories I admired enormously when

I was learning my craft, and I accompanied the stories with essays explaining why I admired them, what was there to admire. So it was a kind of tutorial anthology. One day I was up at the offices of *Locus* and a member of the *Locus* staff then, this was fifteen, twenty years ago, told me she wanted to be a science fiction writer, and asked how I think she should get started. I said, "Take a look at *Science Fiction 101* and read Alfred Bester's 'Fondly Fahrenheit' and Cordwainer Smith's 'Scanners Live in Vain' and write a story just as good. That will start your career." She looked at me stunned and she began to laugh. It's a huge field, gigantic. Several thousand books get published every year, and when I was beginning my career ten or twenty books were published. There were six or seven science fiction magazines when I began writing. Now if you include all the online ones and desktop ones there are dozens. I don't know how many. Of course, there are an infinite number of would-be writers. So you have a vastly expanded market and vastly expanded ambition. When I was beginning back in the '50s, the number of new writers could be counted on one hand. Now I don't even know them. I went to the Worldcon in London and I went to a party given by the science fiction writers association, and there were two hundred people in the room of which I knew about four. They knew who I was, but I didn't know who they were. That's a little distressing because I used to know everybody. It was just a little gang of thirty or forty and I knew everybody. Now I'm in a group of my colleagues and I have to say to Joe Haldeman, "I don't know anybody."

JW: Do you appreciate when writers introduce themselves or do you prefer to keep a distance?

RS: Oh no. I don't want to keep a distance. I want to get to know them. I'd like them to be relaxed with me. I've had people practically have a convulsive fit upon meeting me, and that's not a good experience for me and it certainly wasn't for them. Trembling and, "I can't believe I'm talking to you." Look, I was a kid once and came up to X, Y, or Z and felt the same way.

A lot of contemporary science fiction...I don't read it. I find a lot of it uninteresting. I find a lot of it baffling. A lot of it is written in the debased modern version of English and style is important to me.

207

It sets my teeth on edge to come upon some of the mannerisms that are now accepted, and so instead of going "harrumph" and bang my cane around, I just don't read it. That, incidentally, is a metaphorical cane. I can still walk!

Lester Del Rey, who had a kind of "Dutch uncle" relationship with me, always told me what I was doing wrong, but in a loving way. Lester used to throw books across the room, and when I would ask him, "Have you read such and such?" he'd say, "I read about ten pages and threw it across the room." I wouldn't do that. I'm not a violent man. I don't read contemporary science fiction.

I always come back from the Worldcon interested in reading the latest thing, and I buy it and I don't read it.

JW: Where do you see science fiction going in the future?

RS: I think science fiction will continue to be published, written. Science fiction I regard as a branch of fantasy, of fiction that allows for the free play of the imagination and fantasy has been written for thousands of years. So why would it stop?

First published in Issue 24 of Galaxy's Edge, *January 2017.*

▌ TONI WEISSKOPF

oni Weisskopf succeeded Jim Baen as publisher of Baen Books, in 2006. She has worked with David Weber, David Drake, Lois McMaster Bujold, Eric Flint, Wen Spencer, Mercedes Lackey, Larry Correia, and many others. Baen is also known for its innovative e-publishing program, founded in 1999, which has expanded under Weisskopf's leadership to include not only titles published by Baen, but also titles from other publishers, all without DRM. Other new programs under Weisskopf include the Jim Baen Memorial Short Story Award (co-sponsored with the National Space Society); the Baen Fantasy Adventure Award, awarded at Gen Con; and the Baen Best Military SF & Adventure SF Reader's Choice Award, presented at Dragoncon. With Josepha Sherman, she compiled and annotated the definitive volume of subversive children's folklore, *Greasy Grimy Gopher Guts*, published by August House. Also holding a degree in anthropology, Weisskoph is the widow of Southern fan and sword-master Hank Reinhardt and the mother of a delightful daughter.

▌▌▌▌▌▌

Joy Ward's original introduction: Toni Weisskopf is Baen's publisher and editor. She has been involved with science fiction fandom since the ancient age of fourteen and been nominated for a Hugo for editing. She has worked with some of the most influential lights in science fiction and is one of the most knowledgeable people on where science fiction publishing is heading. She was recently awarded the 2017 Kate Wilhelm Solstice Award. Congratulations Toni!

Toni Weisskopf: I went to my first science fiction convention when I was fourteen. I've had thirty-six years going to conventions. My first technical fan-ish activity was a letter to the editor that was published in *Asimov's* in 1978. So I've been around science fiction and science fiction fandom for some time.

I knew it was something I wanted to be part of. I was aware that there was not just this really cool genre, but I knew there were mysteries and romances and science fiction and westerns. I read all of these. I had started reading the memoirs of the people in science fiction. Before I went to that first convention I had read Fred Pohl's memoir. I had read collections from the first world fantasy conventions and read the introductions David Drake and guys like that had done. I had read some of the collections of the Hugo award-winning stories with an introduction by Asimov. All of these things referred back to this science fiction fandom, so I knew it existed, I knew some of the history. I had read a good bit of the literature and knew that I liked it. Yeah, I did want to be part of it and that's why I reached out and wanted to be heard. Science fiction, to its credit, heard me. George Scithers was the founding editor of *Asimov's* and when he got a letter from a teenager he published it, because he wanted to encourage young people in science fiction fandom. It worked!

In middle school, I wrote to all of the editors I could find addresses to ask them for help on a research paper on Robert Heinlein. And they answered me. All of them did! Ben Bova answered me and Stan Schmidt answered me. They all had suggestions for me, for my research paper on Robert Heinlein. This was before there were more than one or two books of any kind of scholarly attention paid to Heinlein so it was incredibly helpful. Then later I got to meet them all professionally.

It's a sign of the intellectual openness of science fiction that they are willing to engage with anybody who is interested, and I really like that. There is no judgment based on age, sex, or physical configuration of any kind. It's are you interested in science fiction? Yes, I am. Me too, let's talk. I like that kind of level playing field, and it means you can prove yourself. If you can prove yourself interesting, you can play on the field. The only criteria [is] being interesting.

I like fairness. I always have. I guess it's the border collie in me.

You see your name in print. I got a little one-line response in the magazine. It was kind of a thrill to see my name in the magazine, the same place as Asimov's and all these really good authors and it was the sense of being part of this ongoing discussion. I keep using that phrase but that's what it is. I enjoyed that and always have.

I got involved in science fiction fandom, and any good fanzine editor is always looking for volunteers. People are looking for letters of comment on works that they've done, for input. You write letters of comment to fanzines—people give you their fanzines and just like people write comments on blogs these days, I got involved doing that. When I went to college I started publishing a little fanzine with the college club there. Started doing reviews of books. Essays and articles. I got drawn into it. Writing for other people than writing for my fanzine.

I was going to science fiction conventions and I realized about halfway through college that being a professional editor is what I wanted to do, work in the field in some capacity. Following in the footsteps of Fred Pohl, John Campbell and all those guys. So I started preparing my résumé, picking courses and things like that. My senior year I went to conventions with résumé in hand. I met David Hartwell and talked with him at a convention, went to the Tor party at a Balticon and ran into editors there and was handing out résumés by the hot tub. By the time I graduated there was an awareness that there was a young fan interested in an entry-level job in New York, and if anybody knew anything I would hear about it. And I did!

JW: What is it about science fiction that makes you want to be part of the discussion?

TW: Part of the thrill is being able to take on big questions. With mysteries and mainstreams and Westerns and all that kind of stuff you can take on big questions but that's the job of science fiction. All science fiction takes on big ideas and that's exciting! I like that kind of intellectual exercise. I think it's important. I think it's important work publishing science fiction, writing science fiction, fantasy as well. So, you get the feeling that you are doing something worthwhile. All of these things go into it.

I think the difference between science fiction and another literary genre is that it is more collaborative. Science fiction by its very nature encourages cross-pollination of ideas. It's writers and editors and artists and readers and scientists and engineers and technologists and voice actors and all these people working together to create art and that's a lovely thing to be part of.

I guess it's being part of something.

With science fiction, part of the fun of it is playing around and changing the ideas. If you are writing a mystery and you come up with a really cool way of poisoning somebody and doing a lot for the mystery you are not sharing that. You want the credit for having this cool idea. But in science fiction if you come up with a really cool way of new launch technology or a new way to get energy from the Sun or something, you're going to write your story and you want the credit for the cool idea. But then if other people use this and expand upon it and then toss the ball back to you, it just becomes that much more fun. I guess it's like being in a crowd at a rock concert tossing a beach ball around. It's fun! You want somebody to play with! It's that kind of intellectual beach-ball game.

I like being part of science fiction. I like contributing to it. I like working with creative people. I like working with intelligent people. That's a luxury that a lot of intelligent people don't get. I'm aware everyday how pleasant that can be. The level of communication you can get with your colleagues and your peers is pleasant.

Go back to a formative experience between my freshman and sophomore years in college. I came home and was expected to get a job and worked in a Huddle House doing waitressing third shift— ten p.m. to six a.m. Our rush was at two a.m. when the bars closed. You saw a nice slice of life on that shift. I realized what real work was. I realized how lucky I was to go to college and how lucky I was after I left college to be able to work in a field that I loved in a nice air-conditioned office. Yes, with mice, but so I knew how lucky I was to be able to do the kind of work that I enjoyed.

I like a feeling of accomplishment. As an editor, you are taking joy in other people's accomplishments. You're satisfied when other people do well, when a book you've published wins an award, or when a piece of art that you bought as an illustration gets recognition or is sold to some collector for $10,000. So, it's a joy that you take in the triumph of others. In some ways, it is a more selfless joy. I don't think that makes me morally better than others.

JW: How do you see science fiction changing?

TW: We live in interesting times. The biggest change is the rise in the ease of self-publishing. Self-publishing has been available since printing presses were available. The idea that the author can just take their work and present it to the public is absolutely nothing new. Publishing houses rose to the form that they have because these are services that authors need and value and it is worth something to authors to have others do these things for them. The marketing, the accounting, the sales, all this kind of stuff. The art direction, the text setting, the copy editing. All the many, many things publishers do; they take this job away from the writer so the writer can write. It's not an accident why publishing houses have taken the form that they have. We have had printing presses since Gutenberg. It's a maturer form. So, the fact of self-publishing is not new. The ease of self-publishing is. That is the difference, but the fact of all the functions of self-publishing has not changed. The fact that you can make your work theoretically available to a large audience is true. Finding that audience isn't the problem. The balance between the people who want to do everything themselves, and who have the talent to do everything themselves, and those who don't want to do everything themselves, that is sort of what we are seeing shake out now. Who's going to do this? Who's going to thrive? Who's going to succeed and who's not? You are seeing that play out now.

JW: You're an editor but you are also a reader. Which books have really affected you?

TW: Heinlein, obviously, first and foremost. I'm reading Patterson's biography of Heinlein right now that Tor has published. Even very early in his career he started being the science fiction writer who brought the science fiction genre to a broader audience. He wasn't just the science fiction writer for the small science fiction audience. It shows in his enduring popularity. He took on the big ideas. He took on lots of big ideas. He played with them and he moved them around. His independence changed and how he presented them changed. It's fun. He writes fun stories. The kind of fun I like having. So, Heinlein first and foremost.

I don't think he was the writer who went beyond the genre. He was the writer who explained the genre. He always wrote science fiction and fantasy. There wasn't a question that what he was writing was very clearly rooted in our genre. He just made it accessible to people who weren't familiar with our tropes. It was a large part of why these tropes are now familiar to everyone, everywhere, all over. The advertisement I point out to people now is for mortgages. Mortgages are boring but rockets are cool. Rocket mortgages. Rockets were not cool! Rockets were not cool in the thirties! They were dangerous in the thirties and they were kind of dorky in the fifties. They are cool now but that's because of people like Heinlein and Asimov and Bradbury and Clarke and McCaffrey because of what they did. And *Star Trek* and *Star Wars* and *Lost in Space* and all these things that put our tropes and the way we approach the future and the universe out there to the general public.

One of the things that science fiction is supposed to do is to accustom people to the truth that there will always be change, right? We would like to think that the way things are right here and right now are the way they always have been and always will be. But this is not true. It is one of the central things that science fiction does. It helps the brain become more limber and accept this truth, to run these thought experiments. So, there are all kinds of pleasant and unpleasant things that science fiction can help us deal with. Nanotechnologies and biomechanics and asteroid mining and changes in governments and all kinds of atmospheres and all of the things that are changing in our world, science fiction engages with.

JW: What would you tell a young woman who wants to become an editor?

TW: Read the classics. Try to become familiar with the history of your field. I've always liked history, but I see a lot of resistance in the younger generation or maybe it's just not an awareness history is out there and available to them. See why things are the way they are and where they came from. One of the points I wanted to bring up is we're publishing a book called *Women of Futures Past.* [It came out in September, 2016.] It's an anthology of really good science fiction stories from the beginnings of science fiction, the pulps and present day, people who are still alive and still writing. Authors who happen to be women. There's an idea with the younger people that women need a hand up, that women have not been part of science fiction and it's simply not true. It does a disservice to the people in science fiction who were open to all those who contributed. It's erasing these women from history. Kris Rusch and I, who edited the anthology, really wanted to make sure that there is an understanding that these women were here, they were present, they contributed, and we have always been part of science fiction—an important part. Not a women's auxiliary but just part.

I think that it's in us to make it available to them, to let them know this is here. Obviously, science fiction is about engaging the new. I'm not saying you ignore the new for the old but to appreciate just where you've come from. If we don't make collections like this available then how are they supposed to know? If we don't say, "Hey, look, by the way, this is here!" How are they to know? So, I think that's on us.

JW: How do you want to be remembered?

TW: My reward is I get to do my job. An editor wears a lot of different hats. There's two sides of the editor coin. On the one side is the author-service side. That's helping the author make the book that the author has chosen to write be the best possible version of that book. Sometimes that involves saying this is lovely and write a check. That in some ways is the hardest because you don't get to dink with it. You don't get to put your stamp on it. You say, "Wow, that was great!" Sometimes that involves talking with an author at an initial stage about an idea, bouncing an idea back and forth. Sometimes it involves being more hands on, phrasing for a line, a felicitous line, or any of that kind of stuff. So that's working with the author.

The other side of the coin is protecting the reader from bad things; from trying to put out the authors and stories that will be the most interesting. I see both of these as being equally important, both reader protection and working with authors.

I would think I would like to be acknowledged that I continued Jim Baen's legacy. Jim certainly had a tremendous impact on the field and I would like that people to consider that I did not do damage to his legacy.

I think he was doing important work. He was publishing important books. He was providing a different voice in the chorus that is science fiction so that we don't have a monotone. So I'd like to think that his efforts were not in vain.

First published in Issue 27 of Galaxy's Edge, *July 2017.*

■ LOIS McMASTER BUJOLD ▬▬▬

Lois McMaster Bujold is one of the leading writers in the science fiction and fantasy field, with about seventy titles in print. She started, as an English major in college, but her heart was more into the creative aspect of writing rather than the critical side of reviewing. After college, she started a family and worked for a brief time as a pharmacy technician at Ohio State University. Writing a novelette for practice, she completed her first novel, *Shards of Honor*, in 1983 with help and encouragement from Lillian and Patricia C. Wrede. In 1985 Baen bought her first three completed novels. In the meantime, she had started writing shorts, the first of which sold to the *The Twilight Zone Magazine*, which was her first professional sale. Then *Analog* serialized her fourth novel, *Falling Free*, in the winter of '87-'88 and it went on to win her first Nebula. Since then she has won six Hugo Awards and in 2017 she won the special Hugo Award for Best Series, for her iconic Vorkosigan Saga. She has also won three Nebula Awards, three Locus Awards, and other, accolades.

■■■■■■

Joy Ward's original introduction: Lois McMaster Bujold has won Hugos, Nebulas, Locus awards, and the John Campbell Award. In short, this leading light of science fiction and fantasy has won more awards for taking us to her worlds than almost any other writer in the genres.

Joy Ward: Tell me about your first sale.

Lois McMaster Bujold: I wrote *Shards* in 1983, *Warrior's Apprentice* in 1984, and *Ethan of Athos* in 1985. Then they all sold at the end of 1985 to Baen Books, and that was actually my second sale. The first one had been a short story to *The Twilight Zone Magazine* the prior year.

I'd started on *The Warrior's Apprentice,* and I hit a snag. Get something on your résumé by selling short stories, and then maybe they'll pay attention to your novel. There's all kinds of writerly cargo-cult beliefs about how to sell your first novel or any novel. Some of which are true, most of which are not. But the idea was that you would learn how to write by writing short stories, and then write a novel. Which is wrong because they're two different modes, and you can be good at one and bad at the other. I've known many people where their first sale was the novel. Pat Wrede was one of them.

But it was the little short story called "Barter." It was this little thing about a housewife. Housewife meets an alien, triumphs. Popped that off. I'd done three or four short stories at that time, all of which are currently in reprint as a little e-collection called *Protozoa* at the moment. You can still see these antique little things. I was sending them off and getting rejections. I finally got a hit after five tries. That story. It came as a little teeny postcard in the mail, [and I] had to fish it out of the bottom of my mailbox. I was like, "What? They bought it!" I was very excited.

So that was validation. It said, "Okay, you're on the right track. You can do this." This was a little bit of a reward. On that kind of energy I went and wrote the third novel. We'd been going three years without a paycheck. It was pretty discouraging. So that was the thing that I needed and it gave me something to say in the cover letters, besides, "Here is my story. I've never sold anything." Or, "Here's my story. I've sold to this editor over here." You know. Editors have the herd instinct. They stay together and not be caught out from other editors.

Whatever I wrote had to be something I had internalized. It had to be something I really liked. Which was science fiction, mystery, and remember I was a latecomer to romance so romance wasn't really on my radar. Might've been mystery. I might've gone toward mystery. But I had been reading science fiction since I was nine. It was something that I felt like I knew. Kind of what the markets were.

I was so blown away. I was a little cautious because I didn't know Baen Books from anything. They were brand-new at that point. I wasn't sure whether I should try to get an agent. There was some confusion about that for a while. I didn't know that I could negotiate contracts. I didn't know how. I did not have an agent. So I was very much at sea. Do it now, fix it later. But I sat on the news for a while because I kept waiting for it to evaporate. It's like something was going to happen and it wasn't going to be broken off.

It says, I can write another book. Yes! I can do this. Which turned out to be *Falling Free*. It was interesting. It was the first time I had an editor on the line that I could talk to about, "What do you want to buy? And, I've got this idea and I've got that idea." So *Falling Free* actually came out of a conversation with Jim Baen as I was looking at the material I had and I said, "Maybe I could do something with Arty Mayhew," and it kind of fell flat. I had come up with the idea for the quaddies, this race of free-fall dwellers that Arty would go visit and were on his quest for a headset, or for a ship to go with his neurological headset. But we got to talking about the free-fall dwellers, and that led me back to thinking about the Quaddies, and then thinking about them more, developing their backstory, and then going back. I said, okay, where does this story start? That brought me back to *Falling Free*, to the start of *Falling Free*, which was the beginning of this bio-engineered race in this future history that I was setting up to be. Not aliens, but in process of bio-engineering humanity, such that humanity would speciate from about this period going forward, so that ten thousand years down the timeline, all the aliens would be us. From us. There'd be all kinds of races all over the place that were purposely or accidentally consequential to this, to this period where it was just getting started. So the Quaddies are kind of like the first entry in that idea of human speciation. It's a very biologically-centered future history.

I was thinking mostly of Cordwainer Smith's *Tales of the Instrumentality*. He was this great writer from the '50s, '60s, and, I'm not sure he quite made it to the '70s. But he wrote these amazing stories that never explained anything. But you gradually picked up that, that it was this kind of a world where all these people eventually went back to Earth in their family tree and had all kinds of races.

JW: What have you learned as a writer?

LMB: Arguing with reviewers. You can't argue with someone's reading experience. It was what it was. You can't reach in there and fine-tune and change it to have been a better reading experience by arguing with them. So that's pointless.

There's a lot of talk that circles around every human subject, writing included, that is basically jockeying for social status. Fear of losing social status—that's a big driver. Every flame war has got that underneath it. Somebody is convinced that they're having this status emergency and they must defend themselves. It isn't actually an emergency, just something on your mind. Falling into that trap of taking it too personally. Taking it as a personal attack is one to avoid. So that "I must be professional," is a very good bulwark against that temptation. Even back in the old days, the first rule of writing, and the old pros would tell you is, "Don't respond to critical reviews." You can say thank you if somebody said something nice; otherwise, let it go. That is still absolutely true.

The being an author stuff, and then there's the actual writing and people reading it. So those are two different compartments of things that can happen. I divide them by calling [them] author and writer.

The author stuff is everything that people see you do that makes you think, "I'm gonna be an author." And the writing is the actual writing and the reading and the genuine reader feedback. On the author side, the travel has been amazing. I don't want to do it anymore because I'm getting older and my back doesn't take it. But certainly the convention travel, the international travel [of] getting to go, eventually, all over the world, taught me an enormous amount of things. So that was, that was a high point. Trips to England. Trips to Europe. I've been to Croatia. I've been to Australia. New Zealand. Not sure if Canada counts. A lot of places I would never have thought to go on my own.

To a great extent, certainly Americans and other Westerners, their identity is based on their work. You can have identity based on your family and relationships. You can have identity based on your possessions. You know, I have all this stuff, I must be okay. There's identity based on your interests. Fans, for example. Identity out of that. Hobbies. So identity comes from all kinds of sources. The writing kind of rolls along all those sources together. It's something that people are impressed by.

You get that external validation. "She's the writer. Is she all right?" It makes you interesting. So that's a psychological boost. If you're lucky it gives you an income. And income is another thing that identity is judged by and created by. Gives you the empowerment to do things. Like eat. Survive. Travel. Whatever. Send your kids to college. All those items. So that's kind of on the input side.

Then on the writer's side, [it's] when people read the stuff and feed back to you their experience. A writer is kind of like a deaf composer. You never get to actually find out what art you've made because it's taking place inside somebody else's head. But make a comment. A review. Fan fiction is a kind of response. And you get to kind of see, "What is it that I did?" Every once in a while, someone will write you and say a book "has helped in his struggle with leukemia. He so enjoyed your books." "Thank you, I was in the ICU for three months with my premature baby, and I reread *Barrayar* and it helped me process this." Thank you for this or that experience that people use books to get through.

It always makes me think about the books that helped me do this. So it becomes a paying forward. I've received this from books, now I'm paying it back with books. There's that sense of balance. It's balancing, so to speak. It makes it worth having done. It's a side effect. It's not something I control. Books go out and beyond that I have no notion of where they'll land.

I'm very grateful I haven't heard from anybody giving me the opposite. "Your books made me run out and do evil things." No. Haven't heard of that. So, let's avoid that and have more of the helping people. So claiming the one as a consequence of my books means claiming the other. The potential downside and I don't think I really want to do either one. The books are out there, and this is what people make of them and that's their responsibility. But it's cool that my books were the occasion that they found for help. It makes what otherwise would seem a tenuous and sullied way to make a living seem more valid. It's a validation, I guess. I mean, I make and sell daydreams. How fuzzy is that as a way to make a living?

JW: If you weren't making and selling daydreams what would you be doing?

LMB: I have no idea. Some job, I suppose.

JW: No backup plan?

LMB: I had no backup plan. This was part of the reason that I really worked on this. I was working without a net. These days I could probably get an editing job. Because I know enough now, I could edit. Or do some other writing/publishing peripheral tasks, which I could learn.

JW: Has there been a time when you've thought about stopping the daydreams? Just leaving and saying, I'm out the door.

LMB: I don't know how you turn off your brain. The brain has always worked like this. Sometimes there are slack periods. When I was heading into my sixties and thinking about what retirement means for me as a writer, because I'm self-employed. It so doesn't fit, a standard plan of that life period that they set out for people in the financial planning stuff, for example. It's like, okay, do I stop? I could stop. I don't have to do this for a living anymore. I could do something else. I could do nothing else. I kind of went through a little period there, I was kind of backing off and trying to think, what do I do now that I can do anything? Or nothing. So I did nothing for a little while. I got bored with that. I finally decided that I was going to re-create my writing career as my hobby and do just the parts I liked and skip the parts I didn't like. Sort of like a smorgasbord of all my favorite desserts.

So it turns out to be, I like the writing. I like the self-publishing. And no more book tours. No more of the high-stress things. No more conventions. So, getting rid of the PR tasks. Which, this is one, but

I somehow wasn't able to exclude you guys. Saying no to nice people who like me is really hard to learn how to do. Particularly when they're also the people who send me money. But they would eat you, if you let them. 'Cause if I had convention invitations every other week I'd be flying out of here all the time, and I would never write anything because I would be fried.

I, delightfully, do not know where I am going. I basically freed myself from all prior constraints. I can add some of them back in if I want. But I don't have to. What I have been doing for the last two years, actually, is working on a novella series, which are self-published e-books. As original fiction, not as reprints. Most of my things that we've been talking about here have been reprints of previously published books, professionally published books. That's been fun. That's been doing fine financially, and I've liked being able to do a length other than a novel. The main publishing market is really geared up for novels, and preferably fat novels. There are reasons for this. I think it's kind of the publishing equivalent of those restaurants where they heap the plate with food so they can charge you enough so they can cover all their other costs. The food is the least of it. If they give you a big fat book they can put that $27 price tag on it and you'll hold still for it.

JW: What is it about science fiction? 'Cause it always comes back to science fiction and fantasy as a writer?

LMB: There's a jockeying for position thing [between the two]: "Oh, we must be on the important side! Science fiction must be more important than fantasy." "No, fantasy sells better. We're more important than you." Stop worrying about your importance and just read the damn books.

It's an ego flame war. Ego-driven flame war. How many more of these do we need? There's enough. There's a whole internet full of them. If it floats your boat, go for it. But do it over there. But I understand that when it is fear-driven if I do not, if my book is dissed. If I get a bad review my career is going to sink. Nobody's going to read my stuff. The world is ending. Writers can really wrap themselves around the axle with this kind of negative thinking. I have done it. Some people get into that. Somebody challenges my worldview or what I think, and I must fight back because otherwise, what? That's kind of noise.

JW: What is it about science fiction/fantasy that keeps bringing you back?

LMB: I really am not sure I can say. It's so embedded, ingrained in me by this time. Part of my identity, I guess. Speaking of identity: that it's just the normal way I think about things or the usual way I think about things. I don't know how you can live in the twenty-first century and not have some of that mindset. You're going to have to ask the kids, who don't remember a time when there wasn't an internet, how they're processing the world. I bet it's different. It's just more interesting. It asks more interesting questions. It does more interesting things. It gives better escape hatches, if you want to get out of the world today and be somewhere else for a little while. I think escape literature is under-rated. Whenever it's that *du jour* in certain reviews, and the critique side tends to revolve around political issues, people will seize on this or that particular book because it validates their political agenda. The book is not a piece of art in itself. It is material to prop up whatever theory is being promulgated by whichever critic has gotten off onto it. It's fine for them. That's not what I'm doing: this discussion with historical fiction versus the kind of fantasy that uses historical materials for its world-building. I'm not writing a PhD thesis and I am not writing historical fiction with the serial numbers filed off. What I am writing when I do alternate worlds, pre-industrial fantasy worlds, is it's like found art. I'm taking history and using it the way someone uses old electronic parts to sculpture a horse. It's got nothing to do with, or very little to do with, the history. I'm not out to critique history or say things about history or say things about the present through history. I'm making this horse out of this interesting material. Isn't it cool? Found art.

It's a lot more elbow room. I'm not constrained. I'm less constrained by what actually took place. Most of which is always hideously depressing. I can make it less depressing. There's that.

What I want is to put out stories. It's not this other stuff. It's like, "No, I don't want to say anything. I want you to read the story. Here. But don't let me distract you."

JW: You write about identity, and the search for identity, and becoming.

LMB: A lot of the current heated political arguments are in the arena of group identity. Identify with this group. This group becomes you.

Now the group parasitizes you for its needs. There's a lot of interesting opportunities and dangers over on that side. Personal identity partakes of group identity but is not the same thing. It travels independently. It's biologically routed. Biology is universal. So whenever I'm looking at these questions, I sort of like to push away all the accidents and look for the essence, which is underneath. It's biological. What are our biological drivers? It's like the difference between hunger and cuisine. Everybody experiences hunger. Cuisine is the way we satisfy it, and there's a thousand different ways to do it. Identity is like that; everybody has these needs. We need status. We need connections. We need family, perhaps. We most certainly need parents. This isn't negotiable. We need mentors. We need all kinds of things. But there's a lot of different ways to satisfy those needs. But the needs are universal. So I want to look at those universal things to sort of work down from there to the particularities. Rather than being distracted by the group identity-politics, which is all about politics, which is all about status struggles, ultimately.

Status should not be trivialized as a term. I use it because it's the most generic, the most under-rooted thing that has no particularities to it. But if you think back about what status meant in the state of nature; if you were in the small group living out in the edge in the Paleolithic time; if your status was low in the group; you were the first out of the lifeboat, you were the one that was left behind. You were the one who didn't get fed. So there's a lot of really good reasons for status to be a driver in our backbrains as much as hunger or sex or any of the things that get more biological needs. And I keep wondering why that is.

JW: How do you want to be remembered as a writer?

LMB: How do I want to be remembered? I would like to be remembered fondly. I would like people to still be reading my stuff and getting some pleasure and enjoying the characters, dreaming those daydreams long after I'm gone. That would be cool. I would like to be read with some degree of understanding and pleasure in the far future by readers.

First published in Issue 30 of Galaxy's Edge, *January 2018.*

∎ ROBERT J. SAWYER

Robert J. Sawyer is the author of twenty-three novels and one of only eight people to have won all three of the science fiction field's top awards for best novel of the year: the Hugo, the Nebula, and the John W. Campbell Memorial Award. According to *Locus*, he is the number one award winner as a science fiction or fantasy novelist. He has had seven Hugo nominations (aside from his win), and he's won China's Galaxy Award, Japen's Seiun Award three times, Canada's Aurora Award ten times, Spain's *Premio UPC de Ciencia Ficción* three times, the Robert A. Heinlein Award, and the Hal Clement Award, plus many more. The ABC TV series *FlashForward* was based on Sawyer's novel of the same name, and he served as consultant on the TV series and wrote the nineteenth episode, "Course Correction." Sawyer holds honorary doctorates from both Laurentian University and the University of Winnipeg, and in 2016 was made a Member of the Order of Canada, the highest civilian honor bestowed by the Canadian government and the first science fiction author ever named to the order. In 2018 he was inducted into the Order of Ontario, as well.

∎∎∎∎∎∎

Joy Ward's original introduction: Robert J. Sawyer has won almost every award given in science fiction. He was kind enough to give us a few minutes for an interview at the 2015 Worldcon.

Joy Ward: How did you start writing?

Robert J. Sawyer: I was a science fiction fan from being a little kid. I was born in 1960. I grew up watching *Star Trek* and also watching the Apollo Space Program going to the Moon. In 1968 my father took me to *2001: A Space Odyssey*, which was in its first run in theaters. I got fascinated by the fact that there was this literature about the future. Very shortly thereafter, I realized people wrote these stories professionally. From about ten years old, it was something I wanted to do—write science fiction stories. I have been very, very grateful that it has been doable as a career.

I was living in Toronto, Canada, and that was an interesting fact that it didn't matter where I lived to do this. There are all kinds of professions where you have to go somewhere. If you want to be a film or TV star you have to go to Hollywood. Subsequent to my youth, if you wanted to be in computer science you probably went to Silicon Valley. But you could be an author anywhere. I loved the notion of the portability of the profession. I never wanted to have a nine-to-five job. I never wanted to have anything anybody would call a career with a retirement date built into it. This seemed to be the ideal itinerant thing to do with one's life.

JW: What's the first thing you got published?

RJS: My very first published work was in my university's literary magazine. It was a literary annual called *The White Wall Review*, from Ryerson University in Toronto. Ed Greenwood, who went on to be a very major fantasy and Dungeons & Dragons author [he's a Tor author], was two years ahead of me at that university and was the editor of the magazine. He was sympathetic to "genre" contributions, even though it was the literary review. My first story, a fantasy actually, not a science fiction story, was selected for inclusion. That was the start.

JW: So that was the first time you saw your work in print...

RJS: Yes, and there's a typo in the last line of the story, and they left my middle initial out. I've always written as "Robert J. Sawyer" in homage to Arthur C. Clarke and Robert A. Heinlein and James T. Kirk—and there's my middle initial missing. They left a word out of the last line of the story. So my first experience was, oh, there are frustrations. This is not a dream that is easily realized. But nonetheless it was intoxicating to be in print. It had been a goal. I was only twenty when it first appeared...sorry, I was nineteen, and it was something I wanted to have it happen over and over again.

It is funny for me to use that adjective because I don't drink. I guess whatever highs I've had in my life have come from either reading or writing transformative fiction. It has always been my greatest pleasure, reading a good book. People sometimes say I've read a lot about life prolongation, and they ask why I want to live forever and I say, "Simply, there are just so many books that I haven't read, and they keep writing more! There's no way I'll ever catch up!"

JW: What was your first professional publication?

RJS: My first professional publication, my first professional sale—that is one SFWA recognized, was not a print sale. The Strasenburgh Planetarium in Rochester, New York, had a contest in the summer of 1980, judged by Isaac Asimov, to choose a story to be adapted into a planetarium star show. Mine did not win. The winner turned out to be a lovely little vignette that was not at all suitable for making a planetarium star show out of. It was charming, and the producers realized that they needed something else other than what Asimov had selected. They did adapt the vignette. They had decided to buy two other stories and do a trilogy—a star show that had three science fiction visions of the future in it. The producers had liked my entry even if the good doctor had not. So they reached out to me and asked if they could buy the rights to do it, and they did. It was performed one hundred and eighty-six times in the summer of 1980 in Rochester, New York. I went to see it several times. I dragged indulgent friends to see it repeatedly.

It was very interesting because I was studying radio and television arts at Ryerson University at the same time, with a goal of becoming a screenwriter. That was my aspiration: to write film and television science fiction, not to write novels. So this was my first taste of something actually being produced. I think I would have gone down that route, had it not been for the fact that the year I graduated, 1982, from the top broadcasting program in Canada, was the first year that the CBC, the Canadian Broadcasting Corporation, had had massive layoffs for the first time in its history. There were no jobs, not even beginners' jobs, to be found in the broadcasting industry. So I had to do something else with my science fictional visions. I turned back to print. That took on a life of its own and it was many decades before I came back to scriptwriting.

I guess I really started to be noticed when I was doing short stories for *Amazing Stories* in the 1980s, and in particular the summer of 1988. I had a cover-story novelette in *Amazing Stories* with a beautiful Bob Eggleton cover, which I loved so much that I actually bought the original art from him. It was a marriage made in heaven. It still hangs in my bedroom—the original painting. That story, "Golden Fleece," I expanded from a novelette into a short novel—60,000 words. You can't sell those these days. But I used the novella, the novelette, and the fact that it had been the cover story to attract an agent to represent the expansion.

It's a long time ago now, but it was absolutely lovely, partly because this time there were no typos. All the words were there. My "J." was there, and the Bob Eggleton cover painting was spectacular. It was a wonderful experience! Some of my other friends were publishing in *Asimov's* and *Fantasy & Science Fiction* at the time and even one person in *Analog*, which had bigger circulations than *Amazing* at the time. But none of them had had a cover story. I may not have hit the top market, but I got the cover and that let me hold my head up high in what was the burgeoning Toronto SF community of that day.

It was a damn good story. It was as simple as that. I was very ambitious. It actually probably was a compressed novel. There were so many ideas and bits of business in it. I worked very, very hard on it. It was very wondrous for me that the editor at the time, a fellow named Patrick Lucian Price, had taken a liking to my work. I owe an awful lot of what my career turned out to be to that magazine editor who championed me early on.

It made me feel wonderful! It made me feel that I was on my way!

I definitely knew that the next step had to be a novel. As much as they had actually paid me well for that novella—$1,250 for that novelette! It was a lot of money for a short work. But you had to have a book, if you were going to be a serious writer in this field. I knew that I had to proceed to write books. I didn't have any idea that I was going to be able to write more than one but I was embarking on a career that I had to test and at least see if I could write and sell a book to a major US publisher.

JW: How did you decide what was going to be your first novel?

RJS: It was because this cover-story novelette had been received so well; it just seemed natural to expand it. Also, two of my friends in Toronto, Terence M. Green and Andrew Weiner, both had taken stories of theirs, one from *Fantasy & Science Fiction* in Terry's case, and one from *Asimov's* in Andrew's case, and expanded them to their first novels. So it had seemed like this was the way to do it! The novel isn't coming cold to an editor. You can say, here, it is, an expansion of a work that has already proven to have a certain degree of marketability.

JW: Please tell me about one of the high points in your life involving writing.

RJS: I was very gratified about ten years ago when I got a letter from a young woman who'd just finished her PhD in geology. She had started out by studying paleontology, a science she'd gotten interested in by reading my novel, *Calculating God.* That came out fifteen years ago now. She'd read it in high school and hadn't had any interest in being a paleontologist until she read my book. Ultimately, after an undergrad in paleontology, she'd gravitated toward pure geology. That was an enormously satisfying moment to realize that somebody's whole career and a decade of study, had come out of the inspiration that they had taken from something I'd written. It made me feel quite like I was contributing something to the world other than entertainment, and that was nice.

I think science fiction serves an important social purpose, a societal purpose.

JW: What was another high point of your career?

RJS: Oh, it was winning the Hugo Award for Best Novel of the Year. There's no question about that. We're here on the eve of this year's Hugo Award ceremony, and twelve years ago I was the lucky guy to take home what George R. R. Martin, who presented my Hugo to me, called "the big one." There's no question that nothing before or since has equaled that. I can't imagine anything that could.

It meant that my readers had decided that I had done the job I'd set out to do better than anybody else had done it in the previous year. There's nothing more gratifying than actually having satisfied customers. It made me feel terrific! It made me feel that this very financially risky, career path, eschewing a nine-to-five job, a pension, benefits package—had been the right choice to make.

JW: Where do you see science fiction going?

RJS: You ask where science fiction is going. Will there be science fiction as a separate category of publishing in ten years? When I started publishing with Ace Books, that was the early '90s, and Ace did six titles a month then. They do six titles a month now. Back then, it was five science fiction books and one fantasy book. Now it is five fantasy books and one science fiction book. So, if we extrapolate forward another decade or two, will there be any science fiction at all on their list? Two months ago, there were five fantasy novels and one alternate history novel. We can argue academically that alternate history is a subset of science fiction, but to most of the world it is not perceived as such. In other words, Ace Science Fiction had a month where they did no science fiction. That's sort of like the summer where the snow doesn't melt, where you've started the Ice Age. We may be falling into a science fiction ice age. There will be science fictional properties published as mainstream. Andrew Weir's *The Martian* is a pure quill science fiction novel that says science fiction nowhere on the cover.

I dislike the trend toward endless series. I think it is bad creatively for writers. I think it is bad economically for writers. So many of my friends have been dumped by their publishers because volume four, five, six in a series did not perform well. When they say, "I'll write something different," the publisher will say basically, "But you didn't have fans; that series did. Those fans dried up." So many publishers push to create a series brand. It is very easy to sell the next book in an ongoing series. So you end up with writers who were extraordinarily cutting edge early on, like Orson Scott Card who is still mining the Enderverse thirty years later, instead of giving something new. I don't think that's good for the field.

JW: What else is not good for the field?

RJS: The consolidation of publishers. The fewer markets for us to sell our work. Ace and Roc used to be two separate imprints, two separate companies. Now they are all consolidated under Penguin. Penguin and Random House used to be two separate companies. Del Rey and Bantam, which were consolidated, were two separate companies. Now Ace and Roc and Del Rey and Bantam are all the same company. So what used to be four possible buyers for a science fiction novel, which let you have some competition amongst tastes and competition for getting a better price for your work, have consolidated to essentially one buyer. That is very unfortunate for authors. I think also, very unfortunate for having a plurality of works and a variety of voices in the field. It is no coincidence that the huge debates about diversity in the science fiction and fantasy genres have risen up precisely in the era of consolidation of publishing companies. When you have a single buyer, it is not surprising that you have a limited taste.

There should be more diversity than there is. There is a lack of diversity. You would think there would be more diversity than there is. When Warner was not part of Hachette, Warner used to do the Warner Aspect first novel competition. Betsy Mitchell bought Nalo Hopkinson's first-novel—she's a woman of color. She was the first winner. The second winner was Karin Lowachee, also a person of color. There used to be an opportunity to do that sort of thing. We don't see that happening on an ongoing basis anymore.

JW: You are known for excellent background research.

RJS: It isn't possible to have too much science in science fiction, like it isn't possible to have too much sex in pornography. It is what it is about. I am a research junkie. To be perfectly honest, the only reason I write my novels is to support my research habit. I love being able to follow in whatever vagary of depth any topic that interests me for as long as I want and then completely change what it is that I am pursuing. There are not many jobs that will let you do that. I like to say that being a hard science fiction writer is like being a graduate student who gets to change his or her thesis topic at a whim, as often as he or she wishes. For science fiction to be taken seriously, it has to be realistic. It has to be plausible. I think it is important that it be taken seriously. Any social commentary it can bring to the table can be easily dismissed if the underlying science behind the future that is being portrayed can be easily dismissed. The scaffolding is the science that lets you say, "No, here is something realistic and important that you should be paying attention to."

I am learning things all the time! There's a line from classic *Star Trek* where a woman named Rayna says she's interested in the totality of the universe, and anything else is a betrayal of the intellect. That's what I'm interested in. This genre lets me explore just about everything that exists, did exist, or ever could exist! I can't ask for a bigger platform than that.

JW: Well if you weren't doing this, what would you be doing? Where do you go next? What's the difference for you between doing film or video and doing a book?

RJS: The biggest difference is that at this stage of my career, everything that I write gets published. At this stage of anyone's career in film or television, most of what they write never gets produced. You get paid very well for development work, you get paid very well for drafts that are discarded, you get paid very well to write pilots that nobody ever sees. So you do one for economic reasons, and you do the other because you actually want your vision to be realized. I wish the twain met more often, but they are very different paths.

JW: How do you want to be remembered? You'll be writing for a while yet.

RJS: I don't know that. And I think actually far too many authors continue writing after they've had anything interesting to say, or have the patience to take the time to say it well. So I don't know that. If this twenty-third novel, *Quantum Night,* turns out to be my last, either due to the vicissitudes of the marketplace or because my own interests shift to somewhere else, I'll be content. I've won fifty-four awards for my fiction. I've won the Hugo, the Nebula, the John W. Campbell Memorial Award, thirteen Aurora awards, Lifetime Achievement Award from the Canadian Science Fiction and Fantasy Association, the top science fiction awards in Japan, China, France, and Spain. How do I want to be remembered? As an accomplished and prolific hard science fiction writer who always gave his readers value for their money.

JW: What do the awards mean to you?

RJS: The first one that was really major was winning the Nebula Award. What it meant was, as my editor at the time, John Douglas, put it, "You've gone overnight from being a promising newcomer to an established, bankable name." Since I won the Nebula in 1996, I have not had any economic worries and I don't anticipate any for the rest of my life. It meant that I was a commercially viable author in a very competitive industry. The Hugo, which was subsequent to that, simply added luster to that, but the reality was that it was the major award wins that made it possible for me to be the sole income earner for my family, for decades now, and who have enjoyed a pleasant and prosperous existence on this ball of dust.

JW: What advice would you give young writers?

RJS: Write things that you are passionate about. Never ask what's selling, what's hot, what's the trend, what should I be doing? Write the things you most passionately care about. Write them as surpassingly well as you can. Put everything you can into your work. Try to become a distinctive voice in the landscape. Don't emulate others. Don't do it for commercial reasons. If you are good at what you do, in all likelihood you will find both artistic and economic fulfillment.

If you decide that all you want to do is to churn out carbon copies of things that already exist, you will probably find it a rather empty life.

I have had things that I thought were worth sharing with the world. I think having people talk about one's work after you've gone is at least as important as having them talking about you after you've gone. It is a contribution to human culture that transcends your circle of acquaintances. I am proud to have made my little tiny piece of that.

You know, to be perfectly blunt, my younger brother died two years ago. He died of lung cancer. He didn't expect to be checking out when he checked out. But when he did, he said, "In the end, I can't complain. It wasn't as long a life as I wanted it to be, but it was a good life." Just before he died, he won an Emmy award from the International Academy of Television Arts and Sciences. He'd achieved the top distinction in his career. There'll always be an entry on him in the databases and encyclopedias of his profession. They say you're not dead when the people remember you, but the reality is that the people who remember you will soon be dead too. However, work can live on for centuries. That's the only immortality outside of science fiction that any of us have hitherto obtained.

First published in Issue 21 of Galaxy's Edge, *July 2016.*

▮ HARRY TURTLEDOVE

arry Turtledove writes alternate history, science fiction, fantasy and historical fiction and has won a Hugo Award, two Sidewise Awards for alternate history, and the Hal Clement Award for YA science fiction. With more than a hundred books, a couple of hundred pieces of short fiction, as well as a translation of a Byzantine chronicle and four academic articles published throughout his career, Turtledove is a prolific writer of note. He was an astronomer by original intention, but, after flunking out of Caltech, ended up with a doctorate in Byzantine history from UCLA. He wrote his dissertation alongside the first novel he sold. Along with teaching at UCLA, Cal State Fullerton, and Cal State Los Angeles, he worked as a technical writer for the Los Angeles County Office of Education before resigning from that job to freelance in 1991. He is married to Laura Frankos, herself a writer. They have three daughters (one also a published author) and two granddaughters. Two cats, Boris and Hotspur, run the household with iron, clawed fists.

▮▮▮▮▮▮

Joy Ward's original introduction: Hugo-award-winning Harry Turtledove has had a long and fruitful career making all of us look at history differently. He is known for his alternate history clas-

sics such as **The Guns of the South** *and* **The Toxic Spell Dump**.
With a hundred-plus books in print he is almost a library to himself.

Joy Ward: How did you get started writing alternate history?

Harry Turtledove: I am an escaped Byzantine historian. I have been reading science fiction since I was eight years old. I have the kind of analytical tools that a reasonable SF writer ought to have. I know how to do research. I know how to extrapolate. I also have the tools that a historian picks up on how to analyze the past and what stuff means and how some piece relates to another...and when you put that all together I'm a historian who writes science fiction. So I write a lot of alternate history because I use the same extrapolative techniques and then change one thing to see what happens...except a lot of SF changes the present or the near future and looks at the consequences of change in the farther future. I change the more-distant past and look at the consequences. It's the same thing; it just looks a little different when you start at a different place in the timeline.

I was a junior in high school. I was writing alternate history about Romans in the fourth century AD from Julian's army marching across Asia, crossing the Bering Straits in the middle of winter when it is frozen over, getting down into the Americas. It was massively unpublishable, but it was the first novel I finished.

The first story I sold came from an idea that was suggested by a lady I was then married to, about time travelers going back into the Roman Empire to get manuscripts of Greek and Roman literature—that were still extant then and have since been lost—and committing a murder with a handgun in the process of doing so. The local cop in this Roman town was trying to figure out what happened. That's the first story I wrote that sold. The magazine died before it saw print. I sold it to David Hartwell's *Cosmos*. I did get a check—after some begging and whining, but I did. I got the rights back and I eventually sold it to *Asimov's*.

JW: What made you decide to go into history in the first place?

HT: It was Sprague De Camp's fault, because when I was about fourteen years old I picked up a copy of *Lest Darkness Fall* in a second-hand bookstore. I was going to be a scientist. I read SF because it had science in it, man! I read of his *Lest Darkness Fall*. I had read some other stuff before, so I knew I wanted this book. I started trying to find out how much was real and how much he was making up. A whole heck of a lot of it was real. But I got into CalTech and flunked out of CalTech at the end of my freshman year, because I most severely couldn't do calculus. I spent a year at Cal State LA getting my GPA back up to where my draft board could see it. The year in question was '67, '68…this was a relevant consideration. I ended up at UCLA after that. I ended up with a doctorate in Byzantine history. I would have written something if I hadn't found *Lest Darkness Fall* on that shelf, if somebody had bought it two days before, but I have no idea what. I have the degree I have thanks to that book. I've written most of the things I've written because it comes from things that I've learned turning into a historian. Thanks to that book I'm married to the lady I met when I was teaching at UCLA when the prof I was studying under had a guest gig in Athens. Thanks to that book I have the kids I have, living where I'm living. Other than that, it didn't change my life at all. This is alternate history on the microhistorical level. If somebody else had bought that book a week earlier I might be here talking with you, but we would be talking about different stuff.

JW: What was it like to sell that first story?

HT: When I did that back in the mid-'70s, there was a commercial for Almaden, which was California Plonk, where the guy goes to his mailbox and he opens the envelope and it says, "We're buying your short story. Check for however much is enclosed." Well, I had been submitting stories for a few years and I had had a couple of near misses. I went to the mailbox in my apartment building and there was an envelope. Usually the rule for freelance writers is small envelope good, big envelope bad, because big envelope is your manuscript returning in your SASE [self-addressed, stamped envelope] . I had a small envelope. I opened it and it said, "We're sorry we haven't got back to you sooner, but David Hartwell was out with the flu. We're buying your story called 'Death in Vesunna', and we're paying you, I think it was two hundred and eighty bucks." Something like that. It was like three cents a word, which was decent money in those days, not great. It was maybe fifty yards from that mailbox back to my apartment and I ran them. The lady I was then married to was in there and she said, "What the hell are you making a commotion like that for?" And I showed her! I had been working at this and working at this and I can do this is what it was. I can do this!

The hardest work I ever did was *Ruled Britania* because I was working in a language not quite my own. You know how Plutarch was imitating Thucydides and Xenophon except he was living five hundred years after their time and his language isn't quite the same as theirs? Well, that's what I felt like when I was doing Shakespeare. But I like writing pastiche, I like being other people. I've been a lot of other people on paper. It lets you—it's an exercise in limitation and it's an exercise in freedom because you are somebody else. I could pretend to be Shakespeare, Samuel Pepys, J. D. Salinger. That was my daughter's fault. It was another idea that I got by accident. My oldest daughter had to read *Catcher in the Rye* and my next-oldest daughter had never heard of it, didn't know what it was and said, "Catcher in the Rhine?" So I did Holden Caulfield except never naming him that. It's Siegfried without a Siegfried story. I wrote it for Esther Friesner for *Chicks in Chainmail*. It was silly. I've been Ernie Pyle. I've been Edward R. Murrow. I've been Mark Twain. The really scary thing, I've been Hemingway, Lincoln. The scary thing about that stuff is you are trying to impersonate somebody who is better than you are. That's intimidating. You know people are going to read all the good stuff and say, yeah, that's how it's supposed to sound, and they are going to read all the stuff that isn't as good and say, oh you jerk! That's you. That's your fault. Of course people say that to me. In the days before the internet, I wrote research-intensive detail-oriented stuff. I have readers who are into detail-oriented research-intensive stuff, and some of those readers will know more about it than you do. In these days they just blast you on message boards, but in those days you would get the eight-page, single-spaced letters in 8-point type that start out by apologizing how brief they are before they start calling you an idiot for all the dumbass things they think you've done. But the thing is, when I was reading that stuff I got to know Poul Anderson because

I wrote him one of those letters. I hope a little more polite, but he was talking about Byzantine things in his Harald Hardrada historical novels. Everybody is going to know more than you do about some of this stuff. You're going to be wrong sometimes. That happens, too. That comes with the territory.

JW: What have been some high points of your career?

HT: I think the first one is recognizing the opportunity in a throwaway line in a letter from a friend of mine. Back in those days before we had email I corresponded with the fine fantasy writer Judith Tarr, and Judy was doing one of the things that writers characteristically do when they talk with other writers. She was pissing and moaning about the cover art for a book she had coming up, and she said, "This is as anachronistic as Robert E. Lee with an Uzi, for God's sake." I looked at that and I thought, that's a good line, Judy. I wrote back to her and I signed my name at the end of the word-processed letter, and I added a hand-scrawled P.S. at the bottom. "Who'd want to give Robert E. Lee an Uzi? Time traveling South Africans maybe? If I write it, I'll give you an acknowledgement." I looked at that and thought I could do something with that. I xeroxed it to make sure I didn't lose it. I was at the beginning of a two-book fantasy contract, so I had some time to do my homework. That's how *The Guns of the South* happened. That was the book that let me quit my day job. Thank you, Judy.

The moment I won the Hugo in '94, that was pretty cool because it was completely out of the blue. I was amazed to be nominated. I did not expect to win at all. Anne McCaffrey said that when I went up and got the Hugo I had to pick my jaw up off the ground before I could say thank you to anybody, by God. It means, to quote Sally Field, "You like me! You really like me!" Of course there's a doubt. Writers are paranoid.

You are never as good as you want to be. Nobody's ever as good as he or she wants to be. You know you do the best you can, and you look at it later and you think, "I could have done that better."

It means, all right, I'll do it in baseball terms. I'm a baseball geek. It means I'm a pretty good regular. I made the all-star teams a couple of times, and the way it looks right now is I ain't going to make the Hall of Fame because I'm not good enough. I'm pretty good, but I'm not good enough for that. So okay. You do the best you can. It's all you can do.

JW: What would it take to get in the Hall of Fame?

HT: To be better than I am, a cross between Robert Heinlein and Ted Sturgeon. I'm good, but you're never as good as you want to be.

JW: How do you get better as a writer?

HT: You write, you read, repeat. Then you write, then you read, you repeat. You write, you read, you repeat. You write, you read, you repeat. That's all you can do. That's all you've got available to you. See how other people do it better than you and try to do it better yourself.

JW: Where do you see your writing going in the future?

HT: Whatever looks interesting. To a degree whatever people are rash enough to pay me for. You don't know where ideas come from. I found one because I was reading a letter. I found one because I made a smart-ass comment at a convention. I was at the World Fantasy Convention in Phoenix in '91. I was on a magic-and-technology panel, and there I was—a John W. Campbell author—on a Joseph Campbell panel. One of the other people on the panel was Alexandra Honigsberg, and Alexandra and I had been friends for years even then. The way we get along is we sass each other. She made the comment that no matter what methodology you use, whether you use engineering or sorcery, it's going to have environmental consequences. I made this smartass crack about toxic spell dumps. I got a laugh from the audience, and among the people I got a laugh from were Poul and Karen Anderson, who were sitting in the front row, which chuffed me. I got enough of a laugh that I scrawled "toxic spell dumps" on my pocket program so I didn't lose it. An hour or so later, after the panel was over, I scrawled on the other side of the program, "environmental perfection agency." That's how *The Case of the Toxic Spell Dump* happened. I had no idea this was going to happen. I had an idea that I liked and I rolled with it.

I had an idea for a book because my daughter collects stamps. One of my daughters is a moderately serious stamp collector and she gets a stamp weekly. To some degree, in all things, hobbies rub off on everybody in the house. They were talking about the early postal history of Albania, of all the uninspiring topics, and they remarked that the first king of Albania is not on any stamps because he was only king for five days. He was this German adventurer who became king of Albania for five days after the Balkan War because they wanted a Turkish prince. He got wind of it. He spoke fluent Turkish because he had served two hitches in the Sultan's army. He was a ringer for the prince. He got to Albania ahead of the prince, in uniform, convinced the locals that he was the prince, was crowned king of Albania, disported himself in the harem that they recruited for him for five days, declared war on Montenegro for the hell of it, and departed with the Albanian national treasure or as much of it as he could stuff in his pockets. He lived into the '50s. Ideas are where you find them.

JW: What kind of advice do you give young writers?

HT: I'll quote Heinlein's laws. "You must write. You must finish what you write. You must refrain from rewriting except to editorial order." That's the tricky one. He didn't mean don't polish it; he meant don't screw around with your main idea. "You must put it on the market. You must keep it on the market until sold." Do all those things and do them over and over and over again, and all of them without failing, and if there is any talent at all you will give it the opportunity to come out.

JW: How will you be remembered?

HT: There will be some graduate students in English messing around with my manuscripts, and I may even be a small cottage industry because I have manuscripts to mess around with because I do first drafts in longhand. So they will actually be able to play with it and say, "Okay, this is what the idiot was doing."

JW: How would you like to be remembered?

HT: I hope I entertain. I hope I make some people think. Past that, what is any writer going to go for?

I'm a writer. I do this for a living. I did my job as well as I knew how.

First published in Issue 23 of Galaxy's Edge, *November 2016.*

onnie Willis is the award-winning author of *Doomsday Book, Bellwether, To Say Nothing of the Dog*, and the two-volume work *Blackout/All Clear*. Her work has won a record eleven Hugo Awards and seven Nebula Awards, winning both awards for the titles "Fire Watch" (Novelette, 1983), *Doomsday Book* (Novel, 1993), "Even the Queen" (Short Story, 1993), and *Blackout/All Clear* (Novel, 2010). She has been named a Grand Master in the field and been inducted into the Science Fiction Hall of Fame. She's well-known both for her comic and her tragic stories, writing across the spectrum. She's also famous for her Christmas stories— "Miracle," "All Seated on the Ground," and "Just Like the Ones We Used to Know," which was made into a TV movie, *Snow Wonder*, starring Mary Tyler Moore. Willis lives in Greeley, Colorado, with her husband, a delightful bulldog, and two spawn-of-Satan cats. She spends nearly every day writing at Starbucks.

■■■■■■

Joy Ward's original introduction: Connie Willis is one of science fiction's living treasures, always taking a fresh look at technology and its effects on humans. We caught up with her at the 2015 Nebulas.

■■

Joy Ward: How did you start writing?

Connie Willis: I wanted to be a writer from the time I can remember. I made up stories when I was a little girl. I loved writing. I did not actually *do* a lot of writing. I wasn't one of those six-year-olds who wrote a lot of stories. I just made up stories.

I made up stories about my dolls. I gave out stories. I wanted to be a writer, and then when I was in sixth grade my teacher gave me a copy of *Little Women* so I knew which writer I wanted to be. I wanted to be Jo March, of course. But at that point it was still sort of a fantasy because Jo lives back in the 1800s and I did not really have a sense that it was a real career people could have. Then I stated reading science fiction and fell in love with all those writers.

I can't say when I wrote my first story, I can't say when it all started. It wasn't one of those big revelation, breakthrough moments. I just always wanted to be a writer.

When my first sale happened—actually, by the time I graduated from college and got married—I really wanted to be a writer. But I did not assume that I could make a living at it. Most science fiction writers didn't make a living at it. I had read Zena Henning's *The People* stories. She was kind of my career hero, because she was a teacher and she wrote during her summer vacations and spring breaks. So that was kind of how I saw myself as doing the writing. I had no ambitions to write novels, so it was possible to be a part-time short-story writer.

I taught for two years and then had a baby. And in those days, they could fire you for having a baby, so then I decided I would be at home raising the child. I would seriously start sending out the stories and having this be a secondary income. I had very little success with the science fiction. The first thing I sold was an article to *Grade Teacher* on teaching science with no equipment. Then I wrote a number of confession stories for magazines like *True Romance*. Those were great because I could sell them. But my desire was to write science fiction.

The first sale in science fiction was a story called "The Secret of Santa Titicaca" about talking, sentient Incan frogs, I'm ashamed to say. It was a romantic comedy. So that was kind of a theme in my life. That magazine promptly went belly-up and died. I didn't even know it had made print until I was nominated some years later. In 1980 I was nominated for the New Writer, the John W. Campbell

Award. I was so excited and then I got a call fifteen minutes later saying, "Do you now or have you ever written a story 'The Secret of Santa Titicaca?'"

I said, "Yes, but it wasn't ever published."

He said, "Oh yes, it was." And it was published in the last issue of *Worlds of If* before it went belly-up which meant that all it ever did was to ruin my chances at the Campbell Award. So that was my first published.

Then I had a long dry spell.

In 1980 I started to sell to *Galileo,* and Charlie Ryan was cultivating a lot of new writers; James Patrick Kelly and John Kessel and Nancy Kress and other writers who were brand new. He bought a lot of my stories.

There are lots of ups and downs. I usually tell my writing students that I lived in a little mountain town, and so we didn't get mail delivery; we had a post office box. I went up one day, walked up to get the mail, and here was a pink slip in my box. I thought, oh, it's a present from my grandma. No, it was not.

It was every manuscript coming back, every single thing I had out. I think there were eight manuscripts out. Always before I had been able to comfort myself, "Well this didn't sell, but I have a much better story out with *Omni.*" By the time that came back, "I have a great story with *Asimov's.*"

I had nothing to comfort myself with, and I was really discouraged. Maybe I should just give up. 'Cause there was a lot of pressure, not from my family. Thank God, they were very supportive, but my husband was a teacher. We lived in a world of teachers and they could not understand why I would not get a job teaching and bring in a second paycheck and then we could have two cars and all these things. I really was feeling enormous pressure that I wasn't doing my part financially.

What saved me was I always had to walk to the post office. I always bought extra postage and filled out the self-addressed stamped envelope for the following thing. Buy the postage, and then buy the postage for the next one. I had all this extra postage, and all these manila envelopes, so I'll send them all out one more time. Then one of those stories actually did sell, and that was enough to keep me going until the next sale.

I think very much that writers are always dealing with this fear that they are making absolute fools of themselves. You either know if you are a good architect or not a good architect. You know if you are a good mathematician or not. But with writing you don't know if you're just kidding yourself, that maybe you're a terrible writer. That's one kind of writer.

There's another kind of writer; boundless confidence, even though they're terrible. I see these all the time. They're all convinced that they are God's gift to the world, and they can't even write a coherent sentence. So it's such a dicey business. You have to have confidence—absolute confidence and egotism. If you didn't, you'd never have the courage to send your stories out.

At the same time, you've got to be really, really humble and look at your work and be willing to say, "This is garbage! I'm not doing a very good job here." I think that's a really hard balance to maintain as you go along. You're always falling on one side or the other.

I have always managed to be completely neurotic about everything, so therefore I've never enjoyed any of my successes. I've simply found something to be worried about involving them, but that's better than being one of these people who thinks they're wonderful and they're not.

I don't know that I've been able to walk that line. I fall off periodically. You can get over-confident. A couple of years after I won for *Fire Watch*—the Nebula for *Fire Watch* and "A Letter from the Clearys," the first person to have won two Nebulas at once—I was feeling pretty good. Not cocky but certainly like I was out of the slush pile. Now I'm out of the slush pile. Now, I'll get my stories read. And then nothing happened. I got the same rejections from everybody. It was like, "Wait! I have two Nebulas." Then the temptation to go around saying, "I have two Nebula-winning stories, what's your problem?" was very strong but I resisted it because obviously that sounds awful.

But you will get overly cocky and then you'll come down with a *thunk*. You'll find that you think that you deserve more of an advance than you get, then you say to your agent, "Well, look at me. I'm a Grand Master. I should get this." Then you come down with a *thunk* when they tell you your books don't sell well enough to justify this or you are kidding yourself about your sale or something. There's always something.

One of the things that I was very lucky in was I did not achieve any success until I was in my thirties, so I had a long time to stand around and watch people. And I saw many, many bad examples. I saw people who erred on all sides of the equation. People who would shrivel up and die at the slightest harsh word and never be seen again. People who came on guns blazing and convinced that they were the best writer ever and they died. I just got to see all these bad examples, and that was really good for me because then I was like "I'm not going to do that, and I'm not going to do that, and definitely not going to do that." That was really helpful then when those things started happening.

My neuroses kind of protect me. I'm always anxious and nervous and worried. One time Fitzgerald said to Hemingway, "I want to be the best writer in the world. Don't you?"

Hemingway laughed and said something really mean to him that I can't remember right now. And yeah, I was like yeah, don't you want to be the best writer in the world? Doesn't every writer want to be the best? I did learn that no, that not everybody does. A lot of them are quite happy to earn money and fame and don't much care how they get there. For other people, they are into something else. There's some other goal that they want.

I loved writing stories and I love books. I think what saved me is I have always viewed writing as sort of a holy vocation, like becoming a nun or something. Books are the most important things in the world to me. I wanted to spend my life in that world, and it was a privilege to spend my life in that world. It is a privilege to tell stories. It's a sacred thing that you can affect lives.

I was affected by writers I never met who changed my life, and so I wanted to pass that on. I think that helps a little bit to keep your head on straight.

Books are amazing. I don't want to say a religion because that won't give the right impression. But my Mom died when I was twelve. To say I was poorly equipped for this would be an understatement. It was just a smashing, smashing blow. Part of the smashing blow was the absolute inability of anybody to help or say anything useful whatsoever. People say the most annoying and stupid things when someone dies. They mean well, I guess, but they're absolutely useless. But I had read all these books, and the books were not useless.

By the time my Mom died, I had read James Agee, *A Death in the Family*, and that book is about a smashing blow. I had read *Washed in the Blood of the Lamb*, and in that book he says you never recover from a death. You simply take your place on the mourning bench, a bench that stretches back into time forever. And that was very helpful. I had read Peter Beagle's *A Fine and Private Place* and that was very helpful. It was like when someone saves your life, and they saved my life because I was getting no help from anybody. Here was the help. And so when you have that experience, when you're saved from drowning, you owe them your life. I owe books my life.

Just recently I read Joan Didion's *The Year of Magical Thinking* about the year after her husband died and her daughter was in the hospital. This was the best book I ever read. I wish I had had it when I was twelve, but I'll take it now. It's a wonderful, wonderful book. I hope that someday I can write something that will be as helpful to others as that is to me.

I think when I say religious vocation that's what I mean. Books change lives. They reach out across the years and space and they touch you, change you, and make things possible. I was drowning and saved by books on more than one occasion. So of course I owe them everything.

I think writing is a tremendous responsibility. On the one hand, it's a Spiderman kind of moment. With great power comes great responsibility. So I've always felt that my biggest responsibility is trying to tell the truth, especially when I wrote *Passage*, a book about death. It, of course, is not true in a factual sense because it is a fantasy/science fiction novel. But I had to stay absolutely true to what you really feel and what you really think and what death is really like. I will not budge one inch from what I perceive is the truth because that will be the most help to people.

I have had a number of people who said to me, "I just lost my mother and I was reading *Passage*.... It was so helpful."

I really feel like a success when that book is doing for them what these books did for me.

In the movie of Roald Dahl's *Matilda*, Matilda read lots of books, and the message of all of them was that the authors sent their ideas out like ships on the sea. The message was you are not alone. I thought,

"That's it! That's it! Clearly other people have felt the way you feel and someone else knows. You may be all alone in a very hostile situation in which no one understands you or cares about the things you care about or no one is helpful, but somewhere there is someone who understands and somebody who can reach out to you." To me, that is where the books are truly, truly a salvation.

I do lots of library stuff and speeches about libraries and their importance, so I look for quotes from other writers. It's absolutely astonishing! They all have the same experience that I had. They were saved by the public library. They were saved by books. It's people from totally different backgrounds, from totally different worlds who all found salvation. I think Malcolm X wrote that he was in prison for petty theft or something and they gave him the run of the prison library. He said it was the first time in his life he was a free man. He said, "I had thought that I was the only person who had ever had these thoughts, but then I realized that everybody does," and it changed everything about him. His background is about as different from mine as it could possibly be. So, it's amazing. They work miracles every day. It's great to be able to devote your life to that.

JW: You mentioned having a reader correct you for getting a Candy-land card incorrect. Please talk about the importance of research.

CW: I'm not putting down research. I'm not telling people not to do their research. Do your research. The reason you have to get the Molasses Swamp card right is because you are casting a spell and you are saying to this person, "You think you are sitting in a chair in a house but you're not. You are actually in fourteenth century London, or you are in Baghdad with Ali Baba and the forty thieves," or you are on another planet far, far away. In order to do that, the spell has to be consistent. If you make a mistake it kicks the person right out of that spell and they are right back sitting in their chair, and they may or may not be willing to trust you enough again to be back in that world. So the research is incredibly important no matter how small a detail.

But I think the research, where you're researching the spirit of the piece, the spirit of the time [is the most important]. I bitch constantly, I love the Algonquin Round Table. Dorothy Parker, Robert Benchley, Alexander Walcott and Harpo Marx. Love those people! Love all the stories that they told and all the stories about them. There has never been a decent book or a decent movie about them. I'm so furious. Every time I watch something I'm "Ohhh! They've gotten it all wrong." What they get wrong is the spirit of it. Yeah, everybody looks and sounds exactly like they were supposed to. They've got the clothes right and they've got everything right, but they haven't captured the fun of it. They focus in on all the wrong details. Dorothy Parker was always trying to kill herself. She talked about installing a zipper in her wrist at one point. That doesn't mean that those suicide attempts weren't serious, but they focus on those suicide attempts and forget that these people were young and eager and living this exciting life in New York, starting a new literary trend and having lunch every day. Just like the lunches we have at conventions. And they're so fun! And you can't remember after what everybody did except it was so fun!

And so I intend to write mine. If I live long enough I will write my Algonquin short story and try to get it right and try to capture that spirit, because if you get it wrong, it doesn't matter that you got the horses and the clothes and the guns and every other detail right. It just doesn't matter in the long run because you missed the point completely.

My husband and I are having a fight right now over watching Ken Burns's *Roosevelts*, which is extremely good, and I'm enjoying it a lot. But I feel like there are times when they have completely missed the spirit of what they're talking about.

For instance, they talk about Alice being neglected. This is Teddy Roosevelt's daughter, Alice. They talk about how she was in the limelight of publicity. They talk about how he didn't really spend any time with her because he was mourning his lost wife. They tell you all these things about her. What they totally didn't put in was she was the funniest person on the planet. She was wild and crazy and a cheerful, outgoing, charming young girl. She had a color named after her, Alice Blue. At one point somebody was complaining about her smoking because she was smoking in 1910. Teddy Roosevelt said, "I'm sorry. I can either control Alice or I can run the country, but not both." Which I think is the best thing Teddy Roosevelt ever said. And they left that out!

JW: What's bad about that?

CW: One, it's the truth. It's the real person. It's like you have painted a totally accurate picture of someone, yet it doesn't look anything like them and anyone who knows them knows that is wrong. Even though they can't necessarily say that the nose is wrong and the chin is wrong, they know it's wrong. I feel like you have an obligation to get it right.

We saw at the Art Institute today a small version of the Lincoln statue from the Lincoln Memorial and that's the real Lincoln. It's the real Lincoln. It captures not just the way he looks but his sadness and his pity and his enormous compassion for people. It's all right there. It really looks like him.

So when I'm doing a historical era I want it to be like it really was and capture some of the essence of that period. The Victorian era was one of the silliest eras in history. But then there are other truths.

Even during the decline and fall of the Roman Empire people fell in love, they got married, they had babies, and they had perfectly happy lives. All the elements are present in any historical era and you've got to capture that, that essence, as you perceive it. Of course, it will be very personal. Your perception will be totally different from everybody else's but that's all you have to offer as a writer—your view of things. Then hopefully all the views will be put together and eventually form a better picture of the truth.

I had a huge conversation at lunch about Zelda Fitzgerald. Nancy Kress was saying there's Team Zelda and Team Scott. Of course, I'm saying, "You've all got it wrong. This is not the real Zelda and Scott! I know how this works."

I've looked at the same facts as everybody else and I've come to a different conclusion from everybody else. I'm sure I don't have the real F. Scott Fitzgerald or Zelda, but I have a very powerful impression of them and that is what I think a writer has to do. It's really interesting because only by being intensely biased and personal can you have any chance of approaching impartial truth.

I think writers reach for our bag of clichés. We don't mean to, but we've grown up seeing all kinds of images of things and people and stuff. You don't think about it, you just kind of accept them.

I remember my grandmother, she was telling me how everybody did the laundry on Monday. "You clean those tea towels on Monday? Why did you do the laundry on Monday?"

"I have no idea."

Of course, once the automatic washing machine came in nobody did it, but for a long time after her automatic washer came in, she did do it on Monday, even though she could now do it any day she felt like it. I understand the concept of doing it on a specific day because she had to get out all the stuff and you had to heat the water and you had to do all these things, but I didn't understand why it had to be Monday. I was trying to get to the rationale behind it. I'm sure there was a reason at one point but then everybody else kind of blithely went along with it. I think most of us, that's what we all do most of the time. We couldn't function if we didn't accept most of what society tells us, because you can't fight everything all day, every day. You wouldn't have time to get anything done.

But writers have to look at things differently, and they have to stop, and go, "Wait! Why do we do it this way? Why is that necessarily the way it has always been done? Why should it be done that way? Should we do things differently? Should we think differently?"

Writers…that's what their gift is. It's not so much the writing stuff, though that's a whole set of skills that you have to use to get your ideas across, but it's the ability to look a little askew at things. Look at it a little differently. When I wrote "The Last of the Winnebagos" I had read all these end-of-the-world stories and I had been on a number of end-of-the-world panels. There were always people who were living in the rubble, fighting off mutants, eating canned goods that they found somewhere. Nobody ever seems to be grieving. The first incidence of grieving I ever saw was in the original Mad Max film, where the guy said, "I miss lingerie." It was like, "There. That would be how it would really be." There would be so many things that no longer existed that you would just be heartbroken over. So I thought I want to write a story in which only a small part of the world ends. Just a little bit of it ends so that you're not busy fighting off mutants or eating canned goods or scrambling around the rubble. You can continue in your daily life. Nothing is interfering in your daily life, but you have suffered a smashing blow of some sort and a loss that cannot be dealt with because you are grieving so much.

What I hit on, was [what] I had just read about in an old issue of *Collier's Magazine*…I had read about a mine disaster in Wales back in the 1950s called Aberfann. In it the coal tip came down and smothered the school and killed all the children. Except I think there were three children home sick with the measles. It didn't affect them. They could still be miners; the people were still alive. They could continue to go through their daily lives, but they had lost everything that mattered to them.

So when I wrote "Last of the Winnebagos" what I had happen was all the dogs had died. People are always, "What do you have against dogs?" Nothing! I love dogs. That's why I think it would be so terrible. But they don't really affect anything. If they all disappeared tomorrow I guess PetSmart would go out of business, but science and industry could continue; it's just that it would be this smashing blow, and life would no longer be worth living in many ways. How would people deal with that? Then I could deal with all the things they never deal with in all these end-of-the-world stories because they don't have time. I could deal with the grief and the guilt and the projection and trying to blame somebody and all the other things I saw happening, if you really had had a tremendous loss... that was unbearable, and unbearable to think that you had a hand in it.

I think that's [the] writers' job. Science fiction is so great because it provides this stage on which you can act out these ideas. You can change one thing. You can kill all the dogs. You can have a drug that makes you go from being mentally handicapped to genius level in four days like "Flowers for Algernon." You can have a time machine that takes you into the future then takes you into the past like Phillip K. Dick's "A Little Something for us Tempunauts." When an accident would happen it would trap you in this endless loop of disaster. No other kind of literature can do that...can set up these imaginary thought experiments. You can say, "If we did this what would this be like?" I'm always interested in the stage that this sets for human emotions.

JW: In some ways your writing is more focused on emotions than tech than some other Grand Masters. What's important for you that you focus on the emotional implications?

CW: The tech is there. It's in the background, not the foreground. I think they are equally legitimate approaches, and I love many tech stories. To me, the ultimate one is *Rendezvous with Rama* by Clarke: a story in which all the human characters are completely cardboard and interchangeable. People say, "They're terrible characters!"

No. There's a great character. There's one great character in this book and it's the ship and it's them trying to figure out the alien mind that lies behind that ship. Who cares about the people? This ship is the best thing ever and it is a great character. I do believe you have to have great characters in all your books, but they don't all have to be people. They can sometimes be the tech.

But for me, usually what I'm looking is more of the human response to technology than the technology itself. So when I wrote "Even the Queen," I could have written it as a story about how they discovered this amazing drug so that women didn't have to have their menstrual cycle anymore, and what would be the problems developing it…or I could have written a very political story about what were the political handicaps to try and get something like that past Congress. Or I could have written any number of stories about it, but I thought the most interesting story I could tell would be twenty years after the fact. What is the backlash to this? Because there's always a backlash, and the younger generation never appreciates the sacrifices that the older generation has made so that their lives can be better. That goes all the way back to Egypt. And why don't they? In one way you don't want them to because you don't want them to fight the same battles that you fought. You want them to be free of even thinking about it. At the same time, if they don't know the battles you fought, they're likely to not fully appreciate them. To me that seemed like the most interesting story that I could get out of that piece of tech. But there are many others, I'm sure. Joe Haldeman would have written it one way. Larry Niven would have written it another. That's one of the things I love about science fiction. There are so many different views.

I'm not sure any of them would have written the story my way.

I'll never forget Gardner Dozois when "Even the Queen" won the Nebula and I got up there, somewhat flummoxed, to accept. I said, "I am really kind of surprised that this story won because it's a story about…"

And Gardner shouted from the audience in his piercing Gardner voice, "Tell 'em it's a period piece!"

Beyond horrible and absolutely true. Then someone wrote a review that said science fiction is officially dead. A story about menstruation has now won the Nebula. Okay, if that's the way you feel about it. It's just one more form of tech. Just one more form with all these side effects.

Aside from character, the thing I am most interested in always is how humans interact with technology, but also in the unintended side effects of any and all technology. I've spent half my life on these stupid panels about living forever or becoming robots or—I don't know—or singularity or whatever, and people are like, "It's going to be so great! It's going to be so great!"

I'm like, "What could possibly go wrong?"

They're like, "Nothing's going to go wrong."

I'm like, "Something had gone wrong with every single thing we have ever come up with, so what makes you think that with this particular thing something will not go wrong? Or even if nothing goes wrong with it, that there won't be unintended side effects that we have not considered from this very positive technology."

And they're, "No, no, it's going to be great. It's going to be perfect."

I'm like, "Oh my God."

So I would say, "Unintended consequences, that's all I ever write about. Really, unintended consequences. They always show up." I'm just like, "Really people? You can't think of anything that could go wrong with this?"

It is just so frustrating. They never seem to see them.

JW: How does writing about unintended consequences feed into being part of a holy vocation?

CW: Unintended consequences would be part of the truth about the world. We take one step forward and five back and three sideways. We live in this chaotic system where everything matters, everything counts in unaccountable ways, and our job is to kind of foresee. Ed Bryant said that the ordinary person in 1895 might have been able to predict the automobile. The visionary person would have predicted the interstate highway. The science fiction writer would have predicted the traffic jam. I think that's really true.

One of our functions as science fiction writers is to be constantly going, "Now wait just a darn minute here. This could go wrong. That could go wrong. Do we really want to go down this path? Are we sure that this could happen and that could happen and we really should take that into account?" The Iraq War, for example. Just a little historical knowledge and a little historical thinking about what could go wrong. If you approach the world that way, you live usually a much happier life with fewer blunders of enormous consequences. But also its part of the truth about how the world works. I think the writer's obligation is to tell the truth. Period.

Madelyn L'Engle, you know *The Wrinkle in Time*. A lot of her books have a very religious theme. She said, "When I write the story, I serve the story. The story does not serve my faith. The story does not serve me. I serve the story. My obligation is to tell the truth as well as I can tell it."

That's the part that is so important. You have to be as honest as you possibly can, and I think that will see you through as a writer.

JW: How do you want to be remembered?

CW: Who knows? My husband and I have a quiz book from 1927. It's really fun because we have to answer questions. Who is the secretary of state? No idea. No idea. The science very rarely changes. A lot of the language stuff doesn't change. All kinds of things stay the same. I never recognize any of the writers. I never get the writing questions right at all. These people have sunk without a trace. And they were important enough to be in a quiz. I was an English major. I'm not talking about F. Scott Fitzgerald and Hemingway and even minor writers of the time. I have never heard of any of these people, and it was only fifty years ago. So who knows?

I would like to be remembered in the same way I remember Rumer Godden, who wrote a book called *An Episode of Sparrows*—one of my favorite books. It's about a little girl who plants a garden in a burned-out rubble of a church during the Blitz. It's my first introduction to the Blitz. It got me interested in the Blitz. It inspired in many ways *Fire Watch* and all the Blitz stuff that I did after that. That book is actually a retelling of Francis Hodgson Burnett's *Secret Garden*. So Burnett inspires her, and she inspires me, and I would like to inspire whoever that next writer is in the line. That's how I'd like to be remembered.

Expanded version of the interview that appeared in
Issue 16 of Galaxy's Edge, *September 2015.*

■ LARRY NIVEN ■

L arry Niven graduated with a BA in mathematics (and a minor in psychology) from Washburn University, Topeka, Kansas, in 1962. He made his first sale, "The Coldest Place," in 1964, his love of science driving him to write stories on the cutting edge of scientific discovery throughout his career. Neutron stars were a newly-described phenomenon when Niven first wrote about them in 1966, and the modern-day theories of dark matter inspired him to write "The Missing Mass" in 2000. "Neutron Star" netted him his first of five Hugo awards, and "The Missing Mass" earned an award from Locus. In between, he has written about quantum black holes (following a talk with Steven Hawking) and solar flares, becoming most well known for *Ringworld*, which first saw print in 1970. The novel garnered Hugo, Nebula, Locus, and Ditmar awards for its author and sealed his reputation as a master of hard science fiction. He is also well known for his collaborations, especially with the late Jerry Pournelle.

■■■■■■

Joy Ward's original introduction: Larry Niven, Hugo and Neb-ula-winning co-author of such science fiction classics as **Lucifer's Hammer** *and* **The Mote in God's Eye**, *has seen and been part of more science fiction history than many people. Most people do not* *realize that he played an instrumental role in twentieth-century real-world politics—the SDI, commonly known as the Star Wars Initiative. But in this 2015 interview, Mr. Niven talked about his longtime collaborator, Jerry Pournelle. Since this interview, we have, sadly, lost the brilliant Pournelle. I hope that this interview gives a bit of a window into the depth and breadth of their decades of collaboration.*

Joy Ward: Larry, you are known for your epic collaborations.

Larry Niven: I depend quite a lot more on my collaborators. Collaborating is less lonely. I've been collaborating for most of my career. My career is fifty years old, come December, in terms of being a selling author. The first check came in June of 1964. The first sale was the December issue of *World of Ptavvs*, which probably came out in October or November. So, fifty years.

Forty-odd years ago I collaborated on a novel with David Gerrold and that was fun. So when Jerry Pournelle suggested collaborating, I dove in. That was *The Mote in God's Eye*, which took three years to write. A pain in the ass, but lots of fun.

We sent it off to Lurton Blassingame and to Robert Heinlein, who was a friend of Jerry's. Both of them suggested cutting off the first hundred pages and, uh, various other suggestions too. We did that and had to rewrite, of course, to embed the information in the first hundred pages that we wanted in.

JW: How did you get into writing science fiction to start with?

LN: This was where the ideas were coming from. There was a book in Hawthorne School. Hawthorne was where I went to grade school, and they had a book in which Mars was inhabited by animated carrots and onions at war with each other. Quite a bad book. I could've been turned off by that, but then I discovered Heinlein. Heinlein's *Rocket Ship Galileo*. Nazis on the Moon, but well written, much better written.

JW: How old were you when you discovered Heinlein's **Rocket Ship Galileo?**

LN: Make it ten years old; something like that.

JW: What told you that you wanted to write this?

LN: It just seemed an obvious thing to try. I didn't have an ambition, really, and I locked on to this one—forced myself. I eventually sold something for twenty-five bucks and never looked back.

JW: I think you said your first collaboration was with David Gerrold. How did that come to be?

LN: I invited him on a date for dinner with me and Marilyn Niven. So, this must've been in…in around 1968, four years into my career. We invited him. He showed up without a date. He and I got to talking puns and started writing.

The first character there was Quizzard from the stars, whom we named for Isaac Asimov. Asimov had a translator that wasn't perfect.

JW: How did you end up collaborating with Pournelle?

LN: From *The Flying Sorcerers* it went to a script for *Land of the Lost*. Eventually, three scripts for *Land of the Lost* while he was story editor there. And the ideas were all his.

You always get paid in the TV industry. Getting paid is not the problem.

JW: What would you tell people about your time working with television?

LN: What you do may not appear. Fools may interfere with your precious prose. Also bright people, but they'll look like fools 'cause they're interfering with your precious prose.

When you write a book, it's all yours. When you write a script for TV, it's many people's. You get collaborators and you don't choose them.

JW: How does that work out?

LN: You can get pissed off and go away, or you can make a career out of it and make a lot of money. And not as much fame as you think. The fame belongs to the people who write the books.

JW: So which do you like writing?

LN: There is nothing comparable to the feeling of writing a story when it's really got its grip on your imagination.

JW: Tell me about that.

LN: Okay. I'll tell you a story. Jerry Pournelle and I were at work on *Lucifer's Hammer*. It's getting on toward Christmas season and I remember telling him that *Lucifer's Hammer* had cost me my Christmas season one year. I get a call from Jerry [at] about 10, 10:38 p.m., and he's at work on *Lucifer's Hammer*. He says, "I got a problem here. I want to show how awful things are in the valley outside The Stronghold. I've got the spacemen characters now, Deke Wilson and their men. I wanna show how terrible it all is, but they're not noticing anymore. None of the characters are noticing. What are they gonna see that I can describe? Think about it." And he hangs up.

I thought about it for an hour or two or three. I called him around two in the morning. I said, "I've got it. They're gonna notice a dead kangaroo." Then the astronaut is gonna freak out 'cause he's new to this and he's seeing nothing but corpses.

He loved it, of course, and did not complain about being awakened at two in the morning.

I don't do that a lot, mind you. I've never done that a lot, but it was too good to rest.

You're collaborating in order to get a better story than either of you could write alone. The bad news is you each have to do about 80 percent of the work.

JW: What do you look for in a collaborator?

LN: I don't go looking for collaborators so much as collaborators track me down. Steven Barnes did that. Jerry Pournelle did that. I was at the first BoucherCon. Sunday afternoon a bunch of us were in the restaurant and Jerry suggested writing together. I'd done it with David Gerrold—it must be fun.

And Steven Barnes went a little further than that. He was looking for a career and he figured getting a collaborator who knew something was vital. He started reading my stuff with the intent to keep reading until he could say he admired me. Really, the guy is organized.

JW: When somebody comes to you to collaborate, what are you looking for with them? What tells you this is someone you can work with or someone you can't work with?

LN: Each one has been different. Each collaboration has been different; each collaborative book has been different.

I don't write with an amateur. And I don't need to write with somebody who thinks exactly like me. They're contributing something I don't have. Jerry and I worked it out pretty quickly. Jerry knows military. Jerry knows politics. Jerry does these. Jerry's a better scientist too. Aliens are mine and madness is mine.

A character slogging his way through a sea of troubles, with some success and some background to work with, that's Jerry's. Character gets hysterical, that's mine.

JW: How did you get the hysterical characters?

LN: I've got a little more madness than he does, and it appeared quite quickly.

JW: What is it that Pournelle provides to the collaboration?

LN: Really, structure. He's much better at plotting than I am. He does more of the text. He doesn't do it all, by any means, but he does more of the text. And then he complains that everything people remember about a novel in detail is mine.

JW: What else has, other than a number of bestselling and Hugo-winning novels, what has your collaboration with Dr. Pournelle provided you?

LN: We're good friends and he's a little more ambitious in researching a novel. So there have been some trips. I took him to the River Valley Ranch, which the movie industry calls the Murder Ranch. River Valley Ranch became the foundation for The Stronghold.

JW: Let me kind of backtrack a little bit. You've been in science fiction a long time. What trends are you seeing in science fiction?

LN: First off, fantasy is easier to write. It's become far more popular than it used to be. I was there when the del Reys decided to start a science fiction line and there wasn't any up to then. There's a lot more fantasy being published because science fiction has become a lot harder. Too many readers really understand the sciences, so there's less that you can get away with. It's become less likely that a writer will choose to go with faster than light travel.

JW: What has been one of the high points in your very distinguished career? One that you'd say, "That's got to be the best, or close to the best"?

LN: I met Marilyn a couple of nights before the Hugo awards ceremony at which I won my first Hugo.

I was a new writer. It was 1967. I was just getting to be known but they knew me at MIT. I'd followed a friend into a party thrown by the MIT fans and started having a wonderful time. Then I met Marilyn and we talked a lot. It was crowded. We were lying with our backs against the footrest of a bed. That was that night.

That was also the New York Worldcon at which the elevator operators were throwing a strike. A slowdown strike was going on elsewhere, so you couldn't get anything done at this hotel.

I didn't notice anything. We had dinner in the hotel restaurant, and I didn't notice how bad things were because we were having fun together.

I didn't notice Lester del Rey throwing a salad at a waiter because he couldn't stand being treated like a serf anymore.

JW: How long before you asked her to marry you?

LN: We married September 6, 1969. I may have asked her in April '69.

JW: What effect has she had on your writing? How has she affected your writing as your wife?

LN: Keeps me sane. Marilyn keeps me sane. I'm not sure how organized I would be without her. You're not seeing the piles of paper in this house. We're both being swamped by paper, but it would have been a lot worse without Marilyn's help.

And I made her the heroine of a short story called "Inconstant Moon." That won a Hugo award.

First published in Issue 34 of Galaxy's Edge, *September 2018.*

■ DAVID DRAKE

David Drake graduated from the University of Iowa with a double major in history and Latin, then married Joanne (Jo) and started Duke Law School. The US Army drafted him in 1969, changing his immediate career path to a choice between interrogator or grunt. David chose interrogator and was assigned to the 11th Armored Cavalry Regiment, the Blackhorse, thus spending much of 1970 riding armored vehicles through jungles instead of slogging on foot. He returned to Duke in 1971, completed his law degree, and became Chapel Hill's Assistant Town Attorney while trying to put his life back together through fiction that made sense of what he'd seen and done in the srmy. (It still doesn't make any sense to him.) His writing career took off. Since 1981, he has been a full-time science fiction and fantasy writer, often being credited for helping create the military science fiction genre. Depending on how you count it, he has somewhere between sixty-five and a couple hundred books published. He has one son, a grandson, and lives with his wife in Chatham County, North Carolina.

■■■■■■

Joy Ward's original introduction: David Drake is the author of multiple bestsellers, and a mainstay of Baen Books.

■■

David Drake: I am a conservative and I have no ideology. Everyone dies. Everything dies. The heat death of the universe, eventually. We're all going to die.

When my friend, Mark, got his first digital answering machine, somebody joked in the group, "You know, he can make you have said anything he wants," and I thought about it for a moment and I said, "I can't imagine anything that you would twist my words into that would be worse than some of the things I've actually said." There was a general agreement that in that sense, I am absolutely proof against misquoting because no, I've said worse. I'm not going to pussyfoot around my opinions either.

In high school, one of my teachers was a professional writer on the side. That made me realize that writers are not some godlike group somewhere off there. A writer can be a kid who grew up in Decorah, Iowa, on a farm and began writing professionally while doing other things. The writer, whose name then was Eugene Olson. Mr. Olson had a writing pseudonym, Brad Steiger, which he later changed his name formally to, but he was ten years my senior, quite a young high school teacher and very charismatic—one of the two best teachers I've had in my life that had a great deal of academe. I had always told stories. Seeing him made me realize that I could write them down and I started doing that with the intention of someday I would be old enough and I would.

It allowed me to write my stories down and send them out. That's all it did. I mean, I'd always told stories. I continued to tell the stories. As I say, I'd always said when I was old enough, I'd send one off. When I was old enough, I'd sell the story. I went up to Sauk City, Wisconsin, at eighteen, nineteen. I bought some books. The book that had just come in was the *Inhabitant of the Lake*, which was my first book, first collection of work by an Englishman—actually an Irishman named John Ramsey Campbell, who later wrote professionally as Ramsey Campbell.

There was a picture of him on the back of it and he looked about fifteen years old. He is, in fact, a year younger than I am. I looked at that picture and I said out loud, "Well, I can't claim that I'm not old enough to do it." So, I got home and got back to Iowa, at University of Iowa, and wrote Mr. Derleth asking if I could submit a story for his next original anthology. He grumbled and said yes, and I did. He sent it back saying, "It was a good plot outline. Now, write the story." I expanded to a full 3,500 words.

He edited again and said, "Still isn't right, but I'll edit it. Compare it with the printed version with your carbon to see how not to write a story the next time. Here's a check for thirty-five dollars." That was my first sale.

It was the most crushing acceptance letter I've ever heard. I was so ignorant that I didn't know I was supposed to keep a carbon. I thought I am a complete idiot. I'll admit, I didn't think, "Will I get to have this check framed?" I thought, thirty-five dollars. That was actually a lot of money.... I was earning ninety-five cents an hour as a book page in the University of Iowa Library. I spent it.

Kind of weird. I didn't really have a full feeling of it until I started law school and was accepted on the Law Journal. An older member of the Journal was giving us her little pep talk, how if you do really well, you may be permitted to write a note for the Law Journal, and you can't imagine how it feels to have your name in print and the fun of it. People pay me just to put my name in print. I should be proud of doing a note. I guess that was the most significant result of having sold that story.

JW: Your military experiences obviously fed into your military science fiction writing. Please tell us about that time in your life.

DD: I was drafted with a great number of other college graduates who were drafted in 1969. In 1969, they brought in the draft lottery, but there was that year interim where everybody who was in grad school was a potential draftee. I was drafted. In my squad basic training, the first guy was getting his PhD in physics at the University of Chicago. The Language School, which was for grad students only. As it turned out, one of my closest buddies was getting his degree from Princeton in English.

About a third of my basic training battalion were college graduates, about a third were white kids from Western North Carolina, the remaining third...these are rough figures, but they are roughly correct. About a third were Black kids from intercity Detroit who had about the same educational attainments as the white kids from Western North Carolina, but there were cultural differences.

Then, as they say, there were college graduates. Basic training was an interesting experience for everybody, including the drill sergeants, who were very professional and very good, and very puzzled by a lot of things. They were not hostile to us college kids.

When I came back to the world from Vietnam, and to a degree, I wrote a story that actually sold while I was in Vietnam with the 540 crews. It was a fantasy. I wrote it and then I was typing it up on the unit typewriter. This was back in the base at Qui Nhon. It was Sunday morning and I heard a bang. I turned around and looked through the screened window behind me, and there's this orange bubble. I'm thinking, "What the fuck?" Then there was a louder bang! And a larger orange bubble. Then there was a really big, orange bubble and a louder bang. The bangs were coming through the ground before they got through the air. What happened was the ammo dump had blown up.

Some people, the G-troop, had come in from the field. One of the things you had to do when you came in from the field was store all your ammunition and explosives in the ammo dump. It's Sunday morning and two guys in a deuce and a half head back into the dump and were tossing ordnance out the back to empty the truck. In the field, you don't have much in the way of containers. What they were using for a lot of the odds and sods were mortar cases. These were sort of like orange crates, only they were long and thin with slaps and they would normally hold mortar shells.

The guy tossed them out to the back and the pin—one of the grenade pins was hanging out for a slap. It caught on the tailgate latch of the deuce and a half as it went out. It landed in this pile of other ordnance, smoking. Just a fuse, a five-second fuse. They both jumped in the cab of the truck and got the truck back out around the blast wall when that went off in the middle of a pile of the other ordnance, which set off a larger amount of nearby ordnance, which set off the whole thing.

That was the third explosion. G-troop was being mustered out Sunday morning. I later talked to the wife of the cook with the G-troop. He was doing their morning formation and bang, and he looked up in the sky and there's these black specks and it started falling. They were the fifty-four–gallon drums full of sand that was used as temporary blast walls. There were 155 shells unfused that were falling down. What didn't actually go off, went up and fell. No one was injured.

The church was a huge A-frame with sheet-metal walls next to the ammo dump. The burn [was] around the ammo dump that directed the blast, so none of it was going sideways out.

I know what an explosion looked like…I mean, a really big explosion from about a mile. I know exactly what that looks like, and I finished typing up the story, which had nothing to do with anything military. I got to see a lot of things in Vietnam that I wouldn't otherwise have seen.

JW: What is the driving passion behind your writing?

DD: Keeping myself from killing people. I came back to the world very, very angry. There are a lot of reasons to be angry. I was angry at everything. I was probably angry with myself for what I've done, for what I had become. I knew perfectly well what I'd become, and I was curious about it. If I had not had the writing as a way to put it out, to organize my thoughts, that sort of thing, bad things might've happened. I became a much more dog-end writer, not to be a writer but to give me an outlet. I did not know it. I did not admit it. I didn't admit how crazy I was. I was really crazy. I went back and I finished law school. The transition was, I was in returning barracks at Long Binh and seventy-two hours later, I was in the lounge of Duke University Law School preparing to start my fourth semester.

That is our caring country.

That was in 1971. I finished law school. I don't remember anything of that last year-and-a-half. There are people who consider graduating from a top-rated law school as being the most stressful events in their life. No, they weren't going to shoot at me. I've looked up in the morning thinking, "Nobody's going to shoot at me today."

I came back to the world at some level for two things. One, I was already dead. I'd given myself up for dead during the past year. It wasn't that anything bad had happened to me because bad things had happened.

But it wasn't that. It was just I knew from the beginning that I was not going to survive this year and my body did. My mind really didn't. I mean, the personality that I was really did not survive. I don't mean that dreadful things happened to me. No. Worse things happen to a lot of people I knew, a lot of people. That wasn't me, but I had given myself up.

The other thing was, I thought I was crazy. I wasn't admitting this, but I really, deeply did because nothing made any fucking sense.

My writing was able to put things down in an organized fashion. This happened, that happened. At some level, I think, I was believing that because I was organizing it, that it would make sense. The truth, I finally came to realize, was it didn't make any sense, the whole thing was just as crazy as I thought it was, but I was crazy. My brain had not been harmed. My personality and the fact that I couldn't make sense of this did not mean I had become stupid.

No. I really didn't grasp what was going on, and it really made no more sense than I had thought it did at that time. The writing permitted me to see that. It didn't give me myself back. That's been sort of an incremental process of taking these little pebbles and gluing them back together. I've done a pretty good job at it. I really have, but this is not the person I was in 1968. I don't mean I was a great person. Who wasn't? I mean, he was a kid. I think he deserved better. But regardless, it is what it is. I really did die in that two-year period because it was more than just Vietnam and Cambodia. Basic is just... I watched a guy flung through a second-floor window because he walked on the floor of another squad while they were waxing it for an inspection. Four of them just grabbed him and threw him through the window, screen and all. Listen, if I'd been up there.... The guy was a fuck-up. But all right, he's fucked up. Deal with it.

I was okay with it. "Oh, yeah. It is about time somebody did." That's not civilized behavior. When I say, what I became was something I don't much like, I mean that as much as things to do with automatic weapons and suchlike. If you don't adapt to the situation, you will die, really. If you do adapt, the civilian that you were has died.

The army has got very good, you know. It used to be with training, when people got into combat, only about 15 percent at tops would use their weapons if they saw the enemy. A really, really good high morale unit like the 101st Airborne, 35 percent in the middle of violent fire-fight. Now the percentage is about 90 percent. The army in basic, it teaches you to kill. Not the physical act of hoping that bullet went to the right place, but willingness, the instant willingness to kill. That's a very important thing for soldiers to be able to do. What they have not done, what they can never try to do, what I don't think they can do, was make you a better civilian afterward.

What the army did was give me seventy-two hours and put me back in law school. That was the response of the government of the United States of America.

People have high regard for military and for soldiers now, and that's good. I'm glad they do because believe me, it's a rough job.

Non-vets were treated like shit. I mean, I'm not telling any secrets there, am I? I think the country is not embarrassing itself the way it did in the '70s. But I don't think it makes any difference to the people who've been used up.

JW: How do your stories help people understand the ramifications of war?

DD: I don't know that my stories mean anything for civilians. I frankly don't much care. What I have learned is that guys who've been there and read my stories, the story proves to them that they're not alone and that is huge. Their letters made me finally realize that I wasn't alone either. That is huge. I don't have any secrets of how to become normal. I haven't become normal. I will tell you, I will tell people the truth if they ask a question; they'll get answers. They've realized, there is no point in lying.

I learned that when I was twenty-five. Life is too fucking short. You want to know, I'll tell you. You like it, fine. You don't like it, fine. The truth is true. There were a lot of comments that I was an ex-tremely direct person. Well, yeah. I'm not sure why that should be so unusual, but it apparently is.

I'm writing for myself. *Redliners* is the big one. I've had many people say that it helped them enormously in their PTSD to read *Redliners*. I say the same thing, all of it is true. I believe it has helped a lot of people. It hasn't helped anybody nearly as much as it helped me to have written it, and I had no idea of what I was doing. I was just writing a space opera with a strong military component. That's all I was doing. Until I finished the book, and I felt this huge weight come off me that had been there for twenty-five years.

JW: Why is it, do you think, that people have backed away from military SF, even the people who have been at that sharp end of the stick, and yet, your generation has come out and has actually dealt with it?

DD: Yeah, I don't know. I do know that, if you will, the opinion-makers really very determinedly shat on me.

I didn't have any crusade. I have no ideology. I didn't much before I went over, and certainly haven't since I came back. I wasn't trying to do anything. I was just telling stories, and, I say, trying to keep my own head straight.

People like Charlie Brown were really offended by this. Tom Easton of *Analog* called me a pornographer of violence because I was just trying to tell it as it was.

I knew I was a monster. I knew I was a monster. What was I going to do? Kill him? Don't mistake me, that certainly did cross my mind. I don't mean just in print that he did. He was on a panel at Boston to a room with some hundreds of people. The panel was on the use of violence in science fiction and fantasy. He says, "We're here." Five people in the panel, and I honestly don't remember who the two others were. He says, "On my left here is Joel Rosenberg, who uses violence correctly. On my right is David Drake, who is a pornographer of violence."

I went kind of blank and, as they say, various options crossed my mind, and I don't know, I probably was shut down. But what happened was, Joel Rosenberg jumped up and said, "Everything I know about writing about violence, I have learned by reading David Drake." I looked over at Joel, whom I did not know, and I said, "Would you like my first porn?" If it had not been for Joel, that was some awful situation.

JW: How did that make you feel?

DD: Like a monster. I knew myself better than he knew me, and I knew I was a monster.

I'll tell you a high point. Night Shade Books, they contacted me and wound up doing a collected Hammer's Slammer series in three volumes. I got the first volume pre-pub and I opened it, and I held it in my hand and I thought, "Jesus Christ, I've come home."

This was a validation. I was doing what I was doing. I kept on doing it. I was selling, fine. But I was the poor relation. I sold the first two stories to Baen at *Galaxy*. He bought up the original collection. But it's always mass market, paperback. Suddenly, in my hand is this really nice limited edition hard cover. It really, you know, wow!

Odd. We're talking thirty years. I mean, that's a long time. I hadn't really been aware that I was out wandering that long, but I had. You open the door, "Oh, I'm home." It's a funny question, right?

I had become part of the mainstream. I have always been successful, but this was a stage beyond that. I don't read reviews generally. If I do, I'm likely to be as angry at a good one as I am at a bad one because my experience has been pretty much that reviewers are stupid. I'd rather be praised by a stupid writer than cursed by a stupid writer, but he's still stupid. Okay, look, I'm arrogant and I'm overstating the case, but that is how I feel.

I am a first-rate craftsman. I mean, I am a fine craftsman. I did not call myself an artist and I've never called myself an artist, and I don't call myself an author. I am a writer. I am a very competent writer.

JW: What is important about doing your job?

DD: I did my job. I do my job. I did my job in the Black Horse in the 11th Cav.

I didn't fail the people. I did my job. Maybe they failed. But the thing I got from the Black Horse: we were an elite unit, and nobody believed it more. I mean, this is 1970, for Christ's sake. Nobody believed it more and God knows, we didn't believe in the Republic of Vietnam government because it was a joke. It was a grim, criminal joke, as bad as Iraq. What you didn't know about the Black Horse was that when shit hits the fan, the guy next to you would be doing his job and you would be doing yours. If that is the only thing there is [in] the world, then that is something and that is very important to me that I do my job.

JW: Where do you want to go now with your life?

DD: One foot in front of the other. You haven't gotten anything but honesty from me. I don't mean I'm always right, but I will always tell you what I believed.

JW: How do you want to be remembered?

DD: I don't care. No, I will say it. I want to be remembered as a craftsman and a man who did his job. I did my job.

First published in Issue 33 of Galaxy's Edge, *July 2018.*

CPSIA information can be obtained
at www.ICGtesting.com
Printed in the USA
JSHW032220030221
11527JS00002B/3